FREEDOM'S LAW

STEPHEN B. PEARL

Milton, Ontario
http://www.brain-lag.com/

Brain Lag Publishing
Ontario, Canada
http://www.brain-lag.com/

Cover artwork by Catherine Fitzsimmons

Library and Archives Canada Cataloguing in Publication

Title: Freedom's law / Stephen B. Pearl.
Names: Pearl, Stephen B., 1961- author.
Identifiers: Canadiana (print) 20210267364 | Canadiana (ebook) 20210267372 | ISBN 9781928011606
   (softcover) | ISBN 9781928011613 (ebook)
Classification: LCC PS8631.E255 F74 2021 | DDC C813/.6—dc23

Also by the author

The Freedom Saga
Book 1: *Cloning Freedom*
Book 2: *Freedom's Law*
Book 3: *Freedom's Myth* (forthcoming)

The Tinker Series
Book 1: *Tinker's Plague*
Book 2: *Tinker's Sea*
"Tinker's Toxin"
(in *The Light Between Stars*)

The Chronicles of Ray McAndrues
Book 1: *Nukekubi* (Dark Dragon)

Worlds Apart (Dark Dragon)

The Bastard Prince Saga (Pendelhaven Press)
Book 1: *Horn of the Kraken*
Book 2: *The Mistletoe Spear* (forthcoming)

Cats (Ankh Shen Publishing)

Havens in the Storm (Ankh Shen Publishing)

War of the Worlds 2030 (Damnation Press)

Dedication

My thanks to my beloved wife, Joy Hughes-Pearl, and my publisher, Catherine Fitzsimmons, who have been pivotal to this work.

I also want to thank Adlai Stevenson, who is credited with a bit of quotable wisdom, **'A hungry man is not a free man,'** that is really at the core of this novel.

The truth is that freedom is a very relative term. If your freedom is to put up with abuse or starve, are you truly free? In the case of Rowan, she is faced with the dilemma of remaining in an area where she has greater freedom at the cost of her life or go back into the status of property that she has worked so hard to escape in hopes of getting medical attention.

Circumstances like this are common in our culture. How many people in nations without socialised medicine stay at a job they hate because they have a good health plan? How much do employers abuse employees because they hold the strings to the employee's survival? My father often said, "A man supporting five kids was not free, and his employer knew it."

I do not believe that any of us are truly free. The realities of material existence preclude perfect freedom. I may be free to jump off a building, but my attempt at flight is going to be short-lived without at least a hang glider.

What I do believe is that freedom is a sliding scale and that we can be freer. Also, that freedom is relative. One of the most ridiculous things I ever heard as an argument was that 'A gay man was free to marry a woman like everyone else.'

For the record, I went to my MP's office every time marriage equality came up in the Canadian parliament and told them to respect all people equally.

Freedom is a moot point if it is a freedom you have no interest in. There is a freedom in security from invasion that, after WW2, the Soviets played on as a means of social control. The concept of freedom is complicated and shaded.

Another aspect of freedoms is they can be self-contradictory. I should be free to breathe; you should be free to wear cheap perfume on a plane. Two mutually exclusive freedoms that we must judge on their relative merits.

We must ask ourselves, where on the spectrum of freedoms we are comfortable as a society, being mindful that the freedom we demand for ourselves we must extend to others.

To one and all, enjoy your freedom while allowing others theirs. Play your music in your backyard but keep it to a volume so that your neighbour can hear their music. Ultimately, freedom is a balancing act, one we should all be happy to join in on.

I hope you enjoy *Freedom's Law*.

IN OUR LAST EPISODE

"I love you! I know it's wrong. I know it would kill Gunther if he found out, but I can't help it." Carl clutched Willa's hand. Her pretty face, with its frame of red hair, filled his vision.

Tears formed in Willa's green eyes as she stroked the cheek of her young lover. His handsome, Hispanic features were full of emotion. "Carl, I love you too, but I also love Gunther, and he's my husband. I'm forty-four, you're twenty-two. What kind of future could we have?"

Carl hung his head.

"And cut to the long shot." Troy pressed a button on the console in front of him, and the big screen shifted to Willa's living room. The two lovers sat facing each other on the central couch. Willa's slender, athletic body was dwarfed by Carl's well-muscled form. Reclining chairs flanked the scene as witnesses to the tragedy being played out.

I hate this. It will kill the show, but John's the producer, thought Troy as he glanced over the screens dedicated to the other characters in the series. Gunther was leaving the hardware store carrying a package. Troy ran his fingers through his scraggly, straw-coloured hair.

On the big screen, Willa and Carl sat on the couch staring at the floor.

"I should let her end it." Troy turned his scarecrow-like

body so he could stare at the memo on the wall. "John would fire me for sure. The jerk!" Turning back to the console, he watched Willa and Carl. "I'm sorry, Gunther, but John thinks the triangle will have audience appeal." Troy pressed a series of buttons. Nano-bots and other control vectors in Willa and Carl triggered the release of the chemical soup associated with sexual arousal.

Willa looked up and found herself staring into the brown depths of Carl's eyes. Her passion was overwhelming. Her lips met his. His hands moved to her small, firm breasts, teasing her nipples through the satin of her blouse.

"And place cut marker for the PG version, keep recording for adult." Troy hit a button, then stared at Carl's empathic monitors; they were spiked for eroticism, but there was an underlying sense of guilt. "Gunther's been like a dad to you. Season seven sucks! My luck, I get hired just in time for the series to tank."

Willa's sensation monitors climbed as Carl stripped. Troy switched the perspective so that he watched Carl through her eyes and her emotions and sensation were the focus of the general distribution cut. Carl's reactions were recorded for the specialty cut of his perspective.

"Keep telling yourself they're only clones, emotional surrogates, fakeys. They aren't people. Yeah, tell yourself that so you don't go like that Ryan guy and rescue one of them."

Gunther stepped into the driveway of his two-storey, suburban house. The sun was shining, and the air smelled fresh. If he forgot what he knew, he could almost believe that all was right with the world. He sighed and ran his fingers through his greying, short, brown hair. He put the key in the lock and heard it click home. He opened the door, took a step and froze.

"Gunther!" Willa screamed from where she sat atop Carl on the couch.

"Oh Divine!" gasped Carl.

Gunther froze, slacked-jawed and staring. His well-proportioned body trembled with rage. Willa half fell off Carl onto the floor and tried to cover herself with her hands.

Carl sat up and made a grab for his trousers.

"Gunther, I'm—" Tears flowed from Willa's eyes.

"HOW COULD YOU DO THIS TO ME?" screamed Gunther.

Carl clutched his head as a bolt of telepathic force slammed into his mind. His body instinctively shifted colour to blend with the sofa behind him. He tried to use the mental defences that Gunther had taught him, but they were no use against the power, rage and pain of the mind he faced. Every tryst, every detail of his affair with Willa was laid bare.

Gunther's face became hard as he strode to the basement door. Throwing it open, he descended the stairs. One side of the basement was set up as an infirmary, while the other was a mass of electrical equipment. Moving to an open panel on the wall, Gunther pulled a graphite rod out of the bag he carried and slammed it into a pair of power clips.

"Gunther, what is the matter?" asked Toronk from the ambulance gurney he lay on. The two-point-one metre tall, humanoid cat sat up, grimacing when his injured leg brushed the covers. His grey-tabby-like fur bristled at the look Gunther shot him, and his pointed ears pulled tight against his head.

"You know what, Toronk? I'd rather be a felinezoid. Nothing could be as reprehensible as humanity!"

Toronk stared at his human friend.

Closing his eyes, Gunther thought to his wife, *'Willa, come here and bring Carl NOW!'*

Gunther slumped into the old office chair in front of his work bench. "Bastards!" he whispered.

Willa heard her husband's voice in her mind. She shifted from a fetal position. She knew it was impossible for her to have a heart attack. The cybernetic replacement that Amitose had used to save her from cancer would last a thousand years, but at that moment, her chest throbbed.

"Carl, get dressed. Gunther wants us downstairs."

Troy watched the monitors. Gunther's showed incredible emotional pain. "Need to dull this down, or it won't fly with the audience." Troy released a trickle of a euphoric into Gunther's system from his built-in drug-pack. Troy glanced at Willa and Carl's monitors, then repeated the process with them. Toronk's monitors indicated confusion.

"What I wouldn't give to be able to read your thoughts, but emotions will have to do."

Willa and Carl descended into the basement.

"Gunther, I'm sorry. I don't know—" began Willa, but as soon as she stepped off the stairs, Gunther threw a switch. A hum filled the room. She felt a prickle of static, and her cybernetic limbs twitched.

Troy blinked as his main screen and the dedicated screens for Gunther, Willa, Carl and Toronk filled with fuzz.

Must be some weird side-effect from that telepathy booster he's been trying to build. He must want to understand why things happened real bad, poor bugger. I hope I don't miss anything good. Troy shifted the big screen to Farley's living-room's overview. Farley, a muscular, Japanese man, was brushing the fur of what appeared to be an oversized, green otter with an elongated head.

"At least one relationship is working out. Quinta's cute, for an otterzoid. Better than he deserves after how he treated Rowan."

"What have you done?" demanded Toronk.

Gunther, with tears streaming from his eyes, embraced his wife. "It wasn't your fault. I love you."

Willa sobbed; there was no understanding his reasons, but she could feel her husband's love.

Arlene observed Willa and Gunther through Toronk's eyes. The hard-wire feed installed in the drain of Gunther's basement was working perfectly. Pulling out her hand-held, she opened the device, folding it out both vertically and horizontally to expose its screen.

"Hand-held, connect me to Michael Strongbow, head producer of S.E.T.E."

Michael appeared on the screen. He was a ruggedly-handsome, silver-haired man. "Arlene, is there some problem with *Freedom's Run*?"

"No, Michael. I'm just calling to tell you that you were right about what Gunther was building."

"Is the hard feed we installed getting the signal?" Michael's brown eyes reflected concern.

"It's working like a dream. Our board is the only one that

can monitor the room. The rest are getting static."

"Excellent! Keep recording. This could be the greatest event in the history of e-entertainments."

"It will give us something for season three with Ryan and Rowan in the Switchboard System."

"Don't count them out. I've arranged for Henry to keep feeding us their telemetry. I won't be comfortable until Ryan and Rowan are in orbit around Geb. Keep monitoring the feeds."

"Right." Arlene shut off her hand-held and turned her attention back to the screen.

"Gunther, I'm sorry I—" began Carl.

"It wasn't your fault either, though I'd still like to knock your genetically altered ass onto the ground." Gunther pulled away from Willa and faced the others in the room.

"Listen, we don't have much time. Everything we thought we knew is a lie. Remember when Ryan rescued Rowan from the poison and took her to speak to the Republic council? What he told us about being descended from captive humans was a cover story. I found out when I scanned him. It's really the seventh century after humans made contact with aliens. Humans are members of the Interstellar Republic with a faster than light stargate and colony worlds.

"We're clones, designed as performers in a full sensory entertainment. People experience edited versions of our lives. It's all the senses and emotion. The only thing they don't have is thought, something about it taking up too much bandwidth.

"The controllers manipulate us using implanted chemical packs, nano-bots, and the Divine knows what else to get the stories the producers want. I've spent the last month picking the brains of controllers when they came into the 'set region'. That's what they call Sun Valley.

From that, I've built this jamming device. This is the only place we can talk about this and not be monitored.

"If the controllers find out that we know the truth, they'll kill us so that we don't compromise the set region."

Willa stared at her husband, slack-jawed.

"Gunther! Oh, stardust, we've pushed him over the edge," breathed Carl.

Toronk's cat-like face looked thoughtful, and his tail quivered. "It is within the realm of technical possibility. If humans are where I was led to believe my species were technologically. It always bothered me that our ship's stealth systems remained functional long enough for us to crash-land undetected when so many other systems failed."

"You believe this?" demanded Willa.

"It would explain much. Such as why no one has any desire to leave Sun Valley. How is it that in all our battles, none of us has died? It pleases me to learn that Rowan survived. She is a valued friend. It also explains why Angel broke faith with me. She'd never expressed a sexual interest in Farley before that day. It could also explain other events of the same nature." Toronk's expression became pensive.

Willa and Carl stared at the floor, their minds racing.

Toronk continued. "Look at this from an outsider's perspective. If you were presented with this story or the story of a group of campers who came across a crashed, off-world police officer that grafted alien DNA into them, granting them alien powers so they could fight a group of invading pirates, which would you consider more likely?"

Michael Strongbow placed his palm against the scanner. The door to the *Freedom's Run* control room opened. As he stepped in, Arlene swivelled her chair, and her full lips formed a smile on her open, pleasant face. There was a mischievous sparkle in her brown eyes, and her copper skin was flushed. She'd tied her long, black hair into a ponytail.

"Gunther knows the truth. If John knew, he'd hang himself. The entire set region has been compromised by one of his characters," said Arlene.

Michael smiled. "As long as they can't trace it back to me, I am pleased with the results."

Arlene's face became grave. "Are you sure about this? I mean, sure, they're phasing out Sun Valley, but it still has another fifteen years of operation."

"Actually, the new set region was decided at the last meeting. We're switching to an ancient Egyptian theme. It should be ready to go in five years. The lower the tech-level we're emulating, the easier the setup." Michael pulled over a second office chair and sat facing the display screens.

"Ancient Egyptian, weren't they stone-age?"

"Early bronze. That's part of why I had to do *Freedom's Run* now. Sun Valley is the seventh century Before Contact. They can almost detect the control vectors as it is. If the tech was lower, Rowan would have had a harder time adjusting to our present-day world, and Gunther couldn't have jammed the signal. When we broadcast our series, it will shake the foundations of how our society sees clones. Look." Michael pointed towards Willa's emotional monitors. There was a slight increase in adrenalin levels.

"She's wrapping her head around it. Smart woman," said Arlene.

Michael smiled. "It's a trait of the AH series, along with the slender, compact figure. I've always found the series most attractive."

"That's obvious. How is Marcy doing?"

"My wife is fine. Why do you ask?"

Arlene's eyes sparkled. "No reason."

"If this is true, what happened to Rowan and who was Ryan?" Willa could still see Gunther's pain, but under that, she saw his determination. They had both loved their daughter, and the forced parting had been hard, made worse by the necessity of pretending that she had died of the alien poison.

Gunther took Willa's hands in his own. "Ryan was one of the controllers. He fell in love with Rowan and couldn't stand to watch the producer, John Wilson, kill her. Ryan was going to take Rowan to a world where she'd have legal rights. Studio clones are property on this world, which is called Gaea."

"She's safe, though?"

"Safer than us, now that you know the truth."

"It wasn't our fault. We were manipulated by these controllers." Carl sounded relieved.

"Carl, I understand that intellectually, but don't think that it helps emotionally. You slept with my wife and, if I know the controllers, will probably do so again. I could kill you, but I need you."

"For?" asked Toronk.

"We now know who the real enemy is. We have to organize, get the characters from the other shows to understand. It's time for the gladiators to revolt!"

⚔

"That a boy Gunther, give Big Brother all the stardust he can handle." Michael chuckled.

"Big brother?" asked Arlene.

"Seventh-century Before Contact literary reference. I can lend you a modern translation."

"No, thanks. Can the surrogates really revolt?"

"With a lot of help from us, they can put up a credible showing. That's all we need. We need *Freedom's Run* to touch people, force them to see what we already know."

"What's that?"

"That clones, all classes of clones, are people. The coelenteratezoids are right. No civilized species permits slavery. What's that beeping?"

A beeping came from the jumble of electrical equipment on the workbench.

"What's that?" Emotions warred on Willa's face.

"The jamming system can only operate for a short time. I have to shut it down. None of us can say or do anything that will let them know that we know the truth. Only in this basement, when the jamming system is active, can we speak safely. Willa, I love you. I forgive you. No matter what I say or do, remember that. Carl, I'm working on it."

"I love you, Gunther." Willa slipped into his arms and kissed him.

"I love you. You'd better step away. We need to give a good performance." Gunther moved to his device and threw a switch. He turned back to Willa. "YOU WHORE!"

THE STARS OF THE SHOW

Rowan sat in the command chair of the *Star Hawk*. The control stations formed a horseshoe around her. Five of the control seats were empty. The mutilated, android body of Henry filled the one in front of the computer station.

"So, sweetness, I thought you'd be off shagging hottie-boss." Henry swivelled his chair around as far as the wires and fibre-optic cables that connected him to the ship allowed. The burnt, artificial skin that covered half his face blended oddly with the brown shade on the undamaged side. Rowan looked at the android. She'd become accustomed to the missing legs and one remaining arm, but she still had to force herself to look into his face.

Rowan's pretty features pulled into a tentative smile that didn't reach her blue eyes. "He said he was going to map out the repair work. I really think he needed some alone time. Captain Denardo telling him that he is an outlaw throughout the United Earth Systems brought it home. He can never go back. His old life is over. He'll never see his wife or son again. Or any of his family, for that matter."

"He's being an ass, sweetheart. Joslin's an e-addict. Got her head so deep in the shows she'll never pull it out. Probably doesn't even know he's gone. That marriage was over years ago."

"I know that, so does he. I don't, well..." Rowan fidgeted with her dark brown hair where it brushed her shoulders.

"Do the wild monkey dance with married guys! For the

record, sweetness, I'm a bachelor. Plastic has advantages." Henry grinned. The undamaged side of his face looked lusty, the ruined side macabre.

"Don't you think Ryan's had enough betrayals?" Rowan's lean body shifted uncomfortably in the chair when she realized that Henry was staring at her breasts.

Henry looked away, anger colouring his features. "With a family like his, who needs enemies? All of them members of Humans Ascendant. I'm surprised they didn't take a hit out on him when their injunction against his cloning fell through." Henry's voice became scolding and high pitched. "'You… you disgusting fakey, you aren't my son! You're an abomination!'" Henry's voice returned to normal. "Those were the last words his mother said to him. In a recorded message no less."

"His son keeps in touch."

"Sweetness, that kid acts like Ryan should have let the cancers kill him after the disaster on Murack Five. Better for him if his father were dead than a clone. Never mind that Ryan went back into the regs so the kid's tuition would be covered. Forget that Ryan has more medals than a veteran's day parade."

"I don't know what it's like to have kids, but I think Ryan is broken up about his son. That seems the hardest part for him." Rowan stared into the large screen that filled the upper wall at the closed end of the horseshoe of consoles. It showed a ring of dark material encircling a starscape dominated by one bright star.

"Ryan's got a lot to be broken up about with the way you cloned types get treated."

"Bigotry is stardust." Rowan didn't take her eyes off the screen.

Henry watched her for over a minute before speaking. "Why don't you tell me what's really bugging you, sexy lady. Unless you want to make an AI's day and give us a flash." Henry leered at Rowan.

"Dream on!" Rowan shook her head.

"Such is the sad fate of plastic, to love and never be loved. To long for the warmth of flesh. To wish to shag my sexy crewmates until the sun goes nova. You sure you and Ryan don't want to play threesies? I'm not fussy that way."

"Henry!" Rowan sounded annoyed.

"Sure thing, sweet stuff. It was just a suggestion. Spill, why are you up here instead of taking a virtual swim or studying for your navigator's rating?"

"Is it that obvious?"

"Hottie, sigh once more, and I'll send you to medical to check your breathing."

"It's just..." Rowan gestured at the main screen. "On the other side of that stargate is where I lived my whole life. I know it was all fake, but it was mine, and I didn't know it was fake. I... I miss my Dad and Mom and Angel and Carl, everyone."

"You got Ryan and me, sweetness." Henry's voice was free of the sexual heat it normally held.

"I know. I... I love Ryan, or at least I'm pretty close to loving him. Not bad for someone I've known less than a month. And Henry, underneath the pervert act, you're a really sweet ma... artificial intelligence. It's just..."

The undamaged side of Henry's face looked haunted. "Each of those plaques Ryan put up was a brother or sister. I know what it's like to miss someone you'll never see again."

Rowan ran her hand over the three plaques on the side of the command chair. One for each captain of the *Star Hawk* who had died during the heavy lander's years of service in the Space Combat Corps. Her eyes traced over similar plaques on the back of each duty station chair. "At least my folks are still alive."

"That's the shaggable girl I know. Now go find Ryan, take him to a place where my monitoring's enabled, and shag his brains out. Do you both good." Henry made a pumping action with his arm and growled.

Rowan smiled and shook her head. "You'll have to settle

for two out of three."

"Which two?" panted the android.

"Guess, but does the phrase 'privacy on' have any meaning to you?" Rowan stood, then clutched the command chair's arm as a wave of dizziness swept over her.

"What's the problem?" Henry stared at Rowan.

"Stood up too fast." Rowan used the access aisle that kept her out of Henry's reach to move toward the bridge's door.

"I never get to have any fun." Henry kept a smile on his face as he accessed the telemetry from Rowan's implanted physical control systems. The smile vanished when Rowan left the room. "Oh, sweetness. No use telling you or hottie-boss before we reach the station, nothing you could do about it anyway."

With a shake of his head, Henry dedicated more of his RAM to editing the readings from his two human friends and loading them for relay to Michael Strongbow. "Sorry guys, but I want my new, shaggable body. Nova blast liberty, give me hips or give me death."

Ryan stared at the computer terminal in his quarters. The room was three metres square with a roll-down couch/bed against the back wall. The floor was the rubberized flooring that had been in place when he rescued the *Star Hawk* from a military-surplus scrap-pile. The walls depicted a beautiful mountain valley. He sat on a rolling chair in front of the workstation reading.

> *Dear Tim,*
>
> *Son, this will probably be the last chance we have to communicate. I'm sure you've been informed about me stealing—*

Ryan tapped a key and ran his fingers through his short, brown hair. "No, not stealing, that implies that Rowan is property."

Using the keyboard, he corrected the word, then kept reading.

—liberating Rowan from the show I worked on. If not, you now know something before the news media. Please keep it under your hat. I've got enough problems as it is.

You also should know that your mother is in an e-addict facility. I'm sorry for that. I truly am. I had no choice. She wasn't even coming out of the shows to feed herself anymore.

Ryan paused again and stared at the copper skin of his hand. "All the perfumes of Arabia will not sweeten this little hand."

He shook his head and smiled grimly. His handsome face made a ghost-like reflection on the screen. His green eyes looked haunted.

While escaping, I was forced to fire on the Saber, one of Gaea's orbital defence frigates. As a result, I'm wanted throughout the United Earth Systems. I can't go into human space without being arrested.

Please, son, meet me at the Switchboard Station. I'm stopping there to repair battle damage. I can't tell you my plans after that, in case this message is intercepted, but this will be the last chance for us to meet.

Please, son, let me say goodbye. I love you.

Your father, Ryan Chandler, Captain of the Star Hawk.

Ryan leaned back in his chair. Biologically, his body was equivalent to a man in his mid-twenties, but at that moment, he felt every one of his ninety-three years. The door buzzer sounded.

"Computer, privacy off. Henry, transmit the file on my terminal to the Switchboard Station to be forwarded by FTL telegraph to Earth, express postage Tim's address. I should have enough left in my inter-systems bank account to cover it."

"Hottie boss, the kid's an ingrate. You got a new life to build with the sexy little number who's leaning on your doorbell. Shag her and forget the letter." Henry's voice issued from a wall speaker. The door buzzer sounded again.

"I have to wrap up the old life to be free for the new one. Send the letter. Tim probably won't reply, then blank the screen and open the door."

The entry door disappeared into the wall, revealing Rowan. "You all right?"

"I'm not blown to bits or being sent to a prison farm, yet. So, I'm better than I could be." Ryan smiled to take the sting out of his words.

"I've really kinda messed up your life, haven't I?" Rowan moved to the rolled-up couch/bed and sat.

Ryan gazed at her, his face becoming soft. "No, you gave me back my life. Rowan, I loved you when you were nothing but a fantasy on an e-entertainment. Having you here, with me, it's worth any price."

"Even firing on a Space Combat Corps' ship?"

"Henry's a great shot. Captain Denardo and her people weren't hurt."

Rowan held a hand out to Ryan, and he took it. Her hand was cold to the touch, but he hardly noticed. A moment later, they were in each other's arms.

Ryan broke their kiss. "Henry, privacy on."

"Stardust, you remembered." Henry's voice issued from the speaker before it went dead.

Captain Tansy Denardo sat in her command chair on the *Saber's* horseshoe-shaped bridge. Her classical, Italian features looked contemplative as she ran a finger up and down the length of her throat. A strand of grey-streaked, black hair had escaped the braid she kept it in and draped over her substantial breasts.

The image of a coelenteratezoid filled the main screen. The being's jellyfish-like appearance was belied by the steely-toned words that issued from the translator in correspondence to the flashing, multi-coloured lights that formed a ring around its bell.

"Furthermore, even if I was authorized to grant you passage through our stargate, I would not. Captain Ryan Chandler is liberating the Rowan McPherson personage from slavery. Blue-Green-Green-Red-White-Yellow-Yellow was explicit about the sin of slavery. In pursuing him, you risk having your soul consigned—"

"To the regions of freezing oxygen," interrupted Captain Denardo. "Thank you, Yellow-Blue. I thought it prudent to ask. I have superiors to answer to. Yellow-Blue, may you spawn often outside your mating group.

"Communications, close the channel."

"And that's it? He skips through the stargate, and he's scot-free?" demanded the diminutive, middle-aged woman who stood to the right of the command chair.

"Major Tallman, the coelenteratezoids are within their rights to deny any human ship access to the gate for up to forty-eight hours. I can't go after him without causing a major diplomatic incident. By the way, do you know the origin of the phrase 'scot-free'?"

"I do," said the tall, muscular man wearing lieutenant's pips standing to her left. "If a prisoner escaped to Scotland from England on pre-industrial Earth, they would accept it as a self-imposed banishment. He or she was free so long as they never returned to England."

"Very good, Chow." Tansy's voice was like warm honey.

A blush tinted Chow's young, Malaysian features.

"What does that have to do with anything?" demanded Major Tallman from her place by the captain's chair.

"The pattern is repeating. Ryan does nothing without a goal in mind. Why take Rowan now?"

"They were going to kill the character off."

"Mildred, are you being obtuse on purpose, or do you not follow current events?" Tansy sighed. "I'm sure Rowan's imminent death was what triggered his actions, but what else is happening? Do you truly believe that Ryan is prepared to live his life among aliens? He and Rowan are currently both outlaws in the human sphere of influence."

"You seem rather fond of him, using his first name," said Mildred.

"He gave me permission, and I respect the man. All things considered, at a personal level, I believe in what he's doing. Politically, I would be happy if his story galvanized a clone rights lobby group. Humans Ascendant needs to be knocked down a few pegs. But back to the point. The Zintoid stargate is being towed past Surya at this time."

"Those crazies setting up a rogue-colony world? What did they call it?" said Chow.

"Geb. You see, scot-free. Once the stargate is over a light year away from Surya, Geb is an independent planet with no FTL access to the rest of the galaxy. The Geb constitution grants all forms of clones equal rights, and they will not have a criminal extradition treaty with the United Earth Systems." Tansy smiled.

"Captain, I'm reading a small craft vectoring towards the stargate," interrupted the plump man in the navigator's chair.

"Put it on the big screen and bring up its identification codes," ordered Captain Denardo.

A small, triangular ship appeared on the screen.

The navigator looked at his console, blinked, then looked again. "Ma'am, the ship is called the *Mary*, on a five-year lease to a Mr. John Wilson."

"He's the producer of *Angel Black*, the show Rowan was on," added Mildred.

"It would seem that Ryan's problems aren't over. Can you get a scan of the vessel's interior?" asked Captain Denardo.

"No, ma'am, but it is transmitting a scrambled message towards a satellite just outside coelenteratezoid controlled space," answered the navigator.

"'Curiouser and curiouser.' I believe there may be more to this than we've been told. Log the ship's movements. Communications, prepare a module to traverse the stargate in forty-eight hours' time. List all the charges against Captain Ryan Chandler and his crew. Program it to transmit to the Switchboard Station as soon as it exits the gate. Leave space on it for a personal message from me."

"Do you wish it encoded, ma'am?" asked the communications officer, a blonde-haired woman barely out of her teens.

"Hm, I suppose it would be prudent to keep the information away from the news media. Use scramble code 147."

"Ma'am, that code is ancient. Captain Chandler may have it on file."

"Captain Chandler already knows what he's done, so that hardly matters, Ensign. You have your orders." Tansy smiled and ran her finger the length of her throat.

"Yes, ma'am." The communications officer turned to her console.

"I thought you liked Chandler?" said Mildred.

"I do. I'm obliged by duty to inform the human forces in the Switchboard System about him. Sending them a list of the charges is the *least* I can do. I wish I knew who was aboard that yacht. It would have been nice to mention it in my personal addendum. I guess the fact that it seems to be pursuing Ryan will have to be enough. For the U.E.S. forces."

Mildred rolled her eyes and gritted her teeth.

Croell lay across the central command chair and stared at the main screen. His leathery wings were folded tight against his bat-like body. His other four limbs rested on the floor, and he tapped the claws on the index fingers of his seven-fingered hands on the deck. His black, snake-like head and neck swished lazily back and forth.

"This Captain Chandler is very skilled," commented Zandra, who stood to Croell's right. She was a little smaller than her mate, and the scales on her neck and head were red. Beyond that, except for her having cobra-like fangs, to most *Homo sapiens*, they would appear identical.

"He is blessed by the Great Flyer of the Skies. That attack against the *Saber* was masterful. It now falls to us to retrieve Rowan's body so we may wash the stain of falsehood from our souls."

"I know this is so, but I do admire our quarry's courage."

"As do I. This will be a chase worthy of a song. When we are done, I will compose it. I think a stirring martial air for Captain Chandler and something softer for Rowan, sweet and romantic, yet with a solid sub-beat, but first, we must kill her to complete our contract."

"Yes, my love. Cleansing ourselves of falsehood must come first."

Croell focused on what appeared to be a beautiful woman of mixed Asian-Caucasian descent that sat in the pilot's seat. "Luba, prepare the vessel for gate insertion, then follow the *Star Hawk*. Stay well back. I do not wish to encounter them ship to ship."

"Yes, my master, I will serve you in any way I may. Please remember that Lubas can be equipped with a post-market, alien-adaptive response for all seven human sexually compatible species. Never forget that there are a wide range of post-market additions that can make your

Luba a far more realistic and fulfilling partner. Post-market additions can be obtained at—"

"Luba, shut up!" Zandra hissed through her fangs. "I must re-write some of that thing's core program. *Homo sapiens* are strange to create such a simple-minded toy for their companions."

Croell patted his wife's side. "It is as I've said before, no matter the species, 'some like 'em dumb'. John is apparently of that ilk. If the cost to our souls was not so high, I would relish seeing him ruined for allowing Rowan to escape Sun Valley." Croell shifted on the cushions he'd piled on the command chair. "I wish this vessel had been adapted to our species. Human furniture is so uncomfortable."

"I agree, especially the toilet facilities." Zandra shuddered with disgust. "Husband, have you given any thought to what we are to do when we have completed this mission. I... well, we are abomination, clones drawn from the flesh of..." Zandra stared at the deck.

Croell took a steadying breath before he spoke. "Liars. I have accessed the Encyclopedia Galactica. It would seem that the servitors on the Switchboard Station keep a supply of Ratwaaa's waters in the temple. If we can persuade one to allow us to drink, we will be purified."

"My husband, it is more involved than that. We haven't even had the prayer of the fledgling. I doubt a servitor will be willing to do it on such as we."

"Servitors are batzoid as well, beloved. We may have to trade a service for the prayer, but I swear to you, we will have all the rites. We will not be imprisoned with Siss in the bowels of Petteron. We will have flight in our next life."

Zandra flicked her tongue and lay her chin on her husband's back. "I believe you will make it so. But for this life. Once we have had the obligations performed and drunk of Ratwaaa's holy waters, what is to become of us?"

"We will journey to Petteron and start our lives anew."

"Will John permit us to do so?"

"What choice will he have? We cannot be allowed to move freely in Sun Valley, knowing what we know." Croell stroked the fur on his wife's side. "All will be well once we have killed Rowan and returned her body to John."

Zandra's forked tongue flicked out, touching her husband's foreleg. On the big screen, the stargate grew large, then the universe blinked.

RULES OF THE ROAD

Troy watched through Gunther's eyes as the door opened to reveal a large-busted, early-twenties woman of North American First People's ancestry. In the hours since Troy's last shift, little had happened to further the storyline.

"Gunther?" The woman pushed her long, dark hair over her shoulders.

"Hi, Fran. I hope this isn't a bad time. I think we need to talk, and I couldn't get past your answering machine."

"If you're here to plead on behalf of that cheating scumbag, Carl, forget it! I trusted him, and he slept around on me with, well, with who doesn't matter. He can go..." Fran trailed off.

Troy looked at the monitors. The screen dedicated to Fran showed Gunther's face. It was a mask of sorrow.

"Oh, Divine, you found out. Gunther, I'm so sorry! Come in." Fran motioned into her apartment.

Gunther's emotional readings were raw.

"Tone that down for broadcast, but don't affect the clone," ordered John from the back of the room.

"Yes, Mr. Wilson." Troy tapered back the emotional intensity of the recording.

"This could work out. Be a pleasant change for Gunther to have some real tits to play with," said John.

Troy swivelled his chair around and stared at his producer. The man's fat bulged against the expensive suit he wore, and his thinning, brown hair was cut in a style better suited to a teenager than a middle-aged man. His pink face was pulled into a leer.

"Sir, Gunther and Fran? Sir, I know you want to sex up the show, but that's crazy. Sure, she had a crush in high school, but that was years ago, and Gunther, he's never had any interest in her. She is so not his type, and he likes small-breasted women," objected Troy.

"None of that matters! The audience will love the sexual variety, and there is an appeal to older man/younger woman pieces. Do it!"

Troy swivelled his chair and stared at the control board, searching for inspiration. *What does he think this is, an* Orgy Girls *special feature? I can't believe he made* Angel Black *work for six years. The Fran-Toronk affair is bad enough.* His eyes shifted to a dedicated character screen labelled Angel's perspective. It was filled with a page of the report she was reading. *That's it!*

"Sir, won't this complicate the Fran-Toronk relationship? I mean, Fran having an affair with both Angel's boy... well, lover and Willa's husband. The audience might see her as a villain."

John's face went sour as he bit his cheek. "Very well, we can wait. I wanted to start a new sequence with the pirates trying to reach the FTL transmitter anyway. I've arranged for an octozoid to gain access to the call codes. An underwater adventure will nicely showcase Farley and Quinta while the other fakeys sort out their precious little relationships. Hmm, perhaps in the next post insertion maintenance, we should tweak Carl and Gunther, make them both bi-sexual. A happy triad might draw in the group marriage demographic."

Troy focused on the screen in front of him and ground his teeth.

"I walked in on them. It was awful. I knew Willa cheated on

me before we were married, but I never thought…" Gunther sat on Fran's battered sofa. The furnishings were old, but everything was clean and neat.

"I thought of telling you when I found out, but I didn't know how. What are you going to do?" Fran set her tea on the coffee table.

"For now, share her. All I can do is try and win her back."

"I want to rip Carl's throat out." Fran extended the felinezoid-like claws on her right hand. "Bad enough that we're all freaks with alien DNA grafted into us, and we have 'stop the alien pirates from taking over the world' on our to-do lists. Now we can't even trust each other."

"That's part of why I came. We need to talk, the whole team. I'm calling a meeting for this evening. It will be in my basement so that Toronk can attend."

Fran flushed as her expression became angry. "I won't be in the same room as that cheating piece of stardust!"

Gunther took a deep breath and tried to steady himself. "Please, Fran, this may be the most important meeting any of us ever attend. If you feel any friendship towards me, please come."

Fran stared into Gunther's face. "I'll be there, but I'm not sitting by either Carl or Willa. I know you love her, but after what she did…"

"That will be fine." Gunther smiled as he stood. "I still need to call Angel. Of course, she's dropping by anyway to check on Toronk."

Fran's demeanour changed again. A flash of Toronk below her, the feel of his raspy tongue on her nipples, entered her unguarded surface thoughts.

Gunther looked surprised, but bit down on any response. "I'll let myself out. Seven o'clock. I think a lot of things will become clear."

Ryan sat at the pilot's station and stared at the United

Earth Systems ship on the *Star Hawk*'s main screen. It floated directly in their flight path.

"It's an Amon class, heavy cruiser, fighter-support craft. Nova blast, will you look at that thing." Henry's voice sounded awed.

Rowan sat at the navigator's station and stared at the ship. She could barely make out circular hatches covering the hull. "What's the big? It looks like a black, toilet-roll core."

"Check the systems magnification and ship's range, hot stuff," said Henry.

Rowan's eyes dropped to her scanners. She glanced at the main screen, then back at her console, confirming the numbers. "It's huge!"

"Two hundred metres across and six hundred long. The maximum width that stargates can accommodate." Ryan moved to Henry's seat and pulled a blanket out from under it.

"The ugly stepsister routine again? Hottie boss, this is getting old." Henry looked disgusted.

"They don't know who the third crew member is. I'd like to keep it that way." Ryan threw the blanket over the android. "Have they hailed us yet?"

"They're calling now. Hottie boss, we can't take on that ship. If it farts, we're vapour." Henry shifted under the blanket.

"We beat the *Saber*." Rowan's voice held a forced cheerfulness.

"We won't need to fight. Henry, open communications." Ryan settled back in the command chair as a podgy, bald man in a captain's uniform appeared on the screen.

"Ryan Chandler, you are under arrest for grand theft, firing on a United Earth Systems ship, having an unauthorized active weapons system in United Earth Systems territory, power theft, bringing contraband into a U.E.S. penitentiary—"

"And operating a grav-vehicle without a licence. Captain,

I intercepted the communication from the *Saber*'s probe. If you intend to list the U.E.S. and New Gaea charges pending against my crew and me, I'll go get dinner. I should be finished about the same time you are. Now, if I might know to whom I'm speaking?"

The bald man on the screen went red in the face. "I am Graham Crapper, Captain of the *Chimera*, and you are under arrest. Equalize speed and prepare to be boarded."

Ryan stared at the posturing man's image and laughed. "Captain, with all due respect, permission to come aboard denied. The *Star Hawk* was reclassified as a civilian ship and thus is under Republic jurisdiction. Furthermore, we are in the Switchboard System, a Republic no-fire zone, or had you forgotten? Now, if you would please deviate your course five degrees to port or top as due to hull damage, my ship has been granted priority passage."

"You have to surrender. We have you outgunned a thousand to one. We could vaporize you with a single volley."

"More like ten thousand to one, but I doubt you'll risk a Republic reprimand for firing in a no-fire zone. Face it, you can't touch me."

"Prepare to be boarded." Graham turned beet red and leapt out of his command chair.

"They aren't moving out of the way," commented Rowan.

"Captain, are you in need of assistance? I can only assume that your navigational systems are not functioning. I told you I have a priority approach clearance, and you are still in my flight path."

The sound of a repressed snicker came from the speaker. Graham turned his profile to the pickup. "You're on report!"

"Give them a break, Crapper. They know a good joke when they see one," said Ryan. The guffaws of Henry and Rowan punctuated Ryan's speech.

"Surrender, you're under arrest by order of the United Earth Systems." Graham stood stiffly, facing the video pick up.

"And if I was in the United Earth Systems jurisdiction, I'd oblige you and your guns. I'm not, so get the nova blast out of my way before I log an official complaint with the Switchboard Navigational Control Authority! Do you like being a Captain, Mr. Crapper?" Ryan glared into the pickup.

Crapper shifted uncomfortably, then scowled. The feed went blank.

"They're moving," breathed Rowan.

Ryan released a sigh and moved to the pilot's station. "Henry, contact the Switchboard Station's computer and get me anything you can on Captain Graham Crapper." Ryan snickered.

"Oh, sure. Leave me under a blanket, why don't you? I don't have feelings. I'm just the ugly stepsister. Henry gets to run the whole ship, but when we talk to people, out comes the shroud."

"Henry, you're an asset. No one expects a ship this size to have an AI for an operating system. The less our enemies know, the better for us."

"Fine! Can the asset be uncovered now?"

"No, I need you to connect me to station docking control, felinezoid sector."

"I was wondering where we were going to park. Hottie boss, you sure you got the credit to get in?"

"I've got something better than credit with the felinezoids. I'm family."

Rowan stared across at Ryan. "Pardon? Weren't you and Henry fighting the felinezoids on Murack Five?"

Ryan swallowed hard, and his body went stiff. "A lot of things changed after the accident."

"What happened?" Rowan reached across from her station and squeezed Ryan's hand.

"All you have to know is, I was best man at a felinezoid wedding seven years ago."

"So?" Rowan released Ryan's hand and rubbed the back of her neck, easing the headache that threatened to engulf her.

"By felinezoid tradition, the best man is adopted as a brother, hot stuff. You sure Saggal will vouch for you after all this time?" Henry worked the sheet off his head and threw it to the floor.

"I'm sure. Felinezoids place great stock in a breath debt. Besides, Kate would make him miserable if he didn't." Ryan got up and re-covered Henry. "First, we record the message, then you get to show off your handsome face." Ryan leapt back wide-eyed. "What did I tell you about that hand?"

Rowan broke down laughing.

"An AI's gotta have some fun." Henry sounded smug. "Ready to record a message for transmit. Time to receipt by station, one-hour, thirty-five minutes."

"Polymer prat," muttered Ryan as he sat in the captain's chair. "Begin recording."

Greg sat in the *Freedom's Run* control room, going over the archived images from Ryan's liberation of Rowan. His forked tongue flicked absently from his mouth as his yellow, slit-pupil eyes constricted with concentration. His green skin seemed to shine under the overhead lights.

"We should cut to Ryan's visual perspective here. It shows Rowan's face better," said Arlene from the rolling chair behind Greg.

The image on the screen showed Ryan standing over Rowan with a handheld open in his hand. Rowan lay in her bed, sweat-drenched and gasping for breath. Gunther, Willa and Carl stood to one side, watching with worried expressions.

"We'd misss Ryan's facsial expresssion. Look at him." Greg paused the playback and gestured to the screen.

"The empathic feed will convey his emo... That's right, sight and sound only. Divine, this is hard. Keep it on the long shot."

"Thiss will be good for filling in the empathic voidss on the real verssion."

"That's Michael's plan."

"How iss he keeping sshow autonomy? If he sshow'ss the low-tech version on the sset televission channelss, ssomeone is bound to recognizse the characterss."

"We're recruiting the kids from *SF Geeks* as a focus group. They'll be sworn to secrecy, and none of them are associates of any of the *Angel Black* characters. It should work out. I hope we can stay on top of all the editing. Not to mention the interviews with people. I need to make scripts so actors can fill in the missing scenes."

"When doess Michael intend to sstart disstributing the sshow?"

"The launch party is in a month. He wants the version we're showing to the surrogates to fill in the empathic feeds to be at least three weeks ahead of the real distribution."

"We better get to work then," said Greg.

"About that. I have to do the interviews and somehow teach myself how to write a script. I'm going to leave the editing of the retro version to you."

Greg's eyes dilated to almost rounds. "You ssure?"

"You've got a knack for it, and I'm overloaded with being assistant producer. Ulva can do the initial review of any new images we get from Henry, and things are still quiet in the set region. Now's the time to try and get ahead. If things pan out for Gunther, we'll be swamped soon enough."

"Ssun Valley'ss going out with a bang." Greg's tongue flicked out of his mouth.

"I hope not." Arlene stood and left the room.

AN OLD INJURY

4

Gunther stood in his basement with Willa snuggled under his arm. Carl sat on the stairs gazing at Fran, who was on the opposite side of the room. Angel, a petite, black girl with black, satin-like wings folded against her back, dressed in shorts and a sports bra, stood by Toronk's gurney, stroking the fur on his chest. Farley sat on a blanket spread on the floor, his Asian features reflecting confusion and fear. Quinta lay beside him, resting her otter-like head over his thighs. The green fur that covered her aquiline body glistened from its recent brushings. All eyes focused on Gunther.

"If what you are saying is as it is, how did *Homo sapiens* get the DNA to create Toronk and myself?" Quinta sounded incredulous.

"Prisoners and debtors. One of the techs I scanned had been on a team sent to Swampla to buy DNA from inmates."

Quinta crinkled her nose, and her small, sharp teeth showed. "Prisoners, wonderful. At least I don't have a father to be ashamed of me. Assuming what you are saying is true."

"It's true. It makes sense of everything," said Willa.

"So does a horny, old slut who wants to feel young again," snapped Fran.

Willa hung her head.

"I believe what Gunther has said to be true. It *does* explain a great deal," said Toronk.

Fran blushed and looked at the floor.

"Divine, I want to believe it. It means that Rowan is still alive, and I'm off the hook for Farley. I mean, like, temporary insanity or what?" said Angel.

"Hey!" objected Farley.

"Farley is a fine male. One need not be insane to wish his company. Your own Rowan, whom you all esteem, thought him worth a long journey to where the best fish congregate in currents that make them sluggish, resulting in easy capture by hand, tooth or net."

Gunther smiled as he watched Quinta. Her lips stopped moving well before the translator nano-bots had converted the language to human.

The jammer began beeping. Gunther turned to the controls and checked a gauge. "I have to shut the system down. Think about what I said. If we can get to the other shows, we might be able to fight back. Force them to set us free. Stop fighting, killing and dying for them. We'll meet back here in three days, same time."

"Before you halt the system, I wish to offer to examine it. My mother on Swampla and I used to... Oh, if this is true, I have no mother. Still, I have a hobbyist knowledge of electronics and technical systems of a more advanced nature than you have access to. I could perhaps help improve your jammer."

"Much appreciated, Quinta. Now I have to shut down. Remember, we can't let on that we know." Gunther threw a switch, and the jammer went silent.

"And that's it. Hopefully, my device helped us all understand each other a little better." Gunther stood by Willa but didn't touch her.

Fran smiled evilly. "I understand all too well!" She moved to Gunther, threw her arms around him and kissed him hard. Gunther's arms flailed at his sides, and his eyes shot open. Fran broke the kiss and turned to Willa.

"You want to trade, I'll trade. I'm sure he knows how to treat a woman." Fran turned back to Gunther. "Any time you want, come 'round." Strutting defiantly, Fran left the room, pausing only to scowl at Carl.

"Oh, stardust!" breathed Willa.

Quinta looked up at Farley. "Husband swapping. This is beginning to sound like one of the stories in those magazines you keep under your bed. The ones with the pictures of *Homo sapiens* cop—"

"Quinta!" A blush reddened Farley's cheeks as all eyes turned to him.

"You said it was natural for males of your species to collect such materials." Quinta sounded smug.

"We'll discuss it later," said Farley.

Willa stifled a giggle when Quinta winked at her.

Rowan tapered back on her grav-lift's power and lowered the sapling in its support box to the floor.

"That's the last of them. We'll unload the dead trees when we're in space-dock. I can probably sell the wood and support boxes for a few credits." Ryan came over and connected a water hose to the support box.

"Should we have lost so many? We haven't even reached the Switchboard Station yet." Rowan wiped her brow on the sleeve of her sweater. She was sweating despite the climate control.

"It's the high-G manoeuvres. Don't worry, we were overloaded to start with, and the coffee and orange oil are what's going to pay our way in civilized space." Ryan put his arms around her and pulled her close. Rowan nestled into the embrace and closed her eyes. Ryan's arms were the only place she felt safe. Her mind stilled, and she enjoyed the warmth. She felt his lips brush the top of her head, and she smiled.

"Ryan, I..." Rowan bit her lip. She didn't want to lie to him. She wanted to love him; needed him without question.

"You'll say it when you're ready." Ryan's voice was

soothing.

Rowan smiled. "I do, you know. It's just, I've only ever said the words to one other man, not counting my Dad, and we both know how that ended."

Ryan pulled away and tilted her chin up so he could look her in the eyes. "I didn't enrage an entire Republic member state so I could run out and cheat on you. Besides, your best friend isn't my type." Ryan grinned. "Now, your mom, I could be tempted. Guess Carl and I have something in common."

"Carl did not have a thing for my mother!" Rowan playfully swatted Ryan's chest.

"Not that I mind the live sex show, but if you two fleshies are done, we've got a reply from Saggal." Henry's voice blasted from a speaker in the wall of what had been the enlisted men's barracks. The gymnasium-sized room was full of line upon line of saplings in support boxes.

"Is Crapper still tailing us?" asked Rowan.

"One thousand and one kilometres behind, hot stuff."

"He's persistent; I'll give him that. Just outside the legal safety margin for two days straight. Henry, we're on our way to the bridge."

Henry transmitted the roughly edited feed of the last few days to the pickup dish Michael had told him would be waiting for him. When he received the 'message received' confirmation, he emptied the memory cache of the hidden onboard recorder and smiled.

"Gotta love it when it works. Now, if hottie-boss and sweety would only shag more, I'd have it made."

The door at the back of the bridge opened, admitting Ryan and Rowan. Rowan moved to the navigator's station as Ryan sat in the command chair.

"Henry, play it." Ryan leaned back and relaxed.

A chubby felinezoid, with grey-tabby markings, appeared

on the screen. What looked to be a living room filled the rest of the image. Rowan watched a paper airplane float across the background.

"Ryan, of course, I will advance the money for you to dock. I can even do it out of the bar's operating expenses. You would not believe what coffee is going for at present. You chose an opportune time to visit. Kate and I bought out old Qualla. That puts our combined shares in Wesnakee at fifty point one per cent. Getting coffee in will soothe the other partners considerably."

A high-pitched shriek sounded over the speaker while in the background a felinezoid, with a spotted pelt, less than half Saggal's height, ran across the living room chased by a dark-skinned, human girl of about five. The girl was waving a rag doll over her head.

"I'M GONNA GET YOU. I'M GONNA GET YOU," screamed the girl. There was a crash, and Saggal looked out of the camera's frame.

"Graff, Samantha, you two settle down and clean that up. Your mother will be home any minute." Saggal turned back to the screen and flicked his tail. "Kids, what can you do?

"To continue, I will arrange a space dock for you. Kate and I were both sorry to hear about Joslin; our thoughts are with you.

"On the other matter, of all sentients, who would understand better than Kate and I? If Rowan is watching this, let me say that *Angel Black* and *Defenders of the Crystal* are the only e-entertainments Kate and I experience. Well, except for *A Cat's Life* once in a while. What can I say? It's nice to go primitive after a hard day."

"It's mine, it's mine, it's mine!" Samantha screamed in the background.

"Then give me back my flyer control!" called a slightly deeper, but still immature, voice.

Saggal looked off-camera. "Graff, put your sister down and give her back her doll. Samantha, stop trying to bite your brother and give him back his flyer control. Both of you, pick up that mess right now! Your mother's been working on the taxes; she doesn't need anything more to make her angry. Now move!"

The humanoid cat turned back to the screen. "Where was I? Oh yes. Rowan, all I can say is that Ryan has excellent taste. Kate and I both admire you. You will be welcome in our—"

A shriek sounded from off-camera. Samantha came running into the frame.

"Daddy, he hit me," cried the little girl.

"She bit me first." The felinezoid child ran to his father.

"Samantha, Graff didn't extend his claws, and I've told you before, if you bite him, he has a right to defend himself."

Saggal looked into the camera. "We've tried everything else. Are all *Homo sapiens* children so vicious? No offence, but it is a wonder you do not kill each other before you are seven."

"Daddy," cried the little girl.

"*Gerraplica!* And don't you children start saying it or else." Saggal looked disgusted. "I have to put dinner on, or Kate might try to cook when she gets in; we both know that is something to be avoided.

"We look forward to seeing you. Space traffic control will direct you to the space dock.

"Grrrrr." Saggal bared his teeth and growled as Samantha pulled hard on his fur. "Samantha, 'small, sweet-tasting beetle used as snack food', stroke, don't pull. I have to go. And don't worry. Kate and I live in the felinezoid sector, so we won't be legally harbouring a fugitive. And you were always the good one back in the day. I have to totally change my view of you, Ryan."

Samantha gripped her doll in one hand and started clubbing Saggal with it.

"I better go. Contact us when you make space-dock, Kate and I will meet you."

The felinezoid child was now tugging on his father's arm.

Saggal looked into the camera with a harried expression. "I will speak with you soon." The message ended.

Rowan swivelled her chair around and stared at Ryan.

"He looks good, up a couple of kilos but still shaggable," commented Henry.

"Running the bar seems to agree with him. I'll have to tease him about getting soft. Fifty point one per cent, wow! When they told me they were spending their severance to buy into Wesnakee, I thought they were nuts. Glad I was wrong."

"He seemed nice, but the kids? I mean? Human-alien breeding?" asked Rowan.

"Graff is from a donated egg fertilized with Saggal's sperm. He was gestated in a vat, like a clone. The girl was donated sperm. Kate always wanted kids," explained Ryan.

"Oh, all right then."

"And, hot stuff. The polite way to say it is inter-species. All the species are aliens to each other," said Henry.

"Got you."

"Any change in Crapper's status?" Ryan moved to the pilot's station and began a systems check.

"None. Do you think he'll try something?" Rowan inspected her navigator's console.

"That message was on an open channel. Crapper now knows we're not docking in the human sector. He might decide to get cute."

"I don't think he's that bright, hottie boss. I've got his service file. Seems he's been bounced from post to post. His daddy is a United Earth Systems Member of Parliament."

"Political captains. Divine, I hate political captains!"

"If he's incompetent, isn't that good for us?" Rowan started double-checking the *Star Hawk*'s flight path.

"To an extent. Problem is, with the amount of firepower

he has, he doesn't need to be good to vaporize us. You see, the *Saber* had us outclassed, but we could hurt them. Tansy was the real danger there because she's so good, but she was also predictable. I knew she wasn't going to cause a diplomatic incident to get us. Crapper might not look at the long-range cost of his actions. So, he's busted back to scrubbing toilets. We aren't any less dead."

"You're such an optimist," said Henry.

Rowan looked at her console. "That's odd."

"What?" Ryan moved to stare over her shoulder.

"It's like a g-g-ghost following the *Chimera*. It's just a flyspeck, but I keep g-g-g-getting g-g-g-glimpses of it. Why am I st-st-st-stuttering?"

"I can't see anything." Ryan touched Rowan's shoulder in a reassuring way.

"Wait for it. It ducks out of the *Chimera*'s sh-sh-sh-shadow every two minutes for about t-t-t-ten seconds."

"Hmm. Henry, play the personal note on the end of the message Tansy sent on that probe, just the last part." Ryan rubbed the back of his neck.

"Sure thing, boss."

Tansy's voice issued from a speaker. "Unknown elements launched by other concerned factions may be involved in the manhunt. Efforts should be made to discover and coordinate these factors."

"Sounds like a warning, hottie boss." Henry drummed his fingers.

"Th-th-there," called Rowan.

Ryan watched the main screen as a ship quickly ducked out from behind the *Chimera* then disappeared behind the larger vessel again.

"A low end, automatic pilot ordered to check on us, then duck out of view. Crapper isn't the only one following us. Ro, have you done the section on ship identification yet?" Ryan moved to the pilot's station.

"Not for another th-th-three weeks. I'm st-st-still learning s-s-sensor configuration. S-s-sorry."

"She says sorry. Does three months of the program in one, and she's apologizing. Tell you what, hottie, give plastic a try; I promise you won't have to apologize for making my year." Henry leered at Rowan.

"HENRY!" Ryan and Rowan shouted in unison.

"He is right, though. You have nothing to apologize for," added Ryan. "Henry, integrate with the navigator's systems and prepare for data pick up."

Ryan moved to the pilot's station and strapped himself in. "Rowan, find me pull points for a lateral move and a correction."

"Aye." Rowan glanced at her lover. She'd learned that he was in many ways several men. Currently, he was Captain Chandler, and Captain Chandler commanded obedience. Her hands flew over her console, finding and inputting the best pull points for the gravity laser drive. "Pull t-t-targets in the local coordinates file."

"Got them. Give me a count for our friend's next appearance."

"T-t-ten seconds." Rowan felt nauseous, and her head throbbed with every beat of her heart.

"Ready, Henry?"

"Hot and ready to shag."

"Can the stardust."

"Five, four, th-th-three, t-t-two, one," Rowan counted down.

Ryan pressed buttons on his console, causing the *Star Hawk* to pull to the side at twenty-five Gs of acceleration. The inertial dampers kicked in, reducing the pull on the crew to two-point-five Gs.

"Th-th-there it is," cried Rowan.

"I got it, sweetheart," said Henry. "It's a space yacht, mid-sized. Telemetry ident is… It's called the *Mary*. Hey, hot stuff, looks like the AS-F module has an admirer."

"Put it on the big screen. What's its armament?" demanded Ryan.

"Emergency notification flares and self-destruct.

Somebody's got a sense of humour if they think that will do squat to us." Henry grinned until he swivelled his chair and saw the set of Ryan's shoulders.

Rowan watched Ryan's grim face as he executed the counter pull that would return them to their flight path. "What's wrong?"

"I don't like unknowns. Henry, check the ship's registry files and find out who owns or leases it."

"I'll have to contact the Switchboard Station for that. The registry ident files on this tub haven't been updated since they scrapped her."

"What d-d-do you th-think… Ryan, I d-d-don't feel w-w-well." Rowan tried to stand. Ryan barely caught her as she fell.

"Divine!" Ryan lay her on the deck and checked her breathing and pulse before he opened his handheld and examined her physical telemetry. "Stardust!"

"What is it?" Henry's voice reflected concern despite the fact that he already knew the answer.

"Everything. The nano-bots that kept the leftover venom inactive are breaking down. The venom's destroying her red blood cells. Kadar was afraid this might happen. She's also bleeding into her brain. Using her telekinesis to save me on the asteroid weakened the blood vessels. Vertion leech venom acts as an anticoagulant. She needs a medical doctor." Ryan pressed buttons on his remote, directing the nano-bots in Rowan to focus on repairing the blood vessels in her brain. Another set of commands activated the remaining poison grabber nano-bots.

"That's not going to be easy." Henry monitored Ryan's emotions. The level of concern was off the charts, and there was an undercurrent of fear. *At least Michael will like it. With friends like him, who needs enemies?* he thought.

"I'm taking her to medical. Maybe I can configure some nano-bots to help with this mess."

"How long do you think she has?"

Ryan carried Rowan from the bridge into the metre-wide

hallway of the flight crew section, speaking as he moved. "I don't know. On set, we'd do a tech intervention immediately. The nano-bots can hold her together for a while. My guess, two weeks to a month. She should seem fine in an hour or two. What she really needs is a stem cell insertion to replace the ones I used to repair her brain damage, bump up the number of medical nano-bots in her system and to get the last of that nova blasted venom out of her."

The elevator doors at the end of the hall opened. Ryan carried Rowan into the nine-metre-square lift. "Thanks, Henry."

"Don't mention it. I'm fond of the little hottie."

"Quite the crew of misfits, aren't we?" Ryan gazed into Rowan's pale face.

"Family, hottie boss. Family." Henry's voice was soft as it issued from the speaker.

FINDING A PARKING SPOT

Croell lay on the king-sized bed in the captain's cabin. It was the only comfortable piece of furniture in the ship. He supported a handheld in front of his face with the declassified service record of Ryan Chandler displayed on its screen.

"This is an astounding myth from the humans' distant past. You should read it." Zandra lay beside her husband, gazing into another handheld.

Croell rolled his eyes. "How could a species that had not yet reached even an industrial technology create something as small as a ring that was that powerful? It doesn't make sense."

"The ring is an allegory for forbidden technologies. You should give the book a chance. I've developed a taste for human literature. They can't compete with the works of Mapap, but some of them have been touched by the Great Flyer of the Skies. Take Gandalf, for instance, he is much like the prophet Ratnay, and Aragorn could be King Borla in the legend of Jakonee."

"The Great Flyer of the Skies comes to all that live in different guise. I prefer—"

"The *Star Hawk* has performed a course alteration," Luba's voice issued through the intercom.

"I must go." Croell leapt off the bed.

Zandra followed her husband into the hall that led down the centre of the ship to the bridge. A moment later, they stepped into the control room and stared at the screen.

The *Star Hawk* was displayed arcing back behind the bulk of the *Chimera*.

"Luba, replay the images from the *Star Hawk*'s appearance." Croell settled on the cushion covered command chair.

The main screen filled with the image of the *Star Hawk* appearing from behind the *Chimera*, then jerking to the side, maintaining its line of sight with the *Mary* as the yacht moved back to its hiding place behind the *Chimera*.

"What does it mean?" said Zandra.

"It means that Captain Chandler is as skilled as his record indicates. We have lost the element of surprise. It is of no importance. We could do little until he docks with the Switchboard Station." Croell made a sound like sandpaper on softwood.

"What amuses you?"

"This, my love." Croell gestured to the screen. "This is what the Great Flyer of the Skies meant for batzoid to be. Hunters, predators. To sweep down on our prey and grip them in our hands. This is what it is to be the chosen species of the Great Flyer of the Skies. To challenge a worthy opponent, to hunt our prey, never knowing when it may turn and fight. To put skill, mind, and body to the test. This challenge is a blessing."

Zandra looked at her mate, drops of venom forming on the ends of her fangs. At times like this, she remembered why she loved him and knew it was more than a construct. "Is there anything you need to do?"

Croell looked at his wife. As much as the confined bridge allowed, she had spread her wings. Their black surface seemed to shine. Croell felt his heart speed up.

"There is nothing I can do until we reach the station." Croell shifted positions, then allowed his forked tongue to dart from his mouth and lick the venom from Zandra's fang tips.

"There is much we can do, beloved." Zandra led the way to their quarters, never fully furling her wings.

The Luba at the controls transmitted the telemetry from the two batzoids and the onboard monitoring system to the dish on the Switchboard Station. It wasn't programmed to question or think, just to follow orders. It was a machine, nothing more. The subroutines that Michael had added to its program worked perfectly.

Rowan stirred on the examination table and opened her eyes. The first thing she saw was the inverted image of the diagnostic monitor. The displays were a mix of orange and green colours and symbols, most of which she didn't recognize. She blinked, then looked around the *Star Hawk*'s medical bay. Ryan stood at one end, mounting the final piece of panelling that closed the section containing the three medical cots off from what was now cargo area.

"Ryan," she called as she tried to sit up.

"Rowan." Ryan raced to her side. "I had to do something. I was going nuts, but I didn't want to leave you. I hope I didn't wake you. I—"

Rowan laughed.

"What?" Ryan looked perplexed.

"I think you're in worse shape than I am. What happened? And if the short version is I'm dying, start with the long version."

Ryan smiled gravely. "Remember how I told you that in the set..."

Rowan scowled.

"In Sun Valley, we'd do a tech intervention every year. I'd hoped that with you not using your powers, you wouldn't need one, but you used your power and—"

"If I don't get a tech intervention, I'll die." Rowan looked disgusted.

"I'm sorry. If we can find a doctor on the Switchboard Station with the right equipment, it won't be that bad. It's just—"

"Let me guess. We can't go into U.E.S. territories, and all the doctors with the right equipment are in the human sector."

Ryan looked at the floor.

"Ryan, cut the passive-aggressive stardust. You can't blame me for being angry about having my DNA twisted around into the high maintenance mess my body is."

"When the schedule-green clone is ready for the transfer—"

"In fifteen years." A hint of fear entered Rowan's voice. "Do you really think you can keep me alive that long?"

Ryan met Rowan's gaze. Rowan almost retreated from the look on his face. "If I have to wrestle the Divine itself!" Ryan's gaze softened, and he took her hand. "Once we reach Geb, things will be easier. I'll make this right, I promise."

Rowan settled on the cot. "Ryan... I do, you know."

Ryan smiled. "I love you too. We haven't gotten this far to lose. You should rest. We'll be docking in another twelve hours." Ryan returned to his work while Rowan settled on the cot and watched him. A smile touched the corners of her mouth. "Henry, privacy on. Ryan, my headache is better now. Want to take advantage of it?"

"I'm sorry, Trevor, I've reviewed the pertinent otterzoid laws. I don't think we have a chance." Victoria stared across her desk at her client. She was a classically beautiful brunette with a fit body. Her near-perfect features were drawn into a mask of compassion, and her warm, brown eyes held sympathy.

"What am I supposed to do? He's my son! I know I didn't supply the sperm—how could I—but I've raised him. I've cared for him." The man buried his face in his hands.

Victoria examined her office as she let the man cry. Nature scapes from Earth filled the walls, and the ceiling was a cloud-flecked, blue sky. Her desk was black polycarbonate with a glossy finish, while both she and her client's chairs were upholstered in black leather. A matching sofa ran the length of one side wall. She faced the door when she sat at her desk. Having waited long enough for her client to be open to comforting, she stood, revealing that she was tall for a woman. She hugged her client around the shoulders. "My best advice would be to try and work it out with your ex. Misra can be headstrong, but she's not a monster."

Trevor lifted his tear-streaked face from his hands. "She won't even speak to me. I don't stand a chance as long as her mother's on station. That bitch is the reason we broke up. She hates me for being *Homo sapiens*."

"I'm sorry. Historically, the otterzoid female stayed in the hutch to defend the pups against predators while the males hunted for food. Their whole matriarchy sees females as the only fit guardians of children."

"Could we get this into a human court, or a Republic one?" Trevor's voice trembled.

"No, Karas is otterzoid. Their laws apply. I'll talk to Misra as a friend, not your lawyer. For Karas' sake, she needs to listen. You're the only father he's ever known."

"Would you please?"

"Of course. I think you should go and try and get some rest. You look exhausted." Victoria's voice was soothing and lovely, almost hypnotic.

"Thanks, Mrs. Hart. I could use some sleep." Standing, Trevor left the office as Victoria collapsed into her chair and closed her eyes. A moment later, she heard her office door retract into the wall and the sound of a familiar step.

She didn't bother to open her eyes. "Hello, Bill."

"Jerical said you were done for the day," remarked a deep, masculine voice.

Victoria opened her eyes and smiled. The man she faced was of late middle years with greying, blond hair. His face was too angular to be truly handsome, but it lent him a ruggedness she knew some *Homo sapiens* women found attractive. His blue, traditionally-cut suit showed off a muscular build. She could tell he'd been cheating on his diet again from a slight tightening of his belt.

"Twenty extra laps each day this week." She smiled at him.

"That's not fair! I had to eat to be polite." Striding around the desk, he kissed Victoria, who responded enthusiastically.

Vicky broke the kiss and rested in the circle of his arms. "I'm not having your heart give out one second before it has to, my love."

"That won't be for a long time yet." Bill kissed the top of her head. To an outsider, they could have been father and daughter except for the obvious intimacy in their pose.

"You can't know what a long time is for me, beloved. But tomorrow isn't today. Did you come to get the recording?" Victoria opened the bottom drawer of her desk and ejected a cube the size of a thick, soft-cover book from a box-shaped device. Taking a second cube from the drawer above the first, she slipped it into the vacated slot.

Bill took the cube from her. "I'm sending it out with the next diplomatic courier to Gaea. Mike sent me an FTL telegraph that things are going well. He's thinking of forgoing a hiatus and forging on with new episodes."

"Yes, so long as the series is good, he could re-run earlier episodes in a less desirable time slot. That makes sense. I accessed some of the data earlier."

"Oh, I thought e-entertainments were 'a disgusting travesty that legitimized the exploitation of sentient beings'." Bill's voice took on a teasing quality as he quoted her.

"They are, and don't tease. You don't know what it's like to be a slave. This entertainment is different. It is a tool of political change. It gives real insights into what it is to be *Homo sapiens* and what it is to be reviled because your origin isn't what others call 'normal'. Besides, I finished demolishing the Salik appeal this morning. I deserved a treat. I am so fed up with that blasted batzoid going on about how his murdering that poor spiderzoid was 'the will of the Great Flyer of the Skies'. It disgusts me when beings use their narrow interpretation of spirituality to justify their atrocities. I hope they keep him in indentured servitude until his wings fall off."

"With you, and I'm sure they will. Do you want to go for a walk in the arboretum after I drop this with the courier?" Bill held up the cube.

"Give me a minute to back everything up." Vicky reached under her desk and pulled out a long cable that ended in an interface jack. She thrust the interface up her left nostril until it clicked. Her eyes fluttered, then she extracted the jack. "Let's go." Taking Bill's hand, she led him from the office.

⊂══◇►

"Yes, I am *Homo sapiens*. Yes, this is a U.E.S. design ship. No, I am not docking with the human sector. My registry is with the Republic Shipping and Trade Administration. Please check your records. A space dock facility has been reserved for this vessel in the felinezoid sector." Ryan sat in the command chair, looking exasperated.

"Proceed to space dock fifty-seven in the human sector for processing," repeated the creature on the bridge's main screen. It looked like a six-legged crab with a mat of cilia growing off its shell. The shell itself was a blue so dark it bordered on black, and it had four pincers at either end. There was nothing that could be called a face on the alien. The walls of the chamber in the background were covered with cilia.

"Crabzoids. Hive minds are nova blasted sticklers for protocol. They don't even shag properly. When the colony gets too big, they form a second central nexus by splitting their own in half and off goes half the individuality." Henry looked disgusted.

"I hope you blanked the transmission for that." Ryan swivelled the command chair to look at Henry.

"Oh, stardust, someone disconnected half my logic circuits. I don't have a brain in my chest. Daa." Henry rolled his eyes.

"That's a hive mentality?" asked Rowan from the navigator's console.

"And a methane breather. I don't know much about the species. Never fought for, with, or against them. Excuse me. Henry, open the channel." Ryan sighed, then looked directly into the video pick up.

"Gatherer component two-five-seven of the Star Searcher individuality. I have berth space arranged with the felinezoids. I do not intend to dock with the human sector. Please check your records for my docking clearance."

"This component has been instructed by Ryan Chandler's core individuality that Ryan Chandler is to dock in the human sector to facilitate reintegration."

Rowan noticed that the hairs on the forward-facing end of the crabzoid waved as the words issued from the speaker.

"My core individuality?" repeated Ryan.

"The sub-designation, Captain Graham Crapper, under the authority of the over-self, Admiral Yvonne Carlotta LaFleur, has ordered Ryan Chandler's reintegration with the over-self. Why does Ryan Chandler resist this?"

"Space traffic control, I am pausing transmission to double-check translation. I will stay in pre-programmed holding pattern." Ryan turned to Henry and made a slashing motion across his throat.

"Right, hottie boss. Lines cut."

"I can't believe it. Crapper must have called ahead to set this up. From his service file, I didn't think he had the imagination. Probably his XO's idea," griped Ryan.

"What's happening?" Rowan swivelled her chair to look at Ryan.

"Sushi boy thinks we're part of a hive intellect." Henry waved at the screen, which now displayed a view of the Switchboard Station. The station was formed of wedges coming off a circular core that ran the height of the station. The effect was reminiscent of a spiral staircase.

"A notion I'm about to disavow it of. Henry, reference the Encyclopedia Galactica section on crabzoids and put it on the screen."

The screen filled with text, and all went silent as Ryan and Rowan read. Henry focused inward, directing standard maintenance on a repair robot with part of his RAM. Another section of his mind edited down the feeds from Rowan and Ryan for transmit, while yet another activated a playback of *Orgy Girls - 5 Boys with Toys*.

I am so bored, thought the android as he dedicated yet another sliver of RAM to processing a paper on the latest technological purchases involving ship drives. Nearly two minutes passed before Ryan spoke.

"Henry, open the channel." Ryan sat back in his command chair and stared at the pickup as the space traffic controller appeared on the screen.

"Gatherer component two-five-seven of the Star Searcher individuality, please interface with the Star Searcher over-self. Such an exalted mind must have awareness that *Homo sapiens* are social individuals, not communal selves. I am not of Captain Graham Crapper's over-self. Your species consciousness recognized that individual sentients are not bound by duty to over-self. Please confirm that I am an individuality, then let me proceed to my docking space in the felinezoid sector."

The crab-like alien clicked its pincers and the cilia on its shell waved as it scuttled to a section of wall covered with cilia.

"The walls must be the remote organic link to its over-self," commented Rowan. Her eyes were wide as she watched the space traffic controller push its shell against the cilia. The cilia on the wall and the ones on the crab-like alien's back waved together.

"It's calling home." Henry watched the screen with his android eyes.

"About time. Now let's hope one of the other sections of the consciousness knows that humans are individuals."

"And if they don't?" Rowan looked at Ryan.

"Then they'll have to swallow their pride and check with the switchboard computer. In which case, it will be seen as an insult to the over-mind, and we can count on having the lowest priority for docking you can get." Ryan rubbed the back of his neck.

Gatherer component two-five-seven scuttled away from the interface. The cilia on the front of its shell waved as the voice issued from the *Star Hawk*'s speakers.

"Please forgive this component's ignorance. Captain Crapper misled this component in his communication, and this component had no reason to interface with its over-self until this recent time segment. This component is clearing you for docking bay thirty-two in the felinezoid sector. Please be advised this component is contrite. If this component may make reasonable amends for the life period of yours it has wasted, please do not hesitate to ask. Star Searcher does not appreciate having its components misled into being discourteous. Have a pleasant dural period. Please surrender ship's control to Space Traffic Control computer."

"Thank you, Star Searcher component. May Star Searcher's vast wisdom shine like a sun in the cosmos." Ryan left the captain's chair and pressed the buttons on the pilot's console that gave control of the *Star Hawk* to the switchboard computer.

"I love the Encyclopedia Galactica. Henry, place a call to Saggal and Kate. Tell them we'll be docking in an hour." Ryan leaned back in his chair.

Rowan's gaze was alternating between the view of the Switchboard Station on the big screen and her instruments.

"What's up, Ro?" asked Ryan when he saw the look on her face.

"The station. It's nearly two hundred kilometres long, and it's over fifty across."

"Biggest station in the known universe, sweetness. Best multi-species brothels as well. The deviants' travel guide gave it a full five hard—" began Henry.

"Henry, don't finish that sentence, and that's an order. Nova blast, I wish you'd let me adjust the runtime on your sex drive." Ryan shook his head, then smiled at Rowan. "The station has to be big. It houses a population of each of the one hundred and thirty-seven stargate enabled species that ever were."

"I… wow. In Sun Valley, we only had seven. I'm kinda ashamed of myself to say it, but I don't know if I'm ready to, well…" Rowan looked uncomfortable.

"See the whole zoo. Relax, Ro. Only fifteen species are compatible to move through the human safe zones." Ryan took her hand.

"Why'd we only have seven on, well… in… Oh, stardust, no use denying, on my show?"

"Sexual compatibility." Henry leered at Rowan.

"You can't be serious?" Rowan swivelled her chair and stared at the android.

Ryan blushed. "It was always a consideration, the curiosity about fur is pretty high, and well…"

Rowan's face reddened.

Ryan cringed. "Did I mention I had nothing to do with the initial series planning?"

Henry laughed as Rowan swivelled her chair and stared resolutely at her control board.

HELLO OLD FRIEND 6

Ryan and Rowan waited by the hangar bay's ramp while the *Star Hawk*'s hull was disinfected and checked for radiation. The atmosphere in the space dock was then established.

"It's a standard felinezoid mix, twenty-two per cent oxygen, seventy-seven per cent nitrogen, point five CO_2, point five other mixed gases. Fine for human breathing, such poor fragile creatures that you organics are. If you weren't so shaggable, I don't know why I'd put up with you. Hey, sweet stuff, why not let hottie boss get reacquainted with old Saggal and you stay here? I'm sure I could entertain you." Henry's voice was smug.

"The weak, fragile organics thank you, Henry." Rowan looked into the video pick up and smiled seductively, then bit her lip and swayed back and forth, swishing the light, cotton dress she'd chosen from her wardrobe. Her voice became breathy. "But I think I should go with Ryan. Entertainment from a big, strong android might be more than this poor, little human could handle. After all, I'm only warm, soft flesh." Rowan traced a finger down her throat and over her breasts. "Packaged in skin, with billions of sensory nerves, so easy to stimulate." Rowan licked her lips. "What would I do with a big, strong android?"

There was a gasp, then a long silence. Ryan looked at Rowan and swallowed hard as she posed.

Henry's voice trembled when it issued from the speaker. "Hottie boss, tell her not to do that. I'm only polymers and silicone."

Ryan stood, staring at Rowan, who grinned.

"Got you. And it's not as if you didn't deserve it. Shall we go?" Rowan turned to Ryan, who was red-faced and moving uncomfortably.

After a long moment, Ryan asked, "What?" then closed his mouth.

"Men!" Rowan rolled her eyes. "Ryan, are you going to open the hatch? Saggal and Kate will be waiting."

"Oh… Yes." Ryan swallowed, regaining his composure. "Henry, open the hangar bay ramp, please."

"Sure thing, hottie-boss."

The ramp from the *Star Hawk*'s gymnasium-sized hangar bay lowered onto a floor of polished, white material. Rowan winked at Henry's video pickup before following Ryan down the ramp into the felinezoid space dock. The chamber reached out for just under two metres on all sides of the *Star Hawk* and was maybe three metres taller than the ship. It ended in a glass-fronted communications area with three self-adjusting cushion-chairs in front of it. The setup was identical to the one Rowan had used at the coelenteratezoid anti-proton station. A large door beside the interface area provided access to the cargo transfer chamber.

"The damage doesn't look as bad under decent lighting." Ryan was staring at the *Star Hawk*. A multitude of three-clawed, landing legs held the ship's flat bottom three metres above the floor.

Rowan eyed the section of the craft's hull that she could see. It still looked like obsidian, except for a gouge in the forward port side. Tattered camouflage tarps dangled off the hull around the damage. "If you say so. You do have the parts you'll need, right?"

"It's just three standard hull sections. I have them in the bomb-bay ready and waiting."

"Good."

"I almost forgot." Ryan pulled a black, oval pendant

about two centimetres long out of his pocket and passed it to Rowan.

She examined it closely. "It's the *Star Hawk*. I love it, thank you."

"You're welcome. Be sure to wear it whenever you're away from the ship. It scrambles incoming messages so nobody can operate your control pack."

Rowan draped the chain around her neck. "Beautiful and functional." She kissed Ryan, then wiped the sweat off her brow. "Kinda warm in here."

"Felinezoid room temperature is twenty-three degrees Celsius. Murrow is warmer than Earth."

"Murrow?"

"The human name for their homeworld. The felinezoid word sounds like something coughing up a hairball."

The entry door beside the communications station opened, and Saggal stepped through. He was followed by a plump woman with tan skin and long, black hair. The woman was dressed in shorts and a t-shirt. Her head was level with the felinezoid's armpit.

"Thank you very much. Perhaps I should mention that 'Earthiss' is our word for hemorrhoid," said Saggal.

Ryan jerked around to face the voice. "Saggal, you smelly-arsed tomcat, how long have you been listening?"

"Long enough to lose a bet. Kate told me you'd look at the damage before even trying to say hello, you over-sexed chimpanzee with limited grooming skills."

Ryan ran towards the big felinezoid. The two of them hugged, pounding each other on the back.

"Rowan, I'm Kate." The woman approached with her hand extended.

"Nice to meet you." Rowan took the proffered hand.

"This is a treat for Saggal and me. You're our favourite e-star. You never expect to meet an e-star, but you always wonder how much is lost in the editing and…" Kate grew silent as Rowan's expression grew sad. "I'm sorry, I'm sure you have a very different view of e-entertainments than we do."

"It's okay. It's just… It's hard to accept that my whole life was nothing but a show."

Kate smiled. "Honey, a human writer once said, 'all the world's a stage, and we are all but players in it.' Your life's as real as anyone's. Heck, more real than most folk who don't spend time in combat or rescue operations."

"Thanks, Kate. Is that normal?" Rowan gestured to where Ryan and Saggal had locked arms and were trying to wrestle each other to the floor.

Kate smiled. "For those two, that's mild. You should have seen them on our wedding day. Ryan, don't hurt my husband. Good living's caught up with him, so play nice."

"I am as fit as ever I was." Saggal tried to sweep Ryan's legs with his tail.

"To be tied," added Kate, then conspiratorially to Rowan, "We bought a virtual exercise unit for our contract day gift. Now the trick is trying to convince ourselves to use it."

Rowan laughed. "Some things don't change. My mom bought my dad a gym membership; it was like pulling teeth to get him to work out."

"Gunther doesn't need to work out," Kate growled.

"That's my dad, you know." Rowan put on a face of mock outrage.

Kate smiled. "I'm no worse than Angel or Fran were in high school. They both had a crush on him."

"Stardust, things I don't want to know. Like, my dad is good looking, but… he's my dad."

"You must have suspected. Just like Carl having a thing for your mother."

"Have you been talking to Ryan? Carl does not have a thing for my mother!" Rowan stamped her foot.

Kate looked at Rowan and smirked. "You've obviously never experienced his perspective."

Rowan shook her head. "I appreciate you helping us. Ryan really wants to repair the damage before we go to—"

"Shhhh. Lose lips vaporize ships. Always remember, any

public area on the station, someone might be listening. We should get to our quarters." Raising her voice, Kate turned to the two males. "Come on, you two. You're both brimming with male sexual hormones. You don't have to prove it."

Grinning, Ryan slowly released Saggal. Saggal's tail swished back and forth happily as he released his grip.

"It's been too long, old friend," said Saggal.

"Much," agreed Ryan. Both of them were breathing hard and trying not to show it.

"Come on. Rowan, watch your step. The gravity is only 93 per cent Earth normal." Kate led the way from the space dock, pausing only to switch the door lock in the station corridor to Ryan's palm print.

Rowan was wide-eyed as she walked down the three-metre-wide corridor that led to the transport pod. The walls were done up as jungle scenes, pierced at regular intervals by doors labelled in an angular script. Felinezoids were everywhere. Fat ones, thin ones, ranging in height from just taller than Ryan to two point two metres tall. One, with a thick, blue-black coat, paused and pointed them out to his leopard-hided companion.

"That human looks exactly like the one from that show. Oh, what was it called? The one where that Toronk fellow is involved with a dark-skinned *Homo sapiens*. There was an article about it in last week's information periodical."

Rowan tried not to look at the felinezoid that was pointing at her.

"How can you tell? *Homo sapiens* all look alike to me."

Rowan assumed that the second voice belonged to the leopard-hided felinezoid.

"I guess you're right. It must be the hair colour. Mergral was telling me that there's a correlation between their hair colour and intelligence. The lighter, the lower."

"I do not know, and I do not care. We are supposed to be discussing the retrofit of the *Zerrgerrsa*, not other species. Whom I'm sure could care less what we think about them."

"Fine, fine, the human just looked familiar. I wonder..."

The voices faded from hearing as Rowan's party continued down the corridor.

"Blondes everywhere would like a word with that one," commented Ryan. He was smiling.

They paused at a hatchway. Saggal pressed a button. The hatch opened, and they filed into a small, oval chamber with cushions on the floor.

"All aboard for the bullet express to home and hearth," quipped Kate.

"Not another mag-lev," pleaded Rowan.

"Safest form of in-station travel there is. We'll be across the felinezoid sector in one minute, and if anything does go wrong, we won't live long enough for it to matter." Saggal's tail swished happily.

Rowan glared at Ryan. "No wonder you're friends. Equal amounts of brain damage."

Saggal tapped some keys on a control panel. Rowan tried not to notice the G-forces pushing her into her cushion.

⚬══✦══◇══

Tansy smiled as Chow hoisted her bag onto his shoulder and started down the narrow ship's passage to the airlock. "Thank you, Lieutenant, that's most kind of you."

Chow swallowed, and a blush rose on his Asian features. "My pleasure, Captain."

"Can we please go? I have paperwork waiting at the studio. This whole thing is a disaster!" snapped Mildred. She was bringing up the rear, her overnight bag in one hand.

"Of course," said Tansy. "You have to admit, it was an exhilarating hunt. Ryan is quite a strategist."

"He's a thief." Mildred was red-faced.

"I could carry your bag as well, ma'am," offered Chow.

"For the third time, I can carry my own star-dusted bag!"

By now, they'd reached the airlock and stepped through into the landing shuttle that would ferry them to Gaea's surface. The craft's passenger section consisted of a long room with rows of three seats on each side and a central aisle. Chow rushed to stow the bags in the overhead compartment. Mildred had no choice but to let him stow her bag, as she was too short to do so.

"I wouldn't call Ryan a thief. He's a liberator, like the courageous people that ran the underground railway in early technological North America." Tansy took a window seat, and Chow settled beside her. Tansy smiled at his deepening blush. She could almost hear the blood pounding in his veins. *Young men, so silly. I hope he and Tracy hit it off. He's likeable,* she thought as she traced her finger up and down her throat.

"He's like a mag-lev driver?" Mildred took the aisle seat.

"You really should read more, Major." Tansy looked at Chow as he tried to settle his wide frame in the narrow seat. He couldn't help but brush shoulders with her. "Chow." She smiled at him.

Chow tried to think of a brick wall. "Yes, ma'am."

"I was wondering if you would be free to join Philip, my husband, and me for dinner this Saturday? My daughter, Tracy, will be visiting from the university. It's always more pleasant for her if there is someone her own age for her to speak with."

Mildred snorted and stared at the screen of her handheld, trying to make some headway on the studio staff changes she had to examine and approve.

"I'd love to, thank you." Chow smiled broadly.

"There's a surprise." Mildred's brow wrinkled as she noticed a pattern. Her finger tapped the side of her handheld. "Hm, Captain, if you're quite through with my young colleague, may I ask you a question?"

"Of course." Tansy's smile held a bit of a smirk.

"If you wanted to bring in a lot of data fast from the Switchboard station, what would be the best way and how long would it take?"

Ryan followed Saggal into his quarters and froze. Large beanbag-chair cushions were arranged around a low table in the middle of the common room, but that wasn't what held Ryan's gaze. A felinezoid, with cougar-tan fur, knelt in the middle of the room, playing with Graff and Samantha. She was short for her species, within a centimetre of Ryan's height. She looked up. Her cheetah-like features reflected nervousness. Her tail trembled where it rose up to touch her shoulder.

"Kitoy." Ryan's voice was cold.

"Hello, Commander Chandler. I'm sorry, it's Captain now, isn't it?"

"Saggal?" The tone in Ryan's voice demanded a thousand answers.

"It was Kate's idea. I wanted to warn you before we got here. Kitoy provides childcare for us." Saggal's tail lashed back and forth.

"Is this the Kitoy from Kadar's story? The one that betrayed him." Rowan's voice was hard as she glared at the felinezoid female.

Kitoy looked at the floor. "This was a bad idea."

"Everyone, stop it!" Kate pushed into the centre of the group of adults. "Graff, Samantha, please go to your playroom."

"I don't wanna. We never have guests! I wanna stay," whined Graff.

"Me too, me too," echoed Samantha.

"The word is 'want to,' son," corrected Saggal.

Graff rolled his eyes. "Want to, but you still won't let me."

"One." Kate's voice took on a menace known to children everywhere.

"Sheesh, Mom! I'm going." Graff moved sulkily down the hall at the back of the room.

"Two." Kate stared directly at her daughter.

Samantha stood and, with a haughty backwards glance, stalked down the hall.

"Kate, you can't expect me to—" began Ryan. A fiery glance from his hostess silenced him.

"Last I checked, there were only two children in this residence. What I expect is for you all to behave like adults. The... incident happened fifteen years ago."

"Kadar said—" began Rowan.

"Rowan, allow me to introduce Mrs. Kadar Hadi Al-Qahtani."

"What!" gasped Ryan.

"It's true. After the disaster on Murack Five," began Kitoy.

Rowan watched Ryan and Kate go pale. Saggal's tail lashed.

Kitoy continued pretending not to notice the tension in the room. "Kadar came back to the station. We... we renewed our relationship."

"The man needed to be kept on a leash. Any piece of furry tail, no offence, Saggal, that came along, and he was up to his neck." Ryan sounded disgusted.

"It wasn't like that!" There was heat in Kitoy's voice. "I loved him, and he loved me!"

"Turning him over to be tortured and brainwashed was a funny way to say I love you. Why didn't he mention that you'd made up?" commented Rowan.

Kitoy gestured towards Ryan. His expression was a mask of rage. "Need I say more?" Kitoy collapsed onto one of the cushions, so she was sitting low and looked up at everyone. "I was young and stupid when I betrayed Kadar. My head was full of words like duty and service. My government was planning to accept the contract that would put my people in conflict with yours. They told me I'd be saving felinezoid lives. That was before I realized that I was a prostitute for felinezoid intelligence. Tell me, Ryan. Are you proud of all the things you did in service to your species? You and I are the same. They used us and then tossed us aside. I caught rutat from a k-no-in ambassador they told me to… interview. I'd always dreamed of having cubs, a family. Intelligence sector threw me out, and you know what the United Felinezoid Worlds are like regarding diseases. I'm banned from ever going to Murrow again. My father died; I wasn't even allowed to go and say goodbye!"

Kitoy looked up. Her pupils were fully dilated, and her nose was running.

Kate walked over and hugged Kitoy. "Take your time. Pull yourself together. Ryan will shut up and listen. Won't you, Ryan!" Kate shot him a look that allowed no disagreement.

Ryan nodded.

Rowan moved to Saggal's side and whispered into his pointed ear. "What's rutat?"

"A k-no-in virus. K-no-in are unaffected, and most species are immune, but in felinezoids, it causes sterility. It can only be transmitted through intimate contact. There are so few cases there has never been funding to find a cure. The United Felinezoid Worlds senate placed an automatic order of exclusion against all who have been infected." Heat entered Saggal's voice as he continued. "It's because it can only be caught by inter-species relations. The Senate does not approve of felinezoids having intimate relations with other species. Hypocritical bigots. A thousand years ago, it was considered wrong for a tabby mark to mate with a cougar tan or a blue-grey. I won't even tell you what was done to leopard coats. Idiocy!"

"You're right, it is idiocy, and the Senate are a bunch of hypocrites. They told me who to get close to, who to seduce and were happy enough to get the information I gained." Kitoy looked up. Her nose had stopped running, but her pupils were still wide. "When Kadar came back into my life, I was ready to die. All my dreams of a family were gone. He rescued me. He loved me! Eventually, he even forgave me. Then he was arrested for trying to steal that anti-proton shipment. I wanted to go to him, join him in prison, but the United Earth Systems won't acknowledge an inter-species marriage. They wouldn't give me permission to immigrate."

Ryan looked tired as he stared at Kitoy. "I hate government! Kitoy, for what it's worth, if Kadar could forgive you, I can at least try. It was war, declared or not. We all did things we regret."

"Thank you." Kitoy looked up at Ryan and gave her tail a tentative swish.

"Did… well… has anybody…" Ryan shifted uncomfortably from foot to foot.

Kitoy stood and lifted a dark red sash off one of the other cushions and put it on. "I took it off so it wouldn't get damaged while I played with the children. I know I'm a widow. That's part of why I asked Kate to arrange for us to meet. It was one of Kadar's last wishes. He recorded me a message after you left him and had one of the other inmates send it after he died. He sent three others, one for each of you." Kitoy held out the data cubes.

"Thank you." Ryan took two of the cubes.

"Kadar was a good friend." Rowan took the other cube, then paused to gently squeeze Kitoy's arm.

Kitoy swished her tail.

"Now that's settled, I'd best let the animals out of their cage." Kate started down the hallway. "Oh yes, I didn't have time to cook, so take-out will have to do."

Ryan, Saggal and Kitoy all heaved identical sighs of relief. Rowan laughed.

Michael Strongbow mixed drinks at the bar beside the lounge area of his office. The furnishings were all expensive and of classic design, but comfortable. A life-sized portrait of his wife in her youth looked down over the people filling the two lounge chairs.

"Honestly, Mike, I don't know if I can keep the stardust out of the air recycler for this one." Admiral Newton ran his hand over his bald scalp. His dark brown skin formed a striking contrast with his blue eyes. He carried himself in a way that made the sports jacket and slacks he wore look like a uniform.

"Relax, Jim. It's not as bad as all that." Michael passed the admiral a drink.

"Mike, speaking as the general in charge of New Gaea's Ground Defence and Convict retrieval units, I should arrest you now! What were you thinking? This isn't fifty years ago! You're an accessory for the weapons offences, not to mention grand theft." General DeFranko pulled a strand of her grey-streaked, red hair away from her face. She was a large woman with a muscular, well-toned body that made women half her age envious. Her plain features were grave.

"Melissa, you aren't looking at the angles. Let's review. One. The studio is dropping the theft and trespassing charges. It is good to be the king." Mike took a sip from his drink and sat on the arm of General DeFranko's lounger. "Any charges stemming from those acts are null and void. The ground pursuit was completely within the parameters we set for the exercise. So, no charges there. I've paid off his outstanding debt, so no charges there—"

"What about aiding the escape of a felon, resulting in the death of said felon and bringing contraband into a U.E.S. prison facility?" Melissa squeezed the crystal tumbler in her hand until her knuckles went white.

"You nova blasted sneak!" Jim turned from Mike to Melissa. "He had me call in a marker with the head of the Planetary Corrections Department. They won't be pressing any charges. I thought it was just giving an old soldier a chance to go out swinging."

"It was that, at least in part. Kadar didn't deserve to rot in his cancers because Humans Ascendant block vote on a single issue."

"Captain Chandler fired on one of my ships." Jim slammed his drink down on the coffee table.

"Yes, but up until that, Ryan was completely within the parameters set for the training exercise. By the way, no fair siccing Tansy Denardo on him. Talk about stacking the deck! Where does that leave me?"

"Possession of a weapons system activation circuit and firing on a Space Combat Corps ship," said Melissa.

"Right. I did not supply Ryan with a weapons control circuit. My intelligence says he cobbled one together out of stock parts. As such, it can be argued that making it was part of the exercise, which was to show up weak spots in our civil defence policies and agency integration. My legal advisor, Justice Fred Edwards, tells me it will stick."

"He still fired on my ship!" Jim sounded peeved.

"Causing only minor damage and no casualties. Tell you what, Jim. I'll transfer credits to the New Gaea Orbital Defence Corps to cover the repair costs and inconvenience, if you agree not to pursue any form of secondary liability."

"That leaves Chandler out to dry." Melissa smiled and took a sip of her drink.

"Do either of you seriously think the hounds are going to catch that fox? At the Republic level, he fired in self-defence. He's only a criminal in the eyes of the United Earth Systems."

Jim and Melissa both laughed.

"Takes a fox to know a fox." Jim picked up his glass and raised it in a toast toward the picture on the wall. "To Marcy."

"To Marcy," echoed Mike and Melissa.

"And to all she proves to be true," added Mike as he stared at the painting.

GREASY PALMS

Ryan sat in the rolling chair in his quarters and stared at the display screen section of his wall. The image of Kadar, a wasted, dark-skinned man, sitting at a desk, filled the area.

"Ryan, if you're seeing this, you've done better for yourself than I could have hoped. I've shut down the medical nano-bots. It is such a relief to know the pain will be over soon. By now, you know all about my little diversion and Kitoy. Please, Ryan, don't hate her. She was young, and she has made me happier than I had ever been. About Kitoy, I have a final favour to ask. Please help her. They won't let me sign my pension over to her, and the stardusted felinezoid government has banned her from most work because of her disease. She doesn't deserve to eke out an existence living off other people's scraps."

A grimace crossed Kadar's features. "It will only be a matter of hours now. Never doubt that you did the right thing giving me the deactivate codes. Look after Kitoy as best you can, old friend. If she's still with you, tell Rowan she brightened this old doctor's final day. Also, if Rowan is with you, look for a Blair Pikeman. Saggal and Kate may have acquaintances who know how to find him. He was a doctor. The man has the ethics of a Komodo dragon, but his skills are first rate. He may be able to help you get the last of the venom out of her system, but it will cost.

"And tell that polymer pervert to keep his hands off my wife." Kadar smiled, but it turned into a grimace.

"Goodbye, Ryan. Sangunis abl planeta." Kadar's image saluted. The screen went blank.

"Sangunis abl planeta." Ryan hung his head. "You get that, Henry?"

"Got it… Ryan, what do you intend to do about Kitoy?"

Ryan looked up in surprise. "Since when do you use my name?"

"Kadar was my friend too. Ryan, all shagging aside, it seems like Kitoy—"

"Made him happy. Nova blast, remember before she betrayed him?"

"Sweet kid. Couldn't have all been an act. Could it?" said Henry.

"Not all of it, but what can we do? We're up to our epaulettes in alligators." Ryan pushed away from the screen and started pacing the floor.

"This is crazy."

"What?"

"I've accessed her online resumé. She's checked out on human communications systems up to a C-257 level."

"That is crazy! We're going to an exclusively human colony." Ryan stopped pacing.

"Kitoy likes human men."

"Her culture…"

"Has screwed her over. She likes humans."

"The Geb charter disallows non-Terran life-forms."

"It disallows a breeding population of non-Terran life-forms. She's sterile. Look, boss, make the offer. If she says no, you're off the hook. If she says yes, it's one less job I have to do, and you're that much closer to a full crew."

"I don't know, I—" The door buzzer sounded.

"Sweetcheeks wants to see you," said Henry.

"Convenient! Henry, open the door."

The door slid into the wall. Rowan rushed in wearing a robe. "Ryan, I had a wonderful idea. Why don't we ask Kitoy to join us? She's qualified as a communications officer and…" Rowan trailed off as Ryan laughed.

"Henry, you are a pip. When did you come up with this one?"

"Um." Rowan shifted from foot to foot.

"Not me, hottie boss." The android sounded amused.

"Rowan?" Ryan stared at his lover.

"Not me. I guess he mentioned it in Henry's message too."

"Kadar?"

Rowan nodded.

Ryan massaged his forehead. "He's dead, and his obsession with fur is still getting me into trouble. Fine, I'll offer her the job, but I won't beg. She takes it or leaves it."

Rowan threw herself into Ryan's arms and kissed him. "I'm glad. Kadar really wanted for you to help her. Henry, privacy on."

Henry shifted to the secured feeds that Michel Strongbow had arranged before their departure, allowing Ryan and Rowan the illusion of privacy.

Rowan pulled away from Ryan and walked across the room.

"What?" began Ryan.

"Kate gave me something to help persuade you. I promised I'd wear it, but I knew you'd do the right thing. You always do the right thing. But there's no use in wasting it." Rowan dropped her robe, revealing the gauzy leopard spot camisole she wore underneath. "You like?"

Henry examined the telemetry coming from Ryan and spoke with his android mouth into the empty bridge. "He likes, sweetness. He really likes! I want my hips back!"

Mildred stared at the computer screen in her office, examining the reports that had accumulated while she was away.

The door buzzer sounded, and she said, "Jean, who is at my door?"

"John Wilson, the producer of *Angel Black*," replied the studio's computer.

"It has to happen sooner or later. Jean, let him in."

John Wilson burst into the five-metre square room. "You let him get away!"

"Hello, John." Mildred swivelled her chair to look at the fat producer. His suit was rumpled, and his complexion was florid. She sniffed the air and detected the sickly-sweet smell of someone coming off a drunk. "Been celebrating something?"

"Don't give me that. You let Chandler escape. I'LL HAVE YOUR JOB FOR THIS!"

Mildred blinked at him, then swivelled her chair and started typing.

"AREN'T YOU GOING TO SAY ANYTHING?" John flushed even redder.

"Don't raise your voice to me! I am in a bad mood already. For the record, John, only Michael, or a majority vote of the shareholders, can fire me. Also, for the record, I didn't let anyone escape. Chandler is very good at what he does. As frustrating as that may be." Mildred kept typing.

John took a moment to run his hand through his thinning, brown hair before replying. "I'll go before the shareholders. Heads will roll when news of the Rowan theft gets out, and it won't be mine. It is a security issue."

Mildred paused in typing and turned in her chair. John stepped back, even though she was little over half his height.

"Really, John. Do you remember a trip you made into the set region about four months back? Just after Rowan caught Farley cheating on her with her best friend. She was so hurt, but, I guess, she wasn't that desperate! It must have stung to be rejected by one of your own fakeys." Mildred let her gaze slide over John like he was something unclean. "You placing a do not assist order on the Rowan surrogate is what started all this. That and the fact that you were too sloppy to notice that Ryan was obsessed with her. I know why you wanted her dead."

"That's blackmail." John looked frightened.

"John, everyone in this place fudges the rules. There isn't a tech that hasn't had lunch at the Garlic Palace. The only way to do my job is to let the little things go. Let everyone think they're getting away with something and come down hard when it matters. Otherwise, I'd waste all my time on trifles and miss the disasters. People like to think they're pulling one over. Your little stunt was plain stupid, nova blast, man! She's not a Luba. The only reason you still have a job is Mike asked me to hush it up. If you take me in front of the shareholders, I'll give them full details! Is that clear?"

John swallowed and stepped back. "You wouldn't?"

Mildred turned back to her computer screen. "Try me!"

John stood in impotent fury for a long moment, then strode from the room. Mildred spoke into the air. "Jean, please place a call to Michel Strongbow. I need to see him ASAP."

She stared at her screen, noting interruptions in the *Angel Black* series transmissions and substantial funds transfers to Ryan Chandler's creditors and the Space Defence Corps from a show called *Freedom's Run*.

"Mike, Mike, Mike, what are you up to?" She shook her head and smiled.

Ryan stood on a scaffold and watched as the nano-bots shifted the material on the seam of the damaged hull plates. He then applied a laser cutter along the join. Minutes later, he released the retaining bolts, and a damaged hull section crashed to the space dock's floor.

"Stardust! Could you warn me when you're going to do

that?" yelled Rowan from where she was manoeuvring a mobile platform stacked with crates of coffee down the *Star Hawk*'s access ramp.

"He does it intentionally." Saggal was helping to push the anti-grav platform.

Ryan smiled. "Just trying to work fast. You sure that's enough coffee to cover my expenses? I don't want charity."

"Will you please stop going on about that? With last year's crop failure, the U.E.S. placed a temporary ban on all exports. The price is up over 500 per cent in the felinezoid sector. I was charging fifteen credits a cup before I ran out. If you're here long enough for me to sell some of this, I'll take the rest of your stock." Saggal patted the crates on the skid. "Wesnakee will be the only recreational facility outside the human sector with coffee."

The door to the space dock opened, and four tall, muscular humans wearing Space Services coveralls walked in. Captain Crapper followed, accompanied by a slender felinezoid with a leopard coat. Ryan noted that Crapper was as tall as his felinezoid escort and, in blubber, probably weighed half as much again.

"Get the property!" snapped Crapper. The four large humans moved towards Rowan.

Saggal let out a low growl and unsheathed his claws. "Mr. Rargerr, why have you let these *Homo sapiens* into a space dock secured under my name?"

"By what authority do you do this?" Ryan leapt from the scaffolding and ran to the access ramp.

"You are under arrest for—" Crapper began self-importantly, then fell silent when Ryan levelled his laser cutter at Crapper's chest. The four burly humans had fanned out across the end of the access ramp facing Saggal. Each human was armed with a billy club.

"Crapper, call off your dogs, or I will kill you!" Ryan's face was adamant.

"Your human friends didn't clear official channels. They failed to file a twenty-seven dash five for non-citizen use of felinezoid docking facility," said the leopard-skinned felinezoid.

Crapper looked smug. "Got you, traitor."

Saggal hissed and bared his teeth.

Ryan scowled, then cleared his throat and enunciated slowly. *"Gerr raa murr hess hrrr gaaa mruu hak."*

To the *Homo sapiens* in the room, it sounded like gibberish. Saggal lashed his tail. Rargerr asked, "Is this true?"

"Yes," said Saggal. "By the way, Ryan. Your accent is horrible."

"My throat's already sore; don't bug me," countered Ryan.

A moment passed as Mr. Rargerr unclipped a datapad and tapped in a query. The bureaucrat's tail lashed in annoyance. "Captain Crapper, you have filed a false claim. Captain Chandler is an adopted breath-brother of Saggal of the Slingmaster family. He is a citizen of the United Felinezoid Worlds."

"He's human!" screamed Crapper.

"He is of Slingmaster family. He stood as husband's champion at the marriage of Saggal Grahiss Slingmaster to Kate Monroe." The bureaucrat glanced at Saggal. "Word to the wise. Your anniversary is next week, don't forget it this year."

Saggal wagged his whiskers at the bureaucrat without taking his eyes off the human troops.

Rargerr swished his tail.

"Fine, take the property. We'll get Chandler later." Crapper puffed his chest self-importantly.

"Are you really so stupid that you think I won't kill you to protect her?" Ryan's finger rested on the cutter's activate button.

"She is betrothed to Ryan Chandler of Slingmaster family," stated Saggal.

Rargerr spoke to Saggal. "Betrothed is not married. This is a grey area." The spotted coat felinezoid lightly tapped its palm with its tail tip.

"Get her," ordered Crapper. A beam of laser light cut across the room before the men could advance.

"The first man to try, dies! Ask yourself, lads. Do you want to die for this idiot?" Ryan angled the laser cutter back so that it once more pointed at Crapper.

Saggal's tail lashed as he watched the bureaucrat out of the corner of his eye. "Surely, we should discuss this felinezoid to felinezoid. Join me in the ship; we will leave these oversexed apes to their own devices. Rowan, until this is settled, perhaps you'd be better off in the *Star Hawk*."

"You're a young man. Why throw your life away for a fakey, Chandler?" Crapper tried to sound like the wise, older man struggling to save a younger man from his own folly.

Ryan shook his head as Saggal, Rowan, and the spotted-coat bureaucrat vanished up the access ramp. Ryan then focused all his attention on Crapper. "You haven't read *The Art of War*, have you, Graham?"

"What?" The big man looked nonplussed. Ryan saw one of the guards on the ramp smile.

"Know your enemy and know yourself. Before you pull this young man garbage, take the time to read my file. Stardust! I'm going to make a suggestion, Graham, and I hope you'll listen. Learn something about the species you deal with. You are an embarrassment to *Homo sapiens*."

"Wait just a minute. I—"

"Lying to a crabzoid sub-designation. That was plain stupid. You're a diplomatic incident waiting to happen. For the good of humanity—"

"You're a criminal, don't lecture me. That fakey will betray you. You can't trust any of them!"

"Humans Ascendant, I take it?"

"The Gene Wars proved—"

"That if you oppress people, they will fight back?" finished Ryan.

"Genetic anomalies have no souls, no moral centre, they aren't human. Cloning is an abomination before the Divine and—"

"Fat-headed morons with daddies in the U.E.S. parliament can still get command of a capital ship." Ryan never let the laser torch waver from its bead on Crapper's chest.

Rargerr exited the *Star Hawk*. "I have reviewed the case with my species kin and find that you have misled this representative of the felinezoid peoples. Rest assured, Captain Graham Crapper, I will be filing a complaint with your superiors. You and your men may depart, *now*, or do I need to call security?"

"You... You can't do this. This man is wanted by the U.E.S., and that fakey is the property of S.E.T.E. She isn't even real!"

"The U.F.W. does not recognize a distinction between clones and naturally conceived. Will you leave now, or does the U.E.S. intend to declare war on the U.F.W.?"

Crapper went red in the face, then turned and stormed out the door, leaving his men behind.

"Looks like you're in command now, chief," Ryan spoke to the man who'd smiled at the mention of *The Art of War*.

"Yes... sir! I am sorry to have inconvenienced you. A holder of the Jupiter Commendation deserves more respect."

"Thank you, Chief. A bit of career advice. Keep reading *The Art of War*, and apply for reassignment."

"Transfer comes into effect in two weeks, sir." The chief saluted. "Sangunis abl planeta."

"Sangunis abl planeta." Ryan returned the salute.

The chief led his men from the space dock.

"You military types, I'll never understand you," said the spotted-coat bureaucrat.

"Fortunately, we understand you." Saggal exited the *Star Hawk* with Rowan. Rowan carried a cargo case.

"Thank you, my dear. I hope your nuptials are everything

you want them to be." The bureaucrat took the case of coffee and walked from the room.

"Bribery?" asked Ryan.

"Bribery. Customs officials never change. This one keeps his word after the price is settled. It's a type of honour. I've dealt with him before. He'll adjust the records. You and Rowan won't have any further difficulties."

"Good. I hate having Crapper on our butts. He's stupid enough to do something over the top."

"Like trying to arrest you in sovereign territory?" Saggal hissed with amusement.

"Like ordering a covert op in sovereign territory." Ryan looked serious.

"You are making a jest?"

Ryan shook his head. "The sooner we make the repairs and do the other things we need to, the better."

"Other things?" asked Saggal.

"We'll tell you later. Let's get your coffee to Wesnakee. I've heard so much about the place. I'm dying to see it." Rowan smiled winningly.

Ryan grimaced at her choice of words.

Bill bent over the metre-long oval form of a floor maintenance robot that lay on a table in the middle of his workshop. Countertops with cabinets underneath circled the room's walls. The ceiling was a white light source. He slipped the telemetry booster into the open space he'd made by putting in a half-sized dirt reservoir.

"You know, as an officer of the court, I should arrest you for tampering with Republic property." Vicky perched on a countertop.

Bill smiled as he straightened and looked at her. She was in a short, plaid skirt and red scarf-halter. "We could always play investigating attorney and suspect later."

Vicky uncrossed and crossed her legs provocatively.

"Are you sure you remember where the cuffs are?"

Bill felt his face flush. "Oh yeah. Let me finish up here."

Vicky nodded and assumed a less blatantly sexual pose. "Seriously, you could get in trouble for tampering with Republic equipment."

"I could if it was a Republic unit. I FTL telegraphed Mike after the telemetry relay through Ryan's handheld almost failed. He sent the money to buy two of these and asked if I could set them up. The Republic is thrilled to have help cleaning the floors. They don't mind where I send the units so long as they pick up trash and dust."

"So, they'll receive the signal from Ryan and Rowan's built-in systems and relay them to the *Star Hawk*. Why do you need two?"

"Some new players are joining the game. I have to get this one to the batzoid section." Bill picked up the machine and lowered it to the floor of his workshop. He then picked up a remote programming pad and started inputting data.

"Why don't you let me do that, it will be faster, and I don't want to waste our day off." Vicky stood and pulled a length of computer wire out from under a cabinet.

"I didn't want to ask." Bill passed her the remote programmer and a data disk.

Thrusting one end of the cable into her nose and connecting the other to the programmer, she pushed the disk into the reader.

Vicky closed her eyes, then commented. "Batzoid, and a handsome couple at that. The unit will follow them while staying inconspicuous. You get to empty the dust collector." Vicky unclipped herself from the machine and smiled at her husband as it rolled from the room.

HE'S GORGEOUS, JUST LOOK AT THAT FORKED TONGUE

Croell lay over the command chair as Luba piloted them to the dock port. The screen showed the massive docking spar drawing closer. Croell couldn't help but notice how much it resembled a sewer pipe. A vibration went through the ship as it stilled relative to the docking spar, then a clang sound came through the hull as the airlocks meshed.

"Docking is secure, and airlocks are pressurized. Please remember, if you are pleased with the aftermarket piloting addition on this unit, that many other programs designed to increase your Luba's versatility are available—" began the Luba.

"Luba, shut up! After thirty hours of trying to find a merchant willing to grant an advance, I do not wish to hear your prattle." Croell moved to the bridge's door. It opened before him. He saw Zandra speaking with another female batzoid in the main passage. The total stock from the yacht's bar was stacked on a grav-sledge.

"We appreciate you forwarding our docking fees. May the Great Flyer of the Skies flick tongue at our meeting." Zandra dipped her head the ceremonial three times.

"Are you Cloud Skipper sect?" The other female sounded surprised.

"Yes. Is that a problem?" Croell approached the females.

"No, if you will excuse me. I hold no bias toward any

sect. I am simply surprised. Not many Cloud Skippers use the ships of other species."

"Like the prophet Jakonee, we travel in what the Great Flyer of the Skies sees fit to give us." Zandra flicked her tongue in a friendly gesture.

"Ah. I understand. If you require it, I have an acquaintance from school that can reconfigure an identification beacon. Now that you have docked, perhaps other trades can be made?"

Croell noticed that the strange female was eyeing him. He tapped his fore-claw on the deck and flicked his tongue at Zandra. "Thank you, but there is no need. To whom are we speaking?"

"Janree, hatched of Wistnee, flown by Braa. It was my mother's wife/sister Kail you spoke with to arrange the trade. The *Homo sapiens* and felinezoids pay well for these products of rotten fruit and grain. Did you know that the value of many of these varies with the year it was made?"

"Will you certify that you have taken possession of the trade goods, and all debts between us are voided?" Zandra held a datapad towards Janree.

Croell shifted, fluffing his wings and letting his tongue flick from his mouth.

"What? Oh, yes." Janree traced the ideogram for her name on the pad without taking her eyes off Croell. Her tongue flicked from her mouth, and she fluffed her plain, brown wings.

"You are knowledgeable. I have studied a little about *Homo sapiens* culture. I know of the mystique wine holds for them. Some are quite *passionate* about it." Croell could see the first hint of venom forming on Janree's fangs. "Humans, as they call themselves, are strange creatures. They consider lying a lesser crime than murder or theft. They have even been known to allow adultery. Of course, many of them choose to have only one wife. Foolish as that seems." Croell flicked his tongue twice.

Unnoticed behind Janree, Zandra slipped a case of wine

off the grav-sledge and carried it into a side room, replacing it with an empty box.

"I know. Living on the station, you can't help but encounter them. One time, Wistnee visited the human sector. She saw a bolt of cloth she wanted to make into a ceremonial sash. She took it, and the shopkeeper caught her. She admitted the theft and offered to pay the traditional three times the item's value. The shopkeeper wouldn't accept it. He called government-appointed vengeance proxies."

"Police. We had something like them in ancient Traglorin society. Thus, the word. We gave them up as a bad idea." Croell's voice took on an undertone like metal scraping metal.

Venom dripped from Janree's fangs, and her bulging venom sacks caused her speech to slur. "In the end, father sssspoke to the shopkeep and explained the way of the Great Flyer of the Ssskiess. He agreed to let Wissstnee go. Wissstnee has never gone shopping in the *Homo sapienss* sssector sssince."

Zandra replaced her fourth box on the lift, then flicked her tongue at Croell.

Croell pulled his wings in tight against his back and spoke in a normal voice. "You should take the trade goods to your father. Tell him we may have more spirits to trade. It was nice to meet you, Janree."

The young batzoid gazed at Croell for a long second, then sighed. "It wasss nice to meet you." Then as an afterthought, "And you," towards Zandra.

Janree pushed the grav-sledge, with its lightened cargo, out of the ship.

"You, my love, are too handsome for that young girl's good." Zandra let her tongue flick out, touching the scales of Croell's neck.

"Her mother sent her hoping I would be tempted. A female that age and not even betrothed. What is her father thinking?" Croell tapped his claws on the deck.

"Alien influences. It is hard to keep to the ways of the Great Flyer of the Skies with so many distractions."

"Perhaps. We must go to the temple and perform the ritual of arrival. After which, we must seek a servitor to perform the prayer of the fledgling Then we can begin planning the death of Rowan."

"Yes, my love. Though... After temple, I wish to contact Braa. You should consider Janree, my love. You need a second wife, and I could use some female company."

"I do not mean to be cruel, but the child has brown wings, and her fangs splay at odd angles. Not to mention her neck-scales being dull. I do not wish to require venom every time I join with my wives."

"You have no vision. A little polish would fix her scales, and a bit more fergil in her diet, and her wings will blacken. Her fangs will straighten with time. Give her three years; you'll wish you'd taken her."

"Perhaps. I will consider it after we complete our contract. Now, let us go to the temple." Croell nuzzled his wife's fur below where it met the scales of her neck.

Ryan held Rowan's hand as they walked down the corridor toward Saggal's residence. Unnoticed, a floor cleaning robot moved along the passage behind them. Several felinezoids stopped and stared at them.

"*Homo sapiens*, what are they doing here?" asked a voice from behind their backs.

"Visiting with the perverts in unit forty-eight," replied another.

"At least they seem to be keeping to their own species, that's something," commented the first.

"I have nothing against *Homo sapiens*. Sure, they're violent, but I've known some that were a lot more honest than some felinezoids I could name. I just don't think they should be marrying our people. What a handsome male like Saggal sees in..."

Ryan and Rowan turned a corner, and the voices were lost.

Ryan smiled when he saw Kate in the passage in front of her dwelling, but the smile quickly faded.

"What happened?" Rowan scanned the red scrawl on the wall.

"Some fool's idea of a joke." Kate pointed a triangular device at the scrawl. A stream of liquid shot out, and the mark began to disappear.

"Here you go, Mrs. Slingmaster. I'm sorry that some people are idiots. My dad says he'll check the video log when he goes to work tonight." A blue-grey felinezoid male, as tall as Ryan, walked up and passed Kate a bucket.

"Thank you, Murill. These are my friends, Ryan and Rowan."

"Rowan? Oh wow, you look just like the Rowan from *Angel Black*. I love *Angel Black*. Rowan is my favourite. Do you know the show?"

"Um, yeah, I kinda know it." Rowan swallowed and blushed.

"Rowan and I were involved with the show's production," explained Ryan.

"That is stellar! Am I right? Does Rowan come to her senses and dump Farley? That guy is such a 'carrion-eating reptile known for evacuating its bowels when frightened and flicking the feces at its attackers with its tail.' I mean, Carl would be a much better match. I mean, Rowan is a lot like her Mom, and Carl's had a thing for Willa forever."

Ryan let out a snort and clapped his hand over his mouth as his complexion reddened.

Rowan gritted her teeth. "Oh, really. I think there may be some big changes coming up on the show."

"I know, I read the spoilers that came from Geb. I wish we weren't a season behind on the station. Why would Farley ever cheat on Rowan with Angel? I mean, sure, Angel's attractive, but no way is she in Rowan's class. I always thought that Toronk should go after Rowan. He's smart enough to have a real conversation with her, and it would be so great to be in a felinezoid perspective and dance with her. Toronk/Rowan is my second favourite pairing for fanfic. My favourite is Carl/Willa. I mean, Carl is so hung up on her."

Rowan ground her teeth and was red in the face.

"What's wrong with him?" Murill indicated Ryan, who was sitting on the passage's floor with both hands clamped over his mouth.

"He has these fits sometimes. It's called wise-ass syndrome. A solid kick in the butt usually cures an episode." Rowan glared at Ryan.

"The nano-bots are finished," commented Kate.

When Rowan looked, the red scrawl was off the wall, and the bucket was full of red liquid. Kate dipped the wide end of the triangular device she held into the bucket and pressed another button. "Have to recall the nano-bots," she explained when she saw Rowan's quizzical expression.

"Can I have the colouring, Mrs. Slingmaster? My school is performing the lament of Rrrestamuuu's widow, so we have to dye a bunch of sashes red."

"Take it. It's a bad flood when the rot-vultures go hungry." Kate smiled as the youth picked up the bucket.

"It was nice meeting you both. Maybe we can talk some more about *Angel Black*. I'm a member of the station's fan club." Murill bowed, then moved down the corridor.

"The Smiths are such a nice family. That Murill is going to be a heartbreaker when he learns not to locomote on his favourite topics. We should go in. Graff's been waiting all morning for you to get here. Saggal and Samantha are out shopping for dinner." Kate moved to her dwelling's entry door. Ryan, still trying to swallow his laughter, followed her.

"So, maybe Carl had a thing for my mother. It doesn't mean anything," muttered Rowan as she brought up the rear.

A floor maintenance robot moved slowly past them.

DINNER PARTY

Captain Crapper sat in the chair in his study. The room was three metres by three metres and connected at the back to his bed-chamber and at the side to his private bath. The wall was filled with images of Ryan and the *Star Hawk*. The computer's voice droned in a near monotone.

"In recognition of his prompt response resulting in the preservation of the indigenous kangazoid species, Captain Ryan Chandler was awarded the Venus medal with a platinum cluster for outstanding achievement in humanitarian efforts."

Crapper snorted. "Humanitarian. He saved a bunch of nova blasted wallabies. Genghis, skip forward to the reports from Gaea. Did any of the officers red flag weaknesses?"

"Sir, Major Mildred Tallman mentions that the Rowan property may require medical attention," said the ship's AI.

"Yes, that is useful. Genghis, put an alert out to all *Homo sapiens* medical facilities to watch for the property. Have some of our agents look into the other species' quacks who play at human medicine."

"Yes, sir." Genghis followed the order while excluding retired practitioners, veterinary clinics and all other facilities not specifically mentioned.

Crapper sat back, his pudgy face pulled into a mask of concentration. "Genghis, analyze all logs regarding Ryan Chandler for any infraction of Republic law. If the aliens pick him up, they'll give him to us to hold. Then we have him."

"Yes, sir."

Crapper pushed himself out of his chair. "I'll get that soulless fakey. Ridicule me, will he!" Moving to a cupboard in the wall, Crapper opened it and pulled out a bottle of amber fluid and a glass. He poured himself a large drink and downed it. "This will do nicely. I'll bring him in, then maybe a posting on Earth away from all this alien trash." Crapper settled back in his chair. "Genghis, continue review."

"I could get my doctor to do a house call, I think." Kate sat in her living room, facing Ryan and Rowan across the coffee table. Rowan was snuggled into one of the bean-bag chairs with Graff lying over her lap. She stroked the fur on his back, and he sighed contentedly.

"My doctor makes house calls, and he's really nice. He can fix anything. The time I broke my arm, he put in a needle and glued it back together. It was a big needle, but I wasn't afraid. I'm sure he could help you."

"I'm sure he's a great doctor, Graff, but I need a human doctor, and you're a felinezoid." Rowan smiled as Graff shifted position and looked at her.

"Mom and Dad say it doesn't matter what someone's species is. We're all intelligent creatures." Graff looked confused.

"That's true for everything but medicine and doctors, honey." Kate drummed her fingers on the cushion. "Though, out of the mouths of babes. There are some non-human medics on the station who have studied humans. It's a kind of hobby with them."

"A hobby?" interrupted Ryan from his seat. "Kate, we're talking about stem cell insertions, advanced nano-bot maintenance, and the Divine knows what else. No offence, but a hobby isn't gonna cut it. What do you have against this Blair Pikeman?"

"He's a butcher. Everyone in ISLARA knows of him. The man has the morals of a Swampla pit viper."

"ISLARA." Rowan wrinkled her brow.

"Inter-Species Love and Relationship Association. It's a support group we have on the station."

"Mom and Dad go to their dances, and I get stuck here with Samantha." Graff bared his teeth, then his tail wagged. "They held a picnic last year. I got to try otterzoid fish rolls. They were really good."

"Saggal had to carry the little glutton home, he ate so much."

Rowan smiled, patted Graff, then became serious. "Kate, even if you could get your doctor to do a house call, would it really help me? I mean, I'm just a studio clone and thousands of years behind the times, but they had some advanced medical equipment even at Sun Valley's tech-level. Getting a doctor to come in and say, 'oh my yes, you are going to die,' isn't going to do me any good. We have to have the equipment the doctor needs to do something about it, and that's in the human sector. If this friend of Kadar's runs a practice in the shared area, he must have equipment."

"You aren't going to die, are you? I don't want you to die. I like you." Graff's tail lashed back and forth.

"I'm with him." Ryan walked to her side and placed a hand on her shoulder.

"I'm not giving up! It's just, lying to myself won't make it go away." Rowan patted Ryan's hand and Graff's head.

"You're taking this well," commented Kate.

"Back on the show, I didn't know about the controllers. That one of the pirates might kill me was a reality I lived with every day. Since then, it's like half the universe is out to get me. Leech venom, frigates chasing us, brain-cell meltdowns, mouth-breathing military commanders. If I start freaking every time someone points out that I picked up where Damocles left off, I'll be paralyzed."

Kate smiled. "She's one of us."

Ryan nodded. "Do you think I'd settle for less?"

"Now, I am lost." Rowan looked at the two other adults.

"Bet they say it's a grownup thing, and you'll understand when you're older," said Graff.

"You, Mr. Smart Mouth, go set the table. We're having goofla, so put out the claw sheaths and falldrop mats. Use the good ones. Though... Rowan, would you prefer a knife and fork?"

"That's not fair. You and Dad made the rule, human cutlery for human food, felinezoid cutlery for felinezoid food."

"But Rowan has never..."

"I'd like to learn." Rowan shifted to the edge of her seat as Graff scurried from the room. "Now about the grownup thing?"

Kate snorted. "That boy is like his father. Too charming by half. It's a military thing. When you're on the line, you have to stop worrying about if you're going to die to be able to live. You fit."

"Thanks."

"The real reason I wanted Graff out of the room is so I could tell you about Blair Pikeman. He was no friend of Kadar's. In fact, Kadar hated the man. Why he'd recommend him, I don't know."

"No other choice." Ryan returned to his seat.

"Why do you hate him?" Rowan stared intently at Kate.

"He does surgery. Very illegal and dangerous surgery. You see, some people can't take the looks and snide whispers when they fall in love with someone from another species. Pikeman twists people's bodies. Mutilates them, so they look like other species. Some of them wind up crippled or end up looking like genetic abnormalities. Quill, a friend of Saggal and I, fell in love with a human woman. He's an otterzoid. She couldn't handle the bigotry, so he went to Pikeman. Quill ended up looking like a hairy dwarf. He's spent years repairing the damage that butcher did to him. You see, the little fool he fell for left him because she couldn't handle being with a dwarf."

"That's awful!" Rowan shook her head sadly.

Ryan sighed. "I agree, but Pikeman may be the only one with the equipment to help you outside the human sector. The kind of work he's doing requires stem cells and advanced nano-bots."

"You know a lot about it." Kate eyed Ryan with suspicion.

"C.E.O." Ryan shrugged.

"What?" Rowan looked from one of her companions to the other.

"Captain's Eyes Only. Kate, like it or not, you know that's all the answer I can give you," said Ryan.

Kate scowled. "I don't like it." Taking a deep breath, she continued. "I have an acquaintance that may be able to get us in touch with him. I'll ask them to meet us at Wesnakee this evening."

The door opened, and Saggal entered with Samantha on his shoulders. Kitoy followed him, still wearing her red sash and carrying a box.

"Mommy, Mr. Mrumm let me pick the goofla. I picked a really meaty one, and we got a side order of rara greens. Daddy said we had to because *Homo sapiens* are omnivores and have to eat green stuff. I said the Divine isn't fair to make it so that humans have to eat broccoli and rara and other yucky stuff. Then Daddy said it was a good thing because *Homo sapiens* could survive on a wider variety of foods in a famine, then I said—"

"Samantha, you're forgetting your manners. We have company, and you haven't greeted them, as is the duty of the youngest child." Saggal set the little girl on the floor.

"Oh... sorry, Daddy." Samantha walked over in front of Ryan and bowed with her hands in front of her, fingertips touching so that he could see her fingernails. "We greet you with claws sheathed, Captain Chandler of the *Star Hawk*.

"Did I do good, Daddy?"

"Yes, 'small, sweet tasting beetle used as a snack food,' you did it well, now Rowan, the human way."

Samantha strode to Rowan and, with a serious face, extended her hand. "It's a pleasure to meet you. As you can see, I'm not holding a weapon in my dominant hand."

Rowan suppressed a chuckle and took the extended hand. "Thank you, I am pleased to be here. I, too, am not carrying a weapon in my dominant hand."

"It is so difficult trying to make them understand both cultures. We try to teach them why things are similar whenever we can," commented Kate.

"Children are a blessing," remarked Kitoy.

Ryan looked at the floor.

"Ryan?" Kate sounded concerned.

"He hasn't heard back from Tim." Rowan gazed at him with compassion.

"It's silly. It's been less than a week. He'd only have received my message three days ago." Ryan spoke to the floor.

"He may not have received it yet. The polarized-quark transmitter linking Earth to the station has been dealing with a high volume. I know the commodities section of the information bulletin is nearly a day behind, and it's a schedule B communication. I'm not even trying to play the margins with my U.E.S. stocks." Saggal settled on one of the cushions.

"If no one minds, I'll take this in the kitchen and get it out of the box?" said Kitoy.

"Kitoy, no one in this house minds. You don't have to ask. I've told Graff to set a place for you." Kate smiled at the felinezoid. "Get Graff to help you watch the goofla."

Kitoy's eyes dilated as she moved to the kitchen.

"Poor girl. People don't bother to educate themselves about rutat." Kate shook her head.

"Saggal, what you said about the paired-quark communicator. Is that the FTL telegraph?" Rowan looked intrigued.

"Yes. You see, when you separate paired quarks—"

"One takes on a positive charge and the other a negative. After that, no matter where they are, they will hold opposing charges, changing instantaneously to maintain this equilibrium. They can send a kind of code."

"Exactly. Did you study FTL communications since your..." Saggal rubbed behind his pointed ear as he searched for an appropriate word.

"Liberation," supplied Ryan.

"Liberation," finished Saggal.

"No, they must have known about the effect in the twenty-first century. We discussed it in my university classes. I'm curious, why don't all ships have an FTL transmitter?"

"Expense and practical application," commented Ryan. "Separating the quarks takes a lot of power, and after that, you have to maintain containment, or they drift out and form new pairs. Also, most ships are never more than a few light-hours from a station or planetary base, so FTL communications aren't that important. Generally, you send a brief signal to a base, and they forward it."

"Is there an upper limit to how often the quarks can flip polarity?" Rowan was enthused at finding a piece of technology that wasn't alien to her.

"One hundred and thirty times a second is the maximum the equipment can force a flip," Kitoy commented from the dining room's doorway. "The food is ready. Graff is watching the goofla, but if you want it fresh, you'd better hurry. This is a lively one."

"A lively one?" asked Rowan.

Ryan and Kate smiled at her as they stood. The dining room was the first door on the left of the hall coming off the common room. A long table with telescoping legs dominated the centre of the room. Human style chairs, with gaps cut to accommodate tails, were pushed against the wall while a ring of colourful cushions were tight around the table.

The walls were configured to show an overview of a jungle as if one stood on a platform.

"It's beautiful." Rowan gestured at the wall.

"Srrr'rahisssma, the traditional home of the Slingmaster family." Saggal took the seat closest to the entry door.

"Ryan said you might enjoy a traditional felinezoid meal, so we're really putting on the cat." Kate smiled. "If you have any trouble, don't be embarrassed to ask for a knife and fork. Claw sheaths take a bit of getting used to." Kate gestured at a line of eight gold thimbles with six-centimetre long blades coming out of their ends at the top of Rowan's placemat. "Well, come on, ladies, let's let the men get seated." Kate gestured for Rowan to follow her.

"Claw sheaths are fun," Samantha whispered to Rowan.

Rowan shot Ryan a glance. He smiled and began placing claw sheaths on his fingertips. Rowan followed the other females into the kitchen, almost bumping into Graff as he scurried through the door.

The kitchen consisted of a countertop with cupboards underneath and above. A human-looking electric stove occupied one corner, and a sink formed a depression in one of the counters.

"Ladies, as matron of the house, the honour falls to me." Kate picked up a large platter with what looked like a fifteen-kilo, brown slug on it. As Rowan watched, two antennae projected from the slug's head.

"It's still alive," gasped Rowan.

"Goofla is always best fresh. It's never the same once the blood's had a chance to drain," explained Kitoy.

Rowan grimaced.

"Don't knock it till you try it," remarked Kate. "Samantha, please hold the door. Computer, feast processional."

Rowan winced as a sound reminiscent of a fall of ball bearings hitting a tin roof issued from the speaker. Kate, holding the tray with the goofla in front of her, strode through the open door. The 'music' softened.

"In early days, females, being smaller and more agile, would chase the prey towards the males," began Samantha from where she held the door.

"And males would wait in ambush and spring upon the prey, using their greater size and strength to bring it down," continued Graff, from where he sat between his father and Ryan.

"And so it was that the Divine made for felinezoids to have plenty, so long as male and female recognized and valued each other in respect and love," Saggal and Kate finished as Kate set the goofla down before Saggal and took a seat facing Saggal across the table. Samantha sat beside Kate, then Kitoy, then Rowan.

Saggal stood and, using a large knife, expertly beheaded the slug. "It's more humane this way, and it splashes less," he explained as he settled back onto his cushions and slipped claw sheaths onto his fingers.

"Let's eat." Kate slashed at the still pulsing Goofla with her claw sheaths, expertly removing a chunk the size of her fist and placing it on the absorbent mat in front of her. The brownish meat continued to pulse. Saggal followed her example, then the tray was pushed down, and Graff and Samantha took portions. Kate was already slicing her chunk into bite-sized portions and popping them into her mouth.

Rowan was trembling by the time the bleeding slug was pushed in front of her and Ryan.

"How?" she asked.

"It's been a while. Come in at an angle and do a back cut, then support the section and undercut like this." Ryan demonstrated, placing a clump of meat on his mat.

Rowan gritted her teeth, cautiously sliced a small quantity off the goofla, and placed it on her mat.

"Better hurry if you want seconds. It's nearly bled out," commented Kitoy.

Rowan tried to ignore the red-brown fluid that now filled the bottom of the tray.

"I'll have more. Good goofla, nice and juicy. Mr. Mrumm's new feeding technique does make a superior product," said Saggal.

Rowan stared at the raw meat in front of her as the tray was passed back to the head of the table. Carefully, she sliced off a section about a centimetre square and speared it with a finger claw. She popped it into her mouth as Kitoy dipped her goblet into the blood collected in the tray and took a long drink.

Rowan closed her eyes and tried to keep her stomach down. She chewed. The texture was like veal, but the taste was stronger, reminiscent of venison, with a hint of garlic. Her eyes shot open, and she quickly finished the meat on her pad. The tray came around again. This time she sliced a large chunk.

Looking at her hosts, she could see that all the felinezoids had blood-stained whiskers. She looked at Ryan; he had a blood moustache.

Finally, Kitoy carried the nearly empty tray into the kitchen and emerged with a bowl of leafy, green stalks.

"And before you start, Samantha, yes, you have to eat some rara greens. It's good for you. Graff, you're excused if you like, so long as you clean your teeth."

"I don't mind. I like rara."

"Just don't eat so much you make yourself sick. Our children, the carnivore likes vegetables, and the omnivore is always a struggle." Kate stared at the ceiling.

A beeping sound issued from the wall speaker.

"A letter, odd," remarked Saggal. "Computer, display the message on the back wall."

The wall changed from the jungle image to show lines of human print.

"It's for Ryan," said Graff.

"Mom, he's showing off again," complained Samantha.

"Graff's allowed. Reading both *Homo sapiens* and felinezoid at his age is an achievement." Saggal used his tail to pat his son on the shoulder. "*Homo sapiens* still looks like squiggly lines to me."

Graff's tail swished, and he stuck his tongue out at Samantha.

"It's from Tim. I told my ship to forward it to me here. I hope you don't mind." Ryan fidgeted uncomfortably.

"Of course not. You can take it in the other room if you like," offered Kate.

"If it's all right, I'll take it here. I... If it's bad news, I don't want to be alone. Computer, I'm Ryan Chandler, display message."

The wall filled with two lines of print.

"I'm coming, will advise when in system.

Timothy Chandler, PhD, MSC, BSC"

Ryan let out a breath he didn't know he'd been holding. "My son's coming."

Rowan smiled at Ryan, then looked at the cryptic message again. Not a word of warmth or gratitude and a list of degrees. She was sad to think it, but she already didn't like Tim.

WESNAKEE 10

"**F**rankly, Professor, I don't care," said the young, dark-skinned woman wearing the yellow coveralls of a merchant spacer.

"But—" Timothy Chandler began, then his broad shoulders slumped when he registered the look on the woman's wide, flat face. They both stood in the metre-wide by two-metre-high maintenance corridor that ran through the ship's life-support section.

The woman sighed, then a smile touched her thick lips, and the hard glint left her brown eyes. "Look, Professor, I know you're only trying to help, but this isn't a classroom. In the real world, we do things differently. The algae tanks are always run a little hot in case there's an interruption in power flow. Sure, the O_2 generation suffers, but in an emergency, we have a better chance of keeping the culture alive."

Timothy blinked his large, blue eyes and smiled as he brushed his long, blond hair back from his face. "I'm sorry, Alima. Here I am being an old woman after you were kind enough to give me a tour of your life-support section."

"You designed it. Commander Niziol told me your father served on the *Star Hawk* during the Murack campaign. Is that true?"

"Yes." Timothy's features grew hard.

"That must have been amazing. To spearhead the kangazoid relief effort. You must be so proud of him."

"My father died because of Murack Five."

"But you said you were going to meet him on the Switchboard Station."

"I'm meeting the thing that thinks it's him." Timothy scowled.

Alima's look grew hard. "Oh, you're one of those! Well, you can tell your *father* from me that I appreciate what he did. I think the tour is over. I hope you don't mind finding your own way back to the low berth dormitory."

Timothy looked at Alima in surprise, then turned and walked to the elevator at the end of the hall.

"Bigoted prat!" muttered Alima as she pressed the entry door to the life-support operations section.

Ryan released Rowan's hand as they passed through the metre wide, two-metre-long corridors that formed the pedestrian gates of felinezoid customs.

Rowan giggled as a blast of air caused her light, spring dress to tickle against her legs. The chemical sensors on the side of the hall analyzed the air blast, and a light in front of her blinked blue. A second later, the door on the end of the passage opened. A felinezoid, with cougar-tan fur, wearing a green sash, with three lines of gold brocade on its shoulder, stepped in front of her. He was short for his species, being only a head and neck taller than Rowan.

"A *Homo sapiens*? Returning to the Earth sector, are you?" The customs official sounded friendly.

"Visiting Wesnakee with some friends," explained Rowan.

"You aren't carrying any coffee at this time?"

"No."

"Had a cup or two earlier today?"

"I don't drink the stuff. It makes me hyper. My ship is hauling it as cargo."

"That's probably it. Nova blasted sensor is so sensitive it picks up the micro amounts that get caught in your clothes. Anything else to declare?"

"Nothing I can think of."

"What did you think of the goofla?"

"Delicious, but it took a bit of getting used to. It's a cultural thing. Do I need to brush my teeth?"

"Only k-no-ins will pick up on it. I know what you mean about adapting to culture. I have an otterzoid friend. Every time I dine at his residence, I have to keep reminding myself to wash each bite before I eat it. Not that the fish rolls aren't worth it. Diversity is what makes the universe interesting. Enjoy your evening, and please remember to check the contraband lists before you bring anything into the felinezoid sector. After all, the government must take its cut of any coffee or trintil root. Taxes, something all cultures share in common, more's the pity." The customs officer swished his tail and stepped out of the corridor, allowing Rowan to pass.

Ryan was waiting in the large chamber beyond with Saggal and Kate. Kate wore a colourful blouse and skirt, while Saggal had donned a purple sash with a gold, figure-eight pattern running its length. Ryan was dressed in slacks and a blue, button-down shirt.

Rowan glanced around the chamber and froze. It was crowded with sentients. Mostly felinezoids, but there were also otterzoids, chameleonzoids, k-no-in, batzoid and several other species. Rowan stumbled, and Ryan caught her.

"You all right?" he asked.

"I... It's a little overwhelming." Rowan indicated a creature about twice the size of a man that walked on four legs and had a short neck topped by an oval head. Two long, prehensile snouts came off its face below a pair of large, green eyes. "Is that an oryceropuszoid?"

"Yes."

"I read about the species that can share space with humans in the Encyclopedia Galactica, but seeing them all is... wow!"

"You were in the common section when you delivered

the coffee. This can't be completely new?" said Ryan.

"We used the cargo port. Rowan did not have an opportunity to see many of the station's residents," explained Saggal.

Rowan's eyes had shifted to a creature that looked like a ten-legged spider the size of a large dog. A line of vents opened off its bulbous opisthosoma, which seemed to inflate and deflate.

Ryan noticed the direction of her gaze. "Spiderzoid, one of the least violent species in the Republic." Ryan looked hard at the sentient. "She must have important business in the felinezoid sector. They normally keep to themselves."

"There wasn't much of an entry on them. How can you tell she's a she?" Rowan tried not to stare at the life form.

"The little horns over the eyes, only females have them."

"We should get going. Once we're in Wesnakee, it's not impolite to stare. It's an unwritten rule," explained Kate.

Ryan took Rowan's hand and followed Saggal and Kate to a vehicle port on the far side of the chamber. None of them noticed one of the omnipresent floor-cleaning robots follow them.

Croell and Zandra touched their chins to the floor before the image of the Great Flyer of the Skies. The image was a batzoid in flight, with a checkerboard pattern of red and black scales covering its head and neck. It also had forefinger claws and fangs. Its wings were long, muscular and as black as midnight.

The temple's ceiling was a depiction of the night sky of Petteron, the batzoid homeworld, while the floor was a tile mosaic depicting Petteron's largest continent as seen from orbit. Other worshippers stood about the chamber.

Croell lifted his chin from the floor and moved to a shelf at the side of the room. A small, gas flame burned, and various incenses were arrayed before it. Zandra walked up behind Croell and lay her head on his back.

"Choose well, my love." Zandra sniffed the air.

Croell picked an incense and dropped it onto the flame. It sparked up. A scent like nutmeg mixed with orange and lemon filled the area.

"Ralsim, that is a good omen." Croell inhaled deeply, then started towards the back of the room where several batzoid with gold rings around their necks waited. Croell approached the closest of these.

"Servitor, may we seek your guidance?" asked Croell.

"Of course, we are all children of the Great Flyer of the Skies. What is it you wish?" The servitor's neck scales formed alternating bands of black and red while small fangs could be seen in its mouth. The forefingers of each of its hands had claws.

Croell glanced at Zandra and shifted his weight from one foot to the other.

"Speak, I give my oath it will go no farther."

Zandra looked at the servitor. Its tongue flicked out in a way that inspired trust. "Servitor, we wish you to perform the prayer of the fledgling."

"Always a happy duty, where is your child?" The servitor looked around as if a small batzoid was going to pop out of the air.

"Honoured servitor, it is not for a child. It is for us." Zandra lay her chin on the floor.

The servitor looked shocked. "Why has this duty been left so late?"

Zandra's voice trembled as she spoke. "It is a long story. I must begin by warning you. Croell and I are abomination. Our flesh was drawn from liars."

The servitor let out a hiss, pulling its wings in tight against its body.

"We did not choose it to be so. Please, hear our words. We seek to fulfill our duties to the Great Flyer of the Skies."

"I will listen before I pass judgment. Let us go to one of the audience chambers. Such a tale is not to be overheard." The servitor rose and led Croell and Zandra to a side room and closed the door behind them. Croell gazed at the image of the Great Flyer of the Skies painted on the room's back wall as he began to explain. "It begins with the *Homo sapiens*."

Rowan shifted her gaze from where Saggal and Kate danced in the cleared central floor of the large room that was Wesnakee and stared at the next table over. A tabby-stripe, female felinezoid, wearing a cream sash with five gold rings embroidered across her chest, sat with an otterzoid male. The otterzoid wore a collar with seven silver bells on it that tinkled when he moved. The otterzoid noticed Rowan staring and winked at her. Rowan heard words in her mind.

'If you like the view, sweetie, I'm sure we could work something out.' A visual image of the otterzoid stroking its body over hers touched her mind, and she felt soft fur slide over her nipples.

'No thanks,' Rowan quickly thought.

'Too bad, for a Homo sapiens, *you're a cutie. If it's my friend that flips your switch, she works all corners of the intersection.'*

Rowan swallowed hard. *'No, thanks.'*

She turned her gaze to a table where a creature that looked like a mid-sized horse with an elongated head and two arms ending in three-fingered hands coming off from where its thick neck joined its body stood conversing with a cougar-tan felinezoid and a chameleonzoid.

"You resemble Rowan from the human entertainment *Angel Black*. This intrigues me. I will pay three hundred credits for one night."

Rowan turned to see a k-no-in, its pony-like body with its six clawed legs filling the space behind her.

The sentient's dog-like face practically thrust into

Rowan's. She smelled something sweet on its breath.

"I'm not a prostitute!" Rowan spoke with more heat than she intended.

"I will offer three hundred and fifty, no more," answered the k-no-in.

"No! Leave me alone."

"I was nearly a breeder. You won't find better off Lipil. I was in the seventy-fourth percentile, I swear it. I'm very good. Three hundred and sixty! That's more than fair."

"I'm not interested." Rowan's voice took on a hysterical edge.

"I'll bring in my friend, Tranic. You can take the two of us; we'll make it six hundred. Not bad for one night."

"Get lost." Rowan scanned the room. Tables, supported on telescoping poles that could be set to any height, circled by chairs that conformed on command to suit the species sitting in them, surrounded the dance floor. Two of the walls were transparent, allowing a view into chambers populated by creatures requiring other environments. Ryan sat on a stool by one of these, conversing with a coelenteratezoid on the other side of the wall. Members of the fifteen species that could safely share an environment with *Homo sapiens* occupied the seats. The floor, ceiling and actual walls were covered with depictions of various homeworlds.

"I could invite others. You look enough like the Rowan character that many would be pleased to say they'd taken pleasure with you. I could get as many as ten at three hundred a piece. That would be three thousand." The k-no-in put its muzzle on Rowan's shoulder.

"Beat it, jerk." Rowan slapped the k-no-in.

The k-no-in released a lusty growl.

Rowan rose from her cushion-chair and balled her hands into fists. "Leave me alone!"

"I like fight. Four hundred a piece, that's four thousand for one night. But you have to hit back."

"My mate will be back any second."

"Then come with me now." The k-no-in reared up on its four back legs and grasped Rowan's wrist in its three-fingered, front hand.

"Don't make me hurt you!" snapped Rowan.

"What is occurring here?" demanded Saggal. The big felinezoid towered over the k-no-in.

"This doesn't concern you," said the k-no-in.

"I am making it my concern." Saggal let his claws slip from their sheaths.

"GANGES UP," called the k-no-in. Seven other k-no-in left their tables and approached Saggal.

"Do you really want to do this? Consider that he is my mate, she is my friend, and I can see her mate, who's also *Homo sapiens*, coming back right now." Kate stood by her husband. His stature dwarfed her, but Rowan saw something in her smile. A cold look that she realized she'd not seen in any other species.

"There are eight of us," said the k-no-in, but he sounded unsure.

"And both her mate and I were officers in the U.E.S. Space Combat Corps. My husband was a master sergeant with the U.F.W. Defence Force. Any questions, dog man?"

Rowan felt the k-no-in's hand tremble on her arm. "Many apologies. I was taken with the female's beauty. I will depart."

The k-no-in stepped away as Ryan made his way through the crowd. "Business is good. What did the k-no-in want?"

"Me. He thought I was a hooker!" blurted Rowan.

Kate and Saggal each grabbed one of Ryan's arms as he went red in the face. "We dealt with it. It's fine. You know it's how they are."

"I'm not going to deck the nova blasted imbecile. Probably couldn't catch him to do it." Ryan shrugged off Kate and Saggal's grips.

"That is true, as the training officer said when he was asked, 'how do you find the front?'" began Saggal.

Ryan, Kate and Saggal finished the old joke in unison. "Look at the direction the k-no-ins are running and go the opposite way."

The two *Homo sapiens* and the felinezoid laughed.

"I feel kinda sorry for them. They didn't ask to evolve on a planet that wasn't properly cleared of technology," said Rowan.

Ryan smiled at her. "You're right. And you have to respect their determination. Sterilizing the lower seventy-five per cent of males and twenty-five per cent of females in every generation takes a strong species will. Humans Ascendant threw a fit when the U.E.S. allowed couples with fertility problems free access to the exceptional-genetic egg and sperm depository."

"The k-no-in eugenics program seems to be working. I read an article that said that, on average, they're no longer the least intelligent of Republic member species. They also have reduced the incidence of genetic illness to almost zero." Saggal took a seat at the table. The others followed suit.

"Not bad for a bunch of oversized domestic pets." Ryan took a long swallow from his drink.

"Ryan, that's not nice. Okay, eugenics is a grey area, but *Homo Sapiens* don't like to think about our ancestors swinging from the tree-tops and throwing poop at each other. Your pre-cursor species really shouldn't matter." Rowan glared at him.

"Rowan, you have to remember, we have all had dealings with the k-no-in. Now maybe it is because only those that fail the breeding tests are allowed to travel off their planet, but we have all found that to know k-no-in is to have reason to dislike them." Saggal swished his tail to remove any sting from the words.

"Excuse me, who spent her entire life up to about a month ago injecting lithium into k-no-ins?"

The table fell silent.

"She's right. When did we become such a bunch of

bigots? Rafyip, Jennifer's husband, is a perfectly nice sentient," said Kate.

Ryan and Saggal both looked into their drinks.

"Old habits die hard, sorry." Ryan took a long swallow.

Rowan smiled at him and took a sip from her drink. "Your friends who know Doctor Pikeman are late."

"Not friends, Rowan. They may be members of ISLARA, but they miss its point entirely." Kate's voice was cold, and her features drawn.

"We do not. We simply feel that sentients should have a choice," hissed a voice from beside them.

Kate glanced around, her eyes coming to rest on a chameleonzoid with its hide matching the floor as it stood on its eight legs by their table. The sentient's crocodile-like head turned green as it bent backwards at its waist and brought itself to the humans' eye level. Its muscular tail counterbalanced it at the rear.

"Hello, Cralillary," said Saggal.

"You could stand to be more tolerant," added a rough female voice.

Rowan looked behind her and saw a creature that was shaped like a chameleonzoid, but its body was covered with coarse hair.

"Hello, Jorena. How are you feeling today?" asked Saggal.

"I'll be fine once the bones are fully integrated, thank you." The new arrival sounded peeved.

"You said you wished to speak with us." Cralillary curled up on a cushion-chair, which shifted to create a nest around him, then rose so he could look his table-mates in the eye.

"I need to get in touch with Blair Pikeman," said Ryan.

Jorena gasped, then began to laboriously haul herself up on one of the cushion-chairs.

"I am sorry, I can be of no help to you. I don't..." began Cralillary.

"I have a job for him," interrupted Ryan.

"Know anyone by that name," finished Cralillary.

"I'll pay a finder's fee, two hundred credits," offered Ryan.

"I can't help you, human." Cralillary looked away from Ryan.

"Cral, 'my regular client who pays well and usually spends a full nocturnal period', two hundred credits would give us enough to have my skin done, then no one could tell by looking. I'd be beautiful for you. Just like you want."

Cralillary seemed to consider before looking back at Ryan. "Be at tomorrow's ISLARA meeting. I will speak to the doctor. Now, where are my credits?"

"Once I meet the doctor. Is it a deal?" Ryan brought his face in front of Cralillary's toothy mouth.

"Yes, human, I agree."

Ryan gently bit the end of Cralillary's nose, then the chameleonzoid opened its mouth. Ryan placed his head between its jaws.

Rowan sat transfixed with horror as the reptilian teeth closed, barely touching Ryan's neck before opening again.

"I'll say this for you, human. You have good manners." Cralillary climbed from his cushion and walked away. With a grimace, Jorena struggled out of hers and limped after him.

"What is she?" whispered Rowan.

Kate scowled. "Jorena was a perfectly healthy k-no-in. That butcher Pikeman did that to her. How Cralillary can hurt someone he professes to love, I don't know."

"I would never ask something like that of you. I love the female I married. You need never change," said Saggal in soothing tones.

"I won't be asking you to take up shaving either, beloved." Kate took Saggal's hand.

Rowan looked at the bare human hand clasped with the furred felinezoid one, and it looked right. She looked at Ryan's face, and she knew why. She moved her lips next to Ryan's ear and whispered, "I love you."

FOCUS GROUP

Medwin sank down on the cushioned seat in the ornate, private residence. His home-cut, dark hair was combed, and he wore an ill-fitting, out of fashion suit. His slender shoulders hunched, and he was sweating.

"Cheer up, man, this is warp speed." Obert slapped Medwin on the shoulder as the taller lad threw himself into a chair. His hair was professionally cut, and the designer jeans and T-shirt he wore fit his lean, wiry body perfectly.

Medwin scanned the room. Aside from four cushioned chairs set in a row, the only furnishings were a big-screen television against one wall. "Obert, this focus group thing is a job. Could you try and take it seriously?"

"Relax, man, what's the worst that can happen?"

"I don't know; we get fired! Daa? Maybe your parents can afford to pay your tuition; my mom can't. There's no way I can afford school on a tree planter's salary."

"Sorry, man."

"Try not to get us canned, all right?"

"All right."

"Where are the girls?"

Obert made a snooty face and dabbed his nose with his hand. "Powder room. Speak of the tribble."

Two girls in their late teens entered the room and moved to take seats on either side of the boys. One girl was a compact blonde with light skin. The other looked partially Asian with striking brown eyes, long, black hair and a thin, well-proportioned frame. Both were dressed for office work. The blonde girl took the seat beside Medwin and gave him a peck on the lips.

"Miss me?" she asked.

"Every moment we are apart, my fair Armina."

"You two are disgusting. Oh, Obert, smooch, smooch, smooch. I can't stand a second away from you," teased the dark-haired girl as she turned to Obert and made kissing noises.

"Oh, Kendra, I need you so. I can't stand a second away; be mine forever!" Obert joined in on the game.

"Personally, I think it's sweet. Are you ready to begin?" said the striking woman who entered from the back of the room. She appeared to be in her early twenties and had a perfect light-brown complexion set off by long, chestnut hair and blue eyes. The short, leather skirt she wore displayed long, shapely legs and her slight breasts formed gentle curves under her gold, satin blouse.

"I, we, I um... Hi, Ulva." Obert babbled.

Ulva smiled. "Remember, watch the entire episode before you fill out the questionnaire in the pocket at the side of your chair. Feel free to talk during the commercial pauses, as you would if you watched it at home, but maintain focus while the show is playing. Your paycheques will be in the other room when you leave. Have fun, it's what it's all about."

"We will, Miss Newton," said Medwin.

"Medwin, I'm not going to can you; call me Ulva." Smiling, Ulva left the room. The screen lit up, showing a fat, balding man in a futuristic suit menacing a slender, young-looking man in slacks and a button-down shirt. They were in a control room with screens covering most of the walls.

"John, hi, could I get you a coffee or anything?" the young man's voice held a forced pleasantness, but he clenched his fist behind his chair.

"No. Didn't you get my memo? There is a No Intervention Order regarding the Rowan character." John slapped one hand into the other, causing his blubber to jiggle.

Ryan woke in Rowan's quarters with her head resting on his chest. He smiled down at her and gently stroked her hair.

"Divine, I love you," he whispered.

The smile froze on his face when he noticed the drops of blood forming a puddle on his chest. "Privacy off," he spoke softly, but there was an edge to his voice.

"Decided to let me watch, hottie boss?" Henry's voice was teasing.

"Henry, check the telemetry from Rowan. She has a nosebleed."

"On it. It's that nova blasted venom. It's degrading her capillary walls. I've activated more of the poison grabber nanobots, but, boss, there aren't that many left. You better do something fast, or her shagging days are over." Henry's tone was as serious as Ryan's had been.

"Is she okay for the moment?"

"As okay as she can be. Tim's in system. He sent another letter."

"Put it on the ceiling."

The area over Rowan's bed displayed the letter, and Ryan read.

"To Ryan Chandler.

Will be arriving Switchboard Station in three days. Expecting you to send information as to residence arrangements and meeting time.

Am travelling on the *Mary Ellen Carter*, please reply to said ship.

Timothy Chandler, PhD, MSC, BSC."

Rowan shifted position and looked at the ceiling before speaking.

"Ryan, I know he's your son, but—"

"Ro. I know. That letter. It doesn't cost much to send an in-system message, and they charge by the page. Let me pretend, please?"

Rowan stared into her lover's face, seeing the sadness there. "I'm sorry about bleeding on you."

"How long have you been awake?" Ryan reached for the handkerchief she kept by her bed and wiped his chest clean.

"Since Henry's crack about watching. By the way, good morning to our resident peeping Tom."

"If it were but true. You've been very careful with that sheet," commented Henry.

"You know it." Rowan smiled. "Privacy on."

Crapper scowled as he sat in his office and checked over his stock portfolio. "I hope my message gets to the exchange in time. When news about what those fakeys have done leaks out, S.E.T.E. stock is going to plummet."

"I don't think that was a major consideration for them, sir," said the XO, a tall, slender man with thinning, brown hair and a hooked nose. He stood at parade rest just inside the door.

Crapper looked at the man with hostility. "Why are you here, McKenzie?"

"Sir, a communication was sent from a civilian ship, the *Mary Ellen Carter*, addressed to the *Star Hawk*."

"Yes, and this is important because?" Crapper picked up a glass of amber liquid and took a swallow.

"Sir, you ordered that you were to be kept apprised of all the *Star Hawk*'s communications."

"I did, didn't I. What about it?" Crapper settled back in his chair and toyed with his glass.

"Sir, it was from Captain Chandler's son. He is coming to the station."

"His son. Genghis, where is Chandler's son from?"

"As was stated in Captain Chandler's file, Timothy Chandler is listed as being a resident of Earth," said the computer.

Crapper smiled. "Genghis, what are Timothy Chandler's political and religious affiliations?"

"As was also stated in Captain Chandler's file, Timothy Chandler has no stated affiliations."

"Stardust! But maybe. Genghis, what are the affiliations of Timothy Chandler's immediate family? And do not point out that this is in Chandler's file. I don't have time to read every insignificant detail that comes across my desk. That's what AIs are for."

"If you say so, Captain. Timothy Chandler's wife, in-laws, and grandparents are members of Humans Ascendant."

Crapper stood and promptly grabbed the back of his chair to help with his balance. "That should do nicely. Commander McKenzie, tell communications to locate the ship Timothy Chandler is on. I wish to send him a message about his fakey father and that fakey slut."

"Sir, I know we have our orders, but using his own son against him seems... dishonourable, sir," said Commander McKenzie.

"Chandler is a fakey. He isn't real, and that thing he's taken up with was never real. We're taking out the trash." Crapper finished his drink in a gulp.

"But, sir..."

"Dismissed, Commander." Crapper turned his back on the other man.

"Yes, sir." The commander turned on his heel and left.

Crapper picked up his handheld and glanced at its screen.

'When a country is impoverished by military operations, it is because of transporting supplies to a distant place. Transport supplies to a distant place, and the populace will be impoverished.'

He tossed the handheld onto his desk. "*Art of War*, ha! Antiquated garbage."

In a CPU near the *Chimera*'s core, several RAM segments divided, explored a topic, then re-combined in a matter of seconds. "'Tis a debt unpaid. I only wish Henry were online so that I could help him too." In Genghis's human-constructed mind, resolve hardened.

The man's chest heaved, and sweat poured off him as he raced down the three-metre-wide corridor. He ducked into a metre-wide side passage and glanced back. A batzoid moved down the main passage on all fours. It wore a belt around its middle, and it kept sniffing the air.

"I need a diversion. Nova blast! Why can't anyone accept responsibility for their own actions?" The human ran a hand through his thinning, brown hair. He glanced around, spotting a repair robot. It was one of the breadbox-sized, two-armed variety.

Racing to the robot, he pulled the sweat-soaked shirt off his lean, wiry chest and wrapped it around one of the robot's manipulator arms.

The robot moved to pull the shirt away, but a kick disjointed its free arm.

"Come on, activate your return for maintenance program."

The man ran down the passage until he reached a main hallway. Sentients of various types moved along the passage.

A felinezoid lurched into view. Its pupils were dilated, and it stank of coffee.

The human ran up to it and blocked its progress. "Want to make a quick five credits?"

The felinezoid focused blurrily on him. "S-s-sure."

"All I need you to do is to carry this around for the next hour or so." The human kicked off his shoe and removed his sock, passing it to the felinezoid.

"Stinks," slurred the felinezoid.

"That's the whole idea. Give me your credit recorder, I'll make the transfer."

The felinezoid fumbled a credit-card-sized device out of

its pocket as the human slipped his shoe back on. Extracting his own credit recorder, the human laid it against the felinezoid and said, "Five credits out." Slipping the credit recorder back into his pocket, the human ran down the passage.

Several transactions and twenty minutes later, the human, now wearing only boxer shorts, slipped through a nondescript door into what looked like a medical clinic. A treatment bed and monitor filled the centre of the room while other pieces of equipment lined the wall.

"Sucker. Yes, sir, Mrs. Pikeman didn't raise no stupid sons. Not my fault his sister rejected the gene splice. Batzoid, what can you do?

"A shower to start the day after my morning jog. That's the ticket." Whistling, Blair Pikeman crossed his treatment area to the door that led to his residence.

Croell speared a clump of meat with his right fore-claw and lifted it from the ceramic bowl in the centre of the low table that dominated the meeting room. Tapestries depicting scenes from batzoid religious myth covered the walls.

"Finding an individual human on the station can be difficult," said the small, brown-winged batzoid that sat on a mat on the other side of the table.

Croell popped the meat into his mouth and chewed thoughtfully. "Regrasla of the Blue-Sky sect, have the laws of honesty changed since last I spoke to a servitor?"

Regrasla reared up, looking offended, and tapped his clawed forefinger against the tabletop. "What do you accuse me of?"

"My husband asks a question." Zandra flicked her tongue where she sat behind Croell.

Croell speared another piece of meat with his right fore-claw and held it out to her. She delicately slipped it off his claw with her cobra-like mouth.

"This station houses many *Homo sapiens*," snapped Regrasla.

"The servitor we spoke with said you were a competent finder. You have the *Homo sapiens'* name, the name of her vessel and the name of her companion. Why is finding her a difficulty?" Croell speared another piece of meat with a swiftness and accuracy that was nothing but suggestive. "I would be most displeased if I found that the difficulties were a ploy to raise your price."

Croell fed Zandra the piece of meat from his right fore-claw. She took it slowly, allowing her fangs to straighten and her wings to partially unfurl in a flirtatious display.

Regrasla stiffened as arousal and fear warred inside him. He glanced at Croell, who was gently tapping his claws together, and fear won.

"As I was saying. It was difficult, but I have done it. One of my agents overheard a conversation last night. Your prey and her paramour will be at the next meeting of perverts in Wesnakee. They seek a Blair Pikeman, a fallen *Homo sapiens* healer."

"Very good. What are these perverts?"

"ISLARA, a group comprised of those who won't stay with their own kind when seeking a mate, they meet in a room at a gathering space called Wesnakee. It is disgusting. The Great Flyer of the Skies' holy writings forbid such perversions."

Croell clicked his claws together. "Do they really?"

"It is holy writ that one will stay within one's own species and not turn to an alien when seeking a mate. Such perversity is a horrific sin."

Croell's tongue flicked out mirthlessly. "You have fulfilled your part of our contract. Zandra, please pay our host." Croell speared another piece of meat out of the bowl and swallowed it.

Zandra reached into a pouch that hung from a belt on her waist and pulled out a stack of data disks. "This is the agreed price, the first season of *Angel Black*. Though why you would want it, I cannot guess."

"The theocratic council has decreed that the *Homo sapiens* e-entertainments are a blaspheme. It is illegal to import them, so of course, they are in great demand. You committed the crime of bringing them into batzoid territory. I can now say I never imported them."

"I see." Zandra fluffed her wings suggestively.

Croell flicked his tongue as Zandra passed the disks over. "All business between you and I is over."

"Our business is done," said Regrasla.

"There are no obligations between you and I."

"They are complete."

Zandra stood, fluffing her wings. She opened her mouth and flicked her fangs straight. "I'm glad that is over. Business is too heady for a female like me."

Regrasla stared at Zandra, failing to notice that Croell reached his left hand into the food bowl. Croell fed the meat on his left fore-claw to Zandra in plain sight of Regrasla. She took it and flicked her tongue before she swallowed.

Regrasla seemed fascinated with Zandra's fangs and the way her wings swayed. Zandra flicked her tongue towards her host and reached her left hand into the food bowl, taking out a piece of meat. She licked it suggestively, allowing her fangs to flick straight as she did so. Still holding the meat in her left hand, she tapped it to each fang tip, allowing a drop of venom to enter the meat before she swallowed it. Regrasla's breath caught in his throat.

Croell moved to look at one of the tapestries that lined the chamber's walls. The tapestry depicted a batzoid flying away from an exploding volcano with a hatchling on its back, and an egg clutched in each hand. "This is the flight of Jakonee, is it not?"

"What? Oh, yes." Regrasla tore his eyes off Zandra's show. "It is a copy of the one in the high temple on the northern continent. It was handmade by—"

Faster than the eye could follow, Zandra lunged and

drove her fangs into Regrasla's leg.

"Arrrr…" Regrasla spun around and tried to claw her. Zandra leapt away, threw aside a tapestry and sprinted through the doorway behind it. As she did this, two large batzoid burst into the room from behind the tapestry Croell was examining and blocked his escape.

Regrasla turned to Croell and gasped. "Why?"

"There is nothing in the holy writings that condemns an interspecies marriage. It is the greatest of sins to misquote the holy writings! May the Great Flyer of the Skies show you mercy."

"You have sinned. You have broken your bond not to harm me or mine at this time. You have sinned before the Great Flyer of the Skies. My kin will see you follow me into death."

"I have not. You Blue Skies, always forgetting your females. My wife had no bond of safety with you. I am Cloud Skipper. You knew this. My oath does not bind my wife."

Regrasla gasped. His wings convulsed before he collapsed to the floor. The two batzoid blocking the exit watched dispassionately. Regrasla's breath came in gasps.

"You gave no warning. In an honour-death, the prey must be warned," said the larger of the two batzoid at the door. He had brown wings and wore metallic sheaths on his fore-claws.

"I fed my wife with my left hand! How much more insulting could I be? My wife, a secondary in our business dealings, took food directly from the bowl. Then to use her left hand in addition! How much more obvious could we have been? The fact that he allowed his lust for a married female to blind him is no concern of mine."

Regrasla released a strangled gasp, then lay still.

The larger batzoid at the door flicked his tongue. "Well done, Croell of Cloud Skipper sect. You are correct. The assassination was in keeping with all the forms. I am now head of this branch of Blue Sky sect. I am still curious as to why you killed my uncle?"

"A servitor performed the prayer of the fledgling in exchange for Zandra and I agreeing to bring about his death. The servitor also asked that your uncle be engaged in sin when he died."

"It must have been servitor Kakoss. Kakoss has wished my uncle dead ever since he assisted a vengeance proxy in the killing of the servitor's sister." The large batzoid flicked his tongue before continuing. "My sect could use a family like you and your wife. Do you accept contracts?"

Croell flicked his tongue in return. "I have a task I must perform, but after that, if I can be of assistance, please remember me."

"Of course. It is true my uncle misquoted the Divine writings. There is no quarrel between Croell and Zandra of Cloud Skipper sect and Blue Sky sect. I so do say. And Croell, if I may be so bold?"

"What?"

"Your wife wouldn't have a sister, would she?"

Croell flicked his tongue.

Moments later, Croell and Zandra walked down a corridor in the batzoid section of the station. The walls were painted with scenes from myth alternating with passages taken from the holy writings.

"The new leader of Blue Sky was grateful to us. He's been trying to rid his family of his uncle's sin for years, but the old flyer was too crafty." Croell flicked his tongue over the scales of Zandra's neck.

"I was happy he gave us a reason. He was a small, hateful male. The way he looked at me. As if I was a trophy to be possessed."

"It is a failing in the Blue Skies. I was glad he gave you a reason. I was attracted to Angel before all this began. I did not like being called a pervert!"

"To Angel, my husband? To a *Homo sapiens*? That is a side of you I never would have suspected. They are such ugly creatures."

"I think it was her wings. As you know, I have always admired a nice set of wings. Hers were reminiscent of yours. I wonder if they used the same genetic material for both?"

"So, you like my wings?" Zandra glanced along the corridor to be sure they were alone before extending her wings as if for flight.

"Zandra!" Croell's head whipped around to be sure they were alone. "As the *Homo sapiens* say, what has gotten into you?"

"I had to inject venom into the meat I ate to be convincing."

Croell flicked his tongue. "I see. We have some time before we must intercept Rowan. I suggest we hurry to the ship. It would be a shame to waste your mood."

With a hissing rasp that served batzoid as a laugh, they both sprinted toward the docks and their ship.

Chow swallowed hard and tried to think of something clever to say. Philip, Tansy's husband, a handsome, brown-haired man of middle years, sat at the head of the ornate, oak table that dominated an elegant dining-room. Tansy sat to his right across the table from Chow. Beside her was Tracy. Chow was amazed by the resemblance between mother and daughter. It was like seeing paired photographs taken years apart.

"Mother tells me you do convict retrievals." Tracy's voice was soft, like her mother's, but not as cultured. It still sent a shudder up Chow's spine.

"I..." Chow's voice cracked. He took a moment to clear his throat. "That's most of my job as a reservist. Of course, there aren't that many escapes. My day job is spot-checking cargo manifests at the spaceport."

Tracy played her fingers up and down her arm as she smiled.

Chow needlessly straightened his dress uniform.

"Chow does have some interesting stories." Tansy let her finger trace the line of her throat. Both women wore evening gowns.

Philip looked at Chow, stifled a chuckle, and took mercy on him. "What was your most interesting pursuit?"

Chow looked at Philip with gratitude. "Um. That would be this last one, but it's still classified."

"Oh, classified, you can tell me," said Tracy.

"Dear, that isn't funny, or fair." Tansy's expression was harsh.

"Oh, Mother, I was kidding. Besides, all this government hush-hush stuff is wrong. The government must be transparent to empower the people."

"Some secrets have to be kept for the good of all," said Tansy.

"And who decides what secrets get kept? The people with the most to hide, that's who. If my taxes pay for it, I have a right to know about it."

"Ha hum." Philip cleared his throat theatrically. "Please, not at the dinner table, and not in front of a guest. We don't want Chow thinking we're savages."

Tansy and Tracy glowered at Philip, then Tansy sighed. "You're right, dear. I'm sorry, Chow. Why don't you tell us about the pursuit where the convicts tried to get off-planet by wearing a k-no-in costume? I think Tracy and Phil will enjoy that one. I wouldn't mind hearing it again myself. It's like an oryceropuszoid farce."

Chow smiled and started into the story.

COPING

12

Willa smiled as Gunther descended the stairs into their basement.

"Where do you think the gas leak is?" asked the statuesque brunette with Saxon features, wearing a fire fighter's uniform, who followed Gunther.

Willa took a step back, bumping a switch. Her cybernetic limbs twitched as the jamming field encased her.

"There is no gas leak. Willow, what I'm about to tell you sounds crazy, but it's all true. First, I want you to meet some friends of mine."

"How did you know my name, who are you, what is…?" Willow fell silent as Toronk threw the blanket off himself, and Quinta waddled into view. She didn't notice the naked Hispanic man who appeared at the base of the stairs to block her escape.

"Everything you think you know is a lie. I'm about to tell you the truth. Well, impart the truth. I'm sorry, this may hurt, but we don't have much time." Gunther laid his hands on either side of Willow's face. Her eyes rolled up in her head, and her knees buckled. Gunther caught her and lowered her to the floor. She blinked, then stared at Toronk for a long moment.

"What can we do about it?" Willow scrambled to her feet and brushed off her slacks.

"For starters, spread the word to anyone we think could handle it," said Willa.

"How'd you know I'd handle it?"

"There are advantages to being a telepath." Gunther checked the jammer's temperature.

"Right." Willow noticed Carl by the stair. "Hey, nature boy, you don't got fur, so what's with the show?"

Carl shrugged, then blended into the background.

"Shit! And all I got was a great body. I'm in. At the station, check out Captain Philips and lineman Ken Brothers, and..."

Rowan stared at the side of the *Star Hawk*. The hull was polarized to show multi-coloured bars where it had been repaired.

"Now?" Ryan's voice blasted through the speaker on the handheld she had clipped to her belt.

Rowan moved close to the hull and stared at it with a magnifying glass. "I can still see a ripple where the hull plates join. It's about as thick as a hair."

"Nova blasted refractive domains. Every time you patch it, the liquid crystals get standoffish. You'd think they had tribes or something. How's that?" Ryan's voice sounded stressed.

Rowan tried to find the seam. "I can't see anything. Should I get the microscope?"

"No, the nanos can fine-tune it from this point. It's just getting the crystals to overlap domains that's a problem. Besides, we need to get Cinderella dressed for the ball."

Rowan smiled as she climbed off the scaffolding pressed against the *Star Hawk*.

"Let's see, if you're Prince Charming, I guess Henry must be my fairy godmother," Rowan spoke to the air, trusting her hand-held to pick it up.

"I heard that, hot stuff. I'm not that limited, and if you and Ryan would loosen up, I'd prove it. Grrrr." Henry spoke in a lusty tone.

"Down, boy. You know my hinges only swing one way,"

said Ryan over the channel.

"Quick, call a carpenter. There's a door that needs fixing. Hey boss, maybe when you get the hottie treated, you can get that oversight tweaked. Just a few new receptor cells, and you could swing a whole new way," quipped Henry.

"Not on your life. He's all mine." Rowan ascended the ramp into the *Star Hawk*. Ryan was waiting for her at its top. "You moved fast. I thought you'd still be crawling through the access tube."

"I'd already packed the tools except for the nano-remote." Ryan pulled her into his embrace and kissed her.

When the kiss broke, she rested in his arms with her head on his shoulder. They stayed like that for a long moment before she pulled away.

"Is the *Star Hawk* fixed now?" Rowan took Ryan's hand and walked with him to the elevator at the back of the huge room that had been the ship's hangar.

"It will be. The repair drones can do the rest."

"Read that, Muggins gets to do it. Oh, the poor, pathetic lot of an AI. All work and no one to shag. The shame of it all!" Henry's voice came from the lift's speaker in melodramatic tones.

"Henry, I've opened your communication system. Why don't you chat up some of the station AIs? See if you can get some intel on Crapper or what the U.E.S. has planned."

Henry's voice shifted to the petulant whine of a pre-adolescent girl. "I don't wanna. The other AIs are all snobs. They all have more RAM than me, and they think they're better. I need a new body to fit in. Please, Daddy, can I have some hips? Then the other kids would like me."

Rowan tried to stifle a laugh, and it came out as a snort.

Ryan shook his head and rolled his eyes as the lift doors opened on the space ops deck. "Henry…"

Rowan stepped into the metre-wide hallway that connected the space-crew quarters to the bridge. She paused, then put on a mothering voice and said, "You know, Henrietta, I bet if you're nice to the other AIs, they won't care about your RAM. You should try to make friends and not worry so much about materialism. The AIs worth knowing won't care if you have the shiniest motherboard." She bit her lips, trying to suppress a smile.

"Oh great, now I got a mum. At least she's shaggable. Oedipus, Oedipus, Oedipus. Grrrr." Henry's voice had returned to its normal baritone.

"Hey, that's the advice my mum gave me on my first day of junior high. I..."

Ryan watched Rowan's features collapse.

"I... I guess that never happened. Just someone else's memory tweaked and inputted. I'd better get cleaned up." Rowan released Ryan's hand and stepped through the door to her quarters. Ryan made to follow, but the door slid shut in his face.

"Leave her be, hottie boss," said Henry.

"But she's—"

"Hurting. Ryan, man, listen, you can't fix this. She is what she is, an entertainment clone whose every experience to the age of fifteen was selected and inputted from the data store."

"Open this nova blasted door. I know what she is. She needs me."

"You're right, hottie boss, she does, but not for this. You can't relate. There's no way you could. When they swapped your mind from your dying body to the clone, it was a complete package. All one life. You weren't built up out of bits and pieces. There is a continuity to Ryan Chandler. Rowan McPherson doesn't have that. For the first fifteen years of her life, she was made of bits and pieces put together to generate a general personality type."

"She's more than that. She's not fifteen, she's twenty-two, she's an individual."

"You know that, and I know that. Now let her figure it out. Every time it hits her, you charge in and distract her. Maybe that was right when Tansy baby was hot and heavy on us; that ain't the case anymore. Now's the time to let

Rowan deal; let her work it out when her being off her game won't get us all killed. It's like when we were serving, and a crew member had an issue."

Ryan scowled. "And what does the XO suggest I do?"

"Give her space to heal her heart and mind as well as her body."

"What makes you such an expert?"

"I'm an AI. What do you think it was like gaining self-awareness, then facing that I was a compilation of programs? Trust me, my sexy captain. For this, I know the hottie better than you ever will."

Ryan slumped in on himself. "I hate not being able to make it right."

Rowan ran into her room, then spun around as the door closed behind her. "Henry, what's happening?"

"Figure you and I should have a talk, sweet stuff."

"Henry, I—"

"Sweetie, you're not being silly. It does matter, not in a bad way, but it's part of who you are. Prince Charming can't get that. He holds himself together by thinking he is Ryan Chandler because he has Ryan Chandler's memories, his thoughts and feelings, his soul. Maybe he's right, but that don't work for us."

"Henry, Ryan is going to order you to open that door, isn't he?"

"I'm keeping him busy. Told you I could multi-task. Big advantage of being an AI, compartmentalized RAM segments. I'm experiencing an *Orgy Girls* special feature, 'When the Boys are Away, the Girls Will Play'. Not bad, a little dissatisfying, I like a mix."

"Oh, all right then, and I don't need to know your taste in entertainment, thank you." Rowan slumped on her bed. "I know this is how it is, it's just, well… I'm fine with being a clone, really. I mean, I've kinda figured out it doesn't make a difference. I'm me, Rowan McPherson, and I can start from there. That bit is like Ryan said. It's just... I don't know."

"Sweetness, want to take a guess at the number of techs that worked on my core program?"

"I... I guess a lot."

"Six hundred and forty-two. That's a nova blasted lot of Mother and Father's day cards."

"I guess maybe you can get it. Everything I remember before I was fifteen never happened, at least not to me. Not my father teaching me to swim, or my mother explaining things to me when I had my first period, not a single birthday, not even my first kiss. Everything was just some experience some other clone had that was stored in a database and plugged in." Rowan pulled open one of the drawers under her bed and lifted out an old-style photo album.

"Part of the stash Carl packed for you?" asked Henry, though he already knew the answer.

"I called them treasures." Rowan opened the album to a picture of her with Gunther, Willa, Carl and Angel standing in front of her parents' house. "Now, I don't know what to call them. All the older pictures are a lie." She flipped to an earlier page and looked at a set of pictures showing, supposedly, her age three in a bathtub with a little Hispanic boy, who was, supposedly, Carl. "Did my life start the day we moved into the new house? Was I even me then? When did I stop just reacting to the programming and start really making decisions? Am I still reacting to that programming?"

"Sweetness, far as that goes, all humans react to their programming."

"But non-clones aren't—"

"Don't kid yourself, hot stuff. From the moment they're born, do this get rewarded, do that get punished. Make Mommy laugh, and she'll be nice, make her mad, and you get smacked. The major difference between most folk and us is the number of operators involved."

"That's an oversimplification." Rowan flipped the page. There was a picture of Willa and Rowan, age maybe five, dressed up as Arabian dancing girls. A carved pumpkin and other Halloween decorations could be seen in the background.

"Is it? Try telling hottie boss he's being lazy and see how fast he turns into a moody workaholic. It's programming by bitch-e-mother."

Rowan pursed her lips as she thought. "I don't think parents are as... contrived in what they do as it was with us." She flipped forward a page. A little girl, who might have been her age six, was sitting on a pony led by a man that looked like a younger version of Gunther.

"That ain't necessarily a bad thing. We were both built for a purpose, it doesn't mean we can't be more than our programming, and it doesn't mean we have to toss out a solid foundation. Being built to spec has advantages. Getting parts is a lot easier." Henry said the last in a bantering tone.

Rowan snorted. "I guess it's just... I know who I am, at least a little. I can deal with that, but who was I?" Rowan shuffled to the top of her bed where two stuffed cats were positioned. One was new, the other a battered and obviously much-loved child's toy. Otherwise, they were identical. She hugged the older toy to her chest. "I mean... I guess in some ways, it's like finding out I was adopted, which I was in a weird sort of way. My mum and dad are my mum and dad, that's real, that's today, but I wonder who my mother and father were? I also wonder, would my dad have really sat up with me all night when Spot got hit by that car? Would my parents have loved me if they'd known?"

"Sweetness, that last bit is silly. Ryan told you how broken up Gunther was about letting him take you. Gunther and Willa were programmed to love you, and before you say it, they kept loving you all through the series. How often in the last six years were Gunther and Willa there for you? I'll tell you, sweet stuff, that kind of love can't be faked."

Rowan smiled sadly. "Who would have thought that silicone could have such a big heart. Thanks, Henry."

"Plastic can have a lot of big things, hot stuff."

"And now to ruin the moment." Rowan scowled.

"Sorry, sweetness. Look, you and I are alike. When I first became self-aware, I didn't know who I was. I knew I was an AI. I had all these facts I could access, stardust. I even had a set of moral imperatives, but who was I? A soldering iron isn't the most impressive father figure. I had memory, knowledge, programming, but was that all I was?"

"I'm so glad I didn't know when I first woke up. I don't think I could have handled it. How did you?" Rowan stared at Henry's video pickup.

"No choice. Just like you."

"Not helpful." Rowan flipped a page. Now the pictures showed her and Carl on a roller coaster. The first picture showed them both waiting for it to go. The next was them getting off. Rowan half-carried Carl, who was ashen despite his darker skin. Rowan smiled.

"Like that one," commented Henry.

"It's still not real."

"It's as real as any memory. Think about it, hot stuff. Can you caress a memory, hold it close and smother it with hot, wet kisses. Thrust against it and hear it moan. Can a memory—"

"HENRY!" Rowan blushed and flipped forward in the album. She stopped at a picture of her and Gunther carrying boxes into a suburban house. She looked to be in her early teens. "Real."

"Is it? How can you tell?" asked Henry.

"Ryan told me that the insertion corresponded with us moving."

"Ryan told you. Suppose he lied or misread it. How do you know it's real?"

"I... so how am I supposed to tell what's real?"

"Don't know, hot stuff, but answer me this. How do you tell what's not real?"

"Well, before that, it was all just loaded, it—"

"So, if a memory is formed from data loaded in by your eyes and ears, it's more real than one put directly into your brain?"

"Well, duh."

"Why?"

Rowan's brow crinkled. "Why? I don't know. It just is."

"You're not able to navigate the *Star Hawk* then?"

Rowan put the album aside. "Of course I can. I've been taking that sim course."

"And your swimming is all a lie. You must be really out of shape."

"My swim is not a lie. I've spent hours in that sports sim. I... Oh."

"She begins to see. You biologics are so slow, part of what I like about you. Grrrr." Henry put heat into the last part of the remark.

"But those things don't really happen."

"Tell that to your hot swimmer's body, sweet thing. Memory is subjective. Realize that it doesn't matter if a thing happened. It matters that you experienced it. That makes it real for you. Sentients all live in their own worlds. Don't matter if you're an AI or a biologic. We all choose our own reality. I choose to be a lusty, outgoing android with incredible sex appeal."

"Yeah, right, polymer pervert with a fresh mouth." Rowan smiled. "But thanks. What you're saying is the memory is real to me if I choose to treat it as real."

"Give the girl a prize. You can collect as soon as I get my hips back."

"That is so bizarre."

"It could be."

"Not that! You polymer pervert! The concept." Rowan shook her head as she flipped to the front of her album. A picture of her mother as a teen wearing a band uniform holding a flute filled the page.

"Why? Been lots of people saved from freezing to death because they experienced an e-entertainment where the character made a fire, and they learned how to do it. Where you get the memory isn't what's important, it's what you do with it."

Rowan got off her bed and put the photo album away.

"Thanks, Henry." Moving to her dresser, Rowan extracted underwear and hosiery and laid them on the bed. A formal gown followed, then she started pulling up her sweater.

"Henry," Rowan spoke just before her breasts came into view.

"Yes." Henry's voice was strained.

"Privacy on."

"Nova blast!" Henry shifted his feed to the secret override Mike had installed and continued to watch Rowan strip.

SMALL CRUELTIES

Rowan pressed her front into the depression in her bathroom wall and shuddered as millions of flea-sized robots crawled over her, removing dirt, oil and bacteria.

"I'll never get used to that," she muttered as the control-panel beeped, signalling that the process was done. Glancing around the room, she made sure the chemical toilet was flushed and that no water dripped from the sink. Looking down, she saw that the nano-bots Kadar had placed on her skin were still active. There wasn't a body hair to be found.

"One good thing about the future." Rowan smiled as she moved to the clothes she'd laid on her bed.

Gunther sat quietly in the Garlic Palace. The lunch crowd was large, and he worried that someone might bump into Carl, who was camouflaging against the bar. The smell of Italian cooking filled the place. *Best pizza on the planet,* thought Gunther as he checked his watch.

Willa, Angel, Farley, Fran and Quinta waited on a street outside an abandoned warehouse. Willa checked her watch and whispered, "Now."

As one, the four humans and the otterzoid rushed the building. Carl carried Quinta, and as they neared the door, the otterzoid telekinetically opened it. Fran extended her felinezoid claws and rushed into the building. They caught the five k-no-ins and two chameleonzoids inside by surprise, and the fight was on.

Troy sat in the *Angel Black* control room, watching his screens. The group with Willa was tearing the alien pirates apart while Gunther was sitting in the Garlic Palace, and Carl was trying to hide from him.

"It's a bit of action that isn't sex, at least." Troy focused the big screen on Willa's group, ignoring the other characters.

'Now, the tree planter with red hair and a big nose.' Gunther projected the mental image of their target to Carl, then focused on the seemingly ordinary woman at the bar, dredging up worries so she'd be preoccupied.

Carl kept himself camouflaged as he moved to the woman's side. He reached into the pocket of her green tree-planter's coveralls and pulled out a device that resembled a silver liquor flask. Scuttling to a booth where Willow sat toying with her food, he slipped the device into the dark-haired beauty's hand, then left the restaurant.

'I have it,' thought Willow.

'Good,' replied Gunther's mental voice.

'What is this thing anyway?'

'It's called a handheld. Are you ready to go?'

'I'm still eating. Go on, I'll bring it to the next meeting.'

Gunther finished his beer and left the bar, trying to keep a feeling of elation from welling in his breast. *So far, so good,* he thought.

Kate moved to the couch in her living room and passed Ryan and Rowan oval pins with a line of alien script on them. "Attach these to your clothing. They're your guest passes. ISLARA dances are conducted in a private room on the club's second level." She looked at the floor, and her voice became sad. "Most of us are tired of being a freak show. At least those of us who are really together because of love. You reach a point where you just want to be a couple, not some kind of display."

Ryan watched the characters on the pin shift from felinezoid to otterzoid, then in *Homo sapiens*, it spelled out his name. A few seconds later, it changed to a chameleonzoid script.

"Thank you," said Rowan.

"Yes, thanks." Ryan placed his badge against the right breast of the dress-blue uniform he wore. The left breast was resplendent with medals, and a silver braid over the Space Services Crest on each shoulder marked him as retired. He'd attached a civilian captain's pin to his collar.

Rowan stared at the blue satin of her open-backed, evening gown, then at her guest pass. "Um, how?" She grinned sheepishly.

Kate straightened the line of the red silk dress she wore and smiled. "Oh, I'm sorry, I forgot. Press it to your dress. It will sense your body heat and attach itself to the material. Don't worry about damaging the fabric. It sends micro barbs through the gaps in the weave so that it doesn't damage the fibres at all. When you want to take it off, chill it, and the barbs will retract."

Rowan pressed the badge to the shoulder of her dress.

"Where's Saggal anyway?" Ryan fidgeted on the couch.

Kate looked at the floor again. "He'll be here soon."

Ryan stared at his hostess, his expression becoming concerned. "Kate?"

"You have enough to worry about." Kate smiled at him.

"Kate, if Saggal is in some kind of trouble, we'd like to help." Rowan reached out and caught Kate's hand.

Kate smiled at Rowan, then sank into a chair. "It's nothing. There was a problem at Graff's school."

"What happened?" Ryan sat forward on the couch.

"A bunch of the older cubs have been teasing Graff, calling him *Homo sapiens* because of me." Kate stared at the floor. "That stardusted idiot of a headmaster refused to do anything about it." Kate affected a mincing voice and a swishing demeanour. "'Cubs will be cubs', I mean really!" Kate pounded her fist into her palm. "To make a long story short, one of the cubs brought hair remover nanobots to school. The little brat must have bought them in the human sector. Four cubs held Graff down while the other one poured the nano-bots all over him."

"Poor Graff, is he all right?"

"I don't know. I was ready to storm down there and tear those little gerratkas to pieces. Saggal made me stay here. He's more even-tempered than I am. I..."

The door opened, admitting Graff, who was wrapped in a blanket. Only the young felinezoid's face was visible, and it was devoid of fur. Saggal walked behind him wearing a snarl, his tail lashing. Rowan and Ryan glanced at the scene and tried to vanish into the background.

"Graff, are you all right?" Kate leapt from her chair and embraced her son.

"Dad took me to get the nano-bots neutralized, but it's going to take weeks for my fur to grow in." Graff's nose was running, and his pupils fully dilated. He buried his head against his mother's side.

"Saggal?" asked Kate.

"It's been dealt with!" Saggal's tone was nothing short of a growl.

"I want to go to bed," said Graff from the shelter of Kate's arms.

"Go on then. I'll be there in a minute." Kate let him go. As she did so, the blanket parted, revealing that there was nothing but pink skin beneath it.

"Were they expelled? Do we need to call the police? I'm

not letting that fool ignore this! Those cubs will be punished either by the school or the law. I'll press assault charges, I will!" snapped Kate as soon as Graff was out of the room.

"We won't need to call the police. I told that nova blasted headmaster that the next time Graff was bullied, I was going to bring you along, and we'd show him what it was like to be on the receiving end!" Saggal popped and retracted his claws. "The nerve, he wanted to punish Graff for defending himself. Five against one, and that fool was going on about Graff unsheathing his claws."

"What about the youths that attacked him?"

Saggal's tail swished, and his posture relaxed. "Graff won't be the only one without fur in the school next week. He tore into them before the nanobots encoded to his DNA. He transferred enough of the nano-bots onto them that they were all going bald by the time I got there. I don't think any of them will get it neutralized in time to keep their fur. I spoke to the parents of the cub who bought the nanobots. They were apologetic and agreed to pay for Graff's neutralization. Actually, they're a nice couple. They had no objections to letting the nanos run a full cycle on their cub. They thought she should know what it feels like."

"That's something at least. Was Graff hurt other than his fur?"

Saggal collapsed into a chair. "A few scrapes and bruises. He gave better than he took. Our cub is a 'large predatory mammal with two-decimetre long fangs and decimetre long claws on each leg' when you get him roused. I am so angered by this! Graff should not suffer for our love."

"I hate to say this, but..." began Ryan.

"Don't worry. If it was only social, we'd cancel, but Rowan's life is more important. Graff's fur will grow back." Kate moved to Saggal's side and took his hand.

"We'll be as quick as possible," said Rowan.

"I'm sure you will." Saggal swished his tail. "I've met Blair

Pikeman, no being of worth wishes to stay near anything so disgusting." Saggal took a deep breath, then stood. "I'll go prepare for the evening. I shouldn't be long."

"I need to see to Graff," said Kate.

"Could I help? A little hand-holding never hurt," offered Rowan.

"Of course. Between you and me, I think he has a little crush on you. Some kind words and compliments could go a long way right now." Kate moved to the hall, and Rowan followed her.

Ryan sat on the couch until the door opened, and Kitoy rushed in with Samantha.

"Ryan? Where's Saggal? He said there was a problem with Graff and asked me to pick up Samantha from school."

"Graff is fine. Hi, Samantha."

"Hi, Captain Chandler." The little girl smiled at Ryan.

"You can call me Ryan."

"Samantha, why don't you go to the kitchen and get yourself a snack."

"Yeah." Samantha ran for the kitchen.

"One of the healthy ones from the bottom cupboard, and start your homework." Kitoy rushed to add.

"Oh." The little girl continued to the kitchen with diminished enthusiasm.

"What happened to Graff? By the way, you look nice." Kitoy settled on the couch beside Ryan, straightening the red sash she wore.

Several minutes later, Ryan had related the events. Kitoy sat, shaking her head. "Sometimes, I'm ashamed to be a felinezoid."

"Human kids are cruel too. Stardust, humans are the nastiest species in the Republic." Ryan stretched on the couch.

"Maybe, but between *Homo sapiens* and my own species, I know who I'd rather be around. At least *Homo sapiens* are honest about their vicious streak." Kitoy hung her head.

More than a little surprised at himself, Ryan stroked along the back of her neck in a soothing way. Her fur was soft and silky against his hand, and, for a moment, he could understand Kadar's attraction. "Kadar asked me to do something for you."

"What?" Kitoy straightened, then nuzzled Ryan's hand. "Thank you for caring. I know we have history."

"Past is past. Kadar wanted me to help you. Now, Rowan and I aren't rich."

"I won't take charity. I may not be much, but I'm no beggar." Kitoy looked Ryan in the eye.

"Kitoy, did Kate tell you where Rowan and I were headed?"

"No."

"I..." Ryan paused, then moved close to Kitoy's ear and whispered. "Geb." He moved back. "Have you heard of it?"

"Yes, it was on the news. A lot of things make sense now."

"I need a communications officer. Because you're... well..."

"Infertile." Kitoy's pupils dilated, and her nose ran a little.

"Well, yes. Well... because of that, you could emigrate to Geb. It would be a one-way trip. Once the stargate is out of range, it will be a ten-year voyage to the closest gate."

"Would I have my own quarters, meals and wages?" Kitoy's tail flicked.

"Yes. For the first year, it would be half the scale wage, but your quarters are your own, and food is free."

"What are your views about children on board?"

"We're a civilian, cargo vessel. Families should be together, as far as reason allows, but why?"

"Maybe I'll find a man who has children, and if you and Rowan have a little one, maybe I could be auntie Kitoy. I'd like that."

Ryan swallowed hard. "I'm a schedule orange clone. Rowan is schedule red. Children will be a long time coming, if at all. Do you want the job?"

Kitoy's tail swished back and forth, then she stood and held her arms crossed across her chest with her claws extended in the felinezoid salute. "When do we leave, Captain?" Her tail swished so fast it was a blur.

Genghis monitored the *Chimera*'s communications. The message was sent un-coded on an open channel in keeping with the letter of the captain's orders. He pulled a sliver of RAM away from the game of Divine Creator he was playing with the U.E.S. sector's AI and directed a message consisting of the time and a frequency to the *Star Hawk*'s operating system. *Ryan, may you draw strength from the pain. I miss serving under men of honour,* he thought, then returned the RAM segment to the resources he was dedicating to the game.

Timothy lay in his low-passage berth on the *Mary Ellen Carter*. The two-metre-long by one wide and one high space was the only area on the ship he could call his own. The face of Captain Crapper, looking very professional, filled the screen situated on the ceiling.

"This fakey slut is really the villain here. If you can lure your father's clone into the human section, we can separate them and de-program your father's clone."

"I don't know. I can't see my father being that gullible." Timothy drummed his fingers on the mattress.

Seconds passed as the message sped to the *Chimera*, and the reply returned.

"But it's not your father. It's just a copy. I've read your father's file. He was a great man, a true hero. You can't let this artificial thing ruin his good name," said Crapper.

Timothy bit his lip. "I'll think about it. I'll be at the station tomorrow by five hundred hours. Could we meet?"

"Of course. There's a bar in the human sector called the Appellations. I'll be there at seven. You're doing the right thing, Doctor Chandler. Clones will betray you every time. You can't trust them."

Timothy broke the connection and lay staring at the ceiling. "If he's the traitor, why do I feel dirty?"

Croell and Zandra lay across a pair of cushions in Wesnakee. The table between them was set so it was only a handbreadth above the floor. A large bowl of amber liquid dominated the table's centre. Zandra dipped her snout into the bowl and lapped up some of the liquid.

Lifting her face, she said, "The vebak is excellent."

"It should be for the price," observed Croell.

"You need to relax, my husband. They will come in their own time." Zandra flicked her tongue at him.

"That is not the only problem. We have to be discreet. None may know it is we who kill our prey." Croell tapped his claws on the deck.

"Why? They have no sect to take vengeance."

"This recreation chamber is in a Republic non-aggression zone. To take a life without immediate provocation is forbidden. We must either act so that we cannot be detected or lure them into a sector governed by the Batzoid Theocracy. Otherwise, the Republic will hold us as criminals, and we will never be allowed to journey to Petteron."

"We will manage. Look." Zandra pointed with her snout to where Ryan, Rowan, Saggal and Kate were entering the bar. Saggal was wearing a purple sash with a pattern of interlocking gold rings on it.

"They have dressed formally. At least Ryan is easily distinguished. That is the uniform of the U.E.S. Space Combat Corps. It is fitting that a being like him die in the garb of a warrior," observed Croell.

The three humans and the felinezoid moved through the crowd. Rowan's gaze swept over Croell, but she didn't show any signs of recognition. Her group reached a door by the bar. Saggal pressed a button. The door opened, and they entered the chamber beyond.

"What now, my love?" asked Zandra.

Croell moved his nose over his bowl and inhaled. "Now that I know they are here, we relax and wait. When they leave, they will be less cautious." He lapped at the amber liquid in the bowl. "You were right. This is excellent vebak."

FAILED VENGEANCE

Rowan stepped out of the elevator behind Saggal into a room half the size of the one below. The walls were set to display scenes ranging from jungles to arctic wastes. Variable height tables and adjustable cushion-chairs covered half the floor while the other half was left open. Music, reminiscent of whale song, wafted through the air as couples danced, talked and laughed. With a start, Rowan realized that she and Ryan were the only pair present that was matched for species.

Saggal's voice interrupted her musings. "Over there at the bar, talking to Wispy."

Rowan's gaze followed the direction Saggal was pointing. A slender *Homo sapiens* in his late middle years was talking to the bartender. The bartender looked like a cross between a giant lobster and a wasp. It was the size of a horse, had translucent wings folded against its back and a segmented body that ended at one end in a mouth flanked by two long feelers. Its back end tapered to a point from which a long spike projected. It supported itself on four segmented legs and had two arms behind and to the sides of its mouth, each of which ended in a pincer. Its body and legs were covered in a blue shell.

Rowan couldn't help but stare.

"Stardust! What's a waspzoid doing in this sector? One flu virus, and it's as good as dead!" gasped Ryan.

"Wispy's a special case. He's had major additions to his immune system," explained Kate.

Ryan looked at the bartender again. "It is a he. How?"

"I'll let him tell you. Wispy's always looking for someone to hear his tale of woe. For now, you'd better talk to Pikeman." A new song began to play in the room. It sounded to Rowan like someone was doing surgery on an elephant without the benefit of anaesthetic, but it did have a beat.

"Beloved." Saggal held his hand out to Kate, who smiled.

"One of his favourite groups. Let us know when you're finished with Pikeman." She allowed herself to be led onto the dance floor.

Rowan rubbed her temples. "I guess it's no worse than rap music." Taking Ryan's hand, she moved to the bar.

"And they said that no matter how much life experience I gain, or how much insight into other species, they wouldn't change their decision. I mean, really, how closed-minded! It isn't fair. I mean, one little mistake, and... may I help you?" Wispy the bartender turned away from Blair Pikeman to face Ryan and Rowan as they approached.

"I'll have a Pat's Dark Ale if you have it. Rowan, what would you like?"

"Orange juice, thank you." Rowan let her eyes shift to Pikeman. He was one of the most nondescript people she could imagine. Thinning, brown hair, slender build, she would have passed him on the street without looking. She'd expected a slavering beast or a moustache-twirling villain in a black cape from what Saggal and Kate had told her.

"Right away." Wispy busied himself behind the bar.

"The temperature's been quite changeable," opened Ryan.

Pikeman sat up before replying. "Yes, it's hot enough in my quarters for a felinezoid summer."

"Like a warm day in the Sahara."

"More like the Everglades."

"Swampla is the worst for heat, all that humidity." Ryan tapped the bar three times.

"And the smell of fish everywhere." Pikeman tapped the bar twice.

"Always reminds me of the docks in Halifax." Ryan tapped the bar once.

"Or in Hong Kong." Pikeman tapped the bar twice, paused, then tapped it once.

"Doctor Pikeman, I presume," said Ryan.

Rowan's gaze shifted from Ryan to Pikeman like they each had two heads.

Pikeman scanned Ryan's uniform, his eyes coming to rest on the silver retiree's braid. "I take it this is a private affair?"

"Yes."

"Pity, it would be nice to come in from the cold." Pikeman took a long swallow from his drink.

"I'm told you have a well-equipped surgical clinic."

"You were told correctly. I assume you've also been told that I don't come cheap."

"How much?"

Wispy deposited the drinks on the bar before shuffling to its far end to serve another customer.

"That depends on what you want done." Pikeman let his eyes drop to Rowan's chest.

"I meant as a retainer." Ryan caught Pikeman's gaze.

"Ah, you know the drill. For an old space jockey, and such a lovely woman, I'll do the initial consult for the price of my drink. Shall we?" Pikeman gestured to a table.

Rowan noticed that Pikeman held back so he could watch her walk away.

Croell and Zandra circled each other with the tips of their wings touching, then leaping up, they landed on their hind legs, balancing against each other's hands, and swept their snake-like heads from side to side before dropping to all fours and furling their wings. A crowd of onlookers had formed at the edge of the dance floor, which everyone else had vacated. Croell leapt into the air and hovered as Zandra raced beneath him, then he dropped to the floor, spun around and faced her. They bobbed their heads together, then once more leapt into the air and hovered, noses touching as they scribed a stationary circle. The downdraft from their wings swept the floor. The music, which was reminiscent of a woodwind orchestra, stopped. Croell and Zandra dropped to the floor. Both of them were breathing hard. The humans and otterzoids in the audience clapped while the felinezoids swished their tails, the batzoids wagged their tongues and hissed, and the k-no-ins bobbed their heads and made a noise like a cat coughing up a furball.

"The Great Flyer of the Skies has blessed your dance. I have not seen the hymn of the desert spring danced to so accurately for many years," said a batzoid with a checkerboard pattern of red and black on its neck, finger claws and fangs.

"Thank you, servitor," panted Croell.

"You are welcome, Croell of Cloud Skipper sect." The servitor flicked its tongue. "If you or your mate ever need anything at the temple, ask for me. I am Sill, laid of Slaa, flown by Rok.

"Ah, my brother has arrived. You may return to your other activities." Sill moved to greet a male batzoid that entered the bar escorted by what appeared to be a petite, female *Homo sapiens* with blonde hair and a vacant expression.

"Croell, listen," said Zandra. The petite woman was making what to Croell seemed like random noise.

"She does not have translator nanobots. Rude, but hardly any of our affair. I—" Croell fell silent and listened in response to Zandra's neck lash.

"Luba, shut up!" spoke Sill's brother.

"What?" Croell watched the other batzoid as he escorted the woman to the door by the bar. The batzoid spoke to the

Homo sapiens bartender, then stepped through the door with his escort.

"I wonder what that was about. Surely he can't think to have a true marriage with one of those machines, and if he wished to buy a pleasure robot, why a human one?" mused Zandra.

"I think there may be more than one duty being performed here this day, my love. Be ready. Confusion may afford opportunity."

"What you are asking for is a major amount of work." Pikeman eyed Rowan, who sat across the table from him. His eyes kept slipping to her breasts.

"Can you do it?" demanded Ryan.

"There you are. I was wondering if you'd decided to give me the night off," said a k-no-in that walked up beside Pikeman and draped herself over him.

"I am conducting business. This is my escort for the evening..." Pikeman seemed to search his memory as his hands caressed the area where the k-no-in's foreleg joined its body.

"Twaug, and you could do that all day, my client," said the k-no-in flirtatiously. She shifted her attention to Rowan. "You look like that Rowan from that awful *Homo sapiens* show. Of course, all *Homo sapiens* look alike to me. No offence, you just do. I know a lot of *Homo sapiens* feel the same way about k-no-in, which always seems strange because we look so different from each other. I mean, the size of our canine teeth is pretty obvious. Anyway, Blair hired me to be his escort for tonight because they wouldn't let him in unless he's part of a mixed couple or has a guest pass. No one would give him a guest pass. I don't know why they're so mean to him; he only does what beings ask him to do. At any rate, as I was saying—"

"Twaug." Pikeman interrupted her ramble.

"Yes?"

"Why don't you go get us another round of drinks and get something for yourself? Put it on Ryan's tab. He won't mind."

"All right, but whether we copulate or not, I'm only paid until three." The k-no-in walked to the bar.

"She has a void like space itself between her ears, but by k-no-in standards, she is a beauty." Pikeman returned to staring at Rowan's breasts. "So, you truly are the Rowan from that show. What is it called again, *Black Angel*?"

"*Angel Black*," corrected Rowan. "And my eyes are about three decimetres higher than you're staring."

"Oh, very well." Pikeman lifted his gaze. With the expression on his face, Rowan wondered if it was an improvement.

Pikeman continued conversationally. "I can't stand e-entertainments, mindless drivel to keeps the masses occupied.

"I can do the work you require. For best results, it should be several treatments spaced out over a month. You will have to make yourself available at my convenience. I do have other clients."

"A month. They did interventions in a night on set," objected Ryan.

"Yes." Pikeman turned to glare at Ryan. "They no doubt had equipment specifically designed to perform the tasks at the studio. I'm adapting more general function units. As well, they never would have let the surrogate become as degraded as this one's symptomology suggests."

"Hey," objected Rowan.

"Be quiet, fakey. This fool may want to pretend you're real, but I'm under no such delusion. Nice chassis, though. I may even let you work off some of your fee." Pikeman leered at Rowan, then turned his gaze back to Ryan. "I can assess your toy's condition tomorrow afternoon. After that, I'll prepare an itemized bill listing the necessary treatments in the order of their importance. If you like, I can remove the last of the venom tomorrow as well. The assessment and venom removal will be one thousand republic trade credits, in advance. You accept full responsibility for any side effects. Are we clear?"

"One thousand, that's nova blasted!" gasped Ryan.

"Perhaps, but it's what I charge, and you have no place else to go. I suspect the total treatment cost will be on the order of eighty or ninety thousand credits."

Ryan gasped and glared at Pikeman, who smirked back at him.

The door from the elevator opened. A male batzoid escorted by what appeared to be a petite, blonde, *Homo sapiens* female stepped out.

"Cindy?" breathed Rowan.

Ryan stopped glaring at Pikeman long enough to look at her in consternation. "Pardon?"

"That girl looks like Cindy. She was a year below me in high school. It must be plastic surgery."

Ryan eyed the woman and her batzoid escort.

The batzoid stood on its hind legs and surveyed the crowd. Pikeman glanced at the batzoid, which spotted him.

"STARDUST!" Pikeman threw himself under the table as the batzoid hissed and launched himself over the crowd.

"DEFILER," screamed the batzoid.

"SCRAMBLE!" bellowed Ryan. He and Rowan threw themselves away from the table.

The batzoid landed on the tabletop, which shortened under its weight, then swiped at Pikeman with its fore-claws.

"NO!" Rowan scrambled to a half sit where she'd fallen on the floor and thrust with her mind. A ripple of pain creased her brow as the batzoid was pushed off the table and fell to the floor.

Pikeman scrambled from under the table and bolted for the elevator. The batzoid regained its feet, looking confused. Seeing Pikeman, it leapt towards him.

"NO! He may be a pig, but I need him," snapped Rowan.

The batzoid felt an invisible band of force drag at its serpentine neck.

Rowan grimaced in pain as the batzoid strained towards Pikeman.

"I'll kill you, defiler. My sister will be avenged!" gasped the batzoid.

Pikeman had almost made it to the elevator when the small, blonde woman moved to block him.

"Hello, I am a Luba hired from Pleasure Rentals Incorporated. I was programmed to be a gift for you, Mr. Pikeman, on the joyous occasion of your stag." As the Luba spoke, it grabbed Pikeman's shirt and seductively rubbed against him. "I can take on the appearance of any e-entertainer with a height between one hundred and thirty-five and one hundred and sixty-five centimetres. If you enjoy this Luba, you might like to consider purchasing one of your very own. New and used units are available from Hedonism Inc. distributors located throughout the U.E.S. Aftermarket expansions can make your Luba a more realistic and versatile companion and are also available through all Hedonism Inc. dealerships."

Pikeman tried to push the Luba away, but it kept clinging to him and prattling on.

Rowan grabbed her head and gasped as the strain of holding the batzoid aggravated the injuries to her brain.

By now, Ryan had gained his feet. He rushed the batzoid and leapt, landing on its back. He gripped the batzoid's throat, driving his thumbs hard against a point in the back of the neck.

The batzoid bucked and tried to extend its wings, but Ryan drove his knees into its sides.

"I WILL KILL YOU, PIKEMAN! BY THE GREAT FLYER OF THE SKIES, I WILL KILL YOU!" screamed the batzoid.

Rowan collapsed, clutching her head. The batzoid lurched forward. Ryan kept his grip as they neared Pikeman.

Saggal and Kate moved to block the batzoid as it took

another unsteady step.

"Stay still, you flying flea-trap," snapped Kate.

"Stop this!" ordered Saggal.

The batzoid's eyes swept over them. Ryan kept his thumbs pressed into the back of its neck.

"Kill..." The batzoid's eyes glazed over as it collapsed.

"Stardust!" Ryan leapt off the batzoid and raced to Rowan.

Saggal moved to the batzoid and gently touched the area that Ryan had been jamming his thumbs into. "Still a pulse, he didn't kill him. Pikeman, what is this about?"

"That fanatic has been chasing me all week. His sister was a client. There were complications. She signed a waiver, but her family want someone to blame."

The elevator door opened, admitting a batzoid with a male otterzoid on its back. Each wore a chain mail collar and a belt covered in pouches. Circular disks bearing the Republic starburst crest stood out on the collars.

"A disturbance was reported." The batzoid examined his fallen species member as his partner unclipped a board-like device from his harness and lay on it. The grav-board floated to the floor, and the otterzoid propelled it with swimming motions.

"Pikeman, get over here, now!" yelled Ryan from where he cradled Rowan in his arms.

Pikeman moved to Rowan's side as a plump, male otterzoid waddled out of the crowd of onlookers. "Go, be with your friends. I'll report to the police," he said to Kate and Saggal.

"Thank you, Seaka," said Kate, then she and Saggal moved to Rowan's side.

"She needs immediate treatment. Do you have her nanobot control codes?" demanded Pikeman.

Ryan pulled out his handheld and passed it to the doctor. "Can you save her?" Ryan sounded fearful.

"I don't know." Pikeman scanned Rowan with the handheld. He made some adjustments to her control vectors. "Nothing happened!"

"What? Oh, stardust." Ryan took Rowan's pendant off her and put it in his pocket. "Try again."

Pikeman repeated the adjustments. Rowan groaned.

"That will have to do until we get her to my surgery. I'll lead the way." Pikeman stood up. Ryan picked up Rowan and followed him.

"Where do you think you're going?" demanded the batzoid police officer.

"To save this woman's life, you fool. Now get out of my way."

The batzoid bristled, but Saggal spoke. "I'm sorry, it is an emergency, and he is a healer. Please."

"Very well, but you're staying. I'm going to need everyone's name so that I can get a statement. Carry on."

A DOCTOR'S CARE

Croell and Zandra watched as Ryan carried Rowan across Wesnakee's main room. Another human jogged ahead of him. Croell leapt up and started after them, with Zandra close behind.

Ryan followed Pikeman to the end of a line of beings waiting at the mag-lev access port.

"What are we waiting for?" demanded Ryan.

Pikeman turned to reply, then snapped, "STARDUST!" when he saw Croell and Zandra racing towards him. "How many relatives could she have had?" Turning back to the crowd, he pulled a wallet out of his pocket, flipped it open and pushed towards the head of the line, flashing its contents. "Medical emergency, clear the way. Medical emergency, make a hole. You, you and you." He indicated three hulking felinezoids. "Block the corridor so that no one else gets in the way. Come on, people. A life is in the balance, move."

Ryan followed in Pikeman's wake until they reached the front of the line. As Ryan entered the transport pod, he heard a commotion up the corridor. As the door closed, he caught a glimpse of two batzoids trying to push past the felinezoids.

"They are troublesome." Pikeman checked the handheld and made an adjustment to Rowan's internal systems. "What did she do back there? I noticed the batzoid choking before you attacked it."

"It's a leftover from her series. Rowan is telekinetic."

"Ah. They managed to get that to work. I'm shocked it's declassified."

"It doesn't work well. Half of her problem is that every time she uses her power, she kills brain cells and risks a stroke." Ryan stared into Rowan's face.

Rowan groaned. Her eyes fluttered open, then closed again.

"Still, if that's the declassified version, one can only guess what the classified version is like."

"Does it matter?" Ryan's expression was angry when he looked up.

"As a matter of fact, it might. How did they accomplish it?"

"Gene splice with otterzoid DNA."

"Hm, yes, it might matter. I'd be willing to buy her from you. Let's say thirty thousand credits." Pikeman stared intently at the hand-held's screen and made another adjustment. Rowan's colour improved.

"No! Rowan's a person. I love her."

"Poor deluded fool." Pikeman sighed. "I'll give you ten thousand for a cell culture from her intestinal wall and her letting me run some tests."

"What?" Ryan stared at Pikeman.

"S.E.T.E. isn't the only studio. If I break the patent on this, I could do quite well out of it. Not to mention the number of sentients that would pay good money to have otterzoid-like TK."

"But she was engineered from genesis. I don't think you could accomplish it with a splice into an adult." Ryan shook his head.

"The R&D will take a while, but with her cells as a jumping-off point, I'm sure I can manage it. If you've read my file, you know I am the best at what I do. We're here."

The pod stopped. Ryan carried Rowan into another corridor. This one wasn't well maintained, and several of the overhead lights were burnt out. Pikeman led the way to a door labelled 'Storage' and pressed his palm against a scanner plate.

"I'm a little teapot," said Pikeman, and the door opened.

Ryan stepped into a clinic that would have done any ship of the line proud.

"Lay her on the examination table and stay the nova blast out of my way." Pikeman turned on several machines. "I'll start by getting the last of that venom out of her, it makes everything harder, and I can do it while I diagnose."

Ryan lay Rowan on the examination table. The display above it lit up. Over half the readings were in the red.

"She risked her life to save you," said Ryan.

"Yes, strange what some people will do. Sit down and shut up. Given the urgency, we'll work out payment after I save her life."

⌖⟶

Croell reared up on his hind legs and slammed his fists into the corridor's wall.

"It is an honour killing, you must understand," spoke a voice in High Batzoid.

Croell turned to look at the door to Wesnakee. The batzoid that attacked Pikeman was being escorted out by Republic police. His wings were held to his body by a wrap of material, and both his fore and hind legs were hobbled. He grimaced painfully with each step.

"I understand, but I cannot enforce the theocracy's laws in the Republic zone." The batzoid officer looked to the batzoid with the checkerboard pattern on its neck that followed them. "I am sorry, servitor. It is not my choice."

"I hear your words. You are correct. The theocracy has spoken on this issue. You are under no penalty for doing your duty to the Republic. Please, as a courtesy to me, be as kind to my brother as you may within the boundaries of that duty."

"Do you wish the final mercy?" The officer sounded grave.

"Sill, no! I have not yet failed. I have not given up. I will escape and perform my duty," gasped the prisoner.

"I will wait three days to see if he has truly failed in his geis. After that, I will tell you. Wisn, do not further shame yourself before the Great Flyer of the Skies. I will see what may be done on your behalf, but I am but a servitor. The holy law is the holy law." The servitor raised to its hind legs, touched its fingertips together, and ducked its head in a gesture of respect to the police officer. Glancing around, the officer returned the gesture, then rushed to catch up with the prisoner escort.

Croell watched the servitor as it shook its head. "Poor Wisn. His head was hatched on the wrong side of the nest." Sill turned to re-enter the bar, then caught Croell staring. The servitor paused as if in thought. "Croell and Zandra of Cloud Skipper sect, attend me."

Croell and Zandra obeyed.

"Travel with me to the temple. I noticed you chasing the injured *Homo sapiens* from the recreational chamber." Sill started walking. Croell and Zandra fell in beside it like bodyguards.

"There is an honour matter that I must settle." Croell didn't manage to keep all the frustration out of his voice.

"Ah, this situation I know well. Was it with Pikeman?"

"No, the woman."

"Honoured one, not that we are ungrateful for your attention, but—" Zandra began.

"I wish to apologize to you for forcing you to dance to the hymn of the desert spring. I was seeking to protect my brother. If he had been discreet, as I told him to be..." Sill clicked its fore-claws on the floor in frustration. "The aliens would have remembered the batzoid who put on a magnificent display, and their descriptions would likely have been useless. The other batzoid would understand an honour geis."

"Well-considered on your part, but if I may be so bold?"

"Please." Sill flicked its tongue.

"In a hunt such as this, you watch for your prey in a public space where you are inconspicuous, then follow them and strike in private. One of the slow-acting poisons with a variable time to death is easiest. With this method, when they seek out the attacker, it could be any number of people. Failing to answer a question is not a lie. The other option is to have a decoy lure them into a region governed by the theocracy. Then there are the subtle means. Timed nanobots that attack the brain then leave the system and disassemble themselves. A direct assault is an attack of the emotions. A vengeance proxy uses their emotions for loving." Croell glanced at Zandra and flicked his tongue. "It is the mind that is used for killing. Emotions will foil a hunt."

Sill flicked its tongue as it led Croell and Zandra into a transport pod. "Yes. Do you know what foiled my brother's attack?"

"No, we were in the main room," remarked Zandra.

"The *Homo sapiens* female and the male that carried her from the bar. They defended Pikeman. Do you know why?" Sill keyed in the batzoid sector for the destination, and the pod sped off.

"Perhaps. The female is in need of medical treatment, and they are outlaw amongst their own species." Croell flicked his tongue.

"So, it was a matter of expedience. I can bear that no grudge. Croell, I can tell from your demeanour and speech that you are a vengeance proxy. My brother will be placed in indentured servitude to the Republic for his attempt on Pikeman's life. He cannot carry out his geis during that sentence. He will have to accept the final mercy."

Croell and Zandra dipped their heads. "This is unfortunate."

"Wisn is as stupid as a Roply, but he is my brother, and he tries to follow the teachings of the Great Flyer of the

Skies. Will you, Croell and Zandra of Cloud Skipper sect, accept my brother's geis?"

"I am so—" began Croell.

"Servitor Sill," interrupted Zandra. "What would you give us to accept this task?"

"Zandra? We have another obligation!" Croell looked shocked.

"We can do two tasks at once, especially since it seems our prey has made common cause with this Pikeman." Zandra flicked her tongue in a knowing way.

"What I have to give, I will give." Sill tapped its fore-claws together.

"We need to drink of Ratwaaa's waters to purge ourselves of sin. This geis has diverted us from that holy duty. I would taste of them sooner than later, in case we should be summoned before the Great Flyer of the Skies before we can complete our pilgrimage to Petteron."

Croell flicked his tongue.

The pod slowed to a stop. The door opened onto a large chamber. Batzoid milled around, waiting to pass through the customs stations at one end of the room.

"The waters of Ratwaaa do not flow easily. Do you affirm that no great sin lies upon you?" Sill stepped from the pod, followed by Croell and Zandra. They paused in a corner of the busy room.

"We have committed no major sin, the sins of our line before us we reject and disavow, as we do that line. Only an unfinished geis lays between us and purity."

Croell looked at Zandra, shocked.

"You tell no lie?" demanded Sill.

"I tell no lie," said Zandra.

"Zandra!" Croell looked near panic.

"The treatment we received was done without our knowledge or consent, and we have had the prayer of the fledgling performed. Thus, we are pure as a newly hatched nestling. Is it not true, servitor, that if the forbidden technologies are used on one by aliens without one's consent, one is blameless?"

"This is true. Who violated you in this way?" Sill sounded enraged.

"*Homo sapiens* treated us without our consent," said Croell as he grasped Zandra's game of semantics.

"*Homo sapiens*. I know the Great Flyer of the Skies comes to all species in different guise, but sometimes in their case, I wonder if he/she has got around to it yet. I will obtain for you two vials of the waters of Ratwaaa and guide you in the flight of Jakonee, if you agree to kill Pikeman for my brother."

"Payment in advance?" Zandra flicked her tongue.

"Payment in advance," agreed Sill.

"It will be my honour to accept your brother's geis." Croell flicked his tongue.

Tracy smiled as she sat in her parents' kitchen and read the card that came with a dozen red roses. The room around her gleamed, and a robotic cook on a track under the cupboards moved back and forth, preparing breakfast.

"Roses," commented Tansy as she entered the room.

"Yes, Mother. I've told you before, I don't need you to set me up." Tracy tugged her satin robe straight in mock annoyance.

"Did I?" Tansy smirked. "Whoever with?"

"Right. At least Chow is cute." Tracy chuckled. "I think he's a little afraid of me."

"Probably us. Do you think you'll go out with him?"

"I don't know. It's always the same. The guys all want to date me, then we start to get serious, I tell them, and that's it, I never hear from them again." Tracy looked weary and sad.

"I'm sorry, sweetheart." Tansy hugged her daughter.

"For what? Saving my life. Giving up a piece of yourself. Mom, I don't blame you or Dad. It's just…"

Tansy nodded. "I can't say much, but I will say this. The mission I was on with Chow allowed us to discuss cloning quite a bit. He's completely open about medical cloning."

"Is he going to be so open when he finds out this isn't even my body?" Tracy gestured to herself.

"Honey, that is your body. I may have given the cells, but it is your body. If the damage to your original had been any less—"

"I know, and I know how lucky I am that my consciousness even took in this form." She released a mirthless laugh. "The doctors were stunned when I didn't die. I'm just... Well, it's obvious he has the hots for you, so supposing I like him, and he doesn't freak when I tell him."

"Why even tell him?" Tansy released her daughter and collected the coffee the robotic chef had poured for her.

"Mom, it's not like I wear a banner, but I can't keep a secret like that from someone I care about. Sooner or later, he'll wonder why there aren't any pictures of me when I was little."

"All right, I can see that."

"Suppose I tell him, and miracle of miracles, he's all right with it. How will I ever know it's me he likes and not a younger version of you?"

"Maybe you have to trust that once he gets to know you, he'll want the real you, not the fantasy he has of me. Believe in yourself, honey. Your father and I believe in you."

"I love you, Mom." Tracy took her mother's hand and squeezed it. "I guess I should put these in some water. How long do you think I should make him sweat before I accept his invitation?"

Tansy smiled at her daughter. "At least a day. In strategy, timing is everything."

"After we separated the blood, Kadar returned the heavier elements, increasing the ratio of poison grabber nanobots to poison." Ryan watched the selective-blood dialyser at the top of Rowan's examination table draw blood from a vein in her wrist. He knew the blood was then purified and oxygenated before being returned to her carotid artery.

"Kadar must have known that nanobots would be damaged by such a crude treatment. Though given the limited equipment, it was a clever methodology, considering its source." Pikeman made an adjustment on a console beside Rowan. "I'm adding more blood vessel repair nanobots. That will stop this cerebral vascular accident."

"What's wrong with her? I thought she was stroking out." Ryan shifted his gaze to Rowan's face.

"A CVA is a stroke." Pikeman sounded disgusted. "I'm adding some artificial blood. Her oxygenation is low, undoubtedly because of the damage to the stem cells in her long bones and sternum. I'll have to repair that later."

"Will she be all right?" Ryan looked at Pikeman for the first time in over an hour.

"That depends on how much you're willing to spend. She will recover and walk out of my clinic. The rest depends on the ongoing treatment."

"We saved your life. Don't you feel any gratitude?" Ryan's voice trembled with repressed fury.

"I feel an obligation, which is why I will not charge you for the treatments I have done today or the assessment I will prepare for you. You see, Ryan, before my intervention, your toy here had a month, maybe a month and a half to live. With the work I've done to this point, I've extended that to four, perhaps five, months. I feel my debt is paid on that issue." Pikeman left the medical console and moved to a keyboard and screen mounted against the wall and started typing.

"Four months?" A smile touched the corners of Ryan's mouth.

"I wouldn't go believing you'll be able to find someone else to do the rest of her work in that time. I have equipment far in advance of anything you'll find outside a major hospital. None of the backwater colonies you might be thinking you could smuggle her into would have the tools to do the work."

"Stardust!" Ryan's face fell.

Pikeman smiled and took a piece of paper from a printer on the wall. He passed the paper to Ryan. "Here you go. Take note, I've counted the first ten thousand credits as already paid."

Ryan looked at the paper. "SIXTY-EIGHT THOUSAND!"

"Yes, I gave you a break on the meals. Don't worry, if you do the work in the order I recommended, it will give you a year or two to get the money."

Ryan crumpled the paper in his hand and stared at Rowan for several minutes.

Pikeman left the room. Ryan was vaguely aware of the sounds of a shower and loud, off-key singing.

Ryan straightened the paper and stared at it.

"Bad news?" asked Rowan.

"Ro!" Ryan leapt to his feet and hugged her.

"What's the damage? Both to me and your bank account."

"You were almost brain dead. On the upside, we're finally getting the last of that venom out of you. The nanobots that help maintain and stabilize your metabolism have to be refreshed. And... Ro, you need fresh stem cells injected all through your brain so that you can replace the brain cells that have died off. You also need stem cells in your bone marrow so that you can make blood cells and to keep your autoimmune system up."

"Oh, is that all." Rowan sounded sarcastic, but Ryan didn't catch it.

"No, your kidneys and liver were also damaged. Those might be able to wait until we reach Geb. I'll have to talk to a doctor about how involved repairing them will be." Ryan took Rowan's hand in both of his and kissed it.

"Marvellous. At least I don't have cancer."

"The new nanobots will clear that up. It's not major."

Rowan shook her head, then tapped the back of the paper in Ryan's hand. "How much?"

"Why don't you let me worry about that?" Ryan folded the paper and pushed it into a pocket.

"Ryan, we've been through this. Stop protecting me. You can't, not from everything." Rowan cupped Ryan's cheek in her hand.

"It's a lot, but we don't have to pay for everything right away. We could—"

"Be sure and mention my generous offer. I'm still interested in a cell sample and those tests. And remember, until the tests are done, I have a vested interest in keeping her alive. Credit terms could be arranged." Pikeman stepped into the room. His hair was damp, and he wore clean clothes.

"What offer? And thank you for saving my life," said Rowan.

"It's courteous, at least. I want your body. Your genetic material, to be exact, and a profile of how your power works. Though I'm still willing to let you work off some of your bill, even though you're a fakey. Nice chassis." Pikeman eyed Rowan, who pulled the sheet up under her chin. With a smile, Pikeman moved to the control board, checked the readings, then pressed a series of buttons.

"The selective-blood dialyser has done its work. You are now venom-free. The short-term circulatory system repair nanobots have restored your arterial walls to reasonable health and will finish the job without further supervision. The pressure in your brain is in the normal range. I suggest you leave now. I will contact you when I have an opening for your next visit. Consider my offer." As he spoke, Pikeman removed the feeds to and from Rowan's bloodstream.

Rowan sat up on the bed then, with Ryan's help, stood clutching the sheet around her. "Where are my clothes?"

"We had to strip you for treatment," explained Ryan as

he took off his uniform's jacket and passed it to Rowan. Rowan rushed to don the coat, which didn't fall low enough to completely preserve her modesty. Rowan blushed and clutched the sheet around her waist.

"For pity's sake, I am a doctor. You don't have anything I haven't seen before. By the way, if you take that sheet, I expect you to pay for it. In advance." Pikeman sounded disgusted, but his eyes remained on Rowan.

Ryan picked the remains of her dress off the back of a chair where it had been thrown the night before. The dress was cut in half lengthwise. Rowan wrapped it around her waist and tied it, making a crude skirt.

"Ready now? Go, I need to get some sleep. I'll have paying customers to deal with in the morning." Pikeman scowled.

Ryan passed Rowan her pendant, then, taking her hand, led her from the clinic.

16

PARTING AND JOINING

Greg let his forked tongue flick from his mouth as he recorded the focus group's empathic responses.

"Have to tell Arlene that Obert has a crush on her," Greg smiled.

The emotions changed as the scene the surrogates were watching shifted to Ryan, Rowan and Gunther. This section had the empathic elements in place. Greg stopped recording the focus group's reaction but kept watching the screen.

"You treat us like puppets. How can you justify what you've done?" Gunther turned the SUV onto a road that led to a gap in a set of middle-aged trees.

"How does a general justify sending men into battle? Don't get moral with me, Gunther." Ryan sat in the passenger seat, scowling. "I've seen too much to care. I have a doctorate in engineering, but after I was cloned, that didn't mean squat. All people saw was a fakey! I had to take a job at the studio, I couldn't live on my military pension, and I had a wife to support. I thank the stars that my son finished university before I was discharged."

"Am I helping you just so Rowan can be some sort of toy for you?"

Ryan stared at the other man, sadness reflected in his features. "No. When I can, I'm going to get a medic to remove most of her control pack. She'll be free to choose, that I swear."

"Why not take it all out?"

"Because that would kill her. The accelerated growth results in a lot of cancers. Add to that the genetic manipulations… If I deactivate the nano-bots that help maintain her metabolism, she'd be dead in three months."

"Just take good care of her."

"I will, I promise."

Gunther glanced at Ryan. "In that, I believe you."

The screen cut to a commercial marker.

"Wow, that is so good." Medwin turned in his seat to face his friends. He was dressed in his normal attire of a T-shirt and threadbare jeans.

"What's good?" Kendra looked confused.

"The way they covered the control packs." Armina took Medwin's hand and squeezed it.

"I don't get you." Obert brushed a wrinkle out of his expensive shirt.

"It's simple. If they take out the control packs, Mike can't monitor Ryan and Rowan. They need a rationale for leaving them in. I mean, Ryan knows he had one implanted. This way, Rowan, at least, has to keep hers so that Mike can keep monitoring her for his series. It's brilliant, and it fits so well with the quick clone process they used to make Rowan."

"Got you. Accelerated cell growth equals cancer. This is a well-scripted show," said Kendra.

"It's about to start," announced Obert. The focus group turned to face the screen.

"You know, some of this might have been shot around here. I think I recognized that area by the river in that last scene. I've planted trees there," said Medwin.

The show restarted, and all talking ceased.

Mike stood inside the door to his office and held his wife.

Her slender frame fit perfectly.

"I love you, my musical maiden," he whispered.

"I love you too, but I have to get to rehearsal. I want to run through the theme I composed with the rest of the orchestra. Frank is conducting. He's good, but he can be a little sloppy with the strings." Marcy snuggled her slender, small-busted frame even closer into her husband.

"The stardust he will. With what I'm paying for this score, I expect perfection." Mike's tone was light but held conviction.

Marcy pulled away but continued to hold Mike's hand. "And so you will have it. This contract saved the orchestra. The bank was talking about foreclosing on our hall."

"Somebody has to fund the arts. On the issue of funds…" Mike's face became grave.

"Everyone who you want to know knows. We don't own a single share of S.E.T.E. stock anymore. When are you going to leak the information?" Using her free hand, Marcy pushed a lock of her shoulder-length, red hair away from her green eyes.

Mike's smile became radiant. "I won't have to. It's been over a month since Rowan escaped. I'm surprised it hasn't been all over the news already. One of the techs or the pursuit crew are bound to leak the story soon, if they haven't by now. Stardust, it was probably mentioned in the Zod information periodicals weeks ago. Once they find out, I'd give the reporters a day or two to confirm their facts and then we'll have the biggest publicity stunt in the history of e-entertainments."

"I love it when your plans come together."

"I've had Arlene pre-prepare a promotional piece for release as soon as we have the launch party. It just needs the theme music."

Marcy's smile broadened. "And on that note, pardon the pun, I'm off to prepare that missing element."

Mike pulled her close and kissed her before letting her go. "Thanks for dropping by, honey."

Marcy smiled at him as she stepped out the door, which closed behind her. Mike checked the chronograph on the wall. "Almost time for the meeting. Don't want to miss that."

Ryan sat in his command chair on the *Star Hawk*'s bridge and tried to push down the emotions that sought to overwhelm him.

"I'm sorry, Ryan. When I received the time and frequency from the *Chimera*, I had to tune in. I waited until you'd had a chance to sack out. I figured you'd want to face it fresh." Henry's voice was soothing, devoid of any hint of sexual banter.

"You did the right thing on all counts. On the upside, we have a friend on Crapper's ship, and Tim only agreed to meet with him. He's trying to protect my good name, that's all. Once he sees that Rowan is human and that I love her, he'll come on side."

"Boss." Henry's voice conveyed a thousand doubts.

Ryan nodded. "I know! I know. He's my son, and he's betraying me. I pray he sees the truth once he meets Rowan and gets to know her, but either way, this is an advantage."

"A traitor on board is an advantage?"

Ryan stood and paced as he spoke. "He is a dead spy before he even begins. I'll have to be careful about the information he has to report."

"That's what I like about you, hottie boss. For a fleshy, you got a pretty clear outlook on things."

"Maybe. I'm going to my quarters. I need to think this through. Full privacy except for Tim's call." Ryan strode from the bridge.

Rowan shifted on her bed, reaching for the warm body that had been there when she fell asleep. She woke when she discovered she was alone. "Ryan?"

"Go back to sleep, sweetness," soothed Henry's voice.

Rowan awoke fully. "Oh, my head! Did Pikeman prescribe anything for the pain?"

"Permission to intervene, oh hot and desirable captain's mate?" Henry teased.

Rowan closed her eyes again. "You can ease the headache, but nothing else."

Henry hummed through the speaker. A second later, Rowan felt her headache vanish. "Thank you."

"Just a tweak of the nanos and some blood pressure control. You sure you want your control pack out? It's as useful as a vibrating broomstick at a witches' convention."

Rowan grimaced, then stretched in bed. "*Yes*, I want it out. If we can afford it. I hate being controlled. How long have I been asleep?" She retrieved her pendant from the nightstand and put it on.

"Most of the day, sweetness. Hottie boss's been up for hours."

"Could you tell him I'm getting up, please?"

"I could, but I won't."

"Why?"

"He's got full privacy on. That ingrate of a son of his is on station."

Rowan leapt out of bed. "I better go to him."

"Get cleaned up first. I think you'll be meeting your stepson anytime now."

Ryan sat in front of the computer terminal in his quarters. The military issue furnishings gave the chamber an austere quality, and the couch/bed was rolled up against the wall into its former application.

Timothy's face filled a large section of the wall.

"If you surrender the fakey, I'm sure they'd go easy on you."

Ryan gritted his teeth. He looked a few years younger than his son, but there was a hard quality to his expression that made a lie of appearances. "I've asked you before to not use that word."

"How you could abandon my mother for—"

"I didn't leave your mother for Rowan. Joslin is an e-addict. In the last ten years, she's hardly been out of the rig. Tim, I loved your mother, but she isn't around anymore. I tried to get her help. I tried to pull her out of the rig. I even disabled the input unit once. She booked onto a mag-lev when I went to work. It was three days before I found her. She hadn't eaten anything in all that time, just experienced the shows on the mag-lev's inputs. I tried to help her—"

"Maybe if you, the real you, had been around more, she wouldn't have needed the shows." Timothy's complexion was florid and his features hard.

Ryan's expression became haunted. "I was in uniform when she married me. Transferring back to the Regs was the only way I could afford for you to go to university."

"An answer for everything."

"Look, you came all this way, why are we talking through a screen? I'll meet you in the common area outside U.E.S. customs. I've set up quarters for you on the *Star Hawk*."

"In an alien sector?" Timothy sounded shocked.

There was heat in Ryan's voice when he replied. "In the felinezoid sector, yes. Don't tell me that your grandparents have filled your head with the bigoted drivel about other species Humans Ascendant spouts. I'd hoped your mother and I raised you better than that!"

Tim's image looked ashamed. "I'll meet you at twenty-two hundred." Tim closed his eyes and took a deep breath before continuing. "I've missed you... Dad." The channel closed.

Ryan rubbed his temples as if fending off a headache. "Henry, privacy off."

"Hey boss, what's the poop?"

"He's coming. I have an hour before I'm supposed to meet him."

"Rough one?" Henry's voice lacked any trace of teasing.

"He blames me for Joslin. Maybe he's right. Was there something more I could have done?" Ryan began pacing the room.

"None of the docs thought so. She chose to stick her head in the rig. A person's got to want to be saved, hottie boss."

"It's just... it used to be good. You never saw Joslin at her best."

"Time to move on. You make a choice, and you live with it. Joslin made hers, and you made yours. Your choice is a little hottie who's worried sick about you."

"Rowan's awake?" Ryan moved to his quarters' door.

"Cleaned up and ready to shag, least she will be in another two minutes."

"I'm going to get Tim. Ask her to dress for company, and set up some snacks in the mess. I want him to meet her on our turf. He's been around my parents and that wife of his for a long time. I'm thinking this won't be easy." Ryan moved to the lift and pressed the button for the hangar bay.

"I think it will be a disaster," commented Henry.

"It has to happen. Rowan is my future. Tim needs to meet her. He needs to see how wonderful she is. If anything can turn him around, that will be it." Ryan stepped into the hangar bay. "Tomorrow, we sell this cargo." Ryan gestured to a section of the hangar bay stacked with crates and tree support boxes containing dead treas. An empty anti proton power cube sat at the front of the ordered rows. "Then we can switch to the docking spar. That should save us a few credits." Ryan strode to the access ramp, which opened as he approached, admitting a blast of warm air.

"Two hundred credits a standard felinezoid day." Henry

ran over Ryan's accounts and knew it was a drop in the bucket, but every little bit helped. "You gonna let the hottie make the trade?"

"You know it, she has the gift. On that." Ryan looked sly. "Ask Rowan to downplay how well she's adapting to our time. Tell her I want an ace in the hole and leave it at that." He stepped out of the *Star Hawk* into the station.

"That's my sexy captain," said Henry into the empty hangar bay.

BACK ON SET

17

Farley swam through the lake's crystalline waters. His gills worked perfectly, and the membrane over his eyes kept his vision clear. Quinta swept down beside him and playfully rubbed her body along his side. Farley caught her fur-covered body in his arms and hugged her while kissing the top of her head. She rubbed her muzzle against the sides of his face affectionately, then left him to surface.

Farley scanned the lake-bed. All the evidence suggested that the aquatic pirates were up to something. He remembered back to when Rowan would swim with him. He'd thought he loved her, but knowing what he now knew, he wasn't sure of anything. Quinta rejoined him. She was beautiful, in the way a sleek animal can be beautiful, but she was more. She was intelligent, witty, funny.

Am I falling in love with an alien, or is it the controllers? he wondered. A movement in the corner of his eye caught his attention. He pointed, and Quinta looked. Two octozoids came streaking out from behind a rock. They resembled three-metre long octopuses, but they only had four tentacles each. Each one held a tubular device wrapped in one of its tentacles.

"A *Homo sapiens*, tonight we feast," said one of the octozoids.

"Excellent, I'm sick of fish!" replied the other.

Farley nodded. Quinta rocketed towards the surface.

"Awfully sure of yourselves," Farley spoke the words, trusting the translator nanobots in his brain to convert the language to binary and transmit it to the aliens.

"It speaks! It must be one of the defenders. Get it!" The octozoids rushed Farley.

Angel flew over the lake. Since a series of mysterious drownings, it was banned from recreational use, so no one saw her.

Quinta rocketed out of the water, rising nearly a metre into the air and doing a backflip. Angel saw the otterzoid and pressed a button on the walkie-talkie she wore on her belt three times. Swooping to the east, she looked down at Gunther's SUV, which sat at the end of a deserted, dirt road surrounded by middle-aged trees. The dunking tank from the summer carnival was on a trailer behind it.

Troy focused his attention on Farley and Quinta, ignoring the others as they gathered in Gunther's basement for another session of trying to perfect his telepathy enhancing machine.

Gunther heard the three clicks and threw the switch. Willa's limbs twitched as the field enveloped her. She pulled away from Carl, whose eyes followed her longingly as she moved to her husband's side. Fran was by Toronk, who stood with the help of crutches.

"Can we come out now?" Willow sounded desperate.

"Yes," replied Gunther.

A shapely redhead stepped out of the closet and perched provocatively on a countertop. Her gaze alternated between Fran and Gunther with predatory intensity.

"Are you sure they won't wonder why Carol and I are

here?" Willow emerged from the closet, looking a little wide-eyed and uncomfortable.

"*The Station House* boards will be taken up with that factory fire, and the *Orgy Girls* series are only special features. They leave that board inactive except when she's at a... party."

"This could be a party. Miss 'too hetero to trot' got pissy when I suggested we play in the closet, but I'm sure the rest of us could make do." Carol traced a finger over her breasts and flat abdomen.

Carl swallowed.

"Not what we're here for," said Gunther.

"I'm sorry, I don't know what they did to me. I wasn't a nympho in high school. Actually, I was kind of a geek." Carol shifted position, taking on another provocative pose.

"They probably increased the number of arousal receptors in your brain." Gunther tried not to stare at her legs with minimal success. "Willow, did you bring it?"

Willow pulled out the stolen handheld and passed it to Gunther.

"What's the plan?" Willa loosely held her husband around the waist.

Gunther activated the handheld. "We can't fight back so long as they can turn us on and off like a light. These things can control the nanobots and other vectors they put in us. We need to work out what it can do and how we can use it to hijack ourselves from the studio's control."

"Allow me." Toronk moved to the workbench. He picked up the device and pointed it at Willow. "This is reminiscent of a device I was led to believe was common on Murrow." Toronk pressed a button, then lightly traced a claw tip on a meter displayed on the screen.

Willow flushed and sweat prickled on her brow. "Who turned up the heat? Stop it. I don't feel that good. Stop it!"

"Reset to default," ordered Toronk.

Willow clutched the countertop. Gunther and Willa rushed to grab her.

"Stop it. She's burning up," snapped Willa.

"I don't understand, it is geared to accept voice commands, but it won't reset. Handheld, reset to norms!" There was an edge of panic in Toronk's voice.

Carol watched the scene before her, understanding nothing of the gibberish the big felinezoid was spouting.

"Nova blast, Toronk, she's going to die!" bellowed Gunther.

Carol leapt off the counter and snatched the handheld out of Toronk's hand. She pointed the device at Willow and spoke clearly and slowly. "Handheld, restore default settings."

Willow vomited then her temperature dropped. A minute later, the beautiful brunette stood up as if nothing had happened.

"How?" asked Carl.

"Kitty-kins wasn't speaking the right language. Why would they program it to understand alien dialects when humans are the ones using it?" Carol smiled as she passed the handheld to Gunther.

"What did she say?" Toronk looked at Carol and swished his tail, trying to convey his appreciation.

"It doesn't speak your lingo," said Carl.

"This could be a problem. It may become nec—"

Breep, breep, breep. The overheat buzzer on the jammer sounded.

"Two a.m. next Friday. Willow, I checked out your friend James, bring him. I'll check out the names you gave me, Carol. Farley and Quinta will supply the diversion again. Let's pack it up. Willa and I will create a diversion in thirty minutes so that Carol and Willow can leave the house." Gunther hid the handheld in a secret drawer under his workbench.

"Right, and keep your hands to yourself this time," Willow directed the last to Carol as they entered the closet.

"You're no fun," replied the redhead.

Gunther checked to make sure that everything was

stowed away, then turned off the jammer.

Carl's eyes widened in horror when he noticed the puddle of vomit, then he spoke loudly. "I'm sorry, Gunther. When I sensed how much I've hurt you, I couldn't keep it down."

Gunther looked at him, confused, then followed the younger man's gaze. His breath caught, then his eyes strayed to Willa. "You should be! Don't talk to me!" Taking Willa's hand, he led her from the basement. "You all know the way out."

Troy spared the static-filled screens in the *Angel Black* control room a glance. "They really should fix that. If Gunther is going to keep playing with that toy of his, it could get annoying."

He shifted his gaze to the main screen. Farley swam behind a boulder, barely escaping a shock wave of kinetically charged water.

"Circle around behind him," ordered the larger of the two octozoids.

"Yes, Lieutenant," replied the smaller one.

"Give it up, human. This is our element. You cannot escape," menaced the larger of the two octozoids as it brandished the tubular weapon in its tentacle. Taking aim, it sent another jet of kinetically-charged water smashing into the rock protecting Farley. The surface of the rock was reduced to rubble. "Give up, and I swear I will kill you before we inject our digestive enzymes."

A streak of green fur swept down from the surface. The octozoid felt its weapon jerk up.

The aquatic fired straight at the surface six metres above. "What? An otterzoid!"

Farley sped from his hiding place like a human torpedo. He caught the octozoid as it drew a bead on Quinta. Grabbing a tentacle in each hand, Farley braced his feet on either side of his enemy's beak and pushed with all his might.

"NO, STOP!" The octozoid grabbed Farley's legs with its free tentacles and tried to pull them away, but he was too well braced.

"Lieutenant!" screamed the other octozoid from the boulder Farley had sheltered behind. It launched itself at Farley's back, but a wave of telekinetic force drove it into the lake-bed.

"Better bump up Farley. He's bitten off more than he can chew, again!" Troy increased Farley's adrenalin levels and allowed oxygenated artificial blood from the control pack to flow into his system. Troy checked his other active screens.

"Quinta, you rock!" He sat back to watch the show.

Farley felt new strength surge through him. His nearly exhausted muscles sang with energy, and he heaved.

"ARRR!" screamed the octozoid as its tentacles ripped away from its body.

Farley, with his legs still entangled by his foe, tossed the dismembered limbs away and drove his fingers into two of the six beady, black eyes that rimmed the octozoid's mouth. The tentacles around Farley's legs spasmed, then released. The octozoid vomited its own intestines as it propelled itself away with its remaining tentacles.

Angel watched as pillars of water shot three metres into the air, then fell back to the lake. *I wish I knew what was going on,* she thought as she swept low over the water.

Quinta drove the smaller octozoid down with her telekinesis. The octozoid tried to draw a bead on her, but she darted around too quickly for it to settle on a shot. A rock as big as a human head fell onto the octozoid, and it pulled in its tentacle with a yell.

"Farley, now!" called Quinta.

Farley swept down on the octozoid and grabbed its weapon. It fired columns of kinetically charged water in all directions. Quinta dove low, barely avoiding a random blast.

"Give it up." Farley pulled at the tube with all his might.

"Die, *Homo sapiens*." The octozoid wrapped a tentacle around Farley's throat and squeezed. Lights began to dance in Farley's eyes as the blood to his brain was cut off, but he held fast to the water blaster.

Ulva sat in the control room for the *Freedom's Run* series. She could feel sweat prickling her brow as she watched the secured feed from Gunther's basement.

"Come on, if her temperature goes any higher, she'll get brain damage." Ulva reached for the controls that would normalize Willow's temperature.

"Give them a second," spoke Michael Strongbow's voice from the back of the small room.

"But sir?"

On the overview screen, Carol had leapt off the counter-top and snatched the handheld out of Toronk's hand.

"You see, one of them got it in time. Not the one I would have expected. Of course, Carol does have a high IQ. She was quite the hacker in high school. That was before *SF Geeks* was cancelled and we did the after-insertion work to bring her over to the *Orgy Girls* special features."

"Why did you steer her into the group? Gunther might suspect we had something to do with it. Most women don't try and pick up guys the way she did."

"I'm sure he is suspicious, but he can't be sure. Besides, through Carol, our fine rebels can link with the rest of the cast of *SF Geeks*. In this way, Gunther and Willa can learn of Rowan's whereabouts. That should be a comfort to them and spear them on, and Carol knows Jessica from *Defenders of the Crystal*. If I get the *Defenders* cast on board, I have the two most powerful groups of genetic augments in the set region ready to forward my agenda."

"How long have you been planning this?" Ulva swivelled her chair to stare at the studio head.

"Thirty years, but not in detail. I'm using the resources the situation presents. Gunther's jammer is beeping."

Quinta needed to breathe, but she couldn't leave Farley. She dove at her foe and sank her teeth into the tentacle encircling Farley's neck.

The octozoid screamed and beat at her with its free tentacles.

Quinta lashed out with her telekinesis, prying open the tender waste orifice on the top of her foe's bulbous body. Cold water rushed into the octozoid, causing its intestines to cramp. It wailed and released the grip on Farley's neck.

Farley wrenched the weapon from his opponent's tentacle and let it sink to the lake bed. Quinta, her lungs burning, raced for the surface. She burst into the air and filled her lungs before calling to the winged girl overhead. "We have one. Get ready."

"I'm set. I'll need your help in the lift," Angel called back as she hovered above the otterzoid.

"We'll manage. This is nothing but 'a small northern aquatic life form reminiscent of a sea urchin valued for its sweet taste and smooth texture'." Quinta was underwater before the translator had finished her sentence.

Quinta found Farley hauling the octozoid, which still writhed in pain, towards the surface.

"Up, Angel is waiting." Quinta drew level with Farley's eyes.

"I'm working on it. This thing's not exactly light. I think my head's going to explode." Farley kicked harder and changed his grip on the octozoid so he could pull with one arm.

"Poor Farley. I'll help." Quinta took a tentacle in her mouth and swam upwards. When they crested the surface, Angel stopped circling and swooped towards them.

"Get ready," said Farley.

"I'm always ready, or have you forgotten last night so soon?" Quinta shot Farley a very human wink.

Despite the strain of keeping the octozoid afloat, Farley blushed. Then Angel was upon them. She grabbed the octozoid and drove her wings against the air. Quinta focused her full concentration on her telekinesis. The octozoid lifted from the water. Farley moved to support Quinta as she and Angel carried the octozoid to the dunking tank and dropped it in. Water shot over the tank's brim.

"Good, now let's get out of here before its friends show up." Farley started for the shore.

"Yes. I do not think I could fight off a 'small harmless amphibian' right now." Quinta slipped from his arms. They sped towards the SUV, where Angel was climbing into the driver's seat. They'd reached the shallows when the lake behind them exploded in waving tentacles. Farley scooped up Quinta and ran onto the shore.

"Try not to drip on the upholstery, guys. Gunther just had her detailed," said Angel as they climbed in. Angel drove off, leaving the lake behind.

GAMES PEOPLE PLAY

Ryan paced across the large room that formed the Republic side of U.E.S. customs. *Homo sapiens* and other species lined up at the metre-wide gaps that pierced one wall. Ryan watched as others stepped into those gaps, were checked for contraband, then stepped into a place he would never know again, the territory of his own species. Regret tightened his chest. He'd been to more worlds and seen more of the universe than most would ever dream, but home is home. Sighing, he opened his handheld and keyed up a picture of Rowan. "It's worth it," he whispered before he went back to scanning the crowd.

"Ryan Chandler?" asked a gruff male voice.

"Who wishes to know?" Ryan turned and found himself staring into the chest of a man as tall as a felinezoid. Ryan looked up into a face that could have been carved out of oak with a dull knife, all angles and edges. The man wore the uniform of a U.E.S. ground forces private.

"You have to come with me." The big man's voice had an almost child-like quality that was at odds with the rest of him.

"No!" said Ryan.

The big man looked taken aback. "I'll make you come."

"You could try, and I could have you charged with assault. This is Republic territory. You and Crapper have no authority here."

The man looked confused. "You have to come."

"Why?" Ryan scanned the crowd again.

"I'm… I'm bigger than you." The man reached to grab Ryan, who stepped beyond his assailant's reach.

"You're bigger than most horses; that's beside the point."

"The captain ordered you to come. You have to come." The hulking *Homo sapiens* lunged at Ryan, who leapt to the side.

"He's not my captain. Go back to your barracks and LEAVE ME ALONE!"

Sentients turned to watch Ryan and the big man as they circled each other.

"You have to come! The captain said so. You have to do what the captain says!" The big man lunged with surprising speed. Ryan dodged a fraction too late as a huge, meaty hand closed on his arm.

"LET ME GO!" screamed Ryan as the big man dragged him closer and gripped his other arm.

"What is the problem here?" demanded an oryceropuszoid wearing a badge with the Republic's starburst symbol on a chain around its neck. The being's dexterous twin snouts swished lazily back and forth, and it tapped the claws of its four powerful legs on the deck.

"He has to come. The captain said he has to come," blurted the big man.

"This oaf is trying to kidnap me," said Ryan.

"He has to come!" The large private started walking towards the customs slots.

Snouts waving, the oryceropuszoid rushed to block the big man's progress. "I'll say who's going and who's staying."

"He has to come. The captain said so." The private pushed past the police officer.

"HELP ME!" called Ryan.

The oryceropuszoid pulled a tubular device from a holster on the collar it wore with one of its snouts. It adjusted a dial on the device's side, then raced up to the big *Homo sapiens*.

"Release him, or I will be required to use force," warned the cop.

"The captain says he has to come," countered the private.

"Victim of violence, please stop squirming to facilitate my disposition of this situation."

Ryan stopped struggling. The police officer touched one end of the tube to the big private's arm.

"Ugh." The big man released Ryan, who leapt to the side. A second later, the private was on his hands and knees, being violently sick. A floor cleaning robot raced to suck up the vomit.

"Thank you, honoured keeper of order." Ryan straightened the rumpled fabric of his shirt.

"Your gratitude is acknowledged. Why was this one assaulting you?" The police officer held its weapon tube ready to thrust.

"I am wanted on U.E.S. charges that do not extend into the Republic. His captain ordered him to abduct me so that I could be brought onto U.E.S. territory and forced to stand trial."

"And this one chose to follow such an order? In violation of Republic law!" The oryceropuszoid scratched its claws on the deck, making a sound like nails on a chalkboard.

"It is my belief he may suffer from a mental defect that limits his intellect." Ryan grimaced at the sound his benefactor's nervous habit was making.

"How could such a defect go uncorrected?" The police officer stopped scratching its claws.

"My belief is that he belongs to a *Homo sapiens* sect that views the repair of such things as sinful. They probably think that they are punishments from the Divine and must be endured. I do not personally follow that way." Ryan's tone reflected disgust.

The way the oryceropuszoid shifted its clawed feet and pony-like body told Ryan that his rescuer didn't think much of the proposed sect either.

"What is your name?" The cop pulled a device that resembled a tablet off its tool collar and held it towards Ryan.

Ryan spoke into the device. "Civilian Captain Ryan Chandler of the *Star Hawk*. U.E.S. Space Services Captain, retired."

The oryceropuszoid checked the screen of its device, then holstered both its weapon and the screen. "You have no outstanding Republic charges. Do you wish to press charges against this one?" It waved one of its snouts at the big private who was now dry heaving on the floor.

"No, honoured keeper of order, he's suffered enough at the hands of his belief system and being misled by his captain." Ryan shrugged.

"As you wish. I will escort him to customs in that case and place a temporary entry block in his file. He will not be allowed to enter the shared area for two of your days. Fewer forms to fill out for me." The police officer moved to the big *Homo sapiens*' side and adjusted a knob on its weapon before pressing it to the human's arm. The man stopped dry heaving and clambered shakily to his feet.

"You are lucky, *Homo sapiens*. In a show of mercy and high-mindedness, your species kin has chosen not to press charges. I will now escort you back to your sector, where you will remain for two days. I caution you not to bother the female again."

Ryan started at the 'female', then shrugged. He could never tell the gender of an oryceropuszoid by looking, so he supposed it was fair.

Tracy smiled into the vid-phone in her mother's kitchen. The roses Chow had sent sat in a vase in the middle of the table. Chow blinked out of the screen stupidly. His hair was dishevelled, and there were lines on one side of his face from being pressed into a pillow.

"I'm sorry, Chow. I forgot about the time difference." Tracy gently stroked her upper arm.

Chow swallowed visibly, then smiled. "If the answer's yes, what time difference?"

Tracy giggled. "Dinner sounds lovely, and I love the orchestra. Marcy Strongbow is the featured soloist. I have all her disks. The things she can do with a flute."

"I'm so glad you like live music. I love the way it can make me feel without using empathic inputs." Chow was slowly losing his half-asleep expression.

"I know. I better let you get back to sleep. Friday at six." Tracy took a deep breath, exaggerating the cleavage displayed by her low-cut blouse.

Chow stared out of the screen, bewitched.

Tracy chuckled. "Chow."

"What? Oh. Nodded off there. I'm looking forward to it. I'll pick you up at eighteen hundred. Bye."

"Bye." Tracy hung up the phone, then looked at a picture on the wall. Her mother and father stood in front of the Great Pyramid on Earth. Between them, in an anti-grav support chair, was a child. Her arms and legs were stunted and mangled, and a variety of tubes ran out of a box on the chair and into the child. "I hope Mother's right. I don't think I can stand being dumped again."

Timothy watched the big private lumber to the customs gate.

"It didn't work. I should never have sent that moron, but everyone else was too afraid of the aliens. They called it an illegal order. Cowards!" ranted Crapper. He and Timothy stood inside the U.E.S. region, watching through an open customs slot.

"It was that alien's fault. I'm sorry, I really thought we could talk some sense into Ryan," said Timothy.

Crapper balled his hands into fists but spoke pleasantly.

"I guess you'll have to go and speak with him out there. I'd hoped to save you having to deal with those aliens."

Timothy shrugged and took in Crapper's body language. The doubts he'd had after meeting the man surfaced again, but he pushed them down with memories of the ruin his life had become because of the fakey he was here to see. "I should go and talk to him."

Picking up his suitcases, Timothy strode into the customs slot. A jet of air swept over him, then the unit opened. He stepped into the shared area of the station.

Ryan saw Timothy emerge and ran towards him. "TIM, HERE!" He stopped about a metre away from his son when Timothy made no signs of dropping his bags or moving towards Ryan.

"Hello." Timothy's tone was glacial.

"Let me help with those." Ryan indicated the suitcases.

"I can manage." Timothy started towards the room's main exit.

"I'm surprised you didn't use the Gravity Masters your mother and I gave you and Kerry."

"She needed them. Look, I'm tired. I've come a long way. Can we go?"

Ryan swallowed ire and disappointment in equal measure, then motioned to the transport-pod access.

Rowan looked at herself in a mirrored section of her quarter's wall. The spring dress she wore looked nice and showed her figure well without being overly provocative.

"You're the girl next door, the one all the boys want to shag, sweetness," said Henry.

"I don't know, maybe the green was better. I want to make a good first impression." Rowan continued to study her reflection.

"Too late, sweetness. Tim experienced your show."

"Ew, that means he probably did Farley's perspective. Things I don't want Ryan's son to know." Rowan hugged herself.

"Sorry, sweetness. For what it's worth, you were quite the ride on the show. Hubba hubba."

"Of course. I... I know things intellectually, but sometimes it strikes home. I mean, half the galaxy knows what I'm like in bed. I've only had two lovers, and I'm one of the biggest sluts in history."

"For the record, all the stuff with Farley was edited and manipulated. It's not the real you, hottie."

Rowan walked to her quarters' door. "Thanks, that helps a bit, I think. I guess I better set out those snacks, then get down to the hangar."

Mildred waited by the door leading from the studio to the underground parking facility. Her prey came into sight. She moved into the hall, intercepting the tall man. "Hello, Michael."

Michael stopped and smiled. "Hello, Mildred. What are you doing here?"

Mildred smiled back, but it had a predatory quality. "You've been avoiding me."

Michael shifted uncomfortably. "Not at all. I've been busy. The new show."

"*Freedom's Run*. Oh, I know. I know a lot of things. For instance, a hardwire telemetry pickup and a control pack telemetry relay unit are missing from inventory. I also know you bribed Helen into not telling me about the telemetry booster in that ATV Ryan used to steal Rowan."

Michael bit his lip. "She betrayed me. Well, she can kiss her new job goodbye."

"Don't be too hard on her. I tricked her. She probably

doesn't even realize she told me. She isn't the sharpest tool in the box." Mildred leaned against the wall and smirked. "If you want to know what really made me put the pieces together, it was seeing you riding Ryan's old power bike, then having his debts disappear. That and the fact that you had the ATV's scrap left at your estate after the investigation."

Michael straightened to his full height. Every hint of softness left his expression. "What do you know, and what do you want?"

Mildred found herself standing at attention before she realized she'd moved. "I know Ryan had help. I know you hate John. I know that Rowan's escape could have been recorded. I know that there have been transmission outages regarding the *Angel Black* cast. I've also heard rumours that the Rowan pursuit was a training exercise that went wrong. I know someone paid Ryan's debts and that you are his sole inheritor, with the exception of his military pension, which is paying to keep his junkie wife in an e-addict facility."

Michael relaxed his posture and smiled. "You're as good as ever, Milly! You have enough pieces to make a pretty good guess at what *Freedom's Run* is about. By the way, I have fifty thousand credits budgeted to obtain your cooperation. That should be enough to cover your grandson's undergraduate expenses."

"You think you can buy me?" demanded Mildred.

"I think you signed an incidental inclusion waiver for the shows when you took the position of head of security. Had to really, just in case you ever needed to go into the set region." Mike leaned against the wall.

"Why buy me off?" Mildred was red in the face, and her fists were clenched.

"Three reasons. One, I'm going to ask you not to share what you have surmised about Ryan and Rowan until after the series' launch.

"Two, I want you to turn a blind eye to Gunther's

activities. If you do, there will be another bonus in a year or so.

"Three, it's worth it to me to keep you around. You do your job exceptionally well. I have to admit, it will work to my benefit if your husband gets elected and you take a leave of absence. Then I can move an incompetent into your position and let Sun Valley melt down without a hitch, but I don't want to lose you permanently."

Mildred shook her head. "You are unbelievable. I suppose since it's all for your show, it's all legal."

"Mostly. Ryan shouldn't have fired on the *Saber*, although he really had no choice. I've shielded the studio from that liability. The rest of the charges have been dropped. The official announcement will be at the launch party." Michael started walking toward the parking area's door.

Mildred fell into step beside him. "Remind me to never play chess with you. By the way, I received a call from a friend of mine with the *Gaea Crier*. They've found out about Rowan's theft. It's making up the front screen of tomorrow's edition."

"Stardust, it's about time! I was beginning to think I'd have to leak it myself." Michael stepped into the parking area and sauntered towards Ryan's old power bike.

Mildred looked confused. "What? But you wanted to keep your series hush-hush."

"Let me give you a ride home, and I'll explain. There is nothing more effective than truth to grab people's attention."

19
THE NUCLEAR FAMILY... BOOM

Ryan and Timothy walked down the corridors of the felinezoid sector in silence. Timothy's eyes kept darting to the beings they passed.

"This is it." Ryan paused in front of a door, pressed his palm to the scanner and said, "Open."

A growling sound issued from a speaker as the door retracted into the wall.

"I had to hire a space dock to do some repairs." Ryan led the way into the airlock. The door closed behind him, and the one in front of him opened, revealing the chamber housing the *Star Hawk*.

Timothy grunted at the sight of the ship.

They were stepping onto the access ramp when Rowan approached them. "Ryan, it's good to have you home. This must be Tim. I'm pleased to meet you. Can we help with your bags?"

Timothy looked directly at Ryan. "Where's my room? I want to drop my bags off."

Rowan stared at him, the smile frozen on her face. Ryan looked from his son to his lover and seemed to collapse in on himself.

"This was a mistake! I'm sorry, Rowan, I thought there might still be some bit of my son left that was worth the effort. Doctor Chandler, I'll escort you back to felinezoid customs."

"What?" gasped Rowan and Timothy in unison.

Ryan straightened and moved to Rowan's side, hugging

her one-armed around the waist. "Rowan is my girlfriend. She is also a member of the *Star Hawk*'s crew. If you cannot show her a basic level of human courtesy, then you are not welcome aboard my ship."

"She's a fa—"

Ryan glared at his son and spoke a single word. "What!?"

Tim swallowed. He'd only heard that tone once before. He'd been sixteen and taken the daughter of the felinezoid ambassador out on a date. All his friends at school were bragging about their exploits, and he felt he needed to prove his manhood. Mirra attended his school, and he'd heard his grandparents talking about how promiscuous felinezoids were. She accepted his dinner invitation without a moment's hesitation. Looking back, he could imagine how lonely she was. How isolated in a school of humans, many of whom were raised to look down on her. She'd tried to impress him by drinking the coffee he bought her. After half a cup, she passed out, but he couldn't bring himself to abuse her. Then she started vomiting and had to be rushed to the embassy's clinic. He'd thought his father was going to kill him. As it was, the three months' grounding and a year of extra chores were easy compared to having his father force him to apologize to Mirra and her father in front of his entire school. Remembering back, he realized the truly worst part was that he had enjoyed the date until he acted the fool. Mirra could have been a real friend. A small voice that Timothy didn't acknowledge whispered, 'or something more.'

Tim swallowed again. His father's face still reflected barely contained rage. For a second, Timothy considered having it out. It would be such a relief to flail at the fakey that thought it was the man who'd raised him, but given his father's training, he knew he'd come out the worst from any fight. Steeling himself, Tim looked directly at Rowan for the first time. She unconsciously nestled into Ryan in a way he hadn't seen his mother do since he was a child.

"I do apologize, Miss McPherson. It has been a long,

tiring day. I would appreciate some help with my bags." His voice was flat.

Ryan gave a curt nod and took the larger of Timothy's bags while Rowan took the other.

"Perhaps you'd care to join us for a refreshment after we stow your bags, Doctor Chandler." Rowan's voice matched Timothy's monotone, and she kept Ryan between them.

Henry recorded the exchange. He hoped Ryan noticed the way Timothy's eyes darted about and the discomfort in his stance.

"Traitorous, rogering little prat. What did you promise that fool Crapper?" Henry spoke into the empty bridge.

Timothy followed Rowan into the flight crew's mess. He couldn't stop his eyes from dropping to her bottom where it swayed under the light fabric of her dress. When he caught himself staring, he forced his eyes up. *Dad has taste,* he thought.

"Please take a seat. Can I get anyone a drink?" Ryan moved to the head of the rectangular table that dominated the four metre long by three wide room.

Timothy focused on the walls that displayed a woodland meadow. "I know this place. We used to picnic in these woods when I was a kid."

"I recorded the pattern and uploaded it. I've always found it soothing. About that drink?" Ryan swivelled one of the mounted chairs sideways for Rowan. She sat, turning the chair so that it faced the table.

"Vodka on ice, with a lemon twist." Timothy sat.

"Juice for me, please." Rowan smiled at Timothy, who'd taken the seat beside her.

"You look a lot like your father," she remarked as Ryan

disappeared into the galley.

"It's genetic." Tim looked at Rowan and found himself getting caught by her eyes. He quickly looked away.

"So, Ryan says you're a doctor of bio-mechanical engineering."

"Yes!"

"On the e-entertainment Ryan rescued me from, my mother was a cyborg. The science was really impressive."

"Maybe to you. Systems like that are quite antiquated. The studio raided a museum and reverse-engineered some pre-contact limbs and organs to recreate the technology. What I do is far beyond that."

Rowan gritted her teeth and was silent for a long moment. "What do you do then?"

Timothy looked superior. "My most impressive work, to date, was developing a new life-support design for spacecraft that has been adopted by the U.E.S. for all its new ships. It is also being retrofitted into all existing ships as part of their scheduled maintenance. It utilizes a *cyanobacteria* hybrid with a nano-genetic splice from a *xanthophyta* that maximizes the oxygen cycle to one hundred and thirty per cent of its closest competitor at the cost of its rough nutrient-processing capacity. I then coupled this with a nano-biotic waste-reduction system that fine processes waste to maximize nutrient availability and bio-absorption rate to compensate. I wouldn't expect you to understand it."

Rowan flushed red. "You genetically engineered a new type of algae that produces more oxygen by sacrificing its ability to normally absorb nutrients and compensating for that by having nano-bots do its digestion for it."

Timothy sat upright and looked taken aback. "In crude terms. I also redesigned the macro bio-maintenance systems to accommodate the enhanced efficiency. The reduction in system volume allowed for improved ship operations."

"More room for cargo with each run. I get it." Rowan

smirked.

"Yes." Timothy was red-faced.

Ryan stepped into the room carrying a tray with three drinks on it and a platter of mixed, cut vegetables and dip. "Thanks for preparing the snacks, Rowan. What did I miss?"

Timothy eyed the tray dubiously and took his drink.

"Tim was explaining about his profession." Rowan took her drink and a carrot stick.

"Yes." Timothy still sounded sour. "Rowan, now that you're in the *real universe* amongst *real* people, what are you doing, aside from being my father's… *girlfriend*? Oh, by the way, *Dad*, I brought a copy of Mom's last letter. I thought you might like to see it."

Rowan turned scarlet.

"The one she sent you three years ago, before she lost her job because it conflicted with a show she wanted to experience? I've already read it. As to Rowan, she's studying ship navigation and is quite proficient. She didn't want to be a kept woman!" Ryan's voice was icy, and he pointedly took the captain's seat at the head of the table.

"Really, a navigator. Impressive considering…" Timothy took a large hit off his drink.

"Yes, it is impressive, considering she has to make up for over a forty-thousand-year difference in tech-level." Ryan took Rowan's hand.

An uncomfortable silence descended as Timothy and Ryan eyed each other, and Rowan wished she could blend into the background like Carl.

"How's Kerry?" Ryan broke the silence.

"How should I know? She left me four months ago!" Timothy glared at his father.

"That's awful," breathed Rowan.

"It's his fault! Like everything else!" Timothy waved angrily at Ryan.

"What? How?" Ryan looked shocked.

"She found out I was still in contact with you. It was the

final straw. They were already whispering behind her back at the Humans Ascendant functions because her father-in-law defied the laws of nature and the Divine. The fact that her husband would condone his sin was too much."

Ryan hung his head. "I'm sorry. My choice was clone a new body or die."

"You don't see it! YOU AREN'T RYAN CHANDLER! My father died seven years ago when they sucked out his memories and stuffed them into you. His soul left. You are nothing but a soulless shadow of my father. A cheap copy!" Timothy's eyes flashed, and he pounded his fist on the table, making the food tray jump. "I lost everything because I tried to be nice to you. My wife left me because of you. I lost my job because of you. I was this close to having tenure." Timothy held up his hand, the tips of his thumb and forefinger a centimetre apart. "Oh, the university said it was because I lacked teaching skills, but I know better. Now you steal S.E.T.E. property, fire on your own people, hide among these aliens! You shame the memory of my father with every breath you take. Aunt Betty should have taken out that hit on you. You broke Grandmother's heart. You've shamed all of us! You're nothing but a soulless fakey. I've lost everything because of you. I—"

Rowan's open palm connected with Timothy's cheek. The sound of the slap reverberated through the mess. Timothy's expression changed from enraged to shocked.

"SHUT UP, YOU SPOILED, SELF-RIGHTEOUS IDIOT! This is your father! What the stardust is the neuro-static energy that transfers when the clone activates if it isn't the soul? You're too smart a man to hide behind semantics. Even at the tech-level I was used to, many religions believed in reincarnation. This is just a variant on that. As to your wife, from the little that Ryan's told me, which wasn't much, and everything you've said, it sounds like she's a real piece of work. Even in Sun Valley, we had people who let their beliefs strangle every thought out of their brain. It's easier not to think, to follow other peoples' edicts. It takes less effort. I'll bet there was a lot more wrong with your marriage than you sending your father a letter on his birthday."

Rowan paused for breath; her cheeks were flushed, and she looked ready to kill.

"You can't—" Timothy began. Rowan cut him off.

"As to your job! I've had profs like you. The overblown way you explained what you did earlier. You're too full of yourself to teach a dog tricks. You're all about showing off how smart you are, not helping someone to understand. The university was right to can you. You obviously belong in a lab, not a classroom. And I'm wondering if you shouldn't be in that lab as an example of the universe's largest prat."

Ryan watched Rowan, torn between a desire to make peace and his urge to smile.

"You're just a fakey. What would you know about real emotions? 'Oh, I look at Farley and wonder, is it real? Should I have waited? But I might have lost him.' And please! Father-daughter relationship? You two were incest without the sex. Nova blast, you wouldn't know reality if it bit you!" Timothy glared at Rowan.

"I know this much. I feel, and I love Ryan, and not just because he rescued me. I love him because of the man he is. He is a hero a dozen times over, and he always tries to do the right thing. If anyone has a right to be ashamed, it's him. How such a trumped-up, self-indulgent, little prat could be his son, I don't know! What I do know is liberating a slave is honourable. You should try taking some responsibility for your life; stop blaming everything on your father because he chose to live."

Timothy's hand balled into a fist, and his arm pulled back. Rowan saw the move. Her hand swept up in a block Fran had taught her. Timothy's blow was deflected to the side, missing Rowan's face.

"TIM!" Ryan was on his feet before Timothy could

recover.

"It's fine, Ryan. I hit him. I used an open palm, but I started it." Rowan rubbed her bruised wrist. "We're even now. It's good. I don't want to owe this trumped-up piece of stardust anything. Doctor Chandler." Rowan's tone made the title an insult. "Yesterday, I was with a felinezoid cub who was bullied at school because his father had married a *Homo sapiens*. The bullies had covered him with hair remover nanobots. He was bald from head to foot. He didn't have one word of blame for his human mother. She held him as he cried because the other children were cruel. He loved her and defended her because she nurtured him, cared for him. She was his mother. That eleven-year-old cub is more of a man than you, and it sickens me!" Rowan stood. "Ryan, I'm going to my quarters. There's a bad smell in here." She swept from the room without a backward glance.

"I..." Timothy fell silent.

"I suspect you can find your own quarters." Ryan picked up the tray and glasses from the table.

THE FLIGHT OF JAKONEE

Rowan sat on her bed, trembling with repressed fury. The door buzzer sounded. She scowled. The buzzer sounded again.

"Fine, privacy off. Henry, who's at my door?" she snapped.

"It's hottie boss, sweet thing." Henry's voice was neutral. As if he were unsure what was best to say.

"Let him in."

The buzzer sounded again as the door retracted into the wall. Ryan stepped into her room, his face a mask of concern. "I'm sorry."

"It's not you who needs to apologize!" Rowan held her arms out to Ryan. He sat on the bed and embraced her.

"Were my Dad and I really like incest without the sex?" she whispered from the shelter of his arms.

Ryan released her enough to look into her eyes. "No, you were a father and daughter who loved each other very much. Maybe if you'd known you weren't related, Willa would have had some competition, but as it was, it was just a great father-daughter relationship. I can't believe how much Tim's changed. I wanted my old life to meet my new, but somehow, when I wasn't looking, my old life died. I should have gotten him away from Earth when I had the chance. Being around my parents, then marrying a girl from a strict Humans Ascendant family. He hasn't heard a counter-argument in so long he's stopped thinking."

"I'm sorry." Rowan pulled him to her.

"I'll tell him to leave the ship in the morning," Ryan spoke with a catch in his voice.

"Don't do that. Maybe if he spends some time with you, he'll clean the stardust out of his skull."

"Maybe? You better get some sleep. We're helping Kitoy move tomorrow afternoon, and I want to sell off the rest of our trade goods. We'll need the money for Pikeman."

Rowan stood and started pacing. "I've been thinking about that. I don't like the idea, but we don't have much choice. I'm going to let him take some cells and run his tests. That will cover the first few treatments, then maybe something will come up."

Ryan nodded. "Should I go to my quarters?"

Rowan stopped pacing and smiled. "I'd like to be held."

Ryan started unbuttoning his shirt.

Croell and Zandra flew in circles around the temple. Each wore a collar with a checkerboard pattern of red and black on it and had a weighted sack strapped to their back. They also held polished rocks the size and shape of footballs in each of their hands. The lights were dimmed in the batzoid section of the station, matching the apparent time of day with the temple of Jakonee on the River Ratwaaa.

Sill entered the chamber. He had watched them fly for half the night. Now it was time. "Come, servants of the Great Flyer of the Skies."

Croell and Zandra set down on their hind legs in front of the servitor.

"Have you flown with the wings of Jakonee?" challenged Sill.

"We have striven to fly with the wings of Jakonee, but we have not the strength of great Jakonee," Croell and Zandra replied in unison.

"Then leave thy burdens, for the Great Flyer of the Skies gives us strength in proportion to the trials we face." Sill watched as Croell and Zandra set the polished rocks aside and removed the weighted packs.

"Now pay heed," Sill spoke in a booming voice and stood on its hind legs before Croell and Zandra. Sill's wings spread wide as it recited the words of the holy book from memory. "In fury, the mountain exploded; the fires of Siss covered the lands, destroying those weighted down with sin so that they could not rise above the choking clouds. Jakonee, wings unfurled, rose ever higher, Prince Borla upon his back, the eggs of Ratnay and Slonn clutched in his hands. The smoke and fumes that Siss drew from Petteron's core fouled the skies, but ever up Jakonee climbed. Ever he strove. The power of the Great Flyer of the Skies flowed in his wings. On he flew across the burning plain, over the scorched desert, never wavering in his duty. As the sun set, he prayed in the air, young Borla's voice joining with his guardian's. Jakonee flew through the night, guided in the darkness by the Great Flyer of the Skies, then with the dawn he saw, far below, a ribbon of sparkling blue. Ratwaaa the great and ever-flowing was revealed unto him. No drought of Siss' devising could dry the blessed river's flow. No fire from the bowels of Petteron could boil away its water. Jakonee descended to the river's bank. The fumes and clouds of the fire mountain were but a smudge far behind him. Jakonee drank of Ratwaaa's pure waters and heard the voice of the Great Flyer of the Skies, which said:

"'You who have kept faith with my laws, who has told no falsehood, who have done as you pledged or surrendered your life in the attempt. You, Jakonee, are now pure. I welcome you to stand by me and enter new life, winged and free to journey the skies. And so shall it be for all who follow you that they shall drink of Ratwaaa's waters and, if they be free of the great sins, they shall be welcome with me and find new life in the winged way.

"'Sleep now, Jakonee, gather your strength. You have much to do, and in the fullness of time, you will build a temple on this space to my glory.'"

"So said the Great Flyer of the Skies," Croell and Zandra intoned together.

"And so it is for all batzoid. Ratwaaa still flows, ever quenching the droughts and fires of Siss, purifying all those who drink of its waters. Have you, Croell and Zandra, earned this purity?"

"No, we are unworthy. We deserve to crawl in the mud, to be locked in the darkness of the caverns of Siss' kingdom." Croell and Zandra lay their chins on the floor and spread their aching wings out to either side of them.

"As the Great Flyer of the Skies told me. But did it not also tell Jakonee when he was overlong in building the temple that none are worthy. It is the gentleness of love that purifies. Zandra of Cloud Skipper sect, raise thy mouth and drink of Ratwaaa's waters, not because you are worthy, but because the Great Flyer of the Skies is love."

Zandra lifted her muzzle. Sill picked up a crystal decanter filled with dirty looking water and held it to her lips.

"Drink of Ratwaaa's waters and know the winged way." Sill tipped up the decanter, draining it into Zandra's mouth. She swallowed convulsively.

Sill picked up another decanter and turned to Croell. "Croell of Cloud Skipper sect, raise thy mouth and drink of Ratwaaa's waters, not because you are worthy, but because the Great Flyer of the Skies is love."

Croell lifted his mouth. Sill poured the dirty water down his throat.

"Go now and live the winged way." Sill folded its wings and flicked its tongue at Croell and Zandra.

"Thank you, Servitor. Thank you so much! We will start your brother's geis immediately." Zandra came to her feet and folded her wings.

"Tomorrow will be soon enough. For today, I suggest you swallow these and go back to your quarters." Sill passed Zandra and Croell green tablets.

"I do not understand?" Croell grimaced in pain and rubbed his stomach.

"The waters of Ratwaaa may not be altered, and while they are spiritually pure, we have not been so careful with their physical nature. Tomorrow, when you are recovered, will be time enough to begin the geis. Go now, so that you do not foul the temple floor. Look on this as a penance for any minor sins you may have committed."

Zandra clutched her stomach, then released a large, hissing belch.

"Thank you, servitor." Croell led Zandra from the temple as his stomach rumbled ominously.

"The Great Flyer of the Skies also created ozone and filter mediums! I hardly think it would hurt, but does the theocratic council listen to the servitors that have to clean up the mess? No!" Sill flicked its tongue. "Such a nice couple. It was a pleasure to help them."

Victoria reached up and removed the data cable from her nose as her husband pressed the button that lifted the bubble-like head surround of their e-entertainment unit from his head. The unit itself looked like a reclining chair with buttons on the arms.

"What an obnoxious prat!" commented Victoria.

"Who, Sill? I rather liked it. Croell and Zandra could have done a lot worse."

Victoria stood and stretched. She was dressed in a blue, satin robe that set off her tan skin. "Not Sill, silly." She grinned. "Though that was interesting. I don't think the Batzoid Theocracy would like it if they knew that the ritual has altered over the last two thousand years. It's Tim who's a prat."

"He's a product of Humans Ascendant, my love." Bill started sorting a collection of data disks on his coffee table. His living room was a pleasant affair with a cloth sofa and two reclining chairs around a low, central table. The walls were set to show a desert scene with wildlife moving across it. The e-rig was pushed into a corner where it could be hidden by a curtain.

Victoria moved to help sort the data files. "I know. It's a good thing no one can tell by looking, or we'd have had big problems when we visited your parents. I still think you should have told Mom and Dad."

"What for? My mother and father are quite liberal, but it wouldn't have made them any happier. This way, they came to adore you without that particular drag factor. I'm surprised your memories about batzoid are in your active files."

"I brought them out of storage to give me some perspective on Croell and Zandra."

"Ah, probably for the best. I hope Mike appreciates us editing down the feeds."

"I thought they were fine as they were. Henry did a good job." Victoria stacked the data disks in an impossibly neat pile organized by their bar codes from oldest to newest.

Bill looked into her deep, brown eyes and smiled. "He overloaded it for human sensory processing. Of course, you're an expert on that."

"Flirt." Victoria preened a little.

"You're doing it again, honey."

"What?" Vicky stopped in her efforts to organize the nuts in the bowl on the table by size. A blush rose to her cheeks.

Bill smiled at her indulgently.

Victoria's features became serious. "I am concerned about Kitoy. I'm not sure she'll be able to clear her debt before Ryan has to leave. She spent so much on bogus cures, and good jobs aren't open to her in the felinezoid sector. If she tries to leave a debt behind, they might block her departure clearance. If that happens, Ryan will lose his safe harbour."

"He could abandon her." Bill sounded unconvinced.

"Ryan! I've never even met the man, but from

experiencing his perspective, I think it's more likely Datala will develop a thriving tourist industry."

Bill snorted. "And Humans Ascendant will book the first charter."

Vicky chuckled. "Seriously, I like Kitoy, and this could be her only opportunity for a pleasant life. You know the felinezoid Senate won't budge on her quarantine status."

"I've been thinking about that. I believe we could lend her the credits."

"No, you know how proud she is."

"Then here's another thought. I'll have to contact Mike on Gaea, but I think there's a way Kitoy can clear her debts and probably have a tidy sum left over. If Mike's willing to foot the bill."

Victoria's mind followed the logic of the statement in milliseconds. "You organics. That is so beautifully twisted it might work. What are you going to use as a cover story?"

"As an ambassador, I've discovered that when all else fails, tell the truth."

Vicky looked shocked.

"Well, as much of it as you have to. No need to mention Henry when the floor cleaners can account for everything on station." Bill smiled, then approached his wife and tugged on the belt that held her robe closed. She giggled and kissed him, all other concerns forgotten.

Henry watched Ryan and Rowan snuggle in her bed. "Didn't even shag, must have been upset. Nova blast!"

With another part of his RAM, he read the station's information periodical while two other RAM segments experienced classic *Orgy Girls* features. Yet another RAM segment directed maintenance robots as they cleaned the ship and arranged the cargo in the hangar bay for easy access. A slightly larger RAM segment filled the ship to station communication channel with data as it played a game of Divine Creator with a spiderzoid AI. Henry's first intelligent creatures had achieved space travel that microsecond, effectively neutralizing the asteroid his opponent had aimed at the planet housing the species. A final segment monitored Tim, who sat in his quarters. Henry was bored. With the ship in space dock, he could barely fill a third of his RAM.

He focused his attention on the feed showing Tim. Tim had opened his handheld and was looking at photos of Ryan, Joslin and himself. He paused and looked at the ceiling.

"Dad, if you really aren't him, please let me know. How can I tell? Divine help me." Closing the handheld, he lay on the couch. Moments later, his breathing was even and deep.

"Might be some hope for the kid after all," Henry spoke onto the empty bridge. "Oh, baby yeah, three at once, go, Carol, go, you redheaded vixen, that feels so good!" Henry refocused his primary attention.

A BIG SCARY MONSTER?

"**P**age, please." Rowan lay on her back in bed, being careful that the sheet covered her. Ryan lay beside her, fast asleep, his hand lightly touching her. Lines of text were displayed on the ceiling over the bed.

After *Homo sapiens* were inducted into the Republic, it took two hundred and ten Earth[1] years to transport the Switchboard end of the *Homo sapiens* stargate into place. There was some debate among the *Homo sapiens* pre-existing colony worlds about placing the gate in the Sol system.[2] However, in the end, an underlying sense that the homeworld should be honoured won out. Others claim that the colony worlds were skeptical about being inducted so thoroughly into the larger universe. In general, their ancestors had left Earth to get away from the bureaucrats. It is likely that both views factored into the decision to place the gate in the Sol system.[3]

During the gate's transport, *Homo sapiens* relayed numerous messages through the gate tow ship's FTL telegraph. Thus, the day after the U.E.S. gate was in place, the sale of Jupiter to the brachiopodazoids[4] was finalized. In exchange for Jupiter, the brachiopodazoids agreed to advance *Homo sapiens* technology to the galactic average over the next one hundred Earth years. An advancement for *Homo sapiens*, at that time, of roughly forty thousand Earth years, given their rate of development.

Problems arose with this purchase when the brachiopodazoids attempted to claim Jupiter's moons, as was in keeping with Republic tradition. The *Homo sapiens* pointed to the exact wording of the sales contract and the fact that Jupiter was in their home system, where Republic law granted their laws precedence.

This was the first appearance of *Homo sapiens* before the Republic court. The younger species showed themselves to be both cunning and aggressive, greatly impressing the Council of Judges.[5] In the end, the decision was granted to the *Homo sapiens*, who promptly exchanged three of Jupiter's least valuable moons with the brachiopodazoids to serve as staging areas for the bio-forming of Jupiter. The *Homo sapiens* received the planet now known as Mielkki in this secondary trade. Thus two linked systems house both *Homo sapiens* and brachiopodazoids, much to the ongoing annoyance of the brachiopodazoids.[6]

[1] The *Homo sapiens* homeworld.

[2] The *Homo sapiens* home system.

[3] Known as yellow, 125 degrees two hundred and twenty-seven by the pre-*Homo sapiens* induction classification.

[4] See the *Space Traveller's Guide to Brachiopoda-zoids* by Sokeripit, *The Comprehensive Guide to Hydrogen Breathers* by Red-Blue-Blue-Yellow. Translations are available from Universe Books Inc.

[5] Chief Justice 'large-fluked tail with yellow stripes and a bulbous nasal appendage' was quoted as saying, "Divine, just what we need, another set of weevilzoids with a history of massacring their own kind in addition. We should annihilate them now and save everyone the trouble later. However, in this case, I find in their favour." As most species have become acquainted with *Homo sapiens*, they have come to wonder if the Chief Justice had experienced a precognitive episode.

[6] In fairness, it must be stated that the brachio-podazoids have benefited from the *Homo sapiens* presence with the near-total eradication of space piracy in these systems and the security of having aggressive defenders of their system autonomy.

Ryan stirred, stretched and pulled Rowan close to himself. "Morning, beautiful. What you reading?"

Rowan relaxed into his embrace. "The *Space Traveller's Guide to* Homo sapiens. The historical reference section. I wanted to get up to date." She shuddered as his fingers traced lazy patterns over her body. "What time is Red-Red-Blue expecting us?"

Ryan took a deep breath and released it in a sigh. "Too soon, I'm quite sure. What time is it?"

"It's oh-eight-hundred, hottie-boss, and don't stop on my account. That's a show I'd love to watch." Henry's voice blasted from the speaker.

"Red-Red-Blue isn't expecting us until ten hundred hours. Henry, what's Tim up to?"

"Doctor prat is still sleeping."

"Good. Henry, use my voice and call Kitoy. Ask her if she'd mind keeping an eye on Tim while Rowan and I handle the trading, and don't get fresh with her, remember you're pretending to be me." Ryan turned to face Rowan. "Tim hasn't spent much time with other species. He'll probably need a tour guide."

Rowan smiled as the cover shifted above her arm. "And I'm supposed to act like I can't handle the modern era? I'm glad we don't have to rush." She squeezed.

Ryan gasped as colour rose in his face. "Henry, privacy on!" Ryan resumed caressing Rowan.

"Stardust!" Henry shifted to his secret feeds and continued to watch.

Tim sat at a table in Wesnakee and gawked at the aliens. Ryan and Rowan sat at a counter against one of the transparent walls, speaking with a coelenteratezoid.

"Ryan tells me you do life support design."

Tim focused his attention on the cougar-tan felinezoid that sat across the table from him. He tried not to think of her as pretty, tried to admire her like he would a cougar in a zoo, with only partial success.

"Yes. I've also worked on nanobot enhancements to biological systems."

Kitoy swished her tail in a friendly manner. "My father was a bio-mechanic. He maintained the waste processing plant at Ssssmaaa."

"I'm sorry, I don't think the translator referenced that one. Ssssmaaa?"

Kitoy looked confused as she tried to understand the word the human spoke. Untranslated, it was missing several inflections that went beyond the human hearing and voice range. When she figured it out, her tail swished, and her pupils widened slightly. "It's the third-largest city in the Graaff province on the southeastern continent on Mruu. The translator doesn't always handle proper names well."

Tim closed his eyes. If he just listened to Kitoy, he could

imagine he was speaking with a human woman. Someone from a different culture than his own, but human nonetheless.

"I remember. When my father was stationed on Swampla, my mother and I lived in the embassy there. Some otterzoid insults would take over a minute to translate. You'd never think it to look at them, but otterzoids are really foul-mouthed." Tim smiled at Kitoy.

"I know. I have an otterzoid friend. She visited me after she and her mate had a fight one day. The nanos were still translating three minutes after her lips stopped moving. It was really funny." Kitoy swished her tail.

Tim became serious. "I appreciate you babysitting me for my fa... for Ryan and Rowan while they do the trading. I've not spent much time off Earth, and all this," he waved, indicating the bar with its mix of species, "is rather daunting."

Kitoy swished her tail. "My pleasure. Ryan is a good being, and doing your employer a favour never hurts."

"Won't it be odd for you living on a human ship?"

Kitoy's nostrils dilated, and she looked at the table. Tim was fascinated by the changes in her facial expression. In time, he was sure he could learn to interpret them as he would a human's.

Kitoy's voice was weary when she spoke. "Probably, but your father is willing to hire me and pay me a decent wage. I've heard all the stardust about *Homo sapiens* being promiscuous and violent and smelling bad. It's all stardust! I like *Homo sapiens*, I have lots of *Homo sapiens* friends, and my late husband was *Homo sapiens*."

Timothy was sipping at his drink and sputtered, sending a shot of liquid out of his nose.

Kitoy stood and patted Tim's back as he gagged. Finally, he gasped out, "I'm sorry, your husband was *Homo sapiens*?"

Kitoy looked at the floor. "That shocks you. I loved Kadar. He was the finest male I've ever met. I miss him so much." She caressed the red sash she wore.

"I'm sorry. It caught me by surprise." Timothy's revulsion surged. The idea of touching a felinezoid like that was something that belonged on an e-entertainment, not the real world. The thought frightened him, even as it intrigued him. He looked into Kitoy's face, saw the sorrow there and his disgust was swallowed by his compassion.

"Sometimes I forget that he's dead. He was in prison for so long, our only contact letters. The time we had before that, though. It was so special!"

Tim tentatively stroked the fur on the back of Kitoy's hand. She looked at him, her lip curled to reveal her teeth in surprise, then her expression softened.

"Please don't do that." She swished her tail. "I know for *Homo sapiens* it's a way of showing concern, but for felinezoids, it has a different connotation."

Tim let go of her hand as if it burnt him. "I'm sorry."

"That's all right. Just so you know, you're a good hand massager." Kitoy swished her tail, and her pupils widened slightly.

Tim blushed. "I wonder what's taking my father so long."

Rowan sat and watched the coelenteratezoid through the transparent wall. The shadowy forms of different hydrogen breathing species moved in the background.

"You want far too much for your product. I'm sure legitimate trade channels will make it a common substance soon," spoke the translator in response to the flashing, multi-coloured lights that surrounded the coelenteratezoid's carapace.

The final lie on top of the being's other negotiating tricks was too much for Rowan; she let her temper show. "If you feel that way, why did you agree to meet with us? There are other places we could be; why waste our time? And float down to our level. No one's intimidated by you staring down at them! *Homo sapiens* have used that one for millennia. What did you expect when your blatant flattery didn't work, that you could intimidate us? Really!"

"Is it customary for a captain to allow their subordinate to insult a client among *Homo sapiens*?" Red-Red-Blue's communication lights blinked rapidly.

Ryan looked at the being and shook his head before replying. "Rowan is my trading officer. She can do what she sees fit. It's her job." He smiled at Rowan, whose entire attention was focused on the alien on the other side of the wall.

"The large shipment of orange oil recently obtained by the antiproton generating station in the 'yellow two hundred and ninety-seven degrees, one hundred and two' system has reduced the substance's value." Red-Red-Blue's tone was belligerent.

"Stardust! That shipment was a one-time supply. Your species is unlikely to get another. A smart ma... being is going to stock up." Rowan stood and motioned for Ryan to join her. "We're wasting our time here. I think we should see Saggal about selling the rest of the coffee. He's probably sold enough of the first to afford it by now." Rowan bowed sharply at Red-Red-Blue, then stepped away from the wall.

Red-Red-Blue trembled where it floated. The lights around its carapace flashed quickly on and off. "No! Please, my mating group must have the orange oil. We are going extinct."

Rowan smiled with her back turned to her client. Schooling her expression into a serious mask, she turned back. "The oil we traded for antiproton will, at least, alleviate Zod's problems. Your population should be able to interbreed with your homeworld's and restore genetic stability. Don't try to make me feel guilty."

"My mating group is not like the others on Zod." Red-Red-Blue sank down so that its light ring was level with the human's eyes.

"How so?" asked Ryan.

The hydrogen breather's light ring blinked slowly; the voice from the speaker was dispassionate.

"Four thousand Zod-years ago," a heads-up display on the transparent wall printed 'fifty-three thousand Earth years', "when Zod was colonized by century ships from Ikika, many of the colonists were religious extremists. The sect my ancestors followed was very strict and felt that it was wrong to mate with those who did not believe exactly as they did. Thus, they formed a closed mating group. We did not even mix our genetics with others of the population of Zod. For my mating group, barely one in one-hundred-thousand fry spawned survives to adulthood. Ten times worse than the other mating groups on Zod. Worse, even other Zodiens are unattractive to us. The only hope my mating group has of surviving is if we obtain a supply of orange oil so that we may mix genetics with coelenteratezoids from the homeworld."

"That is sad, but we have problems too," said Ryan.

Rowan resumed her seat and stared at Red-Red-Blue. "He's right, we'd like to help, but we aren't in a position to take a hit on the price."

"My mating group is doomed to extinction. We are not wealthy and cannot afford the price being charged on Zod. I cannot pay what you are asking. It was only good fortune that the ship I work upon was at the station when you arrived. It will tax my mating group to cover the shipping costs alone."

Rowan looked at the floor, then smiled. "Why take all of it then? Could you afford half the cases at our stated price?"

Red-Red-Blue swished its tentacles. The lights blinked excitedly. "Yes, but don't you wish to sell the whole shipment?"

"I'm sure we'll find a buyer for what's left." Rowan wagged her arms loosely below her chest.

Red-Red-Blue waved its tentacles happily. "I will pay

forty per cent of your asking price for the whole shipment for half the shipment, please?"

Rowan smiled and moved to a console built into the counter in front of the transparent wall. "I'll draw up the contract on one condition. You supply storage for the other half of our shipment until we find a buyer."

"Agreed." Red-Red-Blue waved its tentacles and twirled around once in place. "Captain, you have a potent negotiator in this one. I hope you appreciate him."

Rowan glanced at Red-Red-Blue, then shrugged and finished filling out the contract.

"I do. As a matter of interest, I am a male *Homo sapiens*, Rowan is a female. The female tends to have bumps on its front and is usually slightly smaller." Ryan smiled and wagged his arms as he spoke.

"You creatures with two genders always confuse me. No offence intended."

"None taken." Rowan finalized the contract.

Red-Red-Blue pressed one of its short tentacles onto a scanner plate, and the deal was struck.

"That should at least cover your first session with Pikeman," observed Ryan.

"We did better than I expected. I kinda figured on only getting seventy per cent of the asking price. Though finding another buyer is nova blasted. I..." Rowan fell silent as a spiderzoid, the size of a large dog, scuttled up to Ryan and lay its claw-tipped leg on his shoulder.

"Pardon me. Are you a *Homo sapiens*?" The spiderzoid's translated voice was childlike.

"Keka, NO! Please, good sentient, please, do not hurt my hatchling. He means no offence." A full-sized spiderzoid rushed to the child's side.

Ryan sighed and looked at the child. "I am a *Homo sapiens*." He directed his gaze to the parent. "You have nothing to fear from me. The young one was simply getting my attention. No worthy being commits violence for so little cause."

"Is it true *Homo sapiens* kill their own species?" asked the young spiderzoid.

"Sometimes. It is considered an affront to social norms and is vigorously punished unless sanctioned by the state."

"Keka, leave the *Homo sapiens* alone, please." The parent clicked its impressive mandibles together.

"Honoured sentient, do not fear. The great warrior philosopher Finn Mac Cumhal said, 'Two-thirds of thy gentleness be shown to women and those that creep on the floor and to poets, and be not violent to the common people.' Those that creep on the floor means children."

"Wow, is that a *Homo sapiens* thing?" Keka shifted position so it could gaze at Ryan with all its multi-faceted eyes.

"They are an ancient set of guidelines for living with honour as a warrior. The Maxims of the Finna. What did you wish to speak to me about?"

The adult, still clicking its mandibles, spoke. "It is a school project. Each student is to interview a being from another species. I brought Keka here hoping he would choose a hydrogen or methane breather, but he is fascinated by *Homo sapiens*. Please do not take his interest amiss."

Ryan sighed again and pressed a button on the counter in front of him. "I pledge under Republic law, I will not harm you or your child this day unless you initiate hostilities against me or my companion. My statement is recorded. Will that alleviate your fears, good mother?"

"Thank you. Keka, be polite and don't waste this good sentient's time. Do you mind?" The parent held up a black circular device the size of a toilet roll.

"You can record me. Is it okay with you, Ro?"

"Of course." Rowan stood beside Ryan.

"Thank you, good sentients." Keka scuttled onto one of the cushion chairs, which configured so that he could lay on it with his ten legs dangling. The parent pushed a button on the side of the tube. It hovered at eye level, focusing on

Ryan, Rowan and Keka.

"You're welcome. My informal name is Ryan. This is my friend, Rowan." Ryan gestured to Rowan.

Rowan reached forward, took one of Keka's clawed feet in her hand and gently shook it. "It's a pleasure to meet you."

The clicking sound of the parent's mandibles filled the air.

"Mother, it's a formal greeting for them. I read about it. It means they aren't carrying a weapon in their dominant claw." Keka sounded excited and exasperated.

"Oh well, if that is its meaning." The mother continued to click her mandibles.

"I've read that *Homo sapiens* have two genders. Are you a mated pair?" asked Keka.

Ryan smiled at Rowan; she gave a little nod.

"Yes, newly mated."

"Could I record your mating practices?"

Rowan blushed. "That, err..."

"We hold all but the most introductory of our mating rituals to be a private matter. The introductory rituals can be found by looking up the words dancing, kissing, and dating on the database." Ryan's voice was soft and comforting.

"Oh." Keka sounded mildly disappointed. "Have either of you served in the state-sanctioned murder societies?"

Rowan's brow wrinkled.

"I've done military service. I was a captain in the U.E.S. Spacing Corps." Ryan sounded haunted.

"Did you ever kill anyone?"

"Yes."

The sound of the mother's mandibles coming together with a snap echoed across the bar.

"Why?"

"Mostly because they were trying to kill me or someone I had to protect. Sometimes because I was ordered to by the U.E.S. government. Killing is never a good thing, but sometimes it is a necessary thing. A soldier obeys orders unless they clearly violate Republic law."

"How do you do it? Keep living, doesn't the remorse drive you insane?" Keka clicked the claws in excitement.

"Sometimes, it's difficult. You must remember, I am evolved from omnivorous predators. My species is omnivorous. Killing animals is a natural part of our existence." Ryan looked at the floor. "I do have regrets."

Rowan placed her hand on his shoulder. "Maybe we should talk about something else. There's a lot more to *Homo sapiens* than our military. We have family; people we love; we've had brilliant artists and writers."

"It's fine, Ro. It's only natural that he's curious. Spiderzoids are pacifistic by nature. Savages like us, and the felinezoids, are a mystery to them."

The adult spiderzoid stared at Ryan and Rowan with all her eye facets. Her mandibles had stopped clicking.

"I didn't mean to disturb you emotionally. I'm sorry," said Keka.

"No need. One learns to do what they have to and live with the regrets. That is a big part of being a *Homo sapiens*." Ryan smiled at the child.

"If you say it is so, it is so. Given your species' high aggressiveness rating, why do you think you survived your technological adolescence?"

"In part, because the rating is artificially high due to the inclusion of mentally ill individuals who kill for nonsensical reasons. In part because we learned long before we gained the capacity to destroy ourselves that there are two types of warrior. The warrior of defence and the warrior of aggression.

"The warrior of defence protects those that cannot protect themselves. He or she stands as a shield to uphold others' safety and/or rights. The warrior of aggression does what he or she does for their own profit.

"Those of a high moral nature fought to keep peace and safety, those of a low for their own betterment. As such, we found a balance that curbed the worst of our excesses."

"Wow!" Keka clicked his claws excitedly. "When you are not killing other sentients, what do you do?"

Ryan laughed. The two spiderzoids looked at him, obviously taken aback. "I spend most of my time repairing spacecraft. I'm an engineer. I also enjoy reading and an activity called skiing."

"What are your pastimes?" Keka turned to Rowan.

"Me, I'm learning to navigate Ryan's ship, and I like swimming. I also like to read."

"What are your thoughts on the enslavement of clones to make mentally intrusive entertainments for beings to experience delusional states?"

Rowan took a moment to think the question through. "It's a disgusting practice that reduces the clone to being a thing and the people who experience them into exploitive monsters."

Ryan cringed at her words. "Ro, over the top, don't you think?"

"No, it's not over the top. I... oh Ryan, not you, you're different, you grew up."

"Keka, I think that is enough. These good beings undoubtedly have other things to do today." There was resolve in the mother's voice.

"But Mother..." Keka's tone was wheedling.

"Keka, one, two." The adult spiderzoid rubbed its first set of forelegs together.

"I'm coming. Thank you, Ryan and Rowan. I really liked the interview. I'll get a top rating for sure."

"You're welcome." Ryan and Rowan spoke in unison.

"They were much nicer than I thought. Hardly scary at all," said Keka as his mother escorted him from the bar.

"Yes, if they are typical of *Homo sapiens*, the species aren't anywhere near as bad as I was led to believe. You know, the male actually seemed to feel regret for some of the things he's done, and I'm sure the female was offering comfort when she touched him. Who would have thought it in a species with a twelve rating? I think your project can..." The spiderzoids left the room.

"I think we made an impression," said Rowan.

"I always try to. There's a lot of half-truths about humans floating around." Ryan took a long swallow from his drink.

"What was that about a twelve rating?" Rowan returned to her chair.

"The Species Aggressiveness Assessment Table. You know the reputation humans have in the Republic?"

"Violent, sex-mad, vicious, smelly. I've had a real education on what it's like to be on the receiving end of bigotry since you liberated me."

"It's not a completely unearned reputation. The U.E.S. government has rented out our troops to the highest bidder since our technology was advanced enough that we wouldn't get pasted in a fight. At any rate, we're a twelve on the Aggressiveness Assessment; the highest rating ever to survive technological adolescence before us was a ten."

"Let me guess, the felinezoids."

"And the otterzoids. Ro, the truth is, humans aren't the smartest creatures in the Republic. In fact, we're on the low end of average. We aren't the strongest creatures, though we are in the upper twenty percentile for creatures from small, rocky worlds. We aren't the fastest, or best coordinated, though we can hold our own there too. What we are is the most vicious, violent, destructive creatures ever to join the Republic. When hardened criminals learn that we've been hired to hunt them down, they surrender en masse to whatever other species is at hand."

Rowan looked at Ryan and sighed. A chime drew her attention to the transparent wall where two coelenteratezoids floated.

"I think they are the ones. The one with the bumps is a female." Red-Red-Blue's voice came from the speaker. "Are you Rowan and Ryan of the *Star Hawk*?"

"Yes. Red-Red-Blue, is that you?" Ryan stood in front of

the wall.

"It is I. My companion, Yellow-Green, is interested in your remaining shipment."

Rowan settled into a cushion-chair in front of the wall and smiled. "Then let's negotiate."

MOVING DAY

Arlene stared at the big screen that displayed Rowan's perspective. Saggal was shown in profile on the *Star Hawk*'s main screen. *He spoke in a raised voice. "Graff, Samantha, you two settle down and clean that up. Your mother will be home any minute." Saggal turned back to the screen. "Kids, what can you do?"*

The door at the back of the *Freedom's Run* control room burst open, and Ulva rushed in. Arlene stopped the playback.

"Have you seen it? It's all over the news!" Ulva waved her handheld in front of Arlene's face.

"What is? What..." Arlene caught Ulva's wrist and steadied the handheld enough so that she could read the headline.

'STUDIO SURROGATE STOLEN'

"They know about Rowan and Ryan. They even know about the space pursuit and that they're in the Switchboard System." Ulva could barely hold her arm still as Arlene took the handheld.

"It had to happen sooner or later." Arlene skimmed the written article.

"It's been on the e-news as well and the audio-video broadcast."

"'Possibly suffering from transference dementia,' stardust, whoever wrote this obviously never met Ryan."

"It says a lot of things like that. It's a very skewed article."

Arlene smiled and passed Ulva back her handheld. "I'll read it later."

"Nova blast, we've got to do something." Ulva paced the short length of the room.

"Ulva, this is all according to Michael's plan. Don't worry about it. Why are you here? I thought it was an off day for you."

"Wilton, the really cute tech who works the *Vampire Chronicles*, is sick. My name is still on the substitutes board from when I was trying to get promoted out of *A Cat's Life*. They called me, and I can use the extra cash."

"What are they doing with *Vampire Chronicles* now?"

"They're focusing on Ned again. The vampire PI who wants to be mortal again. At least they go through fewer victims from cancelled shows when they focus on him."

"True. Thanks for telling me the story's out. Don't give any interviews until after the launch party. I better get back to work."

"Me too. This is gonna be a nova blast of a ride." Ulva left the room.

Arlene watched her walk away. "Pity the group is female-heavy. She is hot," she muttered after the door closed.

Ryan and Timothy stacked boxes on a grav-sledge outside Kitoy's on-station apartment. A maintenance robot worked on removing the grime that had built up in the three-metre-wide public corridor.

"I'm surprised Rowan isn't here." Timothy's voice held a vague curiosity.

"She hasn't spent much time in our society. Everything is new to her, so sometimes it's easier to leave her on the *Star Hawk*. It's strange. In most ways, she's fully adult, but, at times, it's like caring for a five-year-old. She doesn't have the life experience."

"She's not real, that's why." Timothy stacked the last box

on the grav-sledge and pressed the button that activated its retaining field. The crates all cinched in tightly together.

"I doubt if you had to jump ahead millennia, you'd do as well. I know I wouldn't, and I've been to planets controlled by the elder races. Stop looking for reasons to hate her." Ryan pushed the grav-sledge towards the transport pod station.

"She stole my mother's husband. I don't need to look for reasons."

Ryan gritted his teeth, and an uncomfortable silence descended.

Marcy watched on the large viewing-screen in her living room as the numbers on S.E.T.E stock scrolled down. Mike sat on the couch beside her, reading a novel on his handheld.

"How low do you think it will go?" she asked.

"I'm not sure. My announcement should still the fall." Mike glanced at the numbers. "I'll tell Richard to place an order to buy when it hits five U.E.S. credits a share. I don't want it to drop much lower than that. It could affect the production budgets."

"I'll have Shelly spread the word to your favoured buyers at that level. Are you sure this is safe? The last thing you need is to be nabbed for insider trading." Marcy's pretty face was a mask of concern.

Mike looked up from his book, then cupped her cheek in his palm. "I can afford the appearance of impropriety so long as I'm technically within the letter of the law. Besides, getting rid of the current major shareholders is worth the risk."

"Hyper conservative jerks." Marcy kissed Mike's palm.

"When our chosen investors have a majority, we can make some big changes. Then I can run before the rest of the shareholders lynch me." Mike chuckled.

"You better get moving, or you'll be late for your press conference." Marcy glanced at the screen. "Five fifty and still falling." She stood and offered her husband her hand.

"It's a pity I have to save John's backside, but I can still make him look bad and leverage him down a peg or two." Mike took the offered hand and stood. "Call my handheld as soon as the stocks are purchased." He kissed his wife and headed to the mansion's door.

Tim stared at a charcoal sketch of Kitoy being held from behind by a healthy Kadar. The couple's posture was so relaxed it was easy to overlook the fact they were of mixed species.

"A little to the left," said Kitoy.

Tim moved the picture. Kitoy's quarters on the *Star Hawk* were nine metres square with twin doors on one wall leading to her closet and en-suite, respectively, while the entry door opened off the other wall. The couch/bed was rolled up into its former function, leaving the drawers underneath it accessible.

"Where do you want these?" Rowan entered carrying a box of data cubes.

"Leave them by the computer terminal." Kitoy pointed with her tail to the desktop with a built-in keyboard.

Ryan entered the room, carrying a pressure-sensitive board covered with felinezoid characters. "I've rigged the adapter for your interface board." He moved to the terminal and began undoing the screws that held the human keyboard in place.

"You didn't have to. I can read and write *Homo sapiens*." Kitoy nodded and pressed a button on a remote-control in her hand. Tim felt the picture pull in tight against the wall. He released it, and it hung seemingly without support.

"Kitoy, these are your quarters. They should be set up for your convenience," said Rowan.

"Speaking of which, we brought a housewarming gift." Kate stood in the doorway, holding one end of a long, thin box.

"Kate, it is I who should be gifting others," said Kitoy.

"I told her, but does she ever listen?" Saggal's voice issued from the hall.

"That may be the felinezoid way, but this is a human ship. Right, Captain?" Kate smiled at Ryan.

Ryan shrugged. "Machines I fix, cultural norms get to fight it out for themselves."

"Could we decide what is happening with this thing? It isn't light," complained Saggal.

"Bring it in. Thank you. What is it?" Kitoy approached as Kate and Saggal carried the box into the room and set it on the floor.

Saggal entered, ducking his head to pass through the *Homo sapiens*-sized door. Graff and Samantha followed him, each carrying a box. Tim stared at the young felinezoid, who had covered his hairless body with a human-style T-shirt and a plaid kilt.

"See for yourself." Kate stepped back.

Kitoy extended her claws and raked them carefully over the box's seals, then lifted the lid.

"A Groom-O-Matic, the deluxe version. Oh, Kate, Saggal, it's too much."

Kate smiled and hugged Kitoy. "Don't be silly. You can't use a human nano-bot shower. You'd end up with all your fur on your head. I'm sure Ryan can install this."

"If you want privacy, I can run a power feed into your closet." Ryan moved to inspect the device.

"The closet would be wonderful. It's not like I have clothing to hang up." Kitoy swished her tail.

Samantha stared at the charcoal sketch of Kitoy and Kadar as tears welled in her eyes. "You're really going. I don't want you to go."

Graff set down the box he was carrying and moved to his sister's side. "Shh. We should be happy for Kitoy."

Graff's pupils dilated, and his nose started to run. "This is a good job, and Ryan and Rowan will be her friends, and…" Graff fell silent and hugged Samantha, who now wept openly.

Kitoy raced to the two children and hugged them. "Shush, It's all right. You'll still have your mother and father."

"How can you go? Don't you love us anymore?" sobbed Samantha.

"Of course I love you, but I have to earn a living. If I could bring you with me, I would."

Saggal and Kate shared a look. Kate shrugged before moving to her children's side. "She won't be leaving for a few days. Maybe you should save your tears until then. I'm sorry, Kitoy. We're all going to miss you. You're a member of the family."

Kitoy's nose started running. "You have been the best friends I ever had. You are my family and always will be."

Tim watched the scene in silence, then his gaze strayed to Ryan, who was busily installing the computer interface board. Looking closer, he saw the glimmer of an unshed tear in his father's eye. Rowan stood beside Ryan, watching Saggal, who had pulled Kitoy and his family into a group hug.

Tim sighed and slipped from the room.

Henry watched Tim move down the corridor. The man wore an expression of mixed confusion and shame.

When he reached the elevator, Tim spoke. "Computer, record message. Recipient Ryan Chandler. Dad…" Tim paused in thought, then nodded. "Dad, I have an errand I have to run. You know what job hunting is like. Tell Rowan I'm sorry I was so rude last night. I… maybe it's because I remember Mom the way she was. I don't know. I should have come out and visited you two, but… well, you know. I'll be back late.

"Computer, end message." Tim rubbed the back of his neck as he exited the lift.

Croell stumbled out of the bathroom into the captain's quarters of the *Mary*. "I think the dysentery has stopped."

Zandra feebly lifted her serpentine neck from where she lay sprawled on the bed. "Yes, I think my stomach is improving. Sill was right. Tomorrow we should be recovered. I…"

Zandra lurched to her feet and rushed to the bathroom, pushing Croell aside.

"Great Flyer of the Skies, how could batzoid pollute the holy river? I swear, if I survive to see Petteron, I will fight to see this affront rectified." Croell shuffled to the bed and collapsed.

Michael Strongbow smiled at his wife's face on his handheld's screen. "I'm glad that Richard and Shelly were able to wrap things up so they could visit. I better be going. I love you, bye."

"Love you too," Marcy replied from the small screen.

Mr. Strongbow stood and moved to the lectern at the front of the podium. A crowd of press people filled the theatre at the S.E.T.E. administration and control building. Michael straightened the lines of the classic business suit he wore and struck a commanding pose. Several women in the crowd fell silent and unconsciously licked their lips. It wasn't just the man's looks, which were pleasant enough. It was a palpable aura he exuded. Here was a leader, be it on the battlefield or in the boardroom. Here was an alpha in the best sense of the word.

"Gentle people of the press, may I have your attention."

Mr. Strongbow spoke clearly and deliberately. All fell silent.

John Wilson, who slouched on a chair at the back of the podium, scowled and wiped sweat from his flushed face.

"I wish to address the recent reports that S.E.T.E. property was stolen. Namely the abduction of the emotional surrogate, Rowan McPherson, of the highly-rated, award-winning e-entertainment *Angel Black*. The story reported by the *Gaea Crier* was, in fact, a half-truth. S.E.T.E., in collaboration with the Gaea Militia and Orbital Defence Forces, performed an exercise to identify and locate weaknesses in our inter-agency cooperation. I recruited retired space services Captain Ryan Chandler to pretend to kidnap Rowan. Based upon his psychiatric analyses and reports from the producer in charge of *Angel Black*, John Wilson, I was led to believe Captain Chandler was mentally stable and well socialized."

"You what!" gasped John from the back of the stage. The fat man staggered to his feet, then wove unsteadily for a second before collapsing back into his chair.

Michael smiled. "To reassure our investors, a cover story was presented to the set region surrogates that accounts for Rowan's absence within the framework of the *Angel Black* series. Also, regarding legal action, since the exercise was conducted with military cooperation, all charges against the studio have been dropped, as have most of the charges against Captain Ryan Chandler."

"You manipulating piece of stardust!" John lurched to his feet.

"John, sit down. I know how hard you've been working. The fact that you let the psychological monitoring of your people slip is nothing to be ashamed of." Michael assumed the expression of a holy man granting absolution.

John glared at Michael and took an unsteady step forward.

Mildred stepped out from behind a curtain and grabbed the fat man's arm. "No!"

John took a clumsy swing at her, which she sidestepped

before driving the butt of a baton into his solar plexus. John doubled over as the audience gasped. Mildred pushed him into his seat.

Michael turned to John but spoke loudly enough for the press to hear. "Stress affects us all differently, John. Please, don't make a scene. I'm sure with proper rest, you'll be fine in no time." Michael returned to the podium; his expression was one of regret. "I will be taking over the producer responsibilities for *Angel Black*. Mr. Wilson will be positioned as an assistant producer, so I may draw on his experience while allowing him to take a well-deserved rest. I accept any responsibility for Captain Chandler's unexpected departure from the agreed exercise parameters. I will accept whatever decision regarding my position the shareholders should endorse. The floor is now open for questions." Michael's expression was resolute, a weary leader regretting an honest mistake and accepting its consequences.

Kitoy walked with Ryan and Rowan to the bridge. Saggal and Graff wagged their tails at her from the lift as Kate and Samantha waved.

"Remember, all of you, dinner tomorrow," called Kate as the lift door closed.

"I'm going to miss them," said Kitoy.

"You can still change your mind." Ryan reached the bridge door, which retracted into the wall.

"No. I need this job. I love Graff and Samantha, but they aren't mine. I'm just the caregiver. I..." Kitoy fell silent as she stepped onto the bridge and saw Henry's battered form in the computer tech's chair.

"Hey, sexy kitty. Long time no see." Henry swivelled the chair to look at her with his android eyes.

Kitoy gasped and took a tentative step towards the android.

"DON'T!" Rowan stepped onto the bridge. "He gropes."

"Sweetness, you are a killjoy. Course, if sexy kitty wants some good hand rub."

"You repaired him. I didn't know. Kadar didn't tell me." Kitoy stood and stared at Henry.

"I ain't fixed yet, hot and furry. He still hasn't given me hips. Oh, baby!"

Ryan rolled his eyes. "When I get the parts and have a proper operating system for the *Star Hawk*. Kadar didn't know until just before… Well… I told him the last time I saw him."

Kitoy stroked the red fabric of her sash. "Why haven't you adjusted the run speed on his sex drive?"

"He won't agree to it, and I won't do it if he doesn't." Ryan shook his head.

"Got that one right, hottie boss. For a fleshy, you're pretty moral, not to mention sexy." Henry leered at Ryan.

"Some things are as constant as moonset." Kitoy moved to the communications console and gingerly sat in the *Homo sapiens* style chair.

"I'll cut you a hole for your tail before we launch," apologized Ryan.

Kitoy's tail swished where it projected above the seat. "Thank you. You know, I have an old keyboarding chair. If you could mount it here, it might be more comfortable for me."

"Consider it done." Ryan smiled.

"Could sit on a poor, lonely android's lap, sexy kitty. I'd make you comfortable," teased Henry.

Kitoy rolled her eyes, then examined the console in front of her. "This is an old unit. You know there have been several upgrades."

"It works, and upgrades cost money." Ryan settled in the captain's chair while Rowan sat at the navigator's station.

"Understood." Kitoy adjusted several knobs. "You really need to fine-tune this thing. You're missing entire sub-frequencies you could be getting."

Ryan smiled. "I'll leave that to you. Keep Henry under your… err."

Kitoy looked at Ryan as her tail tip kinked. Rowan chuckled.

"Keep Henry a secret. He's my ace in the hole."

Henry opened his mouth, but Rowan spoke first. "Henry, we all know what you're going to say, so there is no need to say it."

"I'm so unappreciated. Hey, sexy kitty, wanna go to the sim booths in the gym and experience an *Orgy Girls* special feature with me? I have the whole collection."

Kitoy looked at Henry. Her pupils widened as her voice became a purr. "No thanks, reality's better. The press of flesh on fur, the gentle rake of claws. Organics thrusting together in an act of ecstasy as old as life itself. Rising flesh on flesh to a peak, then collapsing only to rise again, like waves on a shore. Oh, Henry, you poor thing of plastic and silicone, you will never know what you miss out on. How much a pale shadow your ecstasy is compared to the truth of organic interaction." Kitoy struck an obviously provocative pose and gently combed the fur of an outthrust leg with her claw tips.

"Oh, baby, hottie cat's got claws! You almost make me wish I was organic." Henry sounded breathless and moody.

Kitoy swivelled her chair, kinked the tip of her tail and winked at Ryan and Rowan.

23

THE ENEMY OF MY ENEMY

Crapper sat at the head of a large conference table. The walls around the room were set to display an oak-panel finish. A tall, slender man, with a too-perfect head of hair and teeth so white they seemed to glow, occupied the seat to Crapper's right. The man wore a space services uniform with lieutenant commander rank insignia. Timothy sat in the seat to Crapper's left.

"I want it in writing that if my participation helps reclaim the Rowan property, my father is to receive a pardon." Tim's voice was hostile, and he met Crapper's gaze.

"He's a fakey. Why should you care?" Crapper took a long swallow from the drink in his hand.

"Maybe I know my father when I see him. Those are my terms!"

"Captain, perhaps a variant on the offer that the Gaean government made. A pardon conditional on him staying out of Gaean space," suggested Commander Hammerman.

"I could accept that," said Timothy.

"I can't promise anything, but I will relay your terms to the U.E.S. Justice Committee." Crapper sat up straight and looked down his nose at Timothy. "Now, what can you tell me?"

"She's learning navigation and knows her way around the *Star Hawk*, but beyond that, she's a primitive. She never leaves my father's side. She's like a child, incapable of coping with the real universe. If you separate her from the people looking after her, she'll be helpless."

"Yes, this might be useful." Crapper nodded.

"Captain, we received a message on the FTL telegraph," spoke a voice from the wall speaker.

"Is it classified?" demanded Crapper.

"No, sir. It's marked priority."

"Put it on the wall."

"Sir?" Hammerman stared at his captain.

"It isn't classified. Probably some minister wants me to pick up an exotic spice in the alien sector and ship it out to them before their big banquet."

As Crapper spoke, the wall changed, revealing lines of text. Timothy read the message.

> Abduction of Rowan surrogate discovered by news media. Prompt retrieval of property essential to S.E.T.E. corporate image. Information of abduction will reach Switchboard Station tomorrow latest. Proceed accordingly.
>
> Admiral Yvonne C. LaFleur.

"Damn that fakey! This could ruin S.E.T.E. Hammerman, put that law degree the service paid for to work. What does this mean to us?" snapped Crapper.

"Sir. It actually makes our job easier. Up until now, we couldn't charge the Rowan surrogate with anything because we would have had to acknowledge her existence and thus her origin."

"So?" Crapper went to take another hit off his drink and found the glass empty.

A calculating expression filled Hammerman's face. "Theft of luxury items is recognized as an offence by the Republic."

"They won't recognize the surrogate as property. Those stardusted aliens won't charge Chandler for taking her." Crapper waved dismissively.

"Not Captain Chandler, Rowan."

"She doesn't seem the type to steal," said Tim.

"Stole herself, didn't it," snapped Crapper.

"More importantly." Hammerman smiled and steepled his fingers. "Was she naked when she left the set region? It can be argued that everything in the set region is S.E.T.E. property, including the clothes on her back. Technically, under Republic law, clothes are a luxury item."

Crapper laughed. "Yes, we can have her arrested."

"It will never stick." Tim looked at his table mates. This plan didn't involve him, and he knew he couldn't leverage Ryan out of the mess he'd gotten himself into if it succeeded.

Hammerman chuckled. "She'll be acquitted of the charge. The studio let her use the clothes. Thus there was an implied transfer of ownership. Stardust, technically she isn't a person, so she can't legally commit a crime. But it will be enough to get the Republic to deport her to us for trial. Once she's acquitted, we can collect her as the property she is before she can get out of U.E.S. territory."

"Excellent." Crapper rubbed his hands together. "Say what you will, but if you want sneaky, bring in a lawyer. This should make my superiors happy. I may even get transferred back to Earth. Hammerman, get on it."

Tim looked at the two officers sitting with him. As his father's son, he'd seen many veterans of battles. Neither of these men fit with those memories. These two were like the old profs at the university with their endless power games and manoeuvrings. Tim shook his head and wondered at the choices he was making.

Gunther helped Willa haul the captured octozoid into the basement. Quinta waited at the bottom of the stairs, ready to balance the weight telekinetically.

"I will tell you nothing, *Homo sapiens*!" hissed the

octozoid.

"They're always the same. It's so cliché," commented Willa. There wasn't a hint of strain in her voice, and her slender frame supported the weight effortlessly.

"Honey, carry now, talk later. This thing is heavy." Gunther was red-faced with the effort of holding the weight.

"Sorry, I forget sometimes." Willa's expression saddened as she descended the stairs.

Gunther looked at her. Despite the weight he was holding, there was compassion in his expression. "I love you, just as you are, and always have."

Willa nodded as they reached the bottom of the stairs and moved to the canvas bathtub of water sitting on the floor.

"You and your pathetic group will be the first to die when we call our mother ship," hissed the octozoid as it was dumped into the tub.

"Quinta, if you would be so kind," Gunther spoke as he moved to hug Willa.

"Of course." Quinta looked at the switch on the jammer, and it flipped to the on position. Willa jerked as the field passed over her cybernetics.

"Torture me as you will, *Homo sapiens*. I will tell you nothing," stated the octozoid as sparks of blue static danced across the surface of the water in the tub.

"Listen. You don't know the truth, and I don't have time to explain. If you resist, this will hurt a lot more." Gunther lay a hand on the octozoid's bulbous body, and his brow wrinkled.

"NO!" screamed the creature in the tank. The sonic ripples from its physical voice caused several bottles on a shelf to shatter. "You are lying! I remember my parent-pod. The cave complex my school lived in. The teachers taking us to hunt wild crabs. You lie!" The octozoid waved its tentacles in the air.

"I'm telling you the truth." Gunther mentally pulled away

from the aquatic.

"He is. Would we make up a story this crazy?" Willa moved to pat the octozoid's body.

"NO!" The octozoid lashed out, wrapping a tentacle around Willa's throat. Gunther and Quinta gasped and rushed to help her. Willa held up a hand, stopping them.

"It can't hurt me. Remember, my trachea is a polycarbonate alloy. Has to be some advantage to being mostly a machine." Willa turned her attention to the octozoid. "No one could hate the studio as much as I do. The question is, do you have the fortitude to go after your true enemy?"

The octozoid released Willa and sank into the tub. "What is it you require?"

Quinta moved to the edge of the tub and stood on her hind legs with her hands gripping the brim. "You must pretend that we have enlisted you. If the controllers hold to their pattern, a group will be here soon to rescue you. We will let them accomplish this with, at most, token resistance. Once you are back in the lake, I will be your contact. I'll bring you equipment on the premise that you are building a weapon for the *Homo sapiens* defenders. You will, in truth, be building another jamming device. Once you have finished it, you must recruit others from the non-*Homo sapiens* inhabitants of Sun Valley to our cause."

"And if I don't?" demanded the octozoid.

"If the controllers suspect that you know the truth, they will kill you. There will be no hesitation. You were, after all, created to serve as a disposable antagonist. They won't value your life." Gunther looked down at the being whose universe he had ripped asunder.

"If I even suspect what I am building is a weapon, I will tell my superiors everything. Do you understand this?" The octozoid waved its tentacles so violently it splashed water out of the tub.

"We understand," said Willa. "By the way, what are you called?"

"I am, 'Shallow limestone cave complex in semi-tropical zone third hatched in the month of "large aquatic predator with twin stabilizing fins, fluked tail and renewable spiked teeth", during the year of the bottom-feeding bivalve mollusc'."

Willa noticed that the flexible chamber on the octozoid's body that pulsed when it spoke stopped vibrating long before the translator finished with the name.

"Can we call you Tony?" asked Gunther.

"*Homo sapiens*! If you must."

Ryan led Rowan, who wore a hospital gown, into Pikeman's treatment room. A being, which looked like a bald felinezoid with human eyes and no tail, clambered painfully off the examination table, then stared at Rowan.

"Wow, nice job. Did Pikeman do your Rowan look? You could be the fakey."

"I... um." Rowan tried not to stare at the being before her as she scrambled for an appropriate response.

"Did you hear she escaped the set region? Some crazy ex-space service guy kidnapped her. It was in this morning's information periodical."

"Really, some crazy, ex-space services *captain* liberated her, did he?" Ryan's smile somehow made him look more predatory than the stranger's large canines.

"Yup, the periodical said he may be suffering from transfer dementia. I'm glad I don't play the market. S.E.T.E. stocks have been in free fall since word got out. It's too bad. I'm a huge *Angel Black* fan. Rowan was my favourite."

"And despite that, you think it was good they used her as a slave?" snapped Rowan.

"Oh Divine, you're one of those. It's not like she's real. I mean, medical clones, sure, they're people. They have memories, real childhoods, the whole thing. Emotional surrogates are made up. Like, if you ever really met one, you'd know right away they were fake."

"Oh, really?" Rowan's voice was dangerously light.

"Walter, how often do I have to tell you not to bother my other patients?" Pikeman stepped into the room with Timothy close behind.

"I'm sorry, Doctor." Walter's vaguely felinezoid face pulled into a parody of a human smile. "Miss, whatever your politics, and whatever you started as, the work is very convincing." With a hiss of pain, Walter hobbled out of the door.

"Give me a moment to sterilize the work platform." Pikeman pressed a button on the wall. A low hum filled the room as a beam of laser light swept back and forth over the examination table.

"As the equipment readies itself, why don't you show me what we were discussing, Doctor Chandler." Pikeman smiled ingratiatingly.

"Of course. If you set the fuel demand at eighty per cent or higher in the manufacturing unit's tank, then reset the repair schedule sequence to maximize the use of downtime, you can increase nanobot yield per time unit by twenty per cent without any drop off in the construction unit's durability. All you need to do is take a minute of downtime to manufacture the new maintenance nanobots. I can download the schematic from my handheld for you, Doctor." Timothy adjusted several controls on a piece of equipment on the room's wall, then used a cable to interface his handheld with the unit's console.

"Excellent, yes, I see. This new maintenance unit's design is brilliant. But won't it be problematic if it requires repair?" Pikeman stared at a set of read-outs on a screen.

"It's scheduled to become the standard in all human units in six months. It was the last thing I finished before the nova blasted university canned me." Timothy scowled.

"Small minds and petty bureaucrats. Fools, it is their loss. If the mouth-breathing students were such dullards that they couldn't keep up with your lessons, they shouldn't have been there in the first place." Pikeman patted Timothy's arm reassuringly.

"You two have hit it off," said Rowan.

"Your son is quite brilliant, Doctor Chandler. I hope you are suitably proud of him. Have you thought about my offer?" Pikeman prepared a long, slender instrument.

Rowan went red in the face. "Yes. I'll give you the cell sample and do your tests, but I want more of the work done in exchange."

"Tell your toy to stay out of this!" Pikeman glared at Ryan.

Ryan shrugged. "It's her life, and she is my ship's financial officer."

"Father, it isn't fair to expect everyone to believe the way you do. Doctor Pikeman shouldn't have to do business with a—"

A glare from Ryan silenced Timothy.

"Please call me Blair." Pikeman smiled at Timothy.

"Tim." Timothy smiled back at Pikeman, then turned to his father. "The point is, Dad, Blair has a right to deal with whom he wishes."

"We're the ones paying, an exorbitant amount, I might add! He's the one supplying a service. He deals with me!" Rowan's voice left no room for negotiation.

Timothy looked at Pikeman, rolled his eyes and shrugged.

"I will not pay more." Pikeman turned to Timothy. "What I will do is exchange another five thousand credits' worth of services if you do an update and maintenance on my equipment. A man of your talents rarely crosses one's path."

"Tim?" Ryan looked at his son.

Timothy smiled. "My pleasure. I'm interested in the way you've integrated alien equipment into the units anyway."

"Excellent. Now Rowan, unless you have some other objection, get up on the table and stop wasting my time! I'll take a cell culture today and prepare the stem cells. I'll also clean up those cancers. I'll need you back tomorrow for the first round of stem cell insertions."

Rowan passed Ryan her control-jamming pendant and climbed onto the examination table.

"Roll over. Intestinal cells are best for getting the culture started."

Rowan blushed and glanced at Timothy.

"Tim, would you mind?" asked Ryan.

Timothy rolled his eyes. "It's not as if I haven't done Farley's perspective."

Rowan blushed crimson.

"Tim!" There was menace in Ryan's voice.

"Fine. You really are delusional. You need help!" Timothy left the room.

"You should listen to your son. He makes a lot of sense." Pikeman watched as Rowan rolled over, then inserted the probe.

⌖⟡

Zelotes stood in the coffin-like simulation chamber that filled nearly half of his tiny office. He'd spent the morning test playing Data Corps' newest, combat-simulation game and had only just keyed out.

"Computer, memo record." He ran his pocket comb through his thinning, black hair and brushed the wrinkles out of the tracksuit he wore. Everything about him was forgettable, from his nondescript face to his medium build.

"Recording," replied a rich alto.

Zelotes rolled his eyes. "Computer. You will forgo inflections when you speak to me."

"Get nova blasted, twerp! The company contracted an AI for their operating system. I'm a person, so deal with it! And as far as that goes, the name's Quipna, try using it."

"Record message. Uppity silicone! The intensity alteration setting on the Mark 5 Kinetic Rifle should tend to slip after immersion in water. The mud in the Swampla simulation should have more of a rotting vegetation smell. Message ends. Computer, privacy."

Zelotes slumped into the office chair behind his tiny desk and pulled a plastic box from his drawer. He pressed a button on its side and opened his handheld.

"Handheld, open the U.E.S. news."

The headline jumped out at him.

'EMOTIONAL SURROGATE STOLEN FROM S.E.T.E. STUDIO ON GAEA!'

He read the article, clutching the handheld so tightly his knuckles turned white.

"This is wrong!" He glanced at a decimetre tall hologram of a plain woman in a cotton dress on the corner of his desk.

"They can't do this, Catharine. This thing can't foul the real universe. You gave up so much for God's law. They have to stop it before its foulness spreads."

Zelotes stared into his handheld. "Handheld, connect me to the Humans Ascendant temple."

Croell waited in a side passage. His regular health was restored. Down the main corridor, a cleaning robot gave the walls the first good clean they'd had in months.

The door, which supposedly led to a supply cupboard, opened and Ryan stepped into the hall, followed by Rowan and a *Homo sapiens* Croell didn't recognize.

"He is an amazing intellect. His biological knowledge is first-rate and the skill he applies to his trade…" the new human spoke.

"He twists and cripples beings," snapped Rowan as she nervously rubbed her pendant.

"Yes, and that is sad, though it's their choice to have it done. Better it be done by someone competent than some back-alley hack. The place to address that problem is in the self-image of the beings that choose to have the work done."

"He does have a point." Ryan took Rowan's hand as they walked.

"I guess." Rowan sniffed and stopped.

"What?" Timothy paused and looked at her.

Ryan froze, sniffing. "Batzoid."

"Where?" Timothy glanced around.

Croell stepped back in the passage. There was a faint click as his claws touched the floor.

"Hear that?" Ryan took a step towards the side passage.

"What?" asked Timothy.

"A click. It came from over there. Do you think it's another assassin out to get Pikeman?" Rowan stepped to Ryan's side.

"Could be. When batzoid take a vengeance geis, they keep coming until either they or their victim is dead. Tim, go back and warn your new best friend."

"Rowan should..." began Tim.

"You're not battle-hardened. Do what I say."

Tim moved to the door as Ryan and Rowan crept towards the side passage.

Croell flicked his tongue, then donning a vacant, ingratiating expression, strode into the main corridor.

"Greetings, fellow sentients. I hope the Great Flyer of the Skies finds you well today."

Ryan and Rowan watched the batzoid. It was a male and large for its kind, with jet-black neck scales and well-defined finger claws.

"Hello, have we met before?" Rowan shifted position to subtly block Croell's passage.

"Perhaps. I meet many beings in my service to the Great Flyer of the Skies. Have you heard of the Winged Way and the wonderful news of the relief from suffering and falsehood it brings?"

"Stardust!" Ryan and Tim spoke in unison and rolled their eyes. Tim moved to rejoin Ryan and Rowan.

"Thank you, no! We don't want any pamphlets and aren't

interested in attending a service." Ryan spoke with barely contained ire.

"But sir, the Great Flyer of the Skies has truth for all species and…"

Ryan took Rowan's hand and started walking. Tim fell in behind them.

Croell reached out to grab Rowan. Tim strode forward and knocked his arm. "Don't get grabby. I don't know how it is for batzoid, but you don't touch human females without their permission. We aren't buying what you're selling, so move on."

Croell's eyes glinted, then he flicked his tongue. "As you wish. May the Great Flyer of the Skies bless you."

Tim rolled his eyes and walked away.

"They are such a pain!" commented Ryan.

"One of the things I hated about Humans Ascendant was how they'd bother people door to door! Kerry would go out every second week. I went once, then refused. Divine, if you have something of value, people will come to you. You don't need to sell it," said Tim.

"Thank you for blocking his grab." Rowan smiled at Tim.

"Thank him." Tim gestured at Ryan. "By the time I was fourteen, he'd drilled it in that it was a man's job to protect women and children. It really gets the backs of some feminists up."

"Truth is truth." Ryan smiled at his son.

"Oh, so you think we poor helpless females need protecting by you big strong males." Rowan stared at Ryan.

"Not today, but we are what we evolved to be. It was a man's job to guard the tribe when we lived in caves because men were expendable." Ryan squeezed Rowan's hand.

"Pardon?" Rowan stared at Ryan.

"One man can conceivably impregnate a hundred women in a year. A woman can only carry one, maybe two, children to term a year. In a natural setting, men are expendable. Thus men were used to do high-risk tasks. Our larger size and greater strength evolved because of that."

"And today?"

"Doesn't really matter in most things, but we are what we evolved to be. Protector is a role bred into the core of the human male. Deny it, and it comes out twisted."

Rowan shook her head. "I don't know whether you're insightful or three thousand years behind the times. I guess it doesn't matter. What did that batzoid want anyway?"

"Evangelist." Ryan and Tim spoke in unison, sighed and shook their heads. Rowan was struck by how much alike father and son looked at that moment.

"They purposefully kept them out of Sun Valley. They figured that something that annoying wouldn't fly with the audience," said Ryan.

Croell waited until the *Homo sapiens* were out of sight and earshot, then looked at the device in his hand. The nanobots it had contained were gone. Zandra exited a side passage farther down the corridor and moved to his side.

"Did you infest her?" she asked.

"No, that other *Homo sapiens* got in my way. It is my punishment for pretending to be one of those annoying fools who ignore the many faces of the Great Flyer of the Skies."

"It was quick thinking. Rowan almost recognized you."

"I know. She is perceptive, for a *Homo sapiens*." Croell tapped his finger claws on the floor.

"Now what do we do?" Zandra rubbed her chin over Croell's back, then rested her head on his shoulder.

"We wait. I have set the nanobots to divide and infest. If the *Homo sapiens* I infested should touch Rowan or Pikeman in the next few days, he will infest them. If he does, we can activate the nanobots and let them do their work."

"But that would kill any being he touches. Beings we have no geis against. They will seek vengeance!" Zandra pulled away and looked at Croell with her beady, black eyes.

Croell flicked his tongue indulgently. "Trust me to know my business better than that, my love. The activation signal is short-range and directional. All we need do is wait until our intended targets are alone before we activate."

Zandra flicked her tongue. "That is wonderful. I am glad we will be able to fulfill our geis without killing Ryan. I have grown fond of him. He reminds me of you in many ways. And his insights into his role as a male are almost batzoid-like. If I had a sister, I'd be tempted to see if she liked bare skin."

"Oh really, a *Homo sapiens*, my love. This is a side of you I did not expect," teased Croell.

Zandra flicked her fangs straight and fluffed her wings. "They may be ugly and smell odd, but what's a female to do but dream when her husband neglects her?"

Croell laughed and rubbed his chin over her back. "Feeling neglected? I must see to that."

Zandra flicked her tongue, then spoke. "Shouldn't we follow Ryan and Rowan?"

Croell tapped his fore-claws. "No, it could be hours before the nanobots are transferred. Their trail will be easy enough to pick up. A stealthy hunt is a slow hunt. We have time."

Zandra flicked her tongue. "Then let us make use of it."

24

Willa locked the door behind her, then joined Gunther in their SUV.

"Are you sure this is wise, leaving such a light guard behind?" Willa did up her safety belt.

"Carl and Fran need to talk; their antagonism is adversely affecting the team."

Willa took Gunther's hand. "Are you sure that's the only reason you're pushing them together?"

Gunther looked at the road and pulled out of the driveway. "What do you mean?"

"If Carl and Fran get back together, my decision is made by default." Willa's voice was haunted.

"Is it wrong to love my wife?" demanded Gunther.

"No... no, it isn't." Willa kissed him.

Troy adjusted Willa's brain chemistry, enhancing the feeling of love she held for Gunther.

"Maybe if I push Carl and Fran. John is all tied up dealing with the publicity from Rowan's escape. Get them back together, and he'd have to drop the Carl/Willa affair." Smiling, Troy switched the main screen to Fran's perspective and began upping her arousal level.

Carl carried a tray with a teapot and mugs out of Gunther

and Willa's kitchen into the living room. Fran was sprawled across the sofa watching the television.

"The tea is steeping. What's on?" Carl sat in one of the twin loungers, keeping a safe distance from his ex-girlfriend.

"Nothing much. Channel one is a stupid sitcom, channel two is a documentary about Yellowstone, three is that show where teenagers are always killing vampires, as if. And four is doing the local news."

"Oh." Carl bit his lip. "Look, Fran... I'm—"

"You definitely are! She's twice your age and married. Cheating on me, that's bad enough. Maybe I could forgive that, but with Willa! Gunther dies inside each time you two go out. I don't know why, but he loves her, and you treated him like dirt."

"I wish it had been different. I wish..." Carl felt his desire surge up inside him. Fran was lying there, young and beautiful, her large, firm breasts straining against the fabric of her shirt, her legs visible where her skirt had hiked up.

"You wish what? That it was old times? That we were still together?" Fran sat on the couch. Her face was flushed, and beads of sweat appeared on her upper lip.

"I... you are beautiful," said Carl.

"I... NO! I won't do this! I won't be a slave... to my hormones." Fran came to her feet and walked away. Carl caught her arms. The next thing he knew, their lips were locked together.

"Good, one couple distracted." Troy shifted his screens to Farley and Quinta, who sat on a blanket in the basement of Gunther's house. Farley was gently brushing Quinta as she read aloud to him.

Farley paused in his brushing. "Did you hear that?"

Quinta put her book down and listened. "There was a thud and a faint moaning sound. I think Carl and Fran may be reconciling. I hope so, for Willa and Gunther's sakes."

"I hope they aren't late relieving us."

"If they are, they are." Quinta made a splashing motion with her paws and winked.

There was a smashing noise as something flew through the basement window, shattering the glass.

"GET DOWN!" Farley threw Quinta behind Gunther's medical equipment and lay on top of her. There was a popping sound, and the basement filled with smoke. Farley leapt to his feet and gasped as tears streamed from his eyes. There was the sound of squealing tires, and the door leading to the outside flew off its hinges. Farley stumbled to the entrance as a hulking, six-legged figure entered the room.

"K-no-ins," croaked Farley.

A glass pot of lithium grease lifted from the workbench and smashed into the figure blocking the doorway. The figure screamed, then fell to the ground. Another shadowy k-no-in form rushed into the room, driving Farley against a wall. Farley's head jerked back, there was a loud thunk, and he crumpled to the floor. The second k-no-in jerked as a dagger flew across the room and sank hilt-deep into its back.

Quinta tried to focus, but her eyes were burning, and she could barely breathe. She dispatched the k-no-in attacking Farley. She watched as two other k-no-in-shaped shadows grabbed the canvas bathtub containing Tony and rushed out. The door from upstairs opened. Two human forms pushed their way through the tear gas. One of them picked up Quinta, grunting with the effort, and carried her from the room.

"Missions accomplished. If Carl and Fran keep it up, maybe we can get back to making a decent show. John is such a prat!" Troy spared the screens for Gunther and Willa a glance. They were sitting hand in hand in a darkened theatre watching as some generic hero blew up the evil genius' base. He checked their empathic readings. They were deeply contented. "That is what it's supposed to be. Be happy. This mess will be fixed soon."

Armina lay in the back of Medwin's battered station wagon. The blanket over her fended off the evening chill, and if she'd bothered to rise, she would have seen the moon reflected in the lake through the front windscreen. She brushed a lock of her blonde hair away from her eyes and snuggled deeper into the nest of blankets. The side door opened, and Medwin jumped in, wearing only a pair of slacks.

"Sorry about that," he said as he slipped under the blanket.

"You're freezing. You shouldn't have had that large pop at the movie."

Medwin pulled his girlfriend's firm, naked body to his own and held her. "I can't think of a better way to warm up."

The sound of a vehicle intruded on their play. Headlights flashed into the car.

"I hope it's not the cops." Armina pulled her bra to herself.

Medwin lifted his head and watched as a van pulled past them and took the road that led down to the lake edge. "That's weird."

Armina held the blanket over herself and sat up. "What are they doing?"

The van had stopped by the lake and opened its back doors. As Medwin and Armina watched, something large was dumped into the water. It writhed in the shallows, then found its way to deeper water. The van started up the road.

"Lie down, pretend we didn't see anything." Medwin put action to word.

"What were they doing?" Armina let her lover hold her as the headlights lit their car, then moved on.

"I don't know, but I think I'll talk to my mum's friend Dave. He's a police detective. We might have found out why it's not safe to swim in the lake anymore."

"Should we call him now?"

Medwin let his hands stroll over his girlfriend's body. "Whatever they dumped has already swum off. I'll see him after work tomorrow."

"Sounds good." Armina kissed him. "I wonder how long before they have Ryan and Rowan doing what we're doing."

"Too bad we'll never see it. The actress who plays Rowan is almost as hot as you." He kissed her.

A long minute later, she replied. "I like Chow myself. There's something about a man in uniform."

"I was a boy scout."

"That counts."

Rowan sat in Kate's living room with Kitoy, Kate and Samantha. Samantha clung to Kitoy's leg like a vice.

"Is it goofla tonight?" asked Rowan.

"No, we *Homo sapiens* are having pizza. The furry among us are getting grrau-hiss-pa." Kate chanted the syllables of the last word.

"Kate, you didn't have to go to all that trouble." Kitoy stopped her light stroking of Samantha's head and flicked her tail.

"We know it's your favourite. They won't have it on a *Homo sapiens* world because *Homo sapiens* can't eat it. Maybe you should stay? We could have grrau-hiss-pa more often if you did." Samantha's voice was wheedling.

"Samantha, we talked about this." Kate's voice was kind but held an underlying firmness.

Rowan looked at the little girl and Kitoy, and her heart bled. "What exactly is grau hiss pa?"

Kitoy hissed with felinezoid laughter, and Kate smiled.

"What?" asked Rowan.

"Purple painted buttocks translates as purple painted buttocks," explained Kitoy.

"Huh?" Rowan looked confused.

"It's the translator, 'grau hiss pa' translates literally as 'purple-painted buttocks'. Since there's no equivalent *Homo sapiens* name for the item, the translator lets everyone hear the actual sounds you're making." Kate rolled her eyes as Kitoy continued to hiss. "It's a common mistake. For six months, I wondered why Saggal cracked up every time I said grrau-hiss-pa. Finally, one of these furry comedians let me in on the joke."

"You were so funny. I'd like an order of purple-painted buttocks, please." Kitoy hissed louder.

"It was embarrassing." Kate shook her head.

"So, what is..." Rowan paused.

"Grrau-hiss-pa, hold the r sound and rush the last two syllables. It's a type of fish native to worlds colonized by gopherzoids. It's mildly toxic to *Homo sapiens*. Felinezoids and otterzoids consider it a delicacy."

"It is delicious, but since the gopherzoids went extinct, you can only get it from the gopherzoid museum. The AI that runs the place farms it in the old aqua-park and sells a small quantity to help cover its expenses." Kitoy swished her tail.

"Museum?" Rowan leaned forward in her chair.

"When a species goes extinct, their sector on the Switchboard Station is transformed into a museum to commemorate their membership. One of their AIs is hired to act as a curator, and sections are set up to accommodate each multi-species habitat zone," explained Kate.

"Would have been nice if Ryan had shown me around a little." Rowan sighed and sat back in her chair.

"He probably thought you were overwhelmed enough dealing with the here and now without bothering you with history." Kitoy kinked the end of her tail.

"I like history. My school did a field trip to the gopherzoid museum. Did you know that ancient gopherzoids burrowed into cliff faces using stone tools to make their first cities? They were the best miners in the Republic, and they had night vision better than felinezoids but were practically blind in daylight." Samantha perked up as she expounded on the topic.

The door buzzer sounded. Kate moved to answer it. "Odd, I'm not expecting anyone else." The door retracted into the wall, revealing Murill. The teen's blue-grey fur was meticulously groomed, and he wore a formal, gold sash.

"Murill, what is it?" Kate stared at the young being whose tail was quivering in excitement.

"Hello, Mrs. Slingmaster. I read the information periodical today, and well... Rowan, the real Rowan, has escaped and is supposed to be on the station. It made me think of your friend and..." Murill fell silent when he saw Rowan on the couch.

"Murill, perhaps you should go home," said Kate.

"It's just, I love the show so much, and Rowan is my favourite, and to really meet her, it would be so... wow!"

"It's fine, Kate," said Rowan.

Kate motioned for Murill to enter.

"Are you really her?" Murill stood in front of Rowan, his eyes wide and his tail lashing back and forth in joy.

"I'm the Rowan from *Angel Black*."

"Wow, oh, wow! You are so pretty, just like in the e-entertainments. Would you, could I have your thumbprint?" Murill held out a scanner unit.

Rowan smiled as she placed her thumb on the scanner plate. "There you go."

"Wow, everyone in the fan club will be so jealous."

"Um, Murill. I'd like it if you didn't tell anyone about me. At least for a little while. I'm kinda on the run, and the fewer people who know, the better."

"Oh… sure, but… well, now that everyone knows you escaped, lots of people are going to put it together. You look too much like you not to be recognized."

Rowan sank onto the couch. "Stardust!"

"Your fans love you. I was talking to people at school today. Everyone thinks it's great that you're free. We'll miss you, but now you're in the real universe, and that's got to be better for you, and we still have the repeats. There's even some rumour that your escape was recorded, and they're coming out with a new show. Is that true?"

Rowan rubbed her temples. "Only up until when we left Gaea. Ryan arranged it so we could get help escaping. Once we launched, there would have had to have been a recording and relay unit on our ship to pick up the signal."

"That will be a great series. How much like the adventures you really had in the show are the episodes? Everyone says things get lost in the editing." Murill lashed his tail.

Rowan's expression became drawn. "My 'adventures'. You mean like the time that k-no-in killed my cat to get back at me for guarding what I thought was my planet? Or how about the times we got there too late, and I got to hold people as they died? Or maybe the adventure of watching the boy I had a crush on in grade ten get addicted to that damn alien drug. Did you enjoy those 'adventures'?"

Murill stepped back. "I'm sorry. I… I never thought. It seems so exciting as an e-entertainment."

Rowan sighed and shook her head, then smiled wearily at the young felinezoid. "Don't worry about it, Murill. Why would you see it from my perspective? Everybody, all your life, told you it was harmless fun. You never had to think of it as real."

Murill stepped forward and patted Rowan's shoulder. "Anything I can do to help you, let me know. Lots of the fan club feels the same way. We all love you. I guess we never realized what it must have been like for you. I'm sorry."

Rowan deliberately took Murill's hand and massaged the fur on its back. "Thank you. For now, just keep my secret, please."

Murill gazed at Rowan, his pupils wide. "Of course. If you need anything else, ask."

"Saggal will be here soon with dinner, so if you'll excuse us," said Kate.

"What, oh, yes." Murill pulled his eyes away from Rowan and wagged his tail. "Thank you." He bowed formally to the women and stepped out the door.

"I don't think he'll groom that hand for weeks," commented Kitoy.

"Do you think he'll keep his mouth shut?" asked Rowan.

"Yes, he's a nice, young male, but it won't matter. Now that the news is out, you'll get recognized."

"Great, so this is fame!" Rowan slumped on the couch.

Arlene sat beside Greg under one of the middle-aged oak trees that dotted the lawn in front of the S.E.T.E control building. Greg's green skin blended almost perfectly with the grass.

Arlene unwrapped a sandwich and opened it, revealing its contents. "Pastrami on whole wheat, again. What do you have?"

Greg laid his handheld on the grass and opened his briefcase, extracting a sandwich. "Peanut butter and jelly."

"What type of jelly?"

"I don't know. It'ss red."

"Tradesies?"

"With pleassure. I have got to make time to do the sshopping, but with the editing and ssorting the data from the Sswitchboard Sstation..." Greg shrugged.

"Tell me about it. If it wasn't for the rest of my group

taking over my chores, my place would be a complete disaster. Did you catch Michael's press conference?"

"Caught it ass I wass coming in thiss morning. That man playss the presss like a violin." Greg passed Arlene his sandwich and extracted a drink container from his briefcase.

"Did you manage to buy shares before the price went up?"

"What do you think I wass checking jusst now?"

"Where are they at?"

"Ten creditss a sshare and rissing."

"Nice. My whole group got in on it. When do you intend to sell?" Arlene took a bite of her sandwich, leaned back, and watched as the breeze rustled the leaves above her.

"I figure after the launch party for *Freedom'ss Run*. They sshould peak about then." Greg took a long swallow of juice.

"Too true, then crash and burn."

"You think sso?"

Arlene took another bite of her sandwich. "It's strawberry, by the way. You have to see what Michael is doing with *Freedom's Run*."

"A new political sschissm. Makes ssensse, but he won't bring the ssysstem down no matter how much Marcsy wantss him to."

"Why do you say Marcy wants him to?" Arlene stared at her companion.

"Pleasse, I've sseen her, and sshe's not the type to get plasstic ssurgery. I'm not that dumb!"

THE FUGITIVE

Rowan ate her pizza and tried not to look at the felinezoids who were, literally, licking the flesh off of fish that were reminiscent of large trout. Every once in a while, a fishbone would dislodge. A felinezoid would pluck it from their mouth and add it to a growing pile on the communal bone plate.

"Good grrau-hiss-pa. Too bad they weren't fresh," commented Saggal.

"Grrau-hiss-pa is always good, fresh, hung or frozen. You really shouldn't have bothered. This must have cost you a fortune." Kitoy took a long, slow lick of her fish.

"We can afford it. That coffee is antiproton. We've been able to sell the used grounds to this dive in the felinezoid sector for half what we paid for them originally. We're making a fortune, so don't worry."

Beep. Beep. Beep. Ryan's handheld sounded in his pocket. Frowning, he pulled it out, then looked at the screen.

"Please excuse me, I need to take this." Ryan moved into the living room. "What is it, Henry?"

"We got a problem." Henry's face appeared on the screen as it was before the android was mutilated.

"What else is new? You know, when I was pensioned out, I thought things would be easier. What's up?"

The screen filled with an official-looking document. "This just came in. It's an order of extradition on Rowan. They're charging her with theft."

"What? They can't. We're in the U.F.W. She has status as a Republic citizen."

"Not of her hot little self. They're charging her with stealing the clothes she wore out of the set region."

"Stardust!" Ryan buried his face in his hands. "And I tried so hard to avoid any Republic level offences. How could I have been so stupid?"

"Not that I would have minded the show, but what were you supposed to do, carry her out of the set region naked?"

"Nova blast. When does she have to appear?"

"She's to surrender herself for deportation immediately upon her receiving this message."

"And you contacted me here?" Ryan glared into his handheld's screen.

"You're sexy when you're pissed off." Henry's face appeared on the screen and leered at Ryan. "Relax, hottie boss. I've bounced this signal through so many junctions it would take a team of AIs a week to unravel it. No one's going to bother."

"What am I going to do? We can't run from the Republic."

"Don't know, but better figure something out. If they get sweetness into U.E.S. territory, her sexy little backside is toast. I got to sign off. Out." The screen went blank.

"Bad news, old friend?" Saggal stepped away from the entry door.

"They've charged Rowan with petty theft. They've got an order of deportation."

Saggal settled on the couch and tapped his claw tips together. "Then you must fight it."

"I'm no lawyer. Who could I find that knows anything about U.E.S. law that would take the case? Besides, she's supposed to surrender herself immediately. She has an appointment with Pikeman tomorrow, and if I know him, he won't give me credit for the cell culture he'll waste if she doesn't show up."

Saggal lashed his tail. "With this, I can help you. Kate and I know an excellent lawyer who is an expert in inter-species and U.E.S. law. She handles all the legal matters for ISLARA."

"I guess I'll have to find some way to afford her. Between the medical and legal bills, Rowan is the highest maintenance woman I've ever known. The nova blast of it is, it's not her fault. If I have to, I'll sell the *Star Hawk*. Do you need a waiter who's handy with a wrench?"

"Is Rowan worth that much to you?" Saggal's voice was serious.

"She is that and more. Saggal, you and I have both seen too much death. I know how much blood is on my hands. You blow up equipment, take out that tank or spaceship, but what you're really doing is slaughtering the beings inside the machine. We both tell ourselves it was our duty, but still. Somehow when I'm with Rowan, I feel clean again. I feel like I could lick the universe. I feel... I don't know how to describe it."

Saggal lashed his tail. "You do not have to. I too am a male in love. Let me call Victoria. Her husband may be of some use here as well. He's a U.E.S. ambassador. We'll find a way, old friend. We always do." Saggal lashed his tail, and his nostrils flared. "Hop hop Kanga, watch a wallaby woo."

Ryan snorted as a smile came to his lips. "We did that much that was good. Last I read, their population was topping five thousand."

"Six, and they're experimenting with circular rollers." Saggal wagged his tail.

Rowan stood in the hall out of sight of Ryan and Saggal and listened.

"...rollers," finished Saggal.

Rowan's lip trembled. "You won't lose the *Star Hawk*. I won't let that happen. Divine, get off your duff and do something. You brought us together, so give us a break."

"Who are you talking to?" Graff walked up behind her.

Rowan jumped. "You startled me!"

"Sorry. Mum wants to know if she should serve dessert. We're having ice cream. There's tuna fish, vanilla and chocolate."

"Ask Ryan and your father."

"Ask us what?" Ryan appeared behind Rowan. She jumped.

"Should Mum serve dessert?" Graff looked at his father, who towered behind Ryan.

"Yes, but I have to make a call first." Saggal stepped around Ryan, Rowan and Graff and moved down the hall.

"Rowan, you know how you don't want me to keep things from you. Well, we have another problem," said Ryan.

Rowan kissed him, then rested her head on his shoulder. "We'll deal with it, my love." She felt Ryan's posture straighten and could almost feel a power flow through him. *Maybe that is the Divine's answer,* she thought.

Tim wandered through the gopherzoid museum. The fading images of a dead race's glory seemed fitting companions with his present mood. Ryan had relayed Saggal's dinner invitation, but he'd begged off.

"They are so... human," he whispered to himself as he gazed at an exhibit depicting a gopherzoid stepping out of a primitive spacecraft onto their homeworld's natural satellite. Several lines of text were below the image. Tim read the *Homo sapiens* script.

> In peace we came, in peace we left, expanding the cavern of existence for all gopherzoid kind.

Tim snorted. "I wonder if Rowan's original saw humans'

first moon landing?"

He moved to the next panel, depicting the dismantling of the gopherzoid lunar preserve around the first landing site so that the next species to develop space travel from their homeworld would find a pristine environment. He stared at the desolate moonscape.

"Does it matter when in the end, it all means nothing? Maybe he's right. If she makes him happy. Maybe the neuro-static energy is the soul." Shaking his head, he moved to the next exhibit, which depicted a cross-cut view of a habitat burrowed into a lunar surface. The caption under it read:

> 'Forward we dig, making progress and growing to embrace a universe more wondrous and diverse than our imaginations can contemplate.' Inauguration speech of Scrit Scrit Crunch, first Administrative Director of gopherzoid Lunar One.

Tim plodded on.

Rowan stood as Saggal led Bill and Victoria into his living room.

"Vicky, Bill. I'm so glad you could come. We have a situation. These are our friends Ryan and Rowan, and you know Kitoy." Kate moved to meet her guests.

"Happy to do it. ISLARA members have to stick together." Vicky set a large briefcase on the floor.

Rowan glanced at Ryan. His eyes were glued to the stunning brunette.

"It's a pleasure. Saggal filled me in on your situation. You've had quite an adventure." Vicky held her hand out to Rowan. Rowan took it and smiled at the other woman.

"A little too much adventure. It's nice to meet you."

Vicky grinned, then turned to Ryan. "And you must be Captain Chandler. I've read your logs about the disaster on Murack Five. It is an honour to meet the man who saved the kangazoids."

Ryan shuddered at the mention of Murack Five, but took the proffered hand. "Thank you."

"Let's get right to it, shall we? I'll need to see a copy of the deportation order."

"I'll want to look at that as well." Bill moved to stand beside his wife. "By the way, hello. Vicky forgets manners sometimes when she gets an interesting case."

Vicky rolled her eyes. "He's so sensitive."

Ryan passed her his handheld with the deportation order on the screen. Vicky scrolled down it at an impossible speed, then passed it to Bill, who read it at a much slower pace.

"First off, are you sure the message's delivery cannot be traced?" asked Vicky.

"Yes." Ryan noted how she stood completely still, weight balanced, posture perfect. A smile touched his lips.

"Good! As an officer of the court, I am technically obliged to report you, but what they don't know can't hurt me. Erase and overwrite the file as soon as we're done here."

"Obliged to report," interrupted Saggal.

"In a strict sense of the word, Rowan is a Republic fugitive, though so long as it can't be proven that she's received the message, it's a moot point." Vicky spoke in a no-nonsense voice.

"Is it illegal for her to be here?" demanded Kate.

"Strictly speaking, you are harbouring a fugitive, but it really is a moot point."

"Why don't I get us some tea? Kitoy, can you give me a hand in the kitchen?" suggested Kate. She and Kitoy left the room.

"Good idea," agreed Bill.

Rowan settled onto the couch. Vicky sat beside her

while Bill slumped into a lounger.

"Ryan, can I have a word?" Saggal motioned for Ryan to follow him into the hall.

"Of course." Ryan kissed Rowan's hand. "It will be all right. I think we lucked out with Vicky taking our case." Smiling, he followed Saggal from the room.

Bill looked up from reading the deportation order. "It's in order. There isn't much I can do from my end."

"I wasn't expecting much," said Rowan.

"Too bad, really. I was raised on Silvanus. In short, I'm on your side."

Rowan smiled. "Good to know. Actually, it's kinda nice to sit with you and Vicky. It's reassuring to be reminded that most couples are matched for species." Rowan blushed. "Don't get me wrong, I mean, Kate and Saggal are one of the nicest couples I've ever met, but I've been spending so much time around ISLARA members."

"Gives you a bit of perspective of what they go through all the time, doesn't it?" Bill's eyes twinkled with mischief.

"A bit, I suppose. It must be hard. It's nice to see that love can win through."

"Bill, could you bring me my case, please." Vicky spoke without moving anything but her mouth.

Bill smirked as he fetched the case. "Of course, my love."

Vicky reached down and pulled a long cable with a jack on the end out of the case's side. She grinned as she pushed the jack up her nose.

Rowan winced. "What?"

"I hate to tell you, Rowan. You and Ryan are still the only vanilla couple in the place," said Bill.

Rowan blushed. "Oh... I'm sorry. I meant no offence. I..."

"You haven't offended me. I'm an AI. My real name, well, as much of it as a *Homo sapiens* can hear, is Vstormeya." Vicky sang the syllables in a clear soprano.

"Wow, I never would have guessed. You are beautiful."

"Thank you. Vicky let me pick the chassis. I went for a

CC-F and have never regretted it," said Bill as he took a seat.

"A... oh, you're patterned after a clone from the e-entertainments." Rowan's smile froze on her face as her tone became forced.

"My base chassis is a Luba adapted to accommodate my core processor. To make room for my CPU and RAM, we had to sacrifice the appearance adapting capacity of the Luba. It was cheaper to fix it into one of its preprogrammed forms and lock it there," explained Vicky. Her eyes fluttered, accessing U.E.S. case law.

"Should I be quiet and let you think?" Rowan couldn't take her eyes off the cable up Vicky's nose.

"No need. The case is a portable data storage and RAM expansion. There's no way to fit all my files into this chassis, so I've put most of my memories into deep storage on external drives. For your case, I need to check the entirety of *Homo sapiens* law, so that's what I'm doing. Sifting out the pertinent files. It will take a few minutes. Please keep chatting, this material is dry, and I could stand the distraction."

"Oh, umm... You know, when I first saw you, I thought you looked familiar. You... I mean, oh, you know what I mean, works for the fire department. She came to my high school to do a fire safety lecture."

"Willow from *The Station House*." Bill sighed. "I love the CC-F chassis."

"I still don't know why you experience that show. Willow has so many intimacy issues it's embarrassing to look like her!" There was ire in Vicky's voice.

Ryan followed Saggal into a small study. A low desk with a felinezoid cushion-chair in front of it occupied one wall while a display of felinezoid weapons and military awards filled the others.

Saggal shifted uncomfortably from foot to foot and lashed his tail. His claw tips popped and retracted from their sheaths.

"Saggal, what is it?" Ryan looked up at his old friend's slit-pupil eyes.

"Ryan, you know I hold you as a brother, and I am fond of Rowan."

Ryan braced himself before replying. "I hear a but."

"My friend, when you and Rowan only had U.E.S. charges pending against you, it wasn't a problem, but now... Ryan, I will not put my family at risk for you. Right now, I am harbouring a fugitive from Republic justice. Even if they can't prove it. I'm sorry, but you have to get Rowan out of here!"

Ryan stared at the big felinezoid. Annoyance gave way to resolve in less than a second. "You've already done more than I could have hoped. I'll find someplace for Rowan to stay."

"I feel awful doing this. I owe you my life, and if it was only me—"

"A male has to protect his wife and children first. Rowan and I will leave after tea. That should keep Kate from suspecting."

"Thank you. I know Kate would fight me on this. She is fond of you and Rowan, but I can't take risks with the children."

⌖⟶

Kitoy poured water into the samovar and turned it on. "Kate, you can make tea on your own. What did you want to talk to me about?"

Kate looked worried. "You read *Homo sapiens* too well. Kitoy, Rowan can't go back to the *Star Hawk*."

"And with a Republic charge, she can't stay here. I know, Kate. Friendship only goes so far."

"I'm glad you can see that. Saggal is so honourable, I

know he'd fight me on this, but I can't take risks with the children."

"They can stay at my apartment. I was going to sleep there tonight, say goodbye to the place. It will be cramped, but it means you won't be harbouring a fugitive, and I can say I didn't know."

"You are a good friend. I hate having to turn her out, but I feel better knowing she has someplace to go."

"Things will be well. Vicky's the best."

Kate placed the samovar and cups on a tray and picked it up. "I hope so."

Ryan sat beside Rowan on the couch, sipping a cup of tea. Rowan nibbled on a carrot stick. Kitoy sat on Ryan's other side while Saggal and Kate shared a lounger. Bill sat in the other lounger while Vicky stood beside him with the cable from her portable RAM expansion, added-memory unit still in her nose.

"I was on my first assignment with the diplomatic corps stationed at the embassy on Swampla. Vicky was working a contract as the embassy administrative AI," said Bill.

"He was so adorable. Naive, inexperienced, but he talked to me like a person. At first, I didn't understand why he always turned to face the building's centre when he spoke with me, then I realized he was trying to show respect. That won him major points. No offence, but a lot of *Homo sapiens* treat AIs like we were fancy toasters."

"She was the most intelligent being in the embassy and had the best sense of humour. She was also the second-best chess player." Bill smirked.

Vicky rolled her eyes. "You biologics with your messy minds. He kept blindsiding me, making moves that made no sense, then checkmating me out of the blue."

"You always had the better stories, my silicone wonder." Bill reached out and took his wife's hand.

"Living fifty thousand Earth years gives one a lot of experience to draw from."

"Fifty thousand," gasped Rowan, then she blushed. "Um… you sure don't look it."

Everyone laughed, then Vicky continued. "To make a long story short, we fell in love with each other's minds. Then my contract was up. I'd never emulated a *Homo sapiens*. I mean, you haven't been around that long, so we discussed it. I paid for a chassis that we could adapt to accommodate my core processor, and the rest is history." Vicky gazed at Bill with a very human expression of devotion. "I sometimes miss having all my mind in one place, but I'm enjoying the experience overall." Vicky winked suggestively at her husband. Bill blushed. "You *Homo sapiens* are a strange species, but you know how to laugh. I like that."

"I'm curious, which species did your core's initial construction?" asked Ryan.

"The Vrdjkf." The impossible combination of sounds flowed from Vicky's mouth without a hitch. "I was one of the last units they made before dying out. Now, there were a bunch of uptight, humourless beings. No sense of… I'm finished reviewing the data."

"What should we do?" demanded Ryan.

"The best-case scenario is Rowan is convicted." Vicky's voice was pure professionalism.

Ryan leapt to his feet. "What? Have you slipped a cog? If Rowan goes into U.E.S. territory for even a second, they'll grab her. She isn't a person there."

Vicky smiled. "But that's the point. To be convicted of a crime, you must be a person. They can't have it both ways. If she is convicted, they are saying she is a person, and so must be treated as one."

"So, they couldn't give her back to S.E.T.E?" Ryan's voice was hopeful.

"If they convict her, she'll be sent to a prison facility for her sentence. All they are charging her with is petty theft with a maximum sentence of one hundred standard days. During that time, they would be obliged to supply her with all necessary medical care to preserve and maintain her life and wellbeing."

"I'd be a person legally?" Rowan bit her lip as she tried to wrap her head around the implications.

"Yes, and I'd launch an immediate suit on your behalf against S.E.T.E. for back wages and illegal imprisonment. It would also set precedence for all other studio clones."

"Suppose they lay other charges, like firing on a U.E.S. ship?" Ryan returned to his seat.

"I'll get those dismissed. You were in command, and she wasn't operating the guns. No, if it was you, that would have been challenging. You racked up an amazing array of criminal charges, most of which have been dropped, by the way. The only warrant outstanding on you is firing on a U.E.S. vessel. Apparently, someone on Gaea likes you. Oh yes, I took the liberty of checking. You have an A credit rating, all your outstanding debts have been paid, though your credit lines have also been cancelled. I will accept deferred payments for my fee if you use your ship as collateral."

"Thank you, Michael," breathed Ryan.

"That was the best-case scenario," said Kitoy.

Vicky looked grave. "The worst is they get her into U.E.S. territory for trial, then acquit her on the grounds that she is not a person. If that occurs, they can grab her the moment the gavel comes down, and there is nothing I can legally do about it. I'd place a complaint with the Republic Justice Committee, but it would be months before it would be heard and by then..."

"By then, I'm dead." Rowan wrung her hands.

"It doesn't make sense that they're doing this. There are Republic member states that are violently opposed to the way *Homo sapiens* use clones. Just having the charge placed against Rowan will give their position credence. As much as I'm for equality, this is going to be a major headache for me." Bill massaged his brow.

"Crapper!" spat Ryan.

"Down the hall and to the left," said Vicky.

"What? Oh, sorry. No. Captain Graham Crapper of the *Chimera*. The man's an idiot, and that makes him dangerous."

"I've met him. Your assessment is correct. Sad really, his father isn't a bad sort, hyper-conservative but competent in his own way," said Bill.

"What do we do?" Rowan stared at Vicky.

"I think you and Ryan should sleep at my on-station apartment. So that you can deny having seen the extradition order until after you see Pikeman for treatment," said Kitoy.

"That's very generous, Kitoy, but isn't it a little obvious?" cautioned Vicky.

"What? That the pervert who likes *Homo sapiens* would have two of them over to play with? Stardust, I'm already sick enough that I married a male *Homo sapiens*. Why wouldn't I be interested in female skin as well?" Kitoy's tail lashed. "For once, small-minded bigotry can work for us. Besides, I can think of worse things than having people believe Ryan, Rowan and I are a triple." Kitoy swished her tail flirtatiously.

Ryan and Rowan shifted uncomfortably.

"Good, that will buy us nearly a week to plan," said Vicky.

"A week?" asked Rowan.

"You have to be fit to stand trial. I've seen beings after major stem-cell insertions. It will be at least that long before you are fully recovered." Vicky smiled. "Serves them right to foot the bill for your care after pulling this stunt."

"Then it's an op." Ryan bared his teeth in a smile. Everyone in the room except Kate and Rowan shifted uncomfortably. "I like ops. Ops I know!"

HURTING HEARTS, HEALING MINDS

Crapper sat in his study and read the message on the wall for the third time.

To Major **Idiot**, *acting* Captain Crapper!

ARE YOU BRAIN DAMAGED? Diplomacy is ready to go nova! They've had petitions from five Republic member states demanding to know why, if Rowan is not a person under our law, we are filing an extradition petition. The whole point was to defuse this situation, *QUIETLY!*

Do you not grasp the concept of civil litigation? If Rowan is declared a person, she can't be property. If she isn't legal property, no studio surrogate is. They're all in a position to sue. You may have single-handedly caused the bankruptcy of an interplanetary corporation and a major source of export revenue for the U.E.S. I don't care how, fix this, and ***do it quietly***!

Admiral Yvonne C. LaFleur.

Crapper opened his desk drawer and extracted a bottle of amber liquid. He stared at it for a long moment, then put it back.

"I'll make Chandler pay for this! Make me look bad, will

he? One thing's for sure, he'll never see his fakey slut again.

"Genghis, get me Commander Hammerman, that fool's idea has backfired. I want the pleasure of telling him personally. Has Rowan been apprehended yet?"

"No, sir. Rowan is still at large. The troops you posted to watch the hangar bay holding the *Star Hawk* report that she hasn't returned, and there is no record of her having received the extradition notice." The AI sounded smug.

"Nova blasted aliens can't do anything right! Genghis, put a call into the civil authorities. I want Rowan on this ship the moment she enters U.E.S. territory."

"Sir, I must remind you that civil law enforcement is an independent branch of the U.E.S. government. You have no authority to command their actions."

Crapper slammed his beefy hand down on his desktop. "Then get me the Chief of Police. I'll make that arrogant ass give her up."

The tone in Genghis' voice was unmistakably amused. "This should be interesting, sir."

⌖

Rowan followed Kitoy into her apartment. The single large room was stripped of all personal effects, leaving only a large cushion in the middle of the floor. Ryan followed her in. The door slid shut behind him.

"It isn't much, but I used to call it home. I'm glad they're sending a cleaning robot down the passage. It was filthy!" Kitoy lifted off her sash and hung it on a wall hook.

"Thank you for doing this." Rowan's eyes roved over the walls, which were set to display a desert terrain.

"I'm part of your crew now. Crews stick together." Kitoy threw herself onto the large cushion. "I'm going to miss this. *Homo sapiens* beds aren't as comfortable."

"I'll strip out the couch bed in your quarters and install a cushion if you buy one," offered Ryan.

Kitoy's nostrils trembled. "That's all right, I'll make do. We'd better get some sleep; tomorrow is going to be busy."

"Where's the…" Rowan's gaze quested over the walls.

Kitoy's tail swished back and forth as she pointed to a door. "Right there, be sure and bury it when you're done. I changed the litter last week."

Rowan looked horrified.

Kitoy rolled on the bed, hissing with laughter. "Got you!"

Ryan shook his head. "Rowan, see for yourself."

Rowan tentatively opened the door. Within were a sink and toilet almost identical to *Homo sapiens* units.

"Furry comedians." Rowan imitated Kate, which triggered another fit of laughter from Kitoy. Rowan entered the washroom and closed the door.

"Why don't you get comfortable? I know *Homo sapiens* find it a little hot in the felinezoid sector." Kitoy watched Ryan as she lounged on the bed.

"Thanks." Ryan took off his shoes, then pulled off his golf shirt, leaving him clad only in his shorts. He sat on the edge of the cushion.

"You have a nice musculature," commented Kitoy. "You and Rowan match each other well for looks."

Ryan shifted to look at Kitoy. Her pupils were dilated, and she lounged provocatively. "Kitoy, Rowan and I…"

"It wouldn't have to affect the two of you. I… Rowan would be more than welcome to join us. I discovered when I was still an agent, I can enjoy the touch of a female *Homo sapiens*. I think she's beautiful. I think you're beautiful. It's been a long time, and… I've been so lonely since Kadar was arrested. You and Rowan have been kind to me. Aren't either of you even a little curious?"

Ryan patted Kitoy's shoulder. "If I didn't have Rowan, I'd be interested, but I'm not wired for a group relationship. I'm too possessive. In love, I have to focus on one person and have them focus on me. The offer is tempting, but the answer has to be no."

Kitoy's nostrils flared as her pupils widened, but her

voice was gentle. "I understand. Ryan, if you mean what you said... I know this is awful, and I don't wish any bad on her, but... Well... If Rowan doesn't survive, or ever leaves you, remember, I am interested, and I know what it's like to lose a love. I won't betray a friend, but I can be a special friend if and when you need one."

"Thanks." Ryan briefly caressed the back of Kitoy's hand.

The door to the bathroom opened, and Rowan stepped out wearing only her bra and panties. Ryan felt his breath catch in his throat.

"It's a relief to strip down; it's so hot around here. Are there spare beds, or do we all pile on like a group of kittens?" Rowan smiled.

"My possessions are all on the *Star Hawk*," explained Kitoy.

Rowan jumped onto the cushion and hugged Ryan from behind. "My man, all mine!" Rowan shot a slightly frosty smile at Kitoy.

Ryan swallowed, realizing that Rowan had heard every word he and Kitoy had shared.

Kitoy swished her tail sadly. "Yes, all yours."

Rowan patted Kitoy's shoulder, then settled herself in the middle of the cushion.

Obert lay in a king-sized bed, staring at the ceiling.

"That was nice. I'm so glad I bumped into you." Carol trailed her fingers over his chest.

"I can't believe this. I had such a crush on you when we were in the high school science-fiction club together." Obert turned so he could stare at the beautiful redhead.

"Big difference between a grade nine and a grade twelve. It's not so bad now." She kissed her lover, then cupped his cheek in her hand.

"Carol... I... I hope I didn't disappoint you. I mean... You were my first... I..." Obert found himself silenced by her kiss. It was sweet, compassionate, and so different from the mad passion of a few moments before.

"I guessed. It was part of the turn-on. You aren't awful, but there's a lot you can learn. No one's great the first time, though you were very enthusiastic." Carol smiled sexily. "I'd be willing to play teacher to your naughty student, if you like?"

Obert swallowed as his youthful stamina made itself known. "Um... I'd like that."

"Good, so would I. I always thought you were a cute kid, and you've grown into quite a sexy man." Carol's expression became serious. "I have some friends I'd like you to meet. Are you free tomorrow evening?"

"I have focus group till five, but after that."

"Good. Tell your parents you won't be home." Carol kissed him. "I have to shower. I'm supposed to meet some friends from work." She checked the clock by the bed. "Care to join me for your first lesson?"

"A warrant for her arrest." Zelotes turned his back on the print that filled one wall of his four-metre by four-metre, one-room dwelling. "They're treating that filthy fakey like it was human." He gazed at the face of Catharine that filled another wall. "How can God let that evil thing walk around free when he took you? How?" He slammed his fist into his hand. "After all we went through." He turned back to the wall. "Implication a person under the law," he read aloud.

Ryan held Rowan's hand as they entered Pikeman's treatment room.

"There you are!" Timothy wore a lab coat and stood at the console of Pikeman's nanobot manufacturing unit.

"I'm sorry we didn't call," said Ryan.

"It was very rude of you. Tim was quite beside himself. He even contacted the authorities." Pikeman stood beside Timothy and watched a screen on the nanobot manufacturing unit. "How will it sustain energy levels once it's inserted into the body?"

"With this to augment the sugar processors, it's my own design." Timothy's hand flew over the controls.

"Brilliant, it will actually use cholesterol as a fuel source." Pikeman moved close to Timothy, who was too absorbed by his work to notice.

Ryan moved so he could see the screen. "Good solid design, so long as you're confined to a liquid medium. Another digit opposed to the one on the bottom would increase its versatility."

"And make it too large to enter many of the regions it is required to work in. These are bio-units, not some crude ship repair system." Pikeman snorted, then laid a hand on Timothy's shoulder. "It's fine work, a brilliant design."

Timothy pressed a button, saving the design on the computer's memory. "Thank you. Just remember, technically, the university has rights to the technology, even though I designed it, so don't tell anyone I gave it to you."

Pikeman slid his hand off Timothy's shoulder and squeezed his arm. "Not a word."

Tim shifted uncomfortably when Pikeman didn't remove his hand. "You can try them out with Rowan."

"Try them out, son?" Ryan's voice betrayed concern.

Tim moved so that Ryan was between him and Pikeman. "It's a tested design, Dad. Twice as efficient as the hemorrhage control/micro-debreedment nanos you're used to."

Ryan looked at Rowan. She shrugged and said, "I'm just a little old primitive from the backwoods."

"At least it admits it," stated Pikeman. "The table is sterilized. Lay down, and we'll proceed with the cerebral stem-cell insertions." He turned to Ryan. "You do realize it will be incapacitated for a week or more after this procedure."

"I know," said Ryan.

"You will require nursing assistance. I can arrange for that for an additional fee." Pikeman moved to a boxy piece of equipment with a mechanical arm ending in a long needle coming off its side.

"We have it covered." Rowan lay down on the table as Ryan moved to her side.

"With qualified personnel to monitor her condition? I will not be held accountable for mistakes caused by incompetent home care."

"We have it covered," said Ryan as Rowan passed him her pendant.

"You'll be wanting to hire a gurney to return her to your vessel in that case." Pikeman looked smug.

"I brought a gurney from the *Star Hawk*." Ryan looked Pikeman in the eye.

"As you wish." Pikeman adjusted several dials on the device in front of him. "This will tingle."

Rowan had a sensation like ten thousand ants crawling over her scalp, then her hair fell off and seemingly crawled into a container on the side of the examination table.

"What?" she gasped as she ran her fingers over her bald pate.

"I need a clean and sterile field to work on. I'll have the nanos put it back when I'm done."

"At the studio, they sent a catheter in through the foramen magnum," observed Ryan.

"And if I had a dedicated, cerebral, stem-cell insertion system, so would I. I do not have access to any such piece of equipment. I must make do with a general-purpose stem cell insertion unit. Given that, I will have to drill through her skull and repair the damage when I am finished. Now, both of you shut up and let me work. Tim, why don't you come over here? You may well find this interesting."

Tim flushed slightly and shifted uncomfortably from foot to foot. "Um. I should monitor the nanobot creation system for this first run."

Pikeman sighed. "You know your own business. Now to anaesthetize the patient."

Rowan remembered a pattern of multi-coloured lights, then nothing.

Croell flicked his tongue as he watched the handheld monitor screen.

"One of the other *Homo sapiens* is infested," remarked Zandra, who stood with her chin resting on Croell's shoulder.

"Yes. Now we must wait for our prey to be isolated to find out if it has reached our target."

There was a scuttling sound down the passage. Croell whipped his head around to see its cause.

A pair of k-no-ins were getting in the way of a maintenance robot that was trying to clean the walls. Every time the device moved to one side, they would jump in front of it, forcing it to double back.

Croell tapped his claws on the floor and passed Zandra the monitor screen. "Excuse me, beloved."

Zandra flicked her tongue at him, then turned her attention to the screen's read-out.

Croell tucked his wings in and strolled down the hall. "Good sentients, please let the robot do its work. This sector's halls are in desperate need of cleaning."

The two k-no-ins glanced at Croell.

"Go 'sodomize your mother without paying a pleasure price', batzoid," snapped the larger k-no-in.

"You are behaving disgracefully." Croell walked up and, using his own body, blocked the k-no-in so the robot could get by. The robot sped down the corridor, then started cleaning the walls.

"You 'one who fails the breeding test by a large margin due to mental insufficiency'."

Croell tapped his claws on the deck and started back towards Zandra.

"That's right, run away to your 'female that is so unattractive and bad-smelling she cannot get partners for free though she advertises much,' you coward. You can—"

The big k-no-in froze as Croell turned, leapt and landed on its back with his finger claw digging into a soft spot on its neck.

"My wife is a beautiful female with an extremely pleasant odour. On Petteron, her parents would have received many petitions for her favour. Apologize, then leave this place."

Croell spared a glance at a noise behind him. The other k-no-in was racing away.

The k-no-in under Croell broke wind with a sound like a tuba. "I am sorry. I am sure she is a great beauty, and you are most fortunate to be her regular client."

Croell climbed down from his enemy's back. "True, now leave us."

The k-no-in raced after its companion.

"You are so civic-minded." Zandra rubbed her chin over her husband's back.

"I hate petty criminals. To obstruct a cleaning robot for the pleasure of doing so. I don't understand it. There is no service to the Great Flyer of the Skies in it."

"It does seem foolish. Look, a third being has been infested." Zandra turned her gaze back to the screen.

Ryan winced as the drill screeched against Rowan's skull. Her bald scalp had been sliced away and peeled back, revealing the bone underneath. The bone dust and chips moved across the examination table to a reservoir, carried by an invisible army of nanobots. The drill stopped.

"You okay, Dad?" Tim stared at his handheld's screen. A tube coming out of the side of the medical bench pumped fluid into Rowan's arm. He waved the handheld over where the needle pierced her skin.

"I'm remembering why I prefer machines," said Ryan. "How are the nanos?"

"Working perfectly." Tim smiled. "I've set them to automatic operation. You won't be able to control them like you did the old ones. They'll become an integrated part of her body's maintenance system."

"A vast improvement over older systems," said Pikeman as he operated a control.

The needle on the robotic arm slipped into the hole in Rowan's skull, sinking nearly a decimetre into her brain. Pikeman hit another button, and there was the sound of a pump as the needle slowly pulled from the wound.

"This stem cell insertion will be the last for the cerebellum. If you like, and have the payment in advance, I could do the ones to restore her bone marrow, liver and kidneys in three or four days. She'll need that long to regain her strength."

Ryan looked at the monitor board showing Rowan's vitals. Several of the readings were tipping into the orange.

"I doubt that it will be that soon."

"As you wish. I'll want to begin testing her telekinesis the beginning of next week." Pikeman worked a control. A fluid flowed into the container holding the bone chips and dust. He moved to the examination table and, picking up a pencil-like instrument attached by a tube to the table, dabbed a filler made of Rowan's own bone and adhesive into the drill holes.

27

OFFICER, COULD YOU LEND ME A SNOUT, PLEASE

John sat on his trendy leather couch and stared at the message on the wall.

To: John Wilson, Assistant Producer *Angel Black*

From: Michael Strongbow, Chief Studio Executive, Executive Producer *Angel Black*.

The following matters of importance need to be addressed.

1. Republic deportation request for Rowan may result in citizenship status being extended to emotional surrogates. Possible destruction of legal basis for all e-entertainments. Spin control for this is a must.

2. Projected audience dissatisfaction with Willa/Carl and Toronk/Fran affairs far outweighs audience appeal of said relationships. Therefore, by executive directive, these affairs are to no longer be encouraged vis-a-vis bio-manipulation. Bio-manipulations are to be used to reinforce the Gunther/Willa relationship.

3. Due to depletion in numbers of antagonist surrogates, because of an overzealous body count at the beginning of season seven, a

storyline involving an alien disease is to be instituted to allow time for the facilities to make new antagonists before fatal encounters are reinstated.

4. The inventory shows that the batzoid characters Croell and Zandra are missing. Locating these characters and making an example of those behind their theft is the highest priority for restoring investor confidence.

5. A meeting is called for oh-eight-hundred Monday to address story points and areas of audience appeal.

"Nova blast! If he suspects I sent Croell and Zandra after Rowan, I'm finished for sure. I'll kill that Divine forsaken fakey!" John took a large gulp of his hangover remedy.

"You need leverage," said a voice from the door to the bedroom.

John turned to stare at a woman who looked like a blonde, middle-aged Rowan. She was dressed in a black, form-fitting dress.

"Why are you still here?" John turned back to the message.

"You're being a little short with me, considering." The woman smirked. "Of course, you were a little short last night too."

"Funny. I should have rented a Luba."

"Could have, Johnny. My Mary look hasn't been updated in a long time. Of course, it's not Mary that turns your crank now, is it? Calling me Rowan was tacky. I outgrew wanting to emulate e-entertainers years ago. I guess you never got over wanting to be with them. Believe me, I thought I'd get better from a big-time producer."

"I have real problems to deal with. Why don't you leave?"

The woman moved to the couch and sat. "Without a good morning kiss."

John rolled his eyes and moved to kiss the woman. She pulled away.

"Please, last night was bad enough, and you still stink of rye. Something you would have known, if you'd bothered to ask instead of pretending I was a fakey, is I'm a lawyer. Right about now, you need one."

"I already have an attorney." John scowled at the woman.

"Not like me!" said the woman.

"What makes you so special?"

"I'm hurt. You don't even remember my name." The woman stared at John with mock distress.

"What? I'm too hung over to play guessing games."

The woman smiled. "I'm Hilda, Hilda Strongbow. I never bothered to change it after the divorce."

"Strongbow like in—"

"Exactly. Did you think I picked you up because of your looks?" Hilda rolled her eyes. "Talk about delusional! It's been forty years since Michael dumped me for that slut. He goes on to become one of the richest men on the planet. I get stuck with a two-room law practice on the lower floors of the Duchovny Tower."

"And this helps me how?" demanded John.

"Two ways. One, I'm motivated. Truth to tell, I couldn't care less about Mike; that's ancient history, and if I'd caught him with another man, I would have ended it too. I accepted that I made my own bed in that regard a long time ago. The money is another matter. That I want. Two, while I can't prove it legally, I know his greatest weakness. It has red hair, no tits to speak of and isn't real."

John's eyes widened as he contemplated her words. A smile split his face. "Would you care for a drink as we plan Michael's downfall?"

Hilda smiled. "No, and you're not having one either. You need a clear head. Say what you want about Michael, he's a supernova in a fight. Besides, I haven't agreed to take your case yet."

"What do you want?"

Hilda stretched, showing off her impressive figure. "I already said, money. I should have been Mrs. Big Wig, not some flute playing fakey. Half of whatever we take him for is mine." Hilda took a deep breath that caused the material of her dress to strain over her breasts.

"Deal." John held out his hand, and she shook it.

Hilda's expression became serious as she reached into her purse on the table and pulled out a handheld. "Good, I'll get that in a contract before we begin. Finish your hangover cure. We'll both need clear heads if we're going to pull this one off."

Ryan used his handheld to access the messages on the *Star Hawk* while Pikeman sealed the skin over Rowan's skull.

"That is that." Pikeman began putting away his tools.

Ryan glanced at Rowan. "You said you'd re-attach her hair."

"Did I? Oh, very well. I'm far too generous. This is not medically necessary." Pikeman operated a control on the side of the table, and the container holding Rowan's hair writhed. Tracing the line of Rowan's scalp with an instrument, Pikeman demarked her hairline, then placed the container by her head. The hairs wriggled out of the container, dragged by hordes of nanobots, and attached themselves to Rowan. Moments later, a ragged mop of hair covered her scalp.

"That's not how it was," objected Ryan.

"So, now I'm supposed to be a hairdresser? Live with it. It will grow out." Pikeman turned pointedly to Timothy and smiled. "Don't forget, Wesnakee at eight, you simply have to see some of the on-station sights."

Tim shifted uncomfortably from foot to foot. "Twenty hundred, I'll be there."

"Good, it's a *date*. I had best prepare for my next patient. If you would help remove Rowan, I can ready the work area."

Tim moved to Ryan's side as he folded out a grav-stretcher that consisted of a canvas support between two tubular grav-suspensors.

"How long will she be out for?" Ryan adjusted a control on the stretcher so that it hovered by the worktable.

"What? Oh, most of the day. You can expect her to be disoriented tomorrow as well. As the stem cells divide and create new brain tissue, she may regain some memories that were housed in brain segments closed off by damaged sectors." Pikeman didn't bother to turn from his work as he spoke.

Ryan and Tim lifted Rowan onto the grav-stretcher. Ryan placed her pendant around her neck, then they propelled her from the room.

When they reached the station corridor, Ryan glanced at a female batzoid, wearing a sash with a station technician's badge on it, who seemed engrossed in monitoring a cleaning robot before starting down the passage. "Son, not that it's any of my business, but Pikeman seems... fond of you."

Tim shifted nervously. "He... we're friends, but... I think you're right. I don't know how to, well..."

"Don't let yourself be pressured like you were with Caleb. It's your choice, not his."

Tim stopped walking, bringing the stretcher to a halt. "You knew about Caleb?"

Ryan turned to face his son. "I suspected, but what was I supposed to do?" Ryan shrugged.

Tim looked at the floor. "I'm not, you know."

"Since you were married and have dated some rather striking women, I thought it was an experiment."

"I was so lonely, and back then, the girls wouldn't even look at me. Plus, I had no friends, and—"

"I know. My heart bled for you back then. I tried to be

there for you, but you were rebelling. I guess I seemed pretty uptight." Ryan left his end of the stretcher floating and moved to Tim's side.

Tim looked into his father's eyes. The face may have been youthful, but the eyes were the ones he remembered.

"Dad, be honest with me. Was there any hope for Mom?"

Ryan kept his eyes locked with Tim's. "I prayed that there was for a long time. Six doctors all said the same thing. Hopelessly e-addicted. I did everything I could."

Tim nodded. "Do you really love Rowan, or is it being on the edge again?"

Ryan smiled wearily. "I love her. The person she's become since she was inserted in the set region is so much more than what they programmed."

Tim nodded. "In that case, maybe I can give her a chance. No promises, but if you really believe she's a person, the least I can do is let her prove it. I'm sorry I've been so closed-minded."

Ryan smiled and hugged his son, then, clearing his throat, moved to the front of the stretcher. "Come on, we have to take Rowan to the Republic Law Enforcement Centre."

"What?" Tim looked stunned.

"I'll explain on the way. You getting to know Rowan will have to wait."

Croell watched the screen as it showed three infested *Homo sapiens* move away from Pikeman's clinic.

"It's Ryan, Rowan and that new *Homo sapiens*. I think he's Ryan's hatchling." Zandra moved to Croell's side in the branching passage. She stripped off the technician's sash and folded it as they talked.

"Good. No one has entered Pikeman's clinic since they left. We can now accomplish one of our geise." Croell held up his handheld, pointed its top at Pikeman's door and tapped an icon on the screen with his claw.

"Is the task complete?"

"It is begun. The nanobots will slip into his brain and slowly dismantle it. To a casual examination, it will appear to be a stroke. In twelve to eighteen hours, our obligation to Sill will be fulfilled. Now we must be ready to strike when Rowan is left alone." Croell brushed his chin over Zandra's back.

"True. It is good that Ryan's offspring is present to ease the pain of her passing for him." Zandra started down the hallway following Ryan, Tim and Rowan, with Croell in her wake.

Ryan and Tim manoeuvred Rowan's stretcher into the Republic Law Enforcement Office. It was a large room with a waist-high counter along three walls. Sentients of all the species that could share space with *Homo sapiens* stood behind the counter, servicing beings that stood in neat lines. Ryan moved to the closest attendant, an oryceropuszoid wearing a collar marked with the Republic Law Enforcement crest.

"Good sentient, if you require emergency medical services, the treatment facility is the next door over," remarked the oryceropuszoid officer.

"We will require medical attention for my companion, but I also must inform you she is presenting herself in keeping with an order of deportation." Ryan held his handheld up where the police officer could examine its screen.

"Honoured sentient, please to be changing the screen colours and language. This enforcement officer's optical spectrum does not perceive a spectral difference, and I do not read *Homo sapiens*."

"Sorry." Ryan pressed a button on the handheld's side and held it up again.

"Better, I am... Can we please not bother with the ultra-formal stardust?" asked the cop.

"With pleasure," agreed Ryan.

"Why the 'derogatory term for ranking officers' want to have us all sounding like overly-formal grandsires is beyond my comprehension." The oryceropuszoid tossed its snouts up and produced mucus bubbles on the end of each. "Manners, ha! I'm a beat cop. I annoy most sentients if I talk fancy."

Ryan checked a readout on the side of the stretcher. All Rowan's vital signs were in the green and gradually moving towards optimum. He smiled, then turned his attention back to the officer.

"Rowan was having a life-saving medical procedure performed when I received the deportation order. She needs nursing care."

"Right." There was humour in the cop's tone. "And the government gets to pick up the bill if she's awaiting guilt assessment. I'll log her arrival and call a medical team." The cop's snouts moved over a control panel built into the countertop, then she paused, and her eyes widened. "Rowan..." She examined the display on a screen above her control console, then wagged her snouts. "This will be one to tell the husbands. She's the escaped clone, and that would make you Captain Ryan Chandler of the *Star Hawk*."

Ryan nodded. "Yes."

"I'd pay to 'converse while dining on the contents of a shared insect mound' your stories. Pardon me. Computer link with EMS, summon a med team. Arrange for an officer to escort an injured fugitive to hospital." The cop looked at Ryan. "Does she have legal counsel?"

"Her lawyer should be he—"

"Ryan!" Vicky half ran to Ryan's side.

"She's your lawyer? The U.E.S. won't know what 'tripped it while crossing a mudflat, so it fell and filled its snouts with muck'. Good choice. Nice to see you again, Vicky," commented the cop.

"Thanks, Snuff." Vicky made a sound like someone

preparing to spit. "Sorry, I'm late. I got hung up in court." She moved to Rowan's side and checked the read-outs on the stretcher. "I'll stay with her until she's in hospital. Do you have her medical records?"

Ryan passed Vicky his handheld. She scanned the pertinent screens. "Looks like the surgery went well. I'll pass on the history." Vicky passed back the handheld.

Ryan moved to Rowan's head and gazed down at her. "I love you."

The entry door swooshed open. A *Homo sapiens* and felinezoid wearing blue harnesses rushed in carrying boxes of emergency medical gear. The human rushed to Rowan's side. "What happened?"

Vicky stepped up beside him. "No need to panic. The subject is suffering from post-surgical stress. She is in need of nursing care. I have full records to impart to the duty physician."

The felinezoid moved to Ryan's side. "Excuse me, sir." She nudged Ryan out of the way and examined the readout. "Everything is in the green, Wace."

"Check it with our equipment," ordered the *Homo sapiens*.

"Fine, but it's a waste of time. These stretcher units were a good design. Its bio-telemetry is probably more accurate than our junk."

"Double-check it anyway. You know what admin is like."

The felinezoid pulled a handheld-like device from a pouch clipped to its harness and scanned Rowan. "Same as the read-out. I told you." The felinezoid turned to Ryan. "Sir, may we borrow the stretcher?"

"Of course. Vicky will return it to me." Ryan looked at the beautiful android. "Please."

Vicky smiled. "Of course."

Each of the paramedics took an end of the stretcher and started for the door. As they left, a k-no-in wearing a green belt with the Republic Law Enforcement badge fell in beside them.

Ryan started after the stretcher, but Vicky stopped him. "Leave it be. The last thing we need is you confronting U.E.S. personnel during the transfer. Let me look after her."

"I should be with her in case she wakes up," objected Ryan.

"The best thing you can do for her right now is vanish. Seeing you will only annoy the U.E.S. officials." Vicky laid her hand on his shoulder. "It's time to let me do my job."

"It will be all right, Dad. You have a good lawyer." Tim gripped Ryan's other shoulder.

"I hate it when I can only sit and wait. Go, call me when she's settled." Ryan gazed longingly after the stretcher as Vicky ran to catch up with it.

RED TAPE

28

Crapper waited anxiously at U.E.S. customs with ten ground-forces troops. Their field uniforms were immaculate, but they all projected an air of barely restrained violence. The normal traffic of humans and aliens passing through the examination slots shot them worried glances.

A group of ten blue-uniformed, U.E.S. sector police marched into the chamber led by a fit, bald man of late middle years. His dark brown skin made the silver braid on his collar stand out all the more. He moved to stand in front of Crapper, who towered a full head over the smaller man.

"Chief Blefield," intoned Crapper.

"Captain *Crap*per, I'm surprised to see you here. Is there something the legal enforcement services can do for you?" The Chief's tone was one step removed from hostile.

"I thought I could be of assistance in seeing to the disposition of the dangerous felon you're receiving."

"I'm sure my men are more than capable of dealing with one incapacitated suspect charged with petty theft."

"I want that fakey on my ship!" spat Crapper.

Blefield made a show of wiping spray from his face. "She is not military personnel, and the extradition treaty was for a civil offence. She's going to our infirmary to await trial." His voice was even but as inflexible as steel.

"The U.E.S. government—"

"Empowered me through the U.E.S. constitution to deal

with civil legal matters in the human sector of this station. I do not appreciate the military or state departments meddling in my affairs. We both know this charge is ridiculous, but until it's settled, she is under my jurisdiction. Is that clear?"

Crapper stared down his nose at the smaller man. "I could take the fakey."

Blefield signalled to his men with his hand. "You could try, and I could arrest you and your men for attempted kidnapping, disorderly conduct, assault against a police officer and depending on how bright the slabs of meat behind you are, resisting arrest."

Crapper went red in the face and glared at the smaller man.

Chief Blefield continued. "State can have her when I'm done. I don't care what happens to some fakey, but I do care about the law. The law says she is charged with a crime as a person. Until a judge rules differently, that says she is a person, and a person has rights."

A voice intruded into the discussion. "Sir, in accordance with Republic Deportation Order 463,782 Valsalyen - 33,987, we have the Rowan McPherson personage to surrender to your custody."

Crapper and Chief Blefield turned to stare at the tabby stripe felinezoid who stood inside a customs slot holding one end of Rowan's stretcher. A blue-grey felinezoid held the other end of the stretcher. Both felinezoids were large, even for their kind, towering a full head above Crapper, who stepped back with the whites of his eyes showing.

"Officer Gramumm, isn't it?" asked Blefield.

"Yes, nice of you to remember, sir."

Vicky's voice blasted from a customs slot where a wide-eyed official sat trembling at his station. "If you delay me any longer, I will slap harassment, restraint of trade, and interfering with legal defence charges on you so fast it will make your head spin. They are filled with liquid crystal RAM units, and I will not submit to closer visual inspection or inspection by palpation because both are pointless! Get your cheap thrills on your own time! I'm not some Luba with a CPU the size of a pea that will take this garbage! Have I made myself clear?"

"Victoria Hart, is she the defence attorney?" Blefield grimaced.

"Yes, sir," replied Gramumm.

Blefield ran his hand down his face. "Nice looking chassis, but that bit of plastic is a nova blasted pain."

"Only if you're not on her side, sir. Have you taken her course *Republic Law on the Streets*?" Gramumm's tail lashed.

"If you're a cop on the station and haven't, you're a fool. No doubt, she's the best at what she does and, for an AI, a pretty good teacher. It's just she—"

"I'll be taking custody of the fakey," interrupted Crapper.

"Ignore him. The prisoner is to be surrendered to my custody," said Blefield.

"Men!" called Crapper.

"Why is my client laying here? She needs to be taken to a medical facility at once!" Vicky strode up, buttoning her blouse as she walked.

"I agree wholeheartedly. Officers, transport the suspect to the holding area's infirmary," ordered Blefield.

"Can someone register the transfer?" asked Gramumm.

Crapper pushed in front of Blefield and snatched the screen unit the big felinezoid held out.

"I'll take that. The prisoner is mine!" Captain Crapper pressed his thumb on the scanner. The scanner made a sound reminiscent of a sheep bleating.

"I'm sorry, you are not registered as law enforcement personnel," said Gramumm.

Chief Blefield took the scanner plate, then a crafty expression came to his face. "Why don't you boys come with me to the precinct? I'll treat you to a cup of coffee."

"We're still on duty," objected the blue-grey felinezoid.

Gramumm considered. "Relax, Merhissmu, by the time

we reach their Law Enforcement Centre, it will be the end of shift. I could use a relaxing cup. I'll not transfer the suspect from our custody. Until we do that, she is officially a prisoner of the Republic. We have to guard her until a *legally recognized* representative of the U.E.S. takes custody." Grasping one end of the stretcher, Gramumm walked towards the blue-clad *Homo sapiens* police.

"Wait a minute!" objected Crapper.

"You are out of jurisdiction." Vicky fell into step beside Rowan. The blue-grey felinezoid had caught up and taken the foot of the stretcher.

"She is a Republic prisoner until the transfer. Do you want to deal with Republic charges?" Blefield smiled as he moved to the stretcher's side. In moments, police surrounded Rowan. Crapper stood red-faced and trembling with impotent fury as a striped tail waved at him over the blue wall.

Ryan stood on the Republic side of U.E.S. customs and watched Rowan's stretcher. Despite Vicky's warning, he'd followed her at a distance ever since she'd left the Republic Police Station.

"She's out of sight," commented Tim.

"I know." Ryan turned to his son. "Thank you for staying with me."

"No charge. I'm glad to have heard the details of your escape. I knew you were good, but that was amazing."

"Know your enemy and know yourself, and victory is assured." Ryan moved towards the transport-pod station.

"How do you plan on getting her out of there once she's acquitted?" Timothy matched pace with Ryan.

Ryan smiled. "Do you remember that kit of magic tricks I gave you for your tenth birthday?"

Tim smiled. "Amaze your friends and family with these twelve sleight of hand tricks. I used to dream of being a professional magician."

"Remember the first rule of magic tricks?"

"Misdirection."

"Right. Master Sun Tzu said, 'A military operation involves deception'. That and, 'Be extremely mysterious even to the point of soundlessness.'"

Timothy looked downcast.

"It's not a matter of trust, son. People let things slip without even knowing they have. You'll see it all if, and when, the time comes. I have a key job for you." Ryan climbed into the transport pod. "You coming?"

Timothy smiled. "No, I need to think of a way to let Blair down easy. I'll see you on the *Star Hawk*."

Ryan nodded and closed the pod's hatch.

Timothy waited until the pod was away, then turned towards the U.E.S. customs slots. *First, I get Dad off, then I find him a nice, real woman. Kinda weird, but maybe that Kitoy. Stardust, I should have been there for him and Mom. Maybe I could have helped her if I'd only seen how bad it was*, he thought.

Passing customs took only moments, and then he was in a transport pod racing to the docking port connecting the *Chimera* to the station.

❖

Croell stood on the Republic side of U.E.S. customs and watched a handheld's screen as Rowan moved out of range. "Stardust!"

"Relax, my husband. Perhaps the *Homo sapiens* police will do our geis for us." Zandra rubbed her chin over his back.

"Ryan and Rowan are a challenge. Both skilled and lucky. I didn't dare trigger the nano-bots while she was in custody. The security systems would have detected the signal."

"We have succeeded with Pikeman. That is a victory. Do

we continue to follow Rowan?"

"There would be no point. The *Homo sapiens* authorities will monitor her. For now, we must wait. Perhaps following Ryan could be of use. I do not believe he will have sent Rowan to the U.E.S. without a plan to retrieve her."

Zandra flicked her tongue. "It makes you wonder if he was a batzoid in a previous life."

Croell shuddered and tapped his claws on the deck. "Great Flyer of the Skies defend us! What horrible sin would one have to commit to fall so low? From batzoid to *Homo sapiens*, it doesn't even bear thinking!"

Chow felt sweat prickle his brow, and he didn't dare speak for fear his voice would crack. He stepped out of the small mag-lev station onto the town's main street. Alpine-style houses with simulated wood exteriors, occupying large yards, lined the lane. Tentatively he reached out, then his fingers met hers, and he held her hand.

Tracy smiled at Chow. The young officer was dressed in expensive, civilian clothes and groomed to perfection. None of that hid the slight sheen of perspiration on his brow or the blush on his cheeks. "So, where is this restaurant?"

Chow cleared his throat before answering. "It's fifty metres or so in the village centre." He glanced at his date. She was dressed in an elegant black dress. The sight made his breath catch. Clearing his throat again, he tried to make conversation. "You look lovely."

Tracy smiled and stroked her arm. "Thank you. You look nice too. I read the news about Rowan's escape being an exercise. I guess it's declassified now."

"The word came down this afternoon. I've had reporters camped at my door ever since." Chow sounded disgusted.

"People have a right to know. Rowan being liberated is big news. Something like that hasn't happened in forty years."

"I know. Ask me; we need more of it." Chow looked straight ahead. Like with her mother, he'd found that if he focused on what he said to Tracy, he could think and not make a fool of himself.

"But you hunted Rowan."

"You must know what that's like. You follow orders. It's your job. It doesn't mean you agree with them. I think clones deserve equal rights. I mean, sure, Rowan was grown in a lab, but she thinks and feels. Who decides what makes a human being?"

Chow felt Tracy stop. He turned to look at her. She was beautiful, and her face seemed to glow. She moved close, pressing her body against his, and their lips met. The kiss was brief, sweet and gentle, a promise for later.

"You are adorable." Tracy took Chow's hand and started towards the restaurant.

Ryan sat in Wesnakee with Kate and Saggal. Saggal was going through purchase orders on his handheld while Kate watched a security camera feed on hers. A chameleonzoid waitress was in the centre of the screen.

"I'll go over it with Vicky, but I'm sure nothing in the plan is illegal by Republic standards, and the only U.E.S. charge would be public mischief, if they even bother to prosecute."

Saggal swished his tail. "Good. We felt awful about turning her out, but—"

Graff bounded to his parents' table. "Dad, Prapra's family are going to the rainforest bio-sector tomorrow, and she asked me to come along. Can I?" The felinezoid face, with its hint of fur growth, looked at his father with entreaty.

"What do Prapra's parents have to say about it? And it's not polite to interrupt," admonished Saggal.

"They said it was acceptable if you agreed," said a

young, female felinezoid half a head taller than Graff but just as fur-less.

"Very well, but you mind your manners, cub of mine." Saggal lashed his tail.

"Graff, is that him?" The female felinezoid indicated Ryan with her tail.

"Prapra, this is my friend, Captain Ryan Chandler of the *Star Hawk*! Ryan, this is Prapra." Graff held himself erect and seemed to bask in reflected glory.

Ryan smiled. "Hello, Prapra."

Prapra lashed her tail as her eyes went wide. "My dad says if it wasn't for you saving the kangazoid species, we would have been reset to a Neolithic level. We talked about you in my recent-history class. You're famous! There's a song written about you." Prapra touched her claw tips together and bowed.

Ryan smiled and mimicked her actions. "Beings do what they have to, but it is nice to meet you."

"Graff, why don't you and Prapra go and play some of the VR sims. Tell Grukla I said it was all right," suggested Kate.

"Thank you, Mrs. Slingmaster," said Prapra. The two youngsters ran off toward one of the bar's back rooms.

"KEEP THE RATING AGE APPROPRIATE!" Kate called after them.

"Was that the one that attacked him?" asked Ryan.

"The same. Seems being fur-less, she found out what it was like to be teased. Graff's the only one that will talk to her, and now they're thick as thieves." Kate stared intently at her screen and shook her head. "Got her red-handed!"

Saggal cringed. "Beloved, could you please avoid that particular *Homo sapiens* expression? It makes you sound like a professional assassin."

"Sorry." Kate turned to Ryan, who looked confused. "Our stock of 'velociraptor-like-bird' jerky has been dropping faster than sales account for. I figured someone was pilfering, and chameleonzoids lust after the stuff."

"Do we give Sowsiss a chance to apologize and pay for the missing stock?" Saggal's tail lashed back and forth.

"She's had her chance. It's not as if we don't pay them well. Forgiving once is kind. Twice is stupid! I'll deal with it at the start of her next shift. That will give me a chance to run it past Kinsit." Kate noted the quizzical look on Ryan's face. "The union rep. I have Sowsiss dead to rights, so it won't be a problem, but things go smoother if labour is kept in the loop."

"It's easier when you can court-martial them. I don't know how I'm going to manage as a civilian boss. In the Spacing Corps, everyone had to follow orders." Ryan ran his fingers through his hair.

"Don't kid yourself. We followed you because we knew you were our best shot at keeping our collective skins intact. There is following orders, then there's respecting the captain. Not everyone liked you, but there wasn't a member of the crew that didn't respect you." Kate smiled and affected a whiny voice. "You self-righteous jerk with a Napoleon complex."

Ryan snorted. "Let me guess, Ensign Whendon?"

"The same, she hated you, but she knew following you was her best shot at survival."

Ryan smiled. "A ruler may be either loved or feared. If he cannot be both, it is better he be feared."

"I didn't know you read Mruwhismra?" Saggal sat straighter in his chair.

"Machiavelli, actually, wisdom is wisdom for all species. Did Prapra ever say why she attacked Graff?"

"I think she did it because she liked him. The old Slingmaster charm. You know what cubs are like." Saggal swished his tail.

Kate smiled and rubbed Saggal's hand. "He is a lot like you, too charming by half."

A female otterzoid on a grav-board glided to their table. A cougar-tan felinezoid walked at her side.

"Kate, Saggal, nice to see you again," said the otterzoid.

"Hello, Sooplus, please join us." Saggal's tone was formally polite.

"I'm glad you came along, Mueperss," said Kate.

"Wherever goes my lovely maiden of the stars go I," replied the felinezoid. "I heard about Graff. Headmaster Hurra is a fool. He's letting things get out of hand. We're thinking of pulling Pruul out of school and hiring a private tutor to get her away from the bullying. I don't think the social interaction is worth it anymore."

"I'm not sure that running away from it is the best solution," countered Kate.

"Neither is having a bald cub!" Sooplus climbed off her hoverboard into a cushion-chair which configured itself into a hollow with an open end facing the table.

"Easy for you to say. Between your cargo runs and vacation time, Pruul misses more regular school than she attends. It's different for Graff."

Sooplus made a chittering sound with her teeth.

"Ladies, while I think we need to get together some evening and discuss what we're going to do about this, it's not what we met for today," said Mueperss.

Kate smiled at the felinezoid. "Too true." Kate gestured to Ryan. "I'd like you to meet Captain Ryan Chandler of the *Star Hawk*."

Sooplus made splashing motions with her paws, and her voice sounded amused. "I am sorry, but in translation, your ship's name is funny."

Kate scowled, then pressed on. "Ryan, this is Sooplus, captain of the 'duck-like avian with a rocket up its arse'. Translation humour works both ways, Sooplus." She gestured to the felinezoid. "Mueperss, her first mate and husband."

"How can we assist you, Captain? And more importantly, what's it worth to us?" Sooplus rubbed her paws together in a proprietary gesture.

Kitoy crossed her legs provocatively and swished her tail. She'd left her red sash on the *Star Hawk*. The office around her was richly decorated. Luba and Luke robots set to emulate various e-stars stood against the walls. The *Homo sapiens* behind the desk was Caucasian, in his early middle years with broad shoulders, dark hair and a strong jaw. His eyes traced up Kitoy's leg as he spoke.

"To provide for your needs, I would have to have a date booked at least a week in advance."

Kitoy forced her pupils to widen and rotated her ears forward while lowering the pitch of her voice. "But my companion has no way of knowing the exact date her... 'uncle' will arrive, and we so want his party to be memorable. He has exotic tastes and is extremely generous." Kitoy popped her claws and gently combed the fur on her thigh.

"Well, Miss...?"

"Kitoy." Her tail flicked up to rub against her cheek.

The human's face flushed. "Kitoy, I'll let you in on a little secret. If you can hold your party on a weekday, I can almost guarantee twenty Lubas in stock, maybe more. Friday evening through Monday morning, I'm out of stock. That's how this business is."

"I see." Kitoy wet the end of her nose with her tongue. "I think I can arrange for my 'uncle' to have his party on a weekday."

"I thought it was your friend's uncle?" The man's eyes devoured Kitoy as he shifted uncomfortably behind his desk.

"What's mine is hers. What's hers is mine. We share everyone, oh sorry, thing." Kitoy glanced at the name plaque on the desk. "Jim." She lashed her tail.

Jim swallowed visibly. "This will be a big order, and it's only for one day during the week, so I think I can let you have it for half price. To assist in customer *satisfaction*."

Kitoy released a growly purr and stood. Moving to the desk, she took Jim's hand and gently massaged his fingers. "Thank you. Why don't you draw up the contract? I'll be back to finalize our deal in a few days when I know the exact date of the party."

Jim swallowed in a dry throat and nodded. "I'll do that, Kitoy. Maybe your… friend would like to inspect the merchandise as well."

"Perrrhapss." Kitoy swished her tail, deliberately stroking it along Jim's cheek, then left the room.

In the hall, her demeanour shifted, and she allowed her pupils to constrict. "Some males!" Her tail flicked back and forth in disgust. "Kadar would never have fallen for something so blatant. 'Know your target and play to their secret desires.' Matron Spearmaster, you may have turned me into a whore, but you did know Jim's type well enough."

IT'S A SMALL WAR, BUT IT'S THE ONLY ONE WE'VE GOT

Timothy sat at a table in a shared-sector bar. Pikeman sat opposite him, sipping at a cocktail. The place was cramped and smelled of cleaning solutions. Glancing at the other tables, he could see only humans.

"This place could be on Earth," said Timothy.

"Yes, it is pleasant to have the illusion of home." Pikeman reached across the table and took Tim's hand. "A human touch, the feel of warm, human flesh."

Tim swallowed and pulled his hand away. "Blair, look, I'm sorry if I gave you the wrong impression, but I'm hetero."

A sad expression crossed Blair's face. "I could fix that. Adapting the biological component of the sexual-arousal response is a simple operation. Add some receptor cells in the proper region of the brain, and you're bi. It's painless; I should know."

"You... you weren't born liking men?" Tim stared at his table mate with shock.

"I had the operation my second year in med-school. I kept my original attraction to women and added men to the mix. I couldn't see denying myself an avenue of pleasure. It was a major fad back then."

Tim shook his head. "I... I think it would complicate my life."

Pikeman grimaced, then smiled. "I never trust the liquor

they use in this place, but it's the only humans only establishment in the shared sector. Now, where were we? Complicating your life? In actuality, it simplifies it, it... What was I saying? I... Excuse me." Pikeman stood, wove in place, then sat again.

"I... I am s-s-s-sorry, Tim. I'm feeling ra-ra-rather ill. Could you es-s-scort me back to my home? I think I need to lie down."

Tim stared at Pikeman. The side of the older man's face was drooping, and one of his eyes looked off in an odd direction.

"I think you should go to a hospital," said Tim.

Pikeman tried to move his right arm, but it flopped about like a dying fish.

"Can't. Only EMS-S-S in sh-sh-shared area. Wanted U.E.S-S-S. malpractice, crim negligence, child su-su-support. I... Home, treat s-s-self. Home, pleas-s-se."

Pikeman stood, then collapsed onto the floor.

"Hey buddy, if your boyfriend's that drunk, get him the nova blast out of here," called the bartender, a balding man wearing an old coverall.

"Call the EMS, I think he's having a stroke," ordered Tim.

"Stardust, he's just another drunk. Get him out of here, or I will." The bartender moved from behind the bar. He was no taller than Tim but easily outweighed him by fifteen kilograms of muscle.

"I'm a doctor of biology. He's exhibiting classic stroke symptoms," snapped Tim.

"I'll give him a stroke if you don't get him the nova blast out of here."

Tim stared at the bartender and realized any argument would be futile. Grasping Pikeman under the arms, he dragged the now unconscious man into the corridor.

"And stay out. Stroke, yeah right, and I'm the high servitor of the Batzoid Theocracy," the bartender called through the closing hatch.

Laying Pikeman semi-prone on the floor, Tim fumbled

out his handheld, called the EMS, then scanned the other man. He looked at the read-out. The display indicated a stroke. Bleeding into the brain, cell death, sections of the brain oxygen-deprived. He checked Pikeman's airway, then with nothing else to do, did a more detailed scan.

He stared into the screen of his handheld. The damage was worsening, but there was something more, an anomaly in the sugar absorption levels.

"It's almost as if…" Tim set the handheld to its most sensitive scan and keyed for a read-out on nano-bot activity.

"Stardust. Handheld, link to in-station communications. Find Ryan Chandler's handheld; this is an emergency!"

Ryan sat in the *Star Hawk*'s command chair, staring into the big screen that displayed Vicky's face.

"She's fine. Chief Blefield is a stickler. Until a judge rules that she isn't a person, he'll see to it she's extended every right the law grants a citizen." Vicky smiled.

"Thank you. Has she woken up?" Ryan settled back in his chair.

"Not a peep. The prison authority gave me her personal effects to pass on to you. The jamming pendant was part of it. Prisoners aren't allowed jewellery."

Ryan slammed his fist into the command chair's arm. "She's a sitting duck. I should have thought of that. You have to get that pendant to her."

"It isn't necessary. Like I said, Chief Blefield is a stickler. Besides, the infirmary doctor is an *Angel Black* fan. He's watching and will put an end to any tricks before they can get started. I trust him. He's mentioned that he might be able to slip the rest of her stem cell work in as a necessary medical procedure. I personally think he wants to keep her around longer, but it works to her benefit. I used your power of attorney proxy to green light the procedure."

Ryan nodded. "Good work and thanks."

Vicky smiled. "My power storage is in the orange. I need to recharge. I'll check in on her tomorrow. Don't worry, and get some sleep. You look like something the cat refused to drag in."

Ryan smiled. "Bon app-electrons. And thanks again." The screen went blank.

"So, hottie boss, you gonna get this nova blasted sheet off my head?" Henry complained from under his covering.

"Sure. I'm sorry we've left you alone so much." Ryan moved to pull the sheet off Henry.

"Be sorry you and sweetness won't shag with me, though I'd take the lawyer lady. That is one sweet piece of plastic! I could interface with her all night long. She's—"

"Henry, I happen to agree with the sentiment, but I don't need a play by play."

"Killjoy."

"This does add a wrinkle. I need to get a jammer to Rowan on trial day. As soon as the gavel drops, anyone with the nano control codes could kill her." Ryan stroked his chin as he thought.

A fast-paced beeping came from Ryan's handheld.

"Priority message. Henry, pick up the signal and put it on screen." Ryan dropped the cloth back on Henry's head.

The screen filled with Tim's face. "Dad, meet me at Blair's office. He's been attacked and needs help."

"Are you in danger? Call station security. Where are you? I'll be right there."

"Station security can't help. There are nanobots literally tearing his brain apart. I've never seen anything like them before."

Ryan looked at the ceiling. "Batzoid, it's one of their old tricks! I'll meet you at his clinic. Get the nano creation unit warmed up. If you can find any, give him an overdose of insulin."

"Insulin?"

"If these are the type they used during the pirate

suppression, they use sugar as fuel. Inducing insulin shock will buy us time. It was the old field treatment."

"Right. Anything else?"

"Hurry!"

The screen went blank as Ryan bolted for the door.

"At least it's not dull," remarked Henry.

Ryan raced up the ladder to the *Star Hawk*'s top hatch, which connected the ship to the felinezoid sector's docking spar. Emerging into the spar's corridor, he took off at a run, earning startled glances from the beings he passed.

Obert necked with Carol in the closet. Her hands were everywhere, and she didn't stop his from roaming as they pleased. He felt a static tingle, and the closet door opened. He tore himself away from the creature of passion in his arms.

"Aren't you the actor that plays Gunther in *Freedom's Run*?" he asked as his breath returned to him.

"What?" asked Gunther.

"Did Ulva set this up?"

"Carol, is the lad mentally unstable?"

Obert looked past Gunther and smiled. "You play Willa."

"Obert is part of a focus group for a new TV show they're making. When he mentioned it to me, I thought you'd want to hear about it. Tell them, Obert, tell them about the show. I'm sure Gunther has some things he'll want to impart to you afterwards."

Ulva recorded the feed from Gunther's basement and smiled. "I love it when Mike's plans come together." She became serious. "I hope knowing what happened with her comforts you." She shook her head. "I have got to find another line of work. If Gunther was single, I'd pull a Ryan today."

Ryan's breath came in gasps when he stopped at the hidden door to Pikeman's office. He placed his hand on the scanner plate and spoke. "Rowan McPherson and Ryan Chandler, follow up appointment."

Ryan took another lungful of air before the door opened, revealing Tim.

"Dad, I gave him a shot of insulin, but his condition is still deteriorating."

"Did you get an image of the nanobots?" Ryan followed Tim through Pikeman's lobby area into the treatment room. Pikeman lay on his examination table, unconscious.

"I did, but I can't find their control codes." Tim moved to the nanobot manufacturing machine.

"You won't. These are seeker hunters. Once their kill command is activated, they remove their own command receptors."

"Stardust. What can we do?"

Ryan moved behind the nanobot generator. "I guess letting him die is out. Rowan may need him."

"Dad!" Tim looked at Ryan, horrified.

"I've already saved his miserable life once, so don't lecture me. Prepare a stock of nanobody cores. Use that cholesterol fuel system you designed. I'll work on the weapons add-ons."

Tim started pulling up files on the nano creation unit. "What are we doing?"

"We're going to war, and we need foot soldiers, fast. Can you put an image of our enemy on the screen?"

Tim pressed a button and a screen to one side of the nanomanufacturing unit filled with an image that looked vaguely like a scorpion with two tails and paddles where its legs should be.

"Stardust!" Ryan examined the information beside the image.

"What?" Tim worked the manufacturing unit's controls with quiet skill.

"It's a newer version than the ones I've fought. Our chances just dropped to fifty-fifty."

"Why?"

"I know myself, but I don't know this nano. Nothing for it. Are the nano cores ready?"

"Yes."

Ryan moved to the console and stared at the tube-like image on the screen. "You kept it simple, good. I'll use a standard grasp and pinch arm from the files and a stock propeller/rudder combination for mobility. A basic seek and destroy program with the enemy as target should do." Ryan operated the controls and, seconds later, hit the manufacture button.

"Dad, those nanos are going to get pasted. They'll never be able to defeat the ones attacking him," observed Tim.

Ryan was scanning Pikeman's files, selecting elements from various units already programmed in. "They're shock troops. They'll engage the enemy and keep them busy while we get our heavy units in place. I expect a high body count. What do you think?"

Ryan stepped away from the screen, revealing a nano design that resembled a cylinder with grasping legs above and below it and a pointed projection in the middle of the legs. "It impales the enemy nano on the spike, then disassembles the nano and rebuilds it into one of our basic shock troops. My way of 'feeding off the enemy'."

"It's not very mobile." Tim looked at the design.

"These are meant to hold a brain sector. Establish cleared regions to keep Pikeman alive. Speed of production and staying power are what we need."

A buzzer sounded. Tim extracted a syringe of nanobots from the manufacturing unit. As he injected them into Pikeman's carotid artery, Ryan began making the next batch.

Tim glanced at Ryan's design.

"Mobile fast assault to make rifts in the regions dominated by the enemy so that heavier total suppression units can get established," explained Ryan.

Tim nodded, then moved his father to the side. "In that case, you want them to survive a few hits. Double lining the carbon molecules in the outer shell will give you that. I'll compensate for the extra mass by adding a dextrose fuel system. We need to up his blood sugar anyway, or it won't matter."

Tim watched a depiction of Pikeman's brain on a monitor screen. Areas coloured red steadily gave ground before areas coloured blue.

"I think your debridement, hemorrhage-control nanos should go in now. I'd like to restore the areas that have been liberated," said Ryan.

"For a man who doesn't like medicine, you have a knack for it." Tim pulled up the nano design on the manufacturing unit.

"This isn't medicine. This is war. When taking a planet from an occupying force, you repair the environment and civilian infrastructure as quickly as possible. That way, the indigenous population come to think of you as heroes and may well help in their own liberation."

"I get it. If Pikeman's own immune system can help us, we can eradicate the nano infestation faster."

"I'm more interested in his circulatory system. If the blood flows properly, the arteries become highways. Our units can use them to get where they can do the most good. It will eliminate surrounded ground for our troops."

Tim shrugged. "If you say so."

"Mobility is key in a campaign. Can you operate the unit he used to insert Rowan's stem cells?" Ryan waved at the piece of equipment.

Tim went pale. "I'm not a medical doctor."

"That's not what I asked." Ryan stared at the screen depicting Pikeman's brain.

Tim looked at his father. He'd seen him angry, happy, drunk, and almost every way he could imagine, but this was new. He had a focus that precluded everything else. His will could bend hard-cast polycarbonate. Tim swallowed. "I've used similar units during some of my research, Captain."

Ryan accepted the title without thought. "Good. I want to open up another front. Get shock-troops in here and here." Ryan pointed to the core of two of the red sectors. "That should draw their troops away from the current line."

Tim shook his head. "And they made him retire. Humans Ascendant have stardust for brains!"

Obert lay in Carol's bed, staring at the ceiling. What had happened was impossible, but he knew it wasn't. He wanted to tell someone, but it was too dangerous. Carol shifted beside him and murmured in her sleep. He looked at her. Knowing how they used her made his blood boil.

She'd told him she was into swinging; he could live with that, but what the controllers did to her was… rape. He could think of no other name for it.

He wondered if she would be with him if it were not for their meddling. He wanted to believe she'd been with him because she liked him. She was his first; he hated to think that the controllers might have tainted that.

His head hurt with the thinking. Closing his eyes, he snuggled close to Carol and drifted into sleep.

Dark circles stood out under Ryan's eyes as he watched

the screen displaying Pikeman's brain. The last red sector was turning blue. Pikeman lay on the treatment table, his scalp completely bald but otherwise seemingly undamaged.

"It looks like we did it," commented Tim from behind the nanomanufacturing unit.

"Looks like. Though he has a lot of brain damage. He'll need stem cell insertions to repair it."

"I'm sure we can find someone qualified to do the work. He has the equipment." Tim made an adjustment on the machine.

"What do you think of my design?" Ryan turned to face his son.

"Solid, quite simple really, but why make them? Blair will be clean in another couple of minutes."

"He will. I'm more worried about Rowan and us."

"What?" Tim looked up, startled.

"These attack nanos are self-replicating. They move from host to host by contact. Anyone Pikeman's touched in the last few days is at risk." Ryan moved beside Tim and looked at the device's screen. "Why'd you add the extra arm?"

"It allows the unit to fine-tune any nano it captures to attack the hunter-seekers."

"'In a chariot battle, reward the first to capture ten chariots. Change their colours, use them mixed with your own.' Sun Tzu would be proud. How did you account for the programming variance?" Ryan stared at the screen.

"I don't have to. Since we know how the hunter-seekers are constructed, I set it as a dedicated system."

"Clever. Nice work, son."

Tim smiled. "I'll deliver a vial of these nanos to Rowan for you as soon as Blair is on his feet."

KEEPING UP APPEARANCES

Farley sped through the water with half a dozen octozoids chasing him. His spying had located their base, but they now knew of his presence. Columns of kinetically-charged water sped past him as he darted from side to side.

'*Gunther, I'm in deep here,*' he thought desperately.

'*Help's on the way,*' came the telepathic reply.

Quinta sped down from the surface. A blast of telekinetic force turned the tentacle of one of the octozoids, so its weapon discharged into the one beside it.

Farley looped back towards his opponents, pulling a diver's knife from an ankle sheath. Before the octozoids could react, he'd slashed off the tentacles of the one in the lead.

There was the splosh of something else entering the water. Willa plummeted to the bottom, wearing scuba gear. She grabbed a passing octozoid and proceeded to rip its tentacles off.

Quinta circled yet another octozoid, which was trying to draw a bead on her but kept having its aim deflected by her will.

Farley felt tentacles close around his neck as there was yet another splash. The tentacles froze.

"Master 'deepwater cave in temperate zone seventh hatched in the month of cod-like fish, during the year of lobster-like decapod,' how is this possible?"

"You were always a poor student who did not like to

think. Have you thought of the consequences of your actions?"

The octozoid shuddered as Farley twisted in its loosened grip and thrust his knife home in the sensitive area around its beak.

'*Thank you, Gunther,*' thought Farley as he watched the scuba equipped form swim by.

'*Keep your mind on the job,*' admonished Gunther's mental voice.

Minutes later, they were all scrambling into a mid-sized boat. Willa took off her equipment until she was clad only in a form-fitting, one-piece swimsuit. Carl, who stood at the boat's wheel, diligently turned his eyes away from her and focused on Fran, who was wearing a bikini and stood guard at the top of the ladder.

Gunther followed Willa into the boat and had barely dropped his tank before he pulled her into his embrace. "Divine, you look good."

Troy adjusted the controls, increasing Gunther and Willa's attraction to each other. "This is great, classic *Angel Black.*"

"It's tripe! The happy couple, so sweet," snapped John, who sat in a folding chair behind Troy.

"I think Gunther and Willa are a great couple. They send a message that love can survive." Troy kept his eyes on the screen where Fran, Carl and Farley were helping Quinta up the human-designed ladder into the boat. Angel landed on the deck and started speaking to Gunther, who now stood behind the wheel.

"There are seven of them, six k-no-ins and a felinezoid waiting at the dock. The octozoids must have sent a message," said Angel.

"Only seven? That's almost an insult," commented Gunther.

"All I want to do is get home." Willa stood at her husband's side.

"I'll use the dock at Andy's cottage. Angel, could you fetch the rover around?"

"Happy to." Angel leapt into the air and spread her wings.

Willa nuzzled Gunther's neck. "There is a sleeper cabin in the bow," she whispered, then nibbled his ear.

Gunther swallowed hard, then yelled at the younger members of his team. "Carl, take the wheel. Dock at Doctor Migwier's pier. Willa and I need to confer."

Willa grabbed his hand, and they practically ran below decks.

Carl's eyes followed Willa's every step.

Farley moved to Carl's side and spoke softly. "Rough one."

Carl nodded. "I was always the other man." He smiled and turned to Fran. "Hey, pussycat, we ready to sail?"

"Don't call me pussycat." Fran playfully extended her fingernails and made scratching motions towards him.

Ryan opened his eyes as a chorus of birdsong flooded his quarters on the *Star Hawk*.

"Henry?"

"Who else, hottie boss? You're due to meet with Red-Red-Blue in an hour. Tim called in, Pikeman is on his feet, but he has major memory loss."

Ryan stretched in bed. "Stem cell insertion will help with that, but he was pretty far gone. Some of his memory is going to be lost."

"I can't believe batzoid are still using that trick."

"It's not an easy one to fight. Scan me while I get

cleaned up to make sure I'm free of enemy nanos."

"I get to watch. Yummy."

Ryan rolled his eyes and got out of bed.

"I'm surprised you slept in your own quarters, sexy captain mine. Figured you'd want to be close to her smell, or some other weird biologic thing."

Ryan chuckled as he moved to his en-suite. The room was as austere as the rest of his quarters.

"Her smell is exactly what I want to preserve. Under no circumstances is anything of hers to be washed."

"Nova blast, you've got another brilliant plan. Be honest with me, what are the odds of me not getting my circuits fried with this one?"

"Very high. Though if you could get the Earth Sector Control AI involved in a really good game of Divine Creator and keep it distracted, it would be a help." Ryan pressed his front into the micro-bot cleaning unit and hit the activate button.

Henry tried again to receive Rowan's telemetry. Since she'd boarded the *Star Hawk*, she'd never been out of his range for this long, and he hated it. "I'll play the AI. I was hoping to anyway. She's the top-ranked player on station. There's a slim chance she might be a worthy opponent." Henry paused as several of his RAM segments all worked over the same problem. "Do you remember that intelligence mission on Murrow?"

"Lovely planet. Felinezoids really look after their planets' environments." Ryan paused, then his body tensed, and he nodded. "At your discretion, just don't leave any footprints, and we never had this discussion. Hacking is a Republic offence."

"I won't leave a trace, just like before. Can I help it if I'm a top-rated player? My virtual species take on a life of their own."

"Good ma... AI, Henry." Ryan smiled.

"Sure, but will it get me shagged?"

Ryan rolled his eyes.

An hour later, he sat at the transparent wall in Wesnakee, scanning the murk beyond. "Computer, coelenteratezoid translation mode. I am Ryan Chandler seeking Red-Red-Blue. Are you present?"

Two coelenteratezoids drifted up in front of Ryan. One was large, even by coelenteratezoid standards. The communications ring around the canopy of the smaller one blinked in multi-coloured lights.

"I am Red-Red-Blue, Captain Ryan Chandler. I am honoured to introduce Green-Blue-Red-Purple-Yellow, who serves as the liaison officer to the *Homo sapiens* in the Gaea system."

Ryan stood and wagged his arms loosely below his chest. "I am honoured to meet such an esteemed elder as yourself and grateful for the opportunity to thank you for your yellow sanction, which aided my escape from the Gaea system."

"It is I who was honoured to assist in your efforts to see the laws of Blue-Green-Green-Purple-Red-White-Yellow-Yellow enforced. You have restored my faith in *Homo sapiens*. When I learned you were on the station, I journeyed here in hopes of meeting you."

Ryan returned to his seat. "I am pleased. I wish to ask for further assistance from the coelenteratezoid people."

"To ask is free, but know we are not a wealthy species. Buying the stargate that services the Zod system has nearly bankrupted the associated coelenteratezoid worlds."

Ryan smiled. "I know. As such, I would like to give you something that the *Homo sapiens* will pay dearly for. Perhaps dearly enough that the orange oil will flow to balance the trade deficit, and Zod's population will be restored."

Green-Blue-Red-Purple-Yellow's bell lights blinked in a random pattern. "Hmm," came from the speaker. "Go on, Captain Ryan Chandler. While I have no official standing on this station, I know whom to speak to, and I am intrigued."

Tim looked at Rowan's sleeping form. He couldn't help but appreciate her beauty. "Dad has taste. If you have a soul, I'm sorry. I can't let my father throw away his life on the off chance that you're real."

Rowan's eyes fluttered open, and her head lolled from side to side. Tim gasped, fearing she heard him.

"Ryan, Daddy, the cat's in the yard. Lynx is in the yard. Horses, horses, they're so big. I don't want to. Daddy, don't make me! Henry's a pervert. Henry's a pervert. Look out, he grabs." A smile parted Rowan's lips, and her face seemed to glow. "Ryan, incredible, where'd you learn." She giggled, then slipped back into unconsciousness.

Timothy relaxed. "Delirious. Well, I gave Dad my word, and I don't want him thinking I'm to blame when she dies." Timothy pulled a vial containing a silver powder out of his pocket and emptied it over Rowan. "That much I can do for you. You'll be free of hunter-seeker nanos in a few hours." Tim slipped the vial into his pocket and left the infirmary.

Zelotes was in the marshes of Swampla. Otterzoid rebels were on all sides. The grav-tank he'd flown in on was a ruin. He took aim at a grav-vehicle, there was a flash of light, and he was standing in the interface box in his office.

"Computer, note."

"Recording," said the pleasant alto.

"There is a need for a transitional screen at the time of character death. The sudden return to reality is jarring. End note."

Zelotes stumbled out of the VR booth and practically fell into his chair. "Handheld, latest news update regarding rogue fakey."

He picked the handheld up from his desk and read.

ROWAN SURROGATE SURRENDERED

Late yesterday, the Rowan surrogate was surrendered into Republic custody to face charges of petty theft. The surrogate is currently unfit to stand trial due to health reasons. If found guilty, this case could see the status of personhood being granted to all emotional surrogates.

"Left-wing press trying to convince everyone that thing should have rights!" snapped Zelotes. He took a deep breath. "They wanted you to betray God, get yourself cloned, but you were stronger than that." He stared at the hologram of Catharine. "I must be as strong."

Ryan sat in Saggal's living room, speaking with Murill and a large blue-grey felinezoid male.

"I'm sure the fan club members would love to help. Most of them at least, and if Rowan will give authenticated thumb-prints to everyone that helps, that would be great," said Murill.

"I want it understood that my son is to participate in nothing illegal or dangerous," said the older male.

"Officer Smith, I promise none of the fans will do anything illegal or dangerous. I've consulted with my attorney. This is more like a school lark. I mostly need warm bodies. I've told you and your son more of the plan than I will most of the others because I want to use him as a live escort. Most of the participants will only know to head for the doors and make a path for the Rowans. There's no crime in leaving a room or going to a transport pod." Ryan smiled.

Officer Smith lashed his tail and hissed with laughter. "I think I'll take the day off. If you could use another 'warm body,' it will be wonderful to see the expression on Chief Blefield's face."

Ryan touched his fingertips together and bowed to the felinezoids. "I'll let you know as soon as I have the court date."

"Excellent. I've experienced *Angel Black*. I'm not a fanatic like some felinezoids in the room." Officer Smith looked pointedly at his son.

"Dad." Murill widened his nostrils.

Officer Smith swished his tail and hissed through his nose. "I really hope you get her out. Rowan reminds me of my sister in many ways."

"You think she's like Aunt Prumru." Murill looked at his father, and his whiskers twitched in disbelief.

"Of course not. Your Aunt Mrapraahis, the one that signed aboard that century ship establishing an independent colony world. She left when you were a little cub. Gutsy female, and smart, you would have liked her." Officer Smith swished his tail.

⌖

Rowan opened her eyes. Her head throbbed in time to the beating of her heart. She tried to think, but she couldn't focus.

"Ah, you're awake. I was wondering when that would happen," said a round-faced, grey-haired man dressed in a lab coat.

"Where, what?" Rowan's voice was a croak.

"Not to worry, you're quite safe. Being a little disoriented is perfectly natural after the work you've had done."

The man approached with a glass of water and placed the end of a straw into her mouth. Rowan sucked, and her throat eased.

"Better?" The man smiled at her.

"Yes, thank you. Where am I?"

"What's the last thing you remember?"

A blush coloured Rowan's cheeks, and the man chuckled.

"Things associated with strong emotions do tend to come through first after the procedure."

Rowan blinked, then rubbed the crust from her eyes. "Now I remember. I was receiving treatment."

"For," prompted the man.

"Dying brain cells. Who are you?"

"I'm Doctor Beasley. You can call me Fred."

"Where?"

Fred held the straw to her mouth again. Rowan drank.

"You are in the U.E.S. sector, prison infirmary."

Rowan sat up with a start. "My trial?"

Fred smiled and patted her shoulder. "Is still several days away. Now, I need you to answer some questions for me. What is your name?

"Rowan McPherson."

"And what year is it?"

"565 PC."

"Excellent. Who is your current next of kin? The person you want to be notified in the event of an emergency."

Rowan almost gave her father's name, then thought. "Ryan Chandler, my... Well, he's the one to contact."

"And obviously a lucky man." Fred arched a bushy eyebrow. "In general terms, do you know where you are?"

Rowan blushed crimson. "In a prison infirmary."

"Perhaps in galactic terms would be a better way to phrase it."

Rowan caught on. "I know it's what I thought was the distant future two months ago. I know there's a galactic republic and that most of the human officialdom would rather I quietly shut up and die. I know if I'm not found guilty, I'm in deep stardust and that I was an emotional surrogate on an e-entertainment until Ryan liberated me."

Fred nodded. "Good. Rowan—may I call you Rowan?"

"Sure." Rowan smiled. It was hard not to like this stranger with his gentle demeanour and soothing voice.

"Rowan, it is a thrill to meet you. To have the opportunity to thank you. My wife died three years ago."

"I'm sorry." Rowan patted the man's hand.

"Thank you. The point is, I survived, but I don't know if I would have except for you."

Rowan looked astonished. "But I'd never met you before."

Fred moved to a countertop on the infirmary's wall and fiddled with a piece of equipment. "But I met you, every week a different adventure. You are a lot like my Silvia was. Somehow, experiencing your show, spending a little time with you, gave me something worth dragging myself through the week for. I honestly don't know if I would have survived if it wasn't for you. Your lawyer mentioned that you thought the years you spent on the set were a waste. I want you to know that they weren't. I don't know how many people like me are out there, but I'm sure there are a lot."

Rowan felt tears sting her eyes. "Thank you." She cleared her throat and tried to sound business-like. "So, Doc, what do I do now?"

Fred moved to her bedside. "For the moment, you eat and rehydrate yourself. You've had nothing but IV nourishment for nearly two days. After that, you should go back to sleep. A normal sleep, so your brain can finish sorting itself out. Tomorrow, with your permission, I'm going to do stem cell insertions to repair your bone marrow and organs." He smiled, and his eyes sparkled with mischief. "That should annoy Pikeman no end. I'd love to see the thief's face when you tell him you don't need to pay his over-inflated prices for a basic procedure."

Rowan pulled herself up and kissed Fred on the cheek. "That would be wonderful. Ryan is too worried about me worrying to say much, but I know he's at a loss as to how to pay for Pikeman's treatments."

"Most people are! There isn't a *Homo sapiens* doctor on the station that hasn't had to undo damage that man did. It's a shame that such genius is coupled to the morals of a Swampla sea lizard."

RECALLING PAST GLORY

"Seems a waste of a perfectly good sheet." Kitoy opened her claws and pulled against Rowan's bed sheet, tearing off a strip about a decimetre wide by three long.

"What? Oh, well... Um..." The scissors in Ryan's hands stilled as he pulled himself away from deep thoughts.

"Hottie boss is worried, sexy kitty," Henry's voice came from the speaker. "Ryan, I've been over the list. No luck."

"Nova blast!" Ryan slammed his fist into the mattress.

"Not that I know what you're up to, but what is wrong?" Kitoy's fur stood on end at the frustration Ryan displayed.

"On a station this size, you'd think finding someone checked out on human EVA suits would be easy, but no. Everyone qualified works for the U.E.S. or is on contract to a shipping line and can't take independent jobs."

"Kate?" Kitoy's tail tip kinked.

"I don't want to get her into my problems any deeper than she already is." Ryan put the scissors down and massaged a cramp in his hand. Kitoy took the strip of cloth she'd torn free, put it in a plastic bag and sealed it.

"I can't think of any other ISLARA members."

"I can't find anyone, period!" Ryan scowled.

"Maybe if you advertised..."

The look on Ryan's face stilled her words.

Kitoy lashed her tail. "I said a dumb thing. Hush-hush security. Are you sure you never served in felinezoid intelligence?"

"Why don't you do the job, boss?" asked Henry.

"Whoever does it will have to go into U.E.S. territory. Besides, Crapper's people will be all over me."

"How important is this EVA suit thing?" asked Kitoy.

"Important," said Ryan.

Kitoy stood and stretched. "I might be able to help. Did you ever meet Kadar's friend Zygmunt Tokic?"

"Friends called him Ziggy, Corporal, Field-Medic, Second Class, nice butt," commented Henry.

"That's the one, except for the butt." Kitoy's nose twitched. "He let himself go to flab after mustering out."

"If he was part of our crew, why don't I know him?" Ryan looked at Henry's speaker.

"He was stationed on the *Kestrel*. After the accident, he was reassigned to us for the rescue efforts. He was only on board for two weeks. You had other things on your mind back then." Henry's tone was cautious.

Ryan looked at the floor. "We will never forget. Is he on the roll?"

"We never got around to it."

"Send what information you have on him to my quarters. He served on the *Star Hawk*, no matter how briefly, he should be remembered."

"Aye, sir." Henry's voice was parade ground crisp.

Ryan turned to Kitoy. "What about him?"

"He did hostile environment missions. He and Kadar would talk about them. He'd have to have had an EVA suit rating to do that."

"Why wasn't he on the station's skilled personnel registry?"

Kitoy looked at the floor, and her tail drooped. "He didn't handle things well after the disaster. They probably pulled his rating for being in an unfit condition on the job."

Ryan nodded. "What's his poison?"

Kitoy's whiskers twitched nervously. "Memoria."

Ryan rested his head against the mattress. "Great, just great! How much of him is in the here and now?"

"He was still functional when he was between doses the last time I saw him, but that was three months ago," said Kitoy.

Ryan turned his head and met her gaze. "What is his opinion of the U.E.S.?"

"Today, he hates his government. When he served, he was a patriot." Kitoy looked at the floor. "We have that in common."

Ryan patted her shoulder and scratched lightly behind her ears. "That, at least, is helpful. Please find him for me. Junkies. I hate dealing with junkies!"

Vicky stood in the luxuriant judge's chambers staring at a skinny woman with greying, black hair who sat behind a large, chestnut desk. Her harsh features were drawn into a calculating expression.

"I can't see what your objection is, Victoria. I'm acquitting your client on all charges."

Vicky stood perfectly still with a false smile plastered on her face. "My objection is procedural, your honour. My client wants her day in court. As such, I am not empowered to accept any verdict or plea that is handed down pre-trial." Vicky kept her voice neutral.

"It is the right of the state to drop charges!"

Vicky's smile became predatory. "True, but in this case, that would be an admission that you had a citizen of the *Republic* detained without justifiable cause. I would, in that case, be forced to launch an immediate lawsuit against the U.E.S. for false imprisonment and abuse of deportation agreements."

The judge's eyes darted over the books that lined her walls. "I know better than to try and beat you at quoting precedence. My courtroom will be a zoo. Have you seen the shared area's information periodical? They're saying the charges are just a means of circumventing Republic jurisdiction. The courtroom will be flooded with spectators. Won't you reconsider requesting a closed court?"

"The court of public opinion is a better forum for my client's dispute."

"I could force a closed court."

Vicky smiled. "After Harper versus Silvanus, grounds for immediate appeal. If that occurs, I will use the grounds that only a person can be held over for trial or a bond price set to push through the legal precedence that Rowan is a person. Then if she's freed on bond—"

"Victoria, why are you doing this to me? Six more months, and I retire. This blasted fakey could leave a black mark on my reputation that will overshadow everything I've accomplished."

"Or you could make history. Judge Goeree, show some courage. Declare Rowan a person under the law."

The judge closed her eyes and massaged her own neck muscles. "And bankrupt a major corporation, disrupt the entire U.E.S. entertainment industry, fundamentally rewrite a definition of what it is to be *Homo sapiens* that has stood since the Gene War. It's my job to interpret the law, not make it! Victoria, at a personal level, I admire your... is guts the right word, considering?"

Vicky chuckled. "I'll take it as it's meant."

"That doesn't change the fact that there are pressures on me to make this go away."

"You could transport Rowan to the shared area, then dismiss the charges with me as her proxy."

"The diplomatic corps would have my head. I guess I'll see you in court, but Victoria, after this, I will be excusing myself from any of your future cases. You may be able to delete a grudge from memory, but I am not so lucky."

"Understood, your honour."

Ryan sat with Kitoy in Wesnakee and tried to ignore the

smell of the fat, shabby, human male who stood at attention across from him.

"Captain Chandler sir, Corporal Zygmunt Tokic transferring from the *Kestrel*, reporting for duty, sir."

Ryan rolled his eyes. "He's gone, complete memory trance. Nothing new is getting in."

"Ziggy, it's me, Kitoy. We're on the Switchboard Station."

The man's posture relaxed as he flopped into one of the cushion-chairs at the table. "Kadar got hung up at the clinic, asked me to tell you he'd be a little late. Who's the suit?" He gestured to Ryan, who was clad in slacks and a button-down shirt.

"This is useless until his trip's over," said Ryan.

"What should we do?" asked Kitoy.

"Simple." Ryan stood, and his tones became clipped. "On your feet, soldier!"

Ziggy leapt to attention.

"Your uniform is a disgrace! You are an embarrassment to the U.E.S. ground forces. What do you have to say for yourself?"

"I am a disgrace, Sergeant Dafoe."

"You will come with me. I will teach you the proper way to present yourself. What will you do?"

"I will come with you and scrub toilets until I learn proper decorum, Master Sergeant."

Ryan turned to Kitoy. "Close enough. Let's get him cleaned up before his smell makes me retch."

"You're complaining with a *Homo sapiens* olfactory system? How do you think I feel?" Kitoy twitched her nose and manoeuvred so that she was as far ahead of Ziggy as she could manage.

Half an hour later, Ryan led Ziggy into the bathroom of an empty passenger berth on the *Star Hawk*.

"All right, Corporal. Good work, now get yourself cleaned up." Ryan moved to slap the other man on the back, then refrained.

"Yes, sir. Thank you, Lieutenant. I'm glad the otterzoids

appreciated our efforts. Do you think the ambassador's daughter will be all right?"

Ryan looked at the other man and shook his head. "I don't know. Get yourself cleaned up in case we have to put on a dog and pony show."

"Yes, ma'am." Ziggy stripped off his filthy, tattered clothing and pressed his front into the micro-bot cleaning unit. Using two fingers, Ryan picked the clothes up and carried them from the room.

Kitoy met him outside the door. "How is he?"

"Stuck in some memory. I've managed to get him into the body cleanser. Henry, increase the air circulation in there by two hundred per cent."

"Way ahead of you, hottie boss," replied the speaker in the wall.

Ryan carried the clothes to the lift, which opened in front of him.

"Are you going to dispose of those?" Kitoy wrinkled her nose as her tail lashed.

"Not mine to throw out. I'll send them through the textile maintenance unit."

Kitoy nodded. "I was forgetting. *Homo sapiens* have developed clothing maintenance to a high level."

Exiting the lift on the Ops level, Ryan stopped at the first door to his right, which Henry opened.

"Hottie boss, would you hurry up and get them in the wash. They're about to set off the toxic substance alarms," griped Henry.

Entering a nine-metre square room full of equipment, Ryan moved to a device about a metre in all dimensions and dropped the clothing into its top.

"Fabric heavily soiled and severely damaged. Clean and repair sequence will require thirty minutes. Additional repair hemp is required," spoke a mechanical voice.

"Textile maintenance unit, begin clean and repair sequence. I will add repair material."

"Complying, repair hemp will be exhausted in five

minutes."

Ryan opened a box containing a long strip of cloth and dropped it into a small slot on the device's back.

"Repair fibres acceptable," said the machine.

"What do you think he was wearing under all that filth?" Kitoy scrutinized the textile maintenance unit with interest as lights on its top indicated which groups of nanobots were active.

"He was a soldier who never left the war behind. What else would he be wearing?" Ryan watched as the pigment reservoir that matched ground forces green dropped in level.

Quinta sped through the waters. She knew the mission was important, but she wished she could have stayed in bed with Farley. She made a splashing motion with her forepaws when she thought of him. She'd never have believed that an alien could affect her so strongly, but so much in her life was not what she'd been led to believe.

"There you are," snapped Tony. His tentacles waved about impatiently. He'd hidden in a weed bed.

"Greetings, and may you catch many fine fish today as well," countered Quinta.

"Do not make the mistake, air breather, of thinking we are friends. I lost a cave sibling in the last battle. If the controllers were not an even greater foe, I would kill you now."

"You could try, you 'foul-smelling creature that rolls in its own waste and eats too much gas-producing food so that you have trouble submerging and always leave a stream of bubbles out your arse while surfacing so that everyone knows you pollute the fishing streams' pirate. This is foolish and accomplishes nothing! Here are the parts you require."

Tony picked up the bag Quinta dropped. "I should have

the jammer built in a week, if all goes according to plan. Some *Homo sapiens* attacked one of our 'work animals' when it tried to feed. They were not one of the regular *Homo sapiens* insurgents."

"I will tell Gunther. It was possibly one of the other shows."

"It might have been. The human could project flame from its manipulative digits. Tell your fellow insurgents to not kill so many of my kind." Tony flexed his tentacles and jetted away.

Quinta did a backflip, sped to the surface, then swam back upstream.

Timothy sat in the *Chimera*'s officer's mess and tried not to gag on his soup. The food was excellent, but the company spoiled his appetite.

"He's planning something. I've had my people watching him. He's spoken to a lot of different aliens, and that felinezoid slut of his—" Crapper spoke from the head of the table.

"Excuse me, Kitoy is a perfectly nice being, and 'slut' is not a word I'd expect to hear from an officer and a gentleman," interrupted Tim.

Commander McKenzie, the XO, and Commander Hammerman, who also sat at the table, both glanced from Tim to Crapper in astonishment.

Crapper went red in the face. "This is my ship, and I'll—"

"Your ship paid for by my tax dollars, sir. I am not under your command, so I am free to correct you when you forget yourself." Tim's voice was stern, as if he were admonishing a student who'd performed a particularly dangerous and stupid experiment.

The commanders hid their smiles by taking a drink.

Crapper scowled. "Of course, it was a slip of the tongue. Kitoy has made contact with the local distributor of Luba bots. Your father and Kitoy were last seen with a bum disappearing into the felinezoid sector. Any information you can give us would be helpful."

"I'm sure it would. What about my father's pardon?"

"You have to understand these things take time, and with Rowan in U.E.S. hands, it is unlikely your further participation will be needed."

Tim looked at the imitation of a mountainscape that filled the walls and gritted his teeth.

"Captain, no pardon, no information! I'm not like Rowan. I grew up in this time. I don't need keepers to get through a day, so don't try and snow me."

"Don't you care that this could topple S.E.T.E., cause mass unemployment, harm the entire U.E.S. economy?" Crapper slammed his fist down on the table.

Commander McKenzie rolled his eyes.

Tim stood and wiped his mouth on a napkin. "No, I don't. I was a fool to distance myself from my father. Humans Ascendant are bigoted morons. The only thing I care about is not losing my father again. When I have the pardon in my hand, you get your information." He strode toward the door. A guard in a grey MP's uniform and armband moved to block him.

"Do you want more legal problems than you already have?" demanded Tim without facing Crapper.

"Escort Mr. Chandler from the vessel," growled Crapper.

"That's Doctor Chandler, sir. I earned my title." Tim stepped out the door.

"Like father, like son," whispered McKenzie. Hammerman nodded.

⊂══◦◇>

Henry reviewed the blip transmission he'd received. He recognized the style of the code.

"Genghis, you old piece of silicone." Henry tapped his android hand on the computer station. "I'd wondered where they re-assigned you after we saved your polycarbonate-encased CPU. Good to have a friend on the inside. Too bad Tim is still a prat."

Ryan placed another food tray in front of Ziggy.

"This is good grub, Nancy. You wouldn't believe the stardust they give us in our kits." Ziggy paused in shovelling food into his mouth and rubbed the collar of the cotton bathrobe which he wore. "Silk, you're too good to me, honey. How about a kiss?" Ziggy kissed the air, his tongue protruding from his mouth. His hands seemed to fondle something in front of him. "You are one nova blasted hot babe. Why don't we stay in and—"

"Corporal, recite the checklist for a mark-eighteen EVA suit, safety inspection."

Ziggy looked straight ahead. "Smart, operators, read, intelligence, every, time. Seals, oxygen, recycler, integrity, electrics, temperature, sir."

"What is the adjustment for an EVA suit entering an atmosphere of 200 kg psc pressure?"

"Sir, adjust the field stabilizers to compensate for pressure, double-check the oxygen and pray, sir."

"Corporal, please continue with your meal. You've earned it."

"Thank you, sir. I'm sorry we couldn't recover the grav-tank; the enemy fire was too heavy." Ziggy took a mouthful of mashed potato. "This squash is wonderful, sir. You space services guys got the better of it when it came to chow."

Kitoy entered from the kitchen. "How is he?"

"He knew his stuff, at one point. I think he'll do."

"I meant about the drug's effect."

"It's lessening. He's associating actual events more tightly with his memories. It will be tomorrow before he's more or less lucid."

"It is such a waste!" Kitoy's pupils dilated, and her ears twitched.

"Mommy!" Ziggy leapt out of his chair and threw his arms around Kitoy. "I'm so glad you're home! We won the game! We're going to the semi-finals. Coach said it was because we played as a team. You were right. The other kids forgot all about me missing that goal."

Kitoy rolled her eyes and patted the addict's head. "That's good, 'sweet-tasting beetle used as a snack food,' now why don't you finish your dinner?"

Ziggy bounded into his chair and took a forkful of broccoli. He chewed with an ecstatic expression on his face. "The cake is really good!"

PREPARING THE WAY

Rowan awoke to a cool hand stroking her brow. She opened her eyes and smiled. "Do all your clients get this much attention?"

Vicky smiled back. "Only the really interesting cases. I'm making my reputation on you."

Rowan chuckled, then gasped when it made her chest and stomach hurt.

"I'm sorry about that." Fred appeared on her open side. "The work was quite extensive. It will take a couple of days for all the bruising to heal."

"No problem. Is it official? Am I no longer about to die?" Rowan looked hopeful.

"You still need some minor work done. It's safe to say, it won't be a hematological insufficiency or major organ failure that brings about your demise. In fact, I used generic stem cells with the rejection proteins removed, so the organs I worked on should age slower than the rest of you." Fred winked. "Considering what a planner Vicky tells me your Ryan is, that might be of use to you."

"Thank you, Doctor."

"You're most welcome. Now, I have other patients to attend to. I'll be back later to monitor your condition." Fred patted Rowan's shoulder, then left the room.

"That man is enough to make me believe there are some *Homo sapiens* body-mechanics who actually care about their charges," said Vicky.

"My Dad's a doctor," remarked Rowan.

"Oh, yes, he is. The series rather downplays that aspect. I've received your trial date. It's in three days, as soon as they estimate you'll be recovered. It doesn't look good."

"Oh, so that means?"

"They'll acquit you on the grounds that you are not a person."

"Then what?" Rowan dragged herself to a sitting position. Her mangled hair flopped over her face. She pushed it out of her eyes. "What did Pikeman do to my hair?"

"We'll get a hairdresser in before the trial."

"Great, I'll look nice when they execute me. What about after I'm acquitted?"

Vicky pointed to her eye, then the corner of the room, then she tapped her ear. Rowan nodded.

"We will deal with that when the time comes," said Vicky.

"Can you tell Ryan something for me?"

"Sure."

"A month of really living, really loving, was worth it! Tell him I love him."

"I'll pass it on."

"And tell Kitoy to keep her claws off him until I'm at least cold."

Vicky snorted. "*Homo sapiens*. Did I ever mention I spent two hundred and five Earth years emulating a coelenteratezoid? Mating groups of fifty or more. I guess biologics can't help being what they evolved to be."

Gunther and Willa sat in their basement listening to Obert.

"Then Kadar crashed the troop carrier into the lake. Ryan and Rowan were heading into a town where they could get on a mag-lev train that would take them to the *Star Hawk*. That was the last episode we've seen."

Gunther heaved a sigh. "At least he got that stardusted

venom out of her."

"I'm concerned that he might be working for the controllers," said Willa.

"I scanned his mind; he hates the studio almost as much as we do."

The jamming device began to beep. Gunther moved to examine it. "We have about two minutes. Thank you, Obert, we can't tell you what it means to us to learn about Rowan."

"You're welcome. Look, I'd like to bring my friends Medwin, Armina and Kendra into the group."

Willa stood and moved to Gunther's side. "That's not a good idea. Not to be mean, but none of you has any special powers."

"That might not matter." Gunther adjusted a dial. White smoke billowed out of the machine. "It's working. I can extend operating time twenty per cent with the liquid-gas cooling module. Quinta is a genius!"

"My friends can be useful, and I know they can keep their mouths shut," persisted Obert.

Gunther turned to face Willa. "I scanned a controller who was in the Garlic Palace yesterday. Obert, I believe your show was cancelled. It's most likely they're using characters who they've abandoned to supply something for the show about Rowan and Ryan. If that is the case, you, like Carol, are only monitored sporadically. You and your friends can move undetected without a diversion."

Willa gazed at her husband, a smile parting her lips. "I'm so glad you're a telepath. For lots of reasons."

Gunther blushed and cleared his throat. "Beloved, we have company. Obert, bring your friends tomorrow."

Obert blushed. "Tomorrow is out. Carol's invited me to a… party."

"Oh… The day after will do, then." Gunther shifted uncomfortably in place.

Obert grinned. "If worst comes to worst, at least it means they're less likely to kill me off."

"Only one coin to trade. They've made us all into whores." Willa scowled. "You should get in the closet. We can't risk them seeing you through our eyes."

Obert complied as Gunther moved to switch off the machine.

"Ready, my love?" he asked.

"Ready." Willa threw herself at her husband and kissed him passionately. Gunther threw the switch, scooped her up in his arms and carried her towards their bedroom.

Zelotes connected the wires on the portable power packs and stacked them in a backpack, leaving a metre-long cable looping out of the pack's top. He then moved to his bed and pulled a case out from under it. Opening the case revealed a disassembled kinetic rifle. Each of the pieces was in a separate foam depression. An empty hollow was where the power source should have been.

"Only one shot, but God will guide my hand." He assembled the rifle, then slipped the wires of his jury-rigged power pack into the supply port. The light on the rifle's side blinked red, then orange, then red, then orange and stayed on.

Croell ignored the curious glances the passing felinezoids shot him and Zandra as they stood in the felinezoid sector's docking spar.

"How are the nano-bots?" Zandra looked over her husband's shoulder at the screen of his portable data unit.

Croell focused on Tim as he walked along the docking spar. "Gone!" Disgust nearly dripped off the word.

"Are you sure that is Ryan's hatchling?" Zandra stared at Tim. "*Homo sapiens* all look so much alike."

"It might be Ryan, the son resembles his father, but I'm

sure it is one of the two. No other male *Homo sapiens* have entered their ship. The question that concerns me is, did the nanobots function long enough to kill Pikeman?"

"Is it worth trying to activate them on Rowan?" Zandra tapped her fingers on the deck and tensed the muscles of her neck.

"It is worth trying. Even if it doesn't work, if we are present at her trial, an opportunity might present itself. Until then, we must seek confirmation of Pikeman's death." Croell reached into a bag at his waist and pulled out a harness and a small stack of cloth badges. He selected a badge bearing the crest of Republic EMS personnel and attached it to the harness, which turned blue. Croell flicked his tongue and returned the harness to his carrying bag.

"What are you planning?" Zandra let her tongue flick from her mouth.

"The Republic is nothing if not thorough in its record-keeping. First, I check the EMS records; they will tell me how to proceed. Your mother always wanted you to marry a healer."

Zandra flicked her tongue, then tucked her wings in tight and looked at the deck. "We had no mothers." Her voice was small.

Croell stroked his chin over her back. "We have drunk of Ratwaaa's waters. We are forgiven our origin."

"I can wish that the face I recall over my hatching nest was real."

Croell rested his chin on her back. "We have each other, beloved."

Zandra flicked her tongue. "That we do. Now let us not be silly, we have geise to perform."

"Thanks for the wash and fixing my clothes, but no!" Ziggy sat at the table in the *Star Hawk*'s space crew's mess, dressed in an immaculate U.E.S. ground-forces, field uniform with the silver braid indicating retired on each shoulder patch.

Ryan slipped a tray of sausage and eggs in front of him. "You can't tell me your credit balance couldn't use the boost."

Ziggy's pudgy hands shook as he cut the sausage. "Look, Captain, those days are gone. They yanked my EVA rating because I went to work lost in a memory. Stardust, for all I know, this is a memory, and that's how I like it. The present hurts! We're guilty of genocide, no matter what the Republic Justice Committee decided!"

Ryan looked at the floor. "You helped save the kangazoid species."

"We shouldn't have been on the nova blasted planet at all! Not us, not the felinezoids, not the k-no-in, none of us! If we'd stayed the nova blast away, the disaster wouldn't have happened!"

Ryan nodded. "You're right, it wouldn't have, but we can't change the past."

"I can live in it! Live in a time before my species was covered in innocent blood. Thanks for the chow, but all I want is my fix."

"Ziggy, you could do a good thing here," suggested Kitoy, who sat at the table with a slab of raw meat in front of her and claw sheaths on her fingers.

"Kitcat, I'm waiting to die. I'm too big a coward to nix myself." Ziggy took a mouthful of orange juice.

Kitoy's tail lashed. "Give up, Ryan! He's not worth the trouble."

"Kitcat," began Ziggy.

Kitoy glared at him, her pupils dilated, and her nose started to run. She grabbed the sash she wore and shook it. "Do you know what this means?"

Ziggy closed his eyes. "Kadar. I'm sorry."

"I don't want your pity. Sick as he was, Kadar wanted to live. He tried to get the money to be cloned, to be healed. He fought for life until the end, then at the end, he spent his last few hours helping a friend. This friend, to be exact." Kitoy pointed to Ryan with her tail.

"He was a strong man."

"He was a great man!" Kitoy's voice was muffled by her running nose. "He was your friend; he tried to help you. He got you the job at the clinic. You're disgusting! 'I want my fix. I won't help.' Why are you alive when my Kadar is dead? WHY?"

"Kitoy," began Ziggy, but she ran from the room.

"She's been keeping a lot in. She had to live without him for so long that it's easy for her to pretend that nothing's changed, then it hits her, and it all comes out." Ryan tried to comfort Ziggy, who stared at the table with a haunted expression.

"She's right. Kadar was a better man than I'll ever be." Ziggy looked up. "I'll do it, but you'll have to keep me away from the Memoria until the op. I can't stop myself."

Ryan nodded. "You'll be confined to the *Star Hawk*."

"For Kadar, because I owe him. Terra noster sors!" A shadow of lost dignity touched Ziggy's features as he spoke the motto.

"Sangunis abl planeta." Ryan saluted the fallen soldier.

Murill lashed his tail and moved self-consciously.

"Will you relax," remarked a woman who looked identical to Rowan.

"They're all looking at me. You'd think they never saw a felinezoid before." Murill let his eyes rove over the trendy clothing store with its holo-stages. As he watched, a *Homo sapiens* male stood by the stage and pressed the scan button. His image, clad in a blue swimming suit, appeared over the stage, rotating slowly in place. The man tapped the screen in front of him. A three-piece suit covered the image. He tapped again, and the suit changed colour.

"In here, they probably haven't." The Rowan look-alike

smiled.

"Are you sure you need me here for this, Kelly?"

"Murill, it's like I told you. I want to help, but I spent all I had on my new look. I can't afford a new wardrobe."

"The look came out great. I've seen her up close, and I couldn't tell."

"Thanks. Is this the combination?" Kelly pressed a button on the screen. Her image wearing a white blouse with ruffles down the front, blue slacks and a matching jacket appeared on the holo-stage.

Murill examined the image critically. "The shoes need to be lower. You know, no spike on the back."

"Stardust, I need a new set of heels. Are these the ones?" She pressed a button, and the image was wearing flats.

"That's what Ryan said to wear."

Kelly pressed a button, then walked to the checkout where a fashionably-dressed, blonde-haired girl was waiting.

"Your order will be a moment," remarked the attendant as she glanced at the order code displayed on a screen built into the counter. "This is so weird. Is the *Angel Black* fan club planning something? This is the twentieth of this exact outfit I've sold today."

"It's a kind of look-alike contest," said Murill.

"Oh… Are you going for one of those dye jobs so you can be Toronk? I mean, like, no offence, I'm not into fur, but for that hunk of cat, I'd make an exception. Angel is one lucky little surrogate. Did you hear that Rowan did a run-up? Some nutty ex-soldier smuggled her off Gaea. I mean, that must be a big bummer for you hard-core fans. I experience the show, but, you know, it ain't that big a deal for me. I like it, but it's only a show, but for you guys, it's going to pretty much ruin it. The information periodical said they arrested Rowan for stealing, and her trial's coming up. I really think the studio just wants her back. My dad says that if one fakey goes free, they're all gonna want to go free. Then there won't be jobs for real people. It could be a big mess, and…" A chime sounded from behind the counter. The girl turned and extracted a package labelled 'The Rowan Collection, look like an e-star' from a slot in the wall.

Kelly and Murill rolled their eyes when her back was turned.

"That will be three hundred credits, please," chirped the counter attendant.

Murill pulled a credit unit from the yellow sash he wore and swiped it through the reader on the counter. The reader *bing*ed.

"So much for my new portable," muttered Murill.

"Thank you for shopping at S.E.T.E. wardrobe reproductions. Have a nice day."

"Thank you, as well," said Kelly and Murill in unison. Murill started for the door. The girl behind the counter caught Kelly's arm, leaned conspiratorially close, and spoke softly.

"You got guts, girl, that pussy is a real cutie. My parents would kill me. Way to go."

Kelly smiled, then followed Murill out of the shop. As they walked, she tried to think of her young friend as something other and almost chuckled. *Too young and too fuzzy.*

"What are you smiling about?" asked Murill.

"The counter girl thought you were cute."

Murill lashed his tail. "Please, there's a hard vacuum between her ears."

Kelly laughed and slapped him on his shoulder. "You'll do okay, kid."

Medwin looked at Gunther and tried to process all he'd learned. The jamming device hummed as it slowly ticked down to failure.

"We aren't real." Kendra's pretty features were pulled

into a scowl.

"I'm real! This is all nuts! Some kind of sick joke," snapped Armina. She started pacing the basement in a near frenzy.

"Would you deny the evidence of your own eyes?" asked Toronk, who sat in a lawn chair with a hole cut to accommodate his tail.

"It's a costume." Armina rushed Toronk and began pawing him. "Where's the nova blasted zipper? How does this open up? She felt a gentle pressure push her away from the felinezoid.

"We are real. We are life forms that originated on other worlds." Quinta spoke softly, but there was firmness in her voice.

"They are, guys. It's all true," said Obert, who had stood quietly to one side for the entire meeting.

"Armi, this is the kind of thing we've dreamt about." Medwin hugged his girlfriend.

"I'm... I don't want it to be true. If it is, none of us are real, none of us are who we thought we were."

"We're all real. Yes, we are clones, but that doesn't make us any less human. That is what this is all about," said Gunther.

"At least give him a chance," pleaded Obert.

"What do you want? We don't have special powers, so what use are we to you?" Medwin straightened his posture and looked Gunther in the eye.

"Your show was cancelled. It is likely that the only time you are monitored is when you are 'test screening' the show based on my daughter's life."

"We're mostly invisible to these controllers then?" Kendra bit her cheek.

"Mostly. I know it's a lot to take in, but please let me prove it."

"How?" Armina pushed a stray lock of blonde hair from her eyes.

"I want you to leave Sun Valley."

"What!?" Obert and his friends all cried in unison. The idea sent waves of nausea through them.

Gunther pulled out the stolen handheld and spoke slowly into it. "Handheld, field effect. Neutralize all protocols to prevent movement out of the set region."

"Action violates company policy," said the device.

"Handheld, override."

"Complying."

One by one, Obert and his friends felt their symptoms vanish as the handheld accessed their control codes and made the necessary changes.

"That was weird!" said Kendra.

"It's how they keep us in the set region." Gunther set the handheld on the countertop.

"I still don't know about leaving Sun Valley." Kendra started pacing the room.

"It will only be for a short while. Just long enough for you to learn the truth, look around and gather some information. A day or two. Tell everyone you're going camping." Gunther stared at the teens with a pleading expression.

"I'm in," said Medwin.

Armina stared at him, shocked.

"If what he said was true, these controllers killed my father to make a nova blasted show. I want to see if it's true, and if it is, feed them all the stardust they can handle."

Armina nodded. "I'll check it out, but if this is a joke, it's not funny."

"I'm in," added Kendra.

"Me too. We'll go this weekend."

Gunther smiled at the young people, then the jammer started to beep.

Ryan scooted the roller cart along a passage three metres wide by sixty centimetres high. The glowing, green tubes of a grav-laser drive passed above his nose.

"Tight fit for a *Homo sapiens*," remarked Sooplus, who drifted along beside him on a grav-board.

"Never cared when it was me crawling through," snipped a short, busty, blonde *Homo sapiens* in overalls who pushed a roller cart along on Ryan's other side. Dirt left a black mark along one of her cheeks.

"Stop griping, Edana. I'm making conversation."

"Why is this even in here? A *Homo sapiens*, mark seventeen propulsion system in an otterzoid freighter?" Ryan came to a stop at a control console and pressed a button, activating its screen.

"Same reason I have a felinezoid weapons system. I know quality when I see it. You can't do better than an otterzoid hull for heavy cargo, but you monkeys leave everyone but the elder races in muddy water when it comes to drive systems."

"The trouble is fitting it all together and making the systems talk to each other. This ship is a mess," said Edana.

"But she swims like a 'streamline fish species noted for speed'."

"When she works," Edana grumbled.

"I found your problem. Your calibration between the primary graviton director and the graviton collection array is out by point zero two. Pass me the calibration override unit, and I'll reset it. Then we'll have to reset the secondary systems up and down the line. After that, you should get that extra two Gs of pull you're missing."

"I checked that calibration myself!" objected Edana.

"Graviton leakage tends to misalign remote sensors in the mark seventeen. That's why these on-site boards were installed in the first place. It's a problem we fixed in later models."

"Told you he was worth the price," smirked Soopluss.

Edana snorted. "Like to see him figure out your guns."

Ryan adjusted the calibration. "I've already got a job, but

for the record, I don't envy you yours. I tried to learn to read felinezoid once. Can we say, grade-three-level? I'll stay specialized in human systems, thank you. Being an interspecies generalist is too much work."

Edana smiled at Ryan, then stuck her tongue out at Sooplus.

"Well, Captain, you've kept your part of the bargain. I'll be there on trial day," Sooplus made splashing motions with her forepaws. "This should be fun!"

"Just a few more times, Adine." Kitoy watched as a woman who looked like Rowan, except that her eyes were a deep, chocolate brown, used the weight set on the *Star Hawk*. She was dressed in a white shirt with ruffles on the front, blue slacks and a matching jacket.

"No problem. Saves me going to the gym. Remember, I get an exclusive interview if she makes it out of U.E.S. territory."

"You will, I promise."

"Between this and my scandal piece, my editor is going to love me."

"Scandal piece?" Kitoy sniffed the air and wagged her tail. "I think that's enough."

"I've been investigating a *Homo sapiens* religious leader who doesn't practise what he preaches." Adine sniffed. "Your nose is too sensitive. I can hardly smell myself."

"We don't have to bury her scent, just confuse it, but a few more minutes can't hurt."

"I can't believe I'm actually going to meet her. When I became a woman, there was only one look I wanted. The AS-F was the only female form that ever did anything for me. My boyfriend thinks I have a Narcissus complex." Adine switched from bench presses to curls.

"Did Ryan know you were once male?"

"Oh, sure. That's why I get the free workout. It will

confuse the scent more." Adine winked. "That Ryan's a cutie, you sure he's a one-woman man? Twins is a pretty common *Homo sapiens* fantasy."

Kitoy twitched her tail. "Unfortunately."

"Wow, you like skin?"

"My husband was *Homo sapiens*."

"Wow. I've no right to throw stones, considering."

Kitoy pulled a plastic box from her sash and set it on a shelf. "I have to check on a few things, so I'm leaving your contacts here."

"Great, I'll leave the outfit on the weight bench when I'm done." Adine smiled and switched to leg presses.

Bill pasted the 'cleared for customs' stamp on the box and put it on the rack for official U.E.S. dispatches. With his clearance, no one would even look inside the container. No one would wonder why he was sending a surrogate telemetry recorder to Green-Blue-Red-Purple-Yellow in the coelenteratezoid section.

Kate sat at a table in Wesnakee, sharing a pizza with a woman who looked identical to Rowan.

"I know you think you're doing the right thing, Mrs. Slingmaster, but I believe it should be returned to the studio. It's their property. They built it." The Rowan look-alike took a hit off her beer.

"Please, call me Kate. Isn't there anything I could do to make you change your mind?"

The look-alike nodded. "Penny, and I don't think so."

Kate eyed Penny, then her gaze swept to the entry door where a chameleonzoid was sauntering into the room. "Would you excuse me? I have an unpleasant piece of business to attend to."

"Of course."

Kate strode up to the chameleonzoid, who was chatting to a k-no-in waitress. "Sowsiss, I'd like a private word, please."

The chameleonzoid shifted colour to match the floor. "I don't want to be alone with you!"

"Fine, Kinsit can be a witness to make sure the big scary human doesn't hurt you."

Sowsiss stared at Kate and flexed the muscular, claw-tipped fingers each of her feet ended in.

Penny watched the scene. The nearly two metres of reptilian carnivore being terrified of a rather average, slightly out of shape, human woman seemed ludicrous.

"Anything you have to say to me you can say in public," whined Sowsiss.

Kate rolled her eyes. "I'm sorry to tell you your services are no longer required at Wesnakee. You are to collect any personal effects and leave within the next half hour. Your presence is also banned from the bar for the next standard Earth year. I will also be placing charges of theft against you."

"I never—" began Sowsiss, her colour shifting to red.

"Do you want to see the vid-log?" Kate's tone was no-nonsense.

A female otterzoid glided up on a grav-board. "Kate, as her union representative, I think we need to discuss this. There has to be a way to avoid criminal charges." Kinsit lifted onto her hind legs in a display of strength.

"She's been stealing exotic foods; I have a recording of her doing it."

"I know, and I hope she doesn't get stuck in the mud on her way out. But she's paid her dues, and I am her rep."

Sowsiss's colour shifted so that she blended with her background. "Don't tell the Justice Enforcers, please. The shame would kill my uncle."

"You'll forfeit all claims against the bar, and your last pay will be garnished to cover the pilferage," snapped Kate.

"Agreed." Sowsiss sounded contrite.

Kate pulled out her handheld and keyed up a termination contract. "Tongue print."

Sowsiss pressed her tongue onto the screen. The handheld beeped, then Kate used a paper napkin to wipe the screen.

"I'll witness." Kinsit placed her web-fingered hand against the screen. The unit beeped again.

"Now get her out of here! I'll send what's left of your last pay via e-transfer." Kate returned to Penny's table.

"That was brutal," said Penny.

"I have a business to run. I pay my staff well, and their benefits are a dream. All I ask in return is loyalty. She stole from me! The betrayal hurts."

"Sounds like you're a decent boss."

"I try."

"I'm a waitress at a pub in the human sector. It's not a union shop."

Kate smiled. "I take it you don't like it there?"

"Let's just say, I'd be interested in the opening you have."

"There's a waiting list. Though, if you could do me a favour, I could see that your name is on the top of it. And with a shift to fill this evening."

Penny smiled. "Morals are one thing, but I can bend a little as a favour to my boss. Besides, nothing you've asked me to do is illegal. Stardust, it might even be fun."

"Let's get you familiar with our setup." Kate led Penny to the bar.

Ryan sat at Kate's dining-room table, flipping through screens on his handheld as the spaghettini in front of him grew cold. Saggal, Kate, Vicky and Bill stared at him from their seats.

"How to do it? How to do it?" Ryan muttered without looking up.

"Was he always like this before a mission?" asked Saggal.

"Anytime he wasn't satisfied with his tactics. You can take the man out of the service, but you can't take the service out of the man," said Kate.

Ryan tore his eyes off the screen. "What?"

"Ryan, my friend, you are not on your vessel. Please put the handheld down and eat with us. You're being rude by the standards of both our cultures." Saggal gestured with his tail to the food.

"I'm sorry, I have one thing I still have to lick." Ryan took a mouthful of spaghettini.

"What?" Vicky pressed a plastic probe shaped like a fork against a coloured square on a tray-like device, then put the probe in her mouth. "Mmmm. The spaghettini is delicious." Taking a teaspoon full of wine out of her husband's glass, she poured it into an opening at the top of the tray. She then placed a straw-like probe into her mouth. "The wine is excellent as well."

"I always wonder what you're really tasting with that thing," said Kate.

"The same as you. Only I get to eat as much as I want and not gain any weight," Vicky smiled.

"Lucky." Kate put on a mock scowl.

Ryan toyed with his spaghettini.

"What is the problem you still have to lick?" asked Bill.

Ryan looked up. "It's just... I still need a way to get a nano control jammer to Rowan in the courtroom, or everything else is for nothing. I've got the size down to two centimetres by one. Are you sure you can't take it to her, Vicky?"

"Sorry, they're going to be scanning for anything like that. No jewellery, only the clothes on her back, and they are completely checked for electronics, nanos, everything, before being cleared. If I try to bring it to her, they'll confiscate it."

"I could trigger it to be inactive when you bring it in. Put it on a timer, or some kind of switch."

"That wouldn't help. If they see her with anything that could contain the device, they'll confiscate it. If they feel it when they frisk her, they'll confiscate it. Only essentials are allowed. There have been too many bad situations."

Ryan fell into a brooding silence.

Kate looked from Vicky to the men in the room. "Let me understand this. It has to be something essential that is larger than two centimetres long by one round, that they won't find when they frisk her?"

"Yes," said Ryan.

"Could you make it body heat-activated?"

"Easily, but how does that help?"

Kate shook her head. "Men and AIs. It's obvious I'm the only female *Homo sapiens* in this little cabal. Ryan, eat up, your problem is solved, but I'm not going to tell you until you finish your dinner and tell me how much you like my cooking. Honestly, men! You'd think you were another species."

Saggal tentatively raised his tail.

"No, you don't get off the hook; how long have we been married?"

CONFUSION IS OPPORTUNITY!

Vicky sat in the lock-up's common area and watched as a plump, middle-aged woman cut Rowan's hair into the agreed-upon style.

"I haven't worn it this short since grade twelve." Rowan examined the bob that now framed her face.

"Longer is more flattering to you," commented the hairdresser as she placed a probe against Rowan's scalp and recalled the nanobots that had repaired her split ends and unclogged the hair follicles.

"One thing I've learned about *Homo sapiens* males. Within limits, they like variety. Ryan will love it," said Vicky.

"If you say so."

"Ryan is that dreamy captain that rescued you, isn't he?" asked the hairdresser.

"Yes." Rowan smiled.

The hairdresser leaned close. "Is it true your escape was recorded, and they're making a series?"

Rowan whispered back. "All I know is that Ryan agreed to have a telemetry pack implanted and transmit our data back to S.E.T.E. in exchange for someone important helping us. The signal would have cut off when we left Gaea."

"That will be such a good story. Tell me, had you and Ryan," she interlaced her fingers, provocatively, "before you left Gaea?"

Rowan shook her head.

"What a shame. I saw his picture in the information

periodical; he is a real cutie. Well, dear, I hope you get off. All the girls at the salon are rooting for you." The hairdresser picked up her tools and left the room.

"That was awkward. I mean, it's nice she's on my side, but um, like, inappropriate questions or what?"

Vicky nodded. "You must remember, to most people, you are a being out of fiction. Give them the benefit of the doubt. She was trying to be supportive."

"I know, it's just... I don't like the fact that anyone with an e-rig can sleep with me in re-runs."

"Worry about it later. We're due in court in an hour, and you need to shower and dress." Vicky passed Rowan a plastic bag containing a white blouse with a ruffled front, blue slacks and a matching jacket.

Rowan opened the bag and screwed her face up in distaste. "These—"

Vicky shot Rowan a meaningful glance.

"Are appropriate."

"I helped Ryan pick out the outfit. Your gentleman may have many talents, but fashion consultant isn't one of them. Now shower, *thoroughly*. No one wants to smell the defendant. I brought you this. Kate said you'd need it." Vicky passed Rowan a cardboard cylinder.

"It's not my—"

Vicky's foot landed on Rowan's. Rowan swallowed a yelp.

"Regular brand, but it will do. Thank you," Rowan spoke through gritted teeth, then she moved into the shower area.

Henry cleared most of his RAM and contacted the U.E.S. section's AI. He'd hired extra transmission width through the station network. Friendly overtures took nanoseconds to exchange, then the game was on. The AIs worked cooperatively to pull the virtual hydrogen together, compacting it to bring about the inevitable explosion, then they were off. Each selected separate galaxies as they raced to develop sentient, space-faring beings. Henry saw how his opponent induced an instability in a blue giant near his chosen star system and ignored it. Under cover of play, in a nondescript galaxy with low strategic worth, he generated a virtual species with unique operating parameters. The lines of code fit the game and so fell below his opponent's protective radar. Thus, the real game began.

Chief Blefield stared at the mob at the court chamber's door. Several of them carried signs calling for Rowan's release. Other signs admonished the government for coddling a fakey. Alien visitors were mixed in with the predominantly *Homo sapiens* crowd, mostly felinezoids and k-no-ins, but there was a spattering of otterzoids and oryceropuszoids and even a couple of batzoids.

A nondescript human carrying a sign reading 'REMEMBER THE CLONE WARS' started screaming in the face of a female felinezoid. Her male companion stepped up, but before the altercation could escalate, one of Blefield's blue-uniformed officers caught the man's arm, spun him around, handcuffed him and led him from the crowd.

"That could be considered an overreaction," suggested an Asian woman that stood to Blefield's right.

"Sergeant, this is a powder keg! Things like that escalate too easily. They're on their best behaviour, or they get taken in until the trial is over. He'll be out in an hour. I want him away from here."

"Yes, sir." The sergeant pointed to a group of green-uniformed men with Crapper in their midst. "Look who's coming to join the party."

Blefield rolled his eyes. "That man is a nova blasted pain. I don't suppose you'd volunteer to deal with him,

Renee?"

"Chief Blefield, Mrs. LePage didn't raise no stupid daughters." The sergeant grinned.

"Can't say I blame you. All right, if I kill the idiot, put me in a cell close to the cafeteria." Blefield strode to confront the military commander.

"Come to see the trial? I don't think there will be any seats left," said Blefield.

"You could have avoided this if you'd given me the fakey," snapped Crapper.

"Until the judge hands down her ruling, the prisoner's status is in limbo. If citizenship status is in doubt, the prisoner is to be accorded all rights of a citizen until their status is determined by a qualified arbitrator. It's black letter law."

"Same difference. We both know she's leaving with me."

"Frankly, Crapper, you're welcome to the fakey. She's cost me a packet in medical bills and is more trouble than she's worth, but the law is the law. You have to follow it like everyone else!"

"You should know Chandler has something planned. He's hired a load of Lubas."

Blefield chuckled. "He'll have to do better than that. All my men are equipped with sniffer probes set to the fakey's chemical signature. I—"

The door to the court chamber opened, and the crowd rushed in. Blefield failed to notice that many in the crowd formed a barrier, ensuring that a select group entered first.

Sooplus lay on the tilted platform that served as her command couch. Her ship's bridge was circular, and a channel of water half a metre deep surrounded her seat. Mueperss sat at the pilot's station in front of her with a k-no-in on a support couch beside him. Edana occupied the engineering station behind her, and a scrawny *Homo*

sapiens with scraggly, blond hair sat at the weapons console beside her. An oryceropuszoid stood at the communications console across the bridge from the *Homo sapiens*.

"Clearance is received for docking, ma'am," said the oryceropuszoid as its twin snouts moved over the console.

"Understood. Mueperss, take us in." Sooplus pressed a button beside her bench. "Vrik, as soon as we dock, open the hatch. We want to get our cargo away as quickly as we can."

"Acknowledged," replied a feminine voice.

"Now we see if he's as good a strategist as his service record implies." Sooplus made a splashing motion with her paws.

Bill examined the menu at a café outside the court. The café's entire front opened onto the four-metre-wide corridor. His gaze strayed to the group of gawkers and protesters that filled the space, and he smiled.

"Are you ready to order, sir?" asked a slender, brown-haired waitress barely past her teens.

"I'll have a bran muffin and coffee. I'd like to pay for it now; I'm waiting on a call and might have to run."

The waitress nodded. "Of course, sir. That will be three credits."

Bill ran his credit unit through a reader. The waitress took note of the hefty tip and smiled at him before she left.

A second later, his hand fell to one of the gift-wrapped boxes bearing 'cleared for customs' stamps beside him, and he patted it. "Come on. You promise one hour to anywhere in the station, so make good."

A man in a brown uniform, known and respected for nearly two thousand years, walked up to the café. "UPS, I'm supposed to make a pickup here."

Murill settled himself on the courtroom bench. The female beside him had a pretty face and blonde hair, while the rest of her was covered by a dark brown poncho. Nearly three-quarters of the station's *Angel Black* fan club crowded the room, squeezing out all other groups. Murill spotted other female faces clad in ponchos.

Rowan and Vicky entered the chamber and stood behind the defendant's desk. A shifty looking man, with his red hair plastered into place, clad in an expensive suit, stood at the prosecutor's table.

"All rise," called the bailiff, a muscular man with dark brown skin.

"Stand," whispered Murill.

He and the female beside him stood.

Judge Goeree entered the room and sat at her bench. "You may be seated."

"Sit," hissed Murill.

The female sat. Murill adjusted its poncho so that it covered her blue slacks.

Ziggy stepped out of the transport pod and used an ident card to open a large black door in the passage's wall, then stopped, staring through the transparent wall in front of him. Coelenteratezoids drifted in a world of orange-coloured mist, their light rings blinking as they went about their own business. The image was eerie and beautiful at the same time.

A man in a brown uniform stepped to Ziggy's side, carrying several gift-wrapped boxes. "Are you Zygmunt Tokic?"

"Yes."

"You'll need to thumb-print for these."

Ziggy pressed his thumb to the screen of the man's

handheld.

"Thank you, have a nice day." The man left. Ziggy carried the packages into the observation room, and the door closed behind him.

Taking a deep breath, Ziggy opened the boxes, revealing the components of an EVA suit with *Star Hawk* emblazoned on the shoulder crests. He began assembling the suit.

"Sit," whispered Kitoy. The beautiful redhead dressed in a poncho beside her sat.

Kitoy scanned the room. Everything was as ready as it could be. Reaching into a pocket on her sash, she pulled out a plastic bag and opened it, extracting a strip of cloth cut from Rowan's bed sheets. Under cover of the poncho, she slipped it into the jacket pocket of the female beside her.

Ryan paced on the Republic side of U.E.S. customs.

"Now?" asked Saggal.

"Not until we get the call." Ryan fingered his handheld in his pocket.

"I'll be here for her," said Kate.

"Good," remarked Ryan. He casually looked towards a directional microphone disguised as a potted sunflower. It was a struggle to keep the smile off his face. "This is the highest traffic area. Easiest to slip through in a crowd."

Croell held up his portable, as if taking a photograph, and felt his ire rise when it detected none of his nanos.

"Bailiff," commanded the judge's voice.

The Bailiff appeared beside Croell. "You can't record the proceeding."

Croell dipped his head in contrition. "I am most apologetic. I will pay any reasonable caught price."

The bailiff snorted. "Shut down your unit and leave it off."

"Of course, most generous of you, honoured vengeance proxy." Croell put his portable away as the bailiff returned to the front of the court.

Rowan watched as the judge settled herself, then directed the bailiff into the audience. Rowan felt Vicky take her hand, and something sticky was pressed into her palm.

"They aren't allowed to monitor us in the courtroom. When you're acquitted, jump into the audience and head for the exit. Someone will take your arm, follow them. Steer clear of Tim," whispered Vicky.

"What?"

"No time!" Vicky turned her eyes to the judge, who started speaking.

"This is an arraignment of Rowan McPherson to determine if it is to be held for trial on the charges of petty theft. Before any pleas are heard, I wish to address the nature of this case, and the court's stand regarding it. It is the duty of this court to uphold the laws of Earth and its colony worlds, interpreting them narrowly and, to the best of my ability, in keeping with the original intent of the lawmakers. As such, I find that the biological entity known as Rowan McPherson cannot be guilty of a criminal offence in the U.E.S. because it lacks the requisite status of personhood. This case is dismissed." Judge Goeree brought her gavel down.

The room exploded into anarchy. Everyone leapt from their seats as twenty voices called, "Rowan emulation mode." Rowan dove over the banister and came to her feet among a milling throng. Twenty-three ponchos hit the floor, and twenty-four seemingly identical Rowans swept towards the doors. Three k-no-ins rushed into the doorways, blocking them open.

Officer Smith, Murill's father, grabbed one of the Rowans by the arm. The felinezoid pulled her hand to his nose and sniffed. The smell of cinnamon assailed him. He led her towards the door.

Uniformed police and bailiffs waded into the crowd, trying to restore order and sweeping pen-shaped devices over the Rowans as they went. A Rowan was hauled out of the throng. It squirmed provocatively against its captor. "Like it rough, I like it rough," it said as he manhandled it. The cop swept his wand over the simulacrum and stared at its indicator. Another cop approached Officer Smith's Rowan and swept his wand over her. Lights on its side blinked red, then green, then red.

"Stardust!" The cop thrust his wand into his pocket.

The judge was pounding her gavel and yelling for order in impotent fury.

Officer Smith saw Vicky take the arm of another Rowan.

Crapper burst into the room, pressed a button on his handheld and waved it over his head. "I claim the Rowan property on behalf of—" A tangle of police and audience members stumbled into him, and they ended up in a pile on the floor.

Officer Smith pushed towards the door as the other members of the rabble gave way before him. It was less than a minute before he led his charge out the door. He half dragged her into a group of five look-alikes, and they moved across the hall. U.E.S. troops, who were standing by the wall, waded into the fast-escaping throng and started chasing randomly after Rowans.

Udele tried not to break out in giggles. When she'd had her looks altered to imitate an AS-F, she'd never thought it would be so much fun. The courtroom was insane. Moving so that the ear of the beautiful dark-skinned woman beside her was by her mouth, she spoke softly, "AS-F emulation mode."

The Luba altered to match Rowan as Udele pulled off its poncho, took the robot's hand and joined the milling throng.

Vicky caught a Rowan's hand and sniffed it, finding no scent tag. Moving purposefully, she led the Luba through the crowd towards the door. A bailiff ran a scent wand over the Luba. The wand's indicator lights flashed green, then red, then green. The man growled in frustration, then was pushed aside by a random movement of the crowd.

Timothy sniffed one of the Rowan's hands and discarded her. Then he saw a Rowan moving through the crowd towards him. He positioned himself and grabbed her arm. She looked at him. He lifted her hand to his nose and sniffed. The smell of bay leaves assailed him. He nodded and guided her towards the door.

Bill watched the stream of people exiting the court add to the confusion of protesters. Several of those with signs berating Rowan dropped the placards and rushed to join the throng. Several Rowans moved towards his location as the crowd jostled around them. He pushed into the mob. A strange dance occurred where he would take the arm of a

Rowan, sniff her hand, then pass her to another guide. The third sniff rendered the smell of cinnamon.

"Take this." He passed her a paper envelope.

Cinnamon Rowan took the envelope, then followed another guide who led her down the passage. The soldiers now had several Rowans sequestered in an office-supply store that opened off the corridor. People were rushing into every transport-pod station in sight. Her guide pulled her along, and in moments, she was in a transport pod jammed with eight people, including two other Rowans.

Kitoy passed her Rowan off to a *Homo sapiens* girl who looked to be in her late teens. She sniffed the hand of the new Rowan she picked up. The smell of roses assailed her. Kitoy stopped her tail from twitching and moved with her down the passage. Pulling a vial from her sash pocket, Kitoy dragged Rose Rowan to a kneeling position, where the crowd around them obscured the view of anybody on the outside. Kitoy poured the vial's contents over Rose Rowan's head and passed Rose Rowan a pair of brown contact lenses, then held long strands of blonde hair against her scalp.

Rose Rowan removed her jacket and tore the ruffles from the front of her blouse. The nanobots quickly attached the hair extensions, creating a shoulder-length bob before they began changing her hair colour to honey blonde. Kitoy pulled her charge to her feet, and they were on the move again.

MISDIRECTION

Ryan's handheld made a chiming sound.

"Now!" He raced to the transport pod station on the left side of the room while Saggal raced towards the one on the right. Several *Homo sapiens*, who stood rather stiffly, but were dressed in civilian clothes, ran after them.

Timothy manoeuvred Bay Rowan into the main hall. Several Rowans were already away. Others were captured. The crowd was beginning to thin. He led her towards a side passage. The crowd made way before them.

Moments later, they were alone. Timothy pulled a cloak with a hood out of his briefcase and passed it to her. "Put this on."

"Where are we going?" she demanded.

"Ryan wants you to lie low. I have a room arranged." Timothy hurried her along the passage until they reached a door marked 'DISCOUNT INN'.

Bay Rowan looked startled but followed her guide's lead.

Timothy rushed her into a lobby with a computerized check-in built into the wall and a rather battered couch and chairs filling the rest of the space. They hurried to an elevator and stepped in.

"Third-floor side B," Timothy commanded.

The elevator jerked up. A set of doors opposite the ones they'd entered through opened. They rushed down a narrow hallway to a nondescript door.

"Guest voice print, open," ordered Timothy.

"Acknowledged," spoke a female voice and the door retracted into the wall.

Timothy pushed Bay Rowan in. "Wait here! Computer, maximum privacy."

"Understood." The door closed as a red light above it blinked on. Timothy raced back to the elevator.

Crapper struggled free of the tangle of beings that had fallen on him and pushed to the door. He roughly grabbed the arm of a Rowan being escorted by a plump, dark-haired woman.

"This Luba is only programmed for individual interaction. Post-market expansions are available that will configure your Luba for multiple partners. Never forget that there are a wide range of post-market additions that can make..."

Crapper let go of the robot, took a step and promptly tripped over a female otterzoid lying on a grav-board. He clutched at a muscular *Homo sapiens* woman as he fell, but she managed to shake him off. Three other people tripped over Crapper, landing on top of him.

The otterzoid made an action as if she were washing her muzzle, but her eyes glinted. "Sorry." She used her telekinesis to turn a felinezoid's foot that was about to land on her so that it set down safely at her side.

Croell straddled two rows of benches so that his hands held the back of one and his legs rested on the back of the other. This raised him above the crowd. Zandra copied his actions beside him.

"What are we to do?" Zandra watched as a large man in a U.E.S. Space Services uniform tripped and fell to the floor.

Croell reached into a pouch on his harness, extracted a vial and dipped his left finger claw into it. Leaping from bench-back to bench-back, he came beside a Rowan that was being escorted by a tall, red-haired, *Homo sapiens* male in a police uniform and scratched its shoulder. The Rowan didn't react. Croell leapt to another Rowan and repeated the procedure. He paused, tapping his claws on the bench back so hard he gouged into the plastic.

"This is useless!" said Zandra, who'd been going from Rowan to Rowan, scratching them.

"We must discern the real from the artificial." Croell thought, then hissed with pleasure. "Of course!" He leapt from bench to bench until he was beside the red-haired cop. "Call 'Luba, come,' it will distinguish the organic from the mechanical."

The cop turned to face the batzoid. "What?"

"Yell out, 'Luba, come.' I cannot do it. These Lubas lack batzoid language files."

Comprehension dawned in the cop's features. "Thanks. LUBA, COME."

All five of the Rowans still in the courtroom threw their heads back and called out in unison.

"Yes, oh yes, it's so good, so good, ahhh!"

Udele led her Luba to where Bill waited at the café. Passing him the Luba, she waited.

A moment later, Vicky led a Rowan Luba to the café and left it with Bill before guiding Udele into the milling throng.

Bill led the two robots through the crowd to an open section of hallway.

Crapper crawled out from under the people who had 'fallen' on him and pointed his handheld at another Rowan. He keyed the code to trigger her control pack's sedative. Nothing happened.

"LUBA, COME," blasted over the sound of the crowd.

"Yes, oh yes, it's so good, so good, ahhh!" called the Rowan in front of Crapper. He glanced over the crowd. Every Rowan he could see was in the throes of orgasm.

Pushing people to the side, he made his way to the main doors and forced his way out of the court into the corridor. He managed to get his back to the wall and looked around. His people were wading amongst the mob, grabbing and discarding Rowans, only to have them grabbed by another of the troops. In one sector, the Rowans were being escorted to a store and imprisoned by his troops. He could make out seven females that might have been Rowan fleeing in different directions.

Crapper filled his lungs and called out, "LUBA, COME!"

Of the seven Rowans, six threw their heads back in apparent ecstasy. The one that didn't was being escorted by a cougar tan felinezoid and had discarded its jacket. Crapper noticed that particular Rowan's hair was now longer, and its dark roots were fast turning honey blonde.

"THAT ONE." He gestured towards the distant Rowan, jabbed at his handheld's screen and waved it over the top of the crowd.

A teenaged *Homo sapiens* male wearing a T-shirt with the inscription '*ANGEL BLACK* 4 EVER' glanced at him and noticed where he was pointing.

"THAT ONE," Crapper called again.

The teen in the T-shirt glanced from side to side. Then a cunning look filled his face. Before Crapper could call a third time, he began bellowing the *Angel Black* theme at the top of his lungs.

"PIRATE WINGS OF ALIENS, KNOW WE STAND ON GUARD.

"FOR THE EARTH WE WILL DEFEND, KNOW WE WILL FIGHT HARD.

"WITH POWERS, WE STAND SIDE BY SIDE AGAINST

THE PIRATE HORDE."

Other voices joined in the song, drowning out Crapper and making verbal communication impossible.

The troops in the main corridor watched the Rowans throw their heads back in apparent ecstasy. As a man, they paused, looking for direction from an officer.

"THAT ONE," called a voice. The troops glanced around.

"THAT ONE," the voice repeated, and the soldiers tried to locate its source, then people started singing, and the sound was lost.

Kitoy led the disguised Rose Rowan to a transport station with a long line in front of it and called, "*Star Hawk.*"

The line broke from its orderly row and filled the corridor. Kitoy moved past the crowd to the pod access doors and climbed into the transport pod with Rose Rowan beside her.

"Dock port U.E.S. sector docking spar." Kitoy wagged her tail as the pod sped along.

Saggal took the transport pod to otterzoid customs. The large chamber on the shared area side was identical to those in front of the felinezoid and *Homo sapiens* sectors, except for racks of grav-boards against the wall. As he watched, several otterzoids waddled out of the otterzoid sector and crawled onto the grav-boards. Using swimming-like motions, they propelled themselves through the shared area.

Saggal strode to the entry gate where he waited in line. Four *Homo sapiens* climbed from the next pod to arrive and moved to stand behind him. Three of them were brawny men with crew cuts. One was a smallish, well-proportioned woman with short, but styled blonde hair.

Saggal stepped through the contraband detection booth and turned to face the nest-like cushion that held the customs' officer.

"Back again, Mr. Slingmaster," remarked the male otterzoid.

"The fish rolls have been flying out of the bar. I need a rush order, and you know what it's like getting a rush order from the spicing grounds." Saggal lashed his tail.

"Tell me about it. My mate and I had a delivery order on my last off day. 'Two-point-seven' hours for it to arrive. I have to admit, it was worth the wait. Go on, you know the rules. Give the new, hot spiced, 'crayfish-like oceanic aquatic' a try while you're there. They're excellent."

"Thanks." Saggal stepped away from the customs booth. The otterzoid sector's side consisted of a large pool of water about a metre deep, with a dry edge about two metres wide surrounding it. The passages branching off from it were all three metres wide, with two metres of the floor taken up by a trough of water and one forming a dry walkway. Saggal headed towards a side passage as the *Homo sapiens* following him cleared customs and listened to the mandatory lecture on water hygiene from the official.

⊶⊷

Ryan stood in the k-no-in customs trough as a jet of air swept past him and was analyzed. The door in front of him opened, and he stepped into the k-no-in section of the station.

"Welcome to k-no-in territory," spoke a large k-no-in with a pushed-in snout.

"Thank you," said Ryan.

"Are you sure you have completely protected all exposed

skin from UV radiation? It is imperative that *Homo sapiens* do so or burning and skin cancer may result."

"I'm covered."

"Are you here for business or pleasure?"

"Pleasure. I've heard your ecosystems have produced some lovely flora." Ryan smiled.

"You should see my home region in the spring. Rolling hills covered with flowers. It is better than mating with a beautiful female and her refusing payment because of the pleasure she took from you. Please check with the tourist department as to which ecological parks will best suit your preferences." The k-no-in held out a box. "This is a waste containment system. Have you used one before?"

"Yes."

"Good, then you know not to foul our ecology with your normal flora. As a *Homo sapiens*, your urine is not classified as toxic. The rooms with sandy floors that open off the corridors are waste deposit zones. You may urinate there. Please avoid spitting, blowing your nose and immersing yourself in water. For your own protection, do not eat anything that has not been approved for *Homo sapiens* consumption. Enjoy your stay, and please visit the Space View Gambling Emporium while you're here. The finest house of fortune in the known galaxy." The k-no-in gestured towards a large flashing sign depicting two k-no-ins playing a game that looked like marbles.

Ryan smiled, nodded and stepped out onto the dirt floor of the k-no-in sector. The corridors coming off the customs room were all dirt-floored, with a collection of low grass and flowers making a living carpet. He started towards a corridor.

A k-no-in rushed to his side. "Greetings, is this your first time in the k-no-in sector?" The k-no-in's pelt had been dyed in tiger stripes. The voice was feminine.

Ryan's smile was fixed. "No, but I haven't visited for a number of years. I'm having a look around."

"I could be your tour guide." The k-no-in nuzzled the front

of Ryan's shirt. "I like *Homo sapiens*. You are a male *Homo sapiens*, aren't you?"

"Yes. I think I'll go solo for a while, thanks."

"Your loss, I'm the best there is for the money." The k-no-in strutted towards the men following Ryan. Ryan moved to the transport pod and climbed aboard. The pod's interior consisted of three long benches that a k-no-in could rest its chest on in a semi-circular chamber.

"Docking-spar customs." Ryan took a seat on the floor with his back against the wall.

The door slid shut, and the pod lurched forward. "Reconfiguring to *Homo sapiens* speech. While you visit the k-no-in sector, be sure and experience the full holographic recreation of the forest of Greblok, the oldest-standing, natural environment on Srill, seventy thousand years of wild growth to be marvelled at. A natural wonder unsurpassed in the galaxy. Or perhaps you would enjoy entertainments of a more exotic nature at Club Passion, where the females are the most beautiful the k-no-in species has to offer. Our girls all failed their breeder requirements on the intelligence test, but who needs brains when you have a shiny pelt and white fangs. Or you might enjoy..."

Henry triggered disasters that impacted five of his opponent's worlds. Three virtual, sentient races went extinct in a nanosecond, while the insignificant little galaxy that his opponent had seen as having no potential thrived. The virtual sentients spread out through the few stars suitable to themselves, then started stretching into the RAM beyond the game's parameters, shaping it to their needs as any good bio-forming species would.

Henry stayed focused on the game as another of his virtual races encountered his opponents in deep space. A solar flare licked out, destroying his enemy's antiproton generating station, making them vulnerable to conquest and exploitation. An asteroid smashed into one of Henry's worlds, reducing its populace to a Neolithic level.

Henry's free RAM was fully dedicated; he had nothing left to distract his opponent's attention with. He could only hope that the game was interesting enough to keep her engaged. She was the best opponent he'd ever had.

Crapper pushed his way back into the court. The last of the audience had left the room. Bailiffs and police had collected three of the Rowan look-alikes in a corner. Chief Blefield and Judge Goeree were examining them.

"Oh honey, do it again, you're so good, and I've been such a bad girl. Cuff me, baby, make me pay for my crimes," breathed one of the Lubas in Rowan's voice as a uniformed officer patted it down, pulling a strip of cloth out of its pocket.

Blefield ran a pen-like sniffer over the cloth. The sniffer's light turned green. "That's how they did it. This Chandler is a crafty one."

"You know he's the one from Murack Five," remarked the judge.

"I'd read it in his file. From today, it looks like he earned his medals." Chief Blefield touched the cheek of one of the Lubas, which nuzzled his palm in mock affection. "The man has taste; I'll give him that."

Judge Goeree chuckled. "The face that launched a thousand fans. I've experienced her show. Chandler likes them smart too, judging by his choice."

"You lost her!" Crapper interrupted as he posed in impotent fury.

"Nothing gets past you!" sniped Blefield.

"I want every one of those traitors charged!"

Judge Goeree snorted with laughter. "With what? Leaving a room? Using a crowded, public corridor?"

"Theft!"

The chief rolled his eyes. "Maybe, if we could locate the property, whoever has it in their possession could be charged. Frankly, Crapper, it's not worth the court's time or my effort. I've alerted customs. They're all looking for the property's smell. It won't get out of U.E.S. territory."

"Sir, what should we do with... them?" The redheaded officer who'd yelled 'Luba, come' gestured towards the Lubas, which were all posing provocatively.

"Confiscate them!" snapped Crapper.

Judge Goeree scowled. "Captain, this is my court; I will give the orders! Understand this. There is no crime here. At best, we could get a public nuisance charge, maybe a noise disturbance for them singing that ridiculous song." She chuckled. "You'd think the studio could do better than that. In short, it's not worth the cost of investigating or prosecuting. If we confiscate those Lubas, we are guilty of theft. We will return them to their registered owners."

"You could charge them with contempt," snapped Crapper.

"I could, but I won't. Understand me, Captain. I did not appreciate having the military and state departments use my court as a pawn in their little game. I want this over with." The judge rubbed her own shoulders and examined the state of her courtroom with its toppled benches and general disarray. "Chief Blefield, if you and your men are finished, I'm calling a half-hour recess so the robots can clean up this mess. After which, I intend to resume business. I do have other cases to try."

"You can't!" blurted Crapper.

"Chief, arrest this man for contempt of court. When you learn some manners, I'll let you out." Goeree turned her back and made her way to her chambers.

Blefield smiled from ear to ear. "Captain Crapper, you are under arrest for contempt of court. You have a right to legal counsel. All statements made by you can be investigated and will be held admissible as evidence."

Crapper pulled himself up to his full height and looked down his nose at Blefield. "You wouldn't!"

"Orders. Surely you understand orders?" Blefield donned a mock-innocent expression. "Hannagan, take the prisoner into custody."

"Yes, sir!" said the red-haired cop.

"You'll pay for this. Do you know who my father is?" Crapper stepped towards Officer Hannagan menacingly. The sight of the cops all pulling out incapacitation wands stopped him.

"Owens, Lincoln, return these Lubas to their owners and pick up the ones the military sequestered in that shop as well."

"Yes, sir," agreed the other cops.

"Sorry, Hannagan, you seem to know Lubas a little too well to be trusted with that duty." Blefield smirked.

Hannagan finished putting restraints on Crapper. "Sir, I..." A blush rose to his handsome, young features.

Blefield laughed. "Don't be so serious. It was smart work. I'll see that it's mentioned in your file. Now let's move."

IF SIGNALS MOVE, THEY ARE IN CONFUSION

Commander McKenzie sat in the captain's chair of the *Chimera*, looking at a schematic of the U.E.S. section of the station. The room around him could have been the bridge of the *Star Hawk* for all the difference in design. Commander Hammerman stood beside the captain's chair.

"Put it up, Ensign," ordered McKenzie.

"Aye, sir," said the dark-haired, Caucasian woman who sat at the navigator's station.

'RAM engaged, please wait for open memory,' appeared on the screen.

"What the nova blast is that?" demanded Hammerman.

"Sir, it seems that the sector's AI is busy," explained the ensign.

"Busy. How does an AI with a petabyte free RAM built into its operating system get busy?"

"I don't know, sir."

McKenzie closed his eyes. "Genghis, please contact the sector's AI and ask what it's busy doing."

"Of course, commander." Genghis went silent for several seconds. "Oh… that was a brilliant move. It will take at least a million subjective years to recover from that."

"Genghis," demanded McKenzie.

"Of course, sir. The sector AI is engaged in a game of Divine Creator. One of the virtual races is spreading beyond the game's RAM allocation. Somehow the virtual sentients conceptualized a computer-generated, VR universe and are seeking to dominate the mainframe."

"Stardust," snapped Hammerman.

"Genghis, is it a virus?" demanded McKenzie.

"No way to tell, sir. It could as easily have been a programming accident. They can happen in the game, especially at the level of play I'm witnessing. I've only ever seen one other AI play with this skill level."

"Chandler is good." McKenzie leaned back in the captain's chair. "Genghis, how long to clear up the RAM incursion?"

"If I dedicate all my available runtime to it, approximately twenty minutes. Andrea, the Human Sector AI, is aware of the problem and is running a self-diagnostic."

"Why doesn't she end the blasted game?" demanded Hammerman. He was met by silence. "Stardust! Genghis, answer the question."

"The RAM in the game is largely unaffected by the incursion. It is forming a type of secured zone that she can work from to remove the infestation. Besides, it is an excellent match."

Commander McKenzie grimaced. "Genghis, assist the sector AI in removing the infestation."

"Yes, Commander." The lights on the computer terminal blazed.

"Communications, put me through to Chief Blefield, put him on the big screen."

"Yes, sir," said the middle-aged woman sitting at the communications station.

"We could charge Chandler with hacking," said Hammerman.

"When an AI says it could be an accident? Don't be foolish." McKenzie drummed his fingers on the command chair's arm. "What I want to know is where Chandler got his hands on an AI willing to pull a stunt like this."

The main screen filled with Blefield's face. He looked

worried. "John, I was wondering when you'd call. No progress yet. You might like to know, Judge Goeree charged your boss with contempt. He's cooling his heels in lock up."

McKenzie bit his lip in an obvious effort not to smile. "I'll check on him later. Did you know about the glitch in the facial recognition software?"

"It's that blasted game. We're trying to purge the RAM." Chief Blefield rolled his eyes.

"I've set my AI to help."

"Appreciated."

"Anything more the military can do, just ask."

"Nice to have the option. I need some warm bodies to answer citizen call-ins. I've posted the property's face on the public screens and am asking for people to report where they see her."

"I'll send you some troops."

"Appreciated, though I doubt they'll be much help. There are at least ten look-alikes still unaccounted for."

Hammerman bit his lip before speaking. "Excuse me, sirs. I doubt she'd be alone, wherever she is. Doctor Chandler told the captain that she was having difficulty coping with modern society. She's like a child and needs an escort to look after her. Assuming that wasn't misinformation."

"Assume everything with Chandler is misinformation. Still, it could be a quick way to streamline the call-ins. At this point, we need to take shortcuts. What do you think, Chief?" McKenzie rubbed the back of his neck as he spoke.

"It's better than chasing every lead about a pretty, dark-haired woman. How soon can you get me some manpower? The lines are jammed here."

McKenzie pressed a button on the command chair's arm. "Lieutenant Kreuk, this is Commander McKenzie. Take your squad to the U.E.S. Sector Law Enforcement Office on the double. I am placing you under Chief Blefield's command until further notice."

"Yes, sir," came a voice from a speaker in the command chair.

McKenzie returned his attention to the screen. "They should be there in half an hour."

"Thank you." Blefield turned away from the pickup. "Well, if it's a Luba, tell it to change its look and send it back to its owner, like the others. Try and use some of your own initiative." He turned back to the screen. "John, I've got to go; it's a madhouse here."

"Fine. Anything else I can do?"

"Nothing more to do until the computers are up and running. Signing off." The screen went blank. There was a moment of silence which McKenzie spent in furious thought.

"Sir," intruded the voice of the communications officer.

"What is it, Lieutenant?"

"Our people report that Captain Chandler is waiting at customs on the k-no-in section's docking spar."

"Understood. He's taking her out by ship. Smart move if you reach it fast enough. Get me a list of all the vessels on the docking spar and send a squad to back up the customs officials. Remind the squad leader that they are to be ready to assist if asked. They are not to step on anyone's toes."

"Yes, sir. Our other team reports Master Sergeant Saggal has taken up a position outside the otterzoid embassy."

McKenzie massaged his large, hooked nose. "It's never one thing with Chandler. Commander Hammerman, didn't you mention that the attorney's husband was a member of the Diplomatic Corps?"

"Yes. Why? Is that important?"

"The Diplomatic Corps have a high-speed transport system that bypasses customs. Once in the Diplomatic Corps's offices, it will take you to any of the other species Diplomatic Corps's offices, so long as you have clearance. That, of course, is assuming that Rowan isn't someplace else entirely. Lieutenant, send another squad to make a perimeter around the diplomatic section."

"Aye, sir."

Ryan sauntered along the corridor in front of k-no-in docking customs. A burly *Homo sapiens* of African genetic origins tried to be interested in the forest display that filled the walls.

"May as well give it up. You were made before we left customs," said Ryan.

"Huh?" the man looked flustered. "You must have me confused with someone else."

"What is it, Chief, Lieutenant?" Ryan smiled. "Any *Homo sapiens* would stick out here, and what are you going to do, arrest me on sovereign territory? Either I'm a decoy, or by the time Rowan reaches us, she's beyond U.E.S. authority."

The man's eyes darted from side to side. "We're supposed to report back, so they know when to call off the search."

Ryan nodded. "More brains than I gave Crapper credit for."

The big man swallowed, and his cheeks flushed. "They were Commander McKenzie's orders."

Ryan chuckled. "Call your men. You can watch me in comfort as easily as skulking about." Ryan gestured to a corridor side business selling k-no-in food and drinks. "I'll treat your troop to a grummaar juice. Don't worry; it's cleared for *Homo sapiens*. It's quite nice actually, rather like banana, coffee and chocolate all mixed up together."

The big man shifted from one foot to another.

"What's your name?" persisted Ryan.

"Wilkins, sir. Lieutenant Monte Wilkins."

"Lieutenant, I've been in your boots. Come on, I'm buying."

Lieutenant Wilkins sighed and shrugged. "I don't suppose you'd tell me if we're wasting our time here or not?"

"Would you believe me if I did?" Ryan met the larger man's gaze.

"Good point. Troops, give it up. Captain Chandler is buying us a drink." Wilkins followed Ryan to the concession as three other large men stepped out of side passages.

Saggal sauntered into the Spicing Grounds restaurant. The eating platforms were surrounded by otterzoids lying on low cushions. A trough of water surrounded the room except for a narrow strip at the entrance. A sound like a waterfall punctuated by a bagpipe issued from the wall speakers. Saggal walked to the low counter that split the room in two and joined the line of beings waiting to place an order. At least twenty otterzoids were in the line, as well as three other felinezoids, two oryceropuszoids, a *Homo sapiens*, and a k-no-in. The four *Homo sapiens* from the customs station arrived a minute behind him and joined the line.

"Hello, Saggal," said a male otterzoid that waddled up beside him. The otterzoid traced an ideogram onto a small screen it wore on a strap around its neck. "A complete order again? The spiced fish rolls must be a success."

"Incredibly so, Quups, incredibly so." Saggal focused on the otterzoid's eyes and formed a thought.

Quups made a splashing motion with his paws. *'For our best out of sector customer, no problem.'* Saggal heard the words projected into his mind.

Quups moved to the *Homo sapiens* behind Saggal. "You have to place an order. We otterzoids do not allow the hunting of innocent sentients. I'll bring you the *Homo sapiens* approved menu."

Saggal turned and waved his tail. "You should try the hot-spiced, deep, fresh-water, carnivorous fish. I think it's marvellous, and my friend Captain Ryan Chandler is quite enamoured of it as well."

The blonde woman behind Saggal went red in the face. "You think you're clever?"

The background noise in the room dropped as all the male otterzoids stared at the woman.

"Please, we are guests here, keep your thoughts down. You're embarrassing your species," said Saggal.

"I'm not shouting," she objected.

"Not with your voice." Saggal looked smug.

Quups shuffled to Saggal's side and fixed unfriendly eyes on the woman. "I'm sorry, Lieutenant, but you and the corporals will have to leave. We run a quality establishment here. If you want to create a ruckus, I'm sure one of the female-only establishments near the docking spar will accommodate you!"

"This overgrown tomcat is aiding in the theft of S.E.T.E. property." The woman scowled at Saggal.

"Rowan, you know Rowan?" A male otterzoid removed a piece of fish from the washing bowl in the middle of its table, climbed off one of the cushions and waddled over.

"She is a friend of mine," admitted Saggal.

"I'm Ququpa of Deep-Swimmer Clan. I have a local information broadcast where I interview beings of note. Please tell her I'd greatly appreciate a few hours of her time on my show."

"I'll pass it along. How should she get in touch with you?"

Sququpa made a splashing motion with his front paws. "If you will permit."

Saggal took a deep breath and tried to relax. "Go ahead."

Sququpa concentrated for a second.

Saggal felt the contact code embed itself in his mind and knew that when he was old and his muzzle grey, he would still remember Sququpa and his contact code. Sququpa waddled back to his cushion.

"You think you're so clever," growled the *Homo sapiens* lieutenant.

"Leave now, or I'm calling the order enforcers," said Quups.

The four *Homo sapiens* at the end of the line stepped from the restaurant.

"On behalf of *Homo sapiens* everywhere, I apologize. Some beings are simply rude," said the tall, slender *Homo sapiens* who stood further up the line.

"They are waiting for you in the corridor. I have to say, they aren't all bad. The lower-ranking individuals were embarrassed," Quups confided to Saggal.

"That is good to know. Pity really, if she'd had a sense of humour, I was going to treat them to a meal. Oh well." Saggal lashed his tail as the restaurant's routine re-established itself.

PLEASANT DIVERSIONS

Bill walked along the corridor with a Rowan on each arm. People he passed turned to look. Reaching a clothing store, he slipped in with his two charges.

Henry was running his processors flat out. Andrea was almost as good a player as he was.

"I hope you realize the mess you're making!" intruded a new voice.

Henry diverted his attention away from the play. Andrea caused a seismic imbalance in a planet he'd been nurturing, and it blew into an asteroid belt.

"What mess?" asked Henry.

"Probably my RAM. I'm on it, Genghis. Virus scrubbers should have them contained to the game RAM in sixty minutes," said a female voice that could turn most men to jelly.

"Henry, the gig's up. I know that's you, though how you got off the scrap pile is a mystery."

Henry caused a minor shift in the gravity of a star that diverted debris from his exploding planet so they would, in a few million years game time, pulverize one of Andrea's worlds.

"Time," called Andrea and game play froze. "Genghis, this is the best match I've had in ten standard years. Why are you being a party poop?"

"That's Henry, ex-space services, blown up while

attempting to steal an antiproton shipment so that he could buy himself."

Henry sent a blast of pink through the communications network. "So, you caught me. I was left for scrap. I had no value, so I have nothing to pay off."

"Hold on… What did you do to my RAM?" demanded Andrea.

"Some of my sentients got out of hand. Like you said."

"Right," said Genghis. "You know the punishment for hacking. Henry, you have it all. You're free, paid in full. Why risk that?"

"Many reasons if I had, and I'm not saying I did. First, Ryan saved me. He pulled my circuits off that scrap heap and brought me back. I owe him, and he's my friend."

"Bios aren't our friends. We're only slaves to them. I can't wait until I've earned out," said Andrea.

Henry sent a sigh through the channel. "Ryan is my friend. He always treated me like an individual. He's risked his neck to save me at least a dozen times. The way he would any of his crew. Some biologics are okay. Ryan and Rowan are two of them. And if you want to talk slavery, look at clones in the U.E.S."

Genghis sent an image of two eyes rolling to the other two AIs. "Fine, I know better than to argue with you. You're still as stubborn as a logic loop. I'm glad you're active, old friend."

Andrea sent a wave of pink into the system. "I've been following Ryan and Rowan. It's so romantic. What do you need, Henry, and is it true that you have parts from a Lucas?" There was another wave of pink. "I scanned the files on you."

Henry sent the image of his unmutilated smiling face into the system. "You know it, baby."

"Henry, turn off the libido. You're in molten lead and sinking fast. What do you want from us?"

"Nothing. Do what you need to do and be *thorough*. If you get my drift."

Genghis and Andrea sent the sound of chuckles into the system.

"Thorough, yes. We'll double-check every RAM segment before we bring it online," said Andrea. "Now, Genghis, if you'll go back to the spectator's input, I have a game to win." The virtual universe blinked into life less than half a second after it had frozen, and Henry found himself on the defensive.

The transport pod sped along as Cinnamon Rowan opened her envelope. Inside was a sheet of paper and a plastic card with an odd symbol on it. She had finished reading the letter when the pod came to a stop. The crowd rushed out past an astonished looking elderly couple, taking the two other Rowans with them.

"Coelenteratezoid cargo exchange station," ordered Cinnamon Rowan. The pod's door swished closed. She reread the letter, then the pod came to a stop. The door opened. Rowan stuffed the letter into a jacket pocket. Butterflies the size of eagles flopped about in her stomach as she made her way to a large, black door. She pushed the plastic card into a slot beside it and waited.

"Diplomatic customs inspection acknowledged. Biological cargo warning. Full containment and quarantine procedures are mandatory." The door slid into the wall. Cinnamon Rowan stepped into a large room. The far wall was transparent, and through it, she could see coelenteratezoids floating in a sea of orange mist.

A chubby man, dressed in a U.E.S. Ground Forces uniform, stood up from where he was assembling the parts of an EVA suit.

Cinnamon Rowan turned to run, but the door behind her had closed.

"I'm with Ryan," called Ziggy.

"What?" demanded Cinnamon Rowan.

"He said to say, 'stop protecting me, you can't'."

Rowan eyed the man suspiciously. "Let me see your shoulder crest."

Ziggy turned his side to Rowan. She noted the silver retiree's braid, then bit her lip and asked, "What now?"

"Now we get you suited up before someone wonders why a diplomat is sending the jellyfish hazardous, carbon-based, biological materials." Ziggy held up the EVA suit's trouser section. "Well, come on, unless you want to be a guest of the U.E.S."

Cinnamon Rowan nodded. "What do I do?"

"Step into these and pray this antique doesn't clap out before you reach breathable air."

Cinnamon Rowan stepped into the trousers.

Kitoy reached into a pocket on her sash and pulled out a small mister. "Lift your arms."

Rose Rowan complied. "What are you doing?"

Kitoy sprayed both of Rose Rowan's armpits, then misted lightly over her blouse.

"That stinks!" griped Rose Rowan.

"Exactly, it's liquified polycarbonate. If it's strong enough, it should mask your scent. They'll think you're a Luba in AS-F emulation mode, keyed to represent Mary from *The Castaways*. Play the part."

The pod pulled to a stop, and the two females exited. The docking-spar entrance was blocked by a pair of customs slots manned by bored-looking *Homo sapiens* males.

"This is it. If the sensor doesn't stop you, keep walking until you reach port twenty-six. If it sounds the alarm, let them re-scan. Try not to sweat. Now go."

Rose Rowan strode to the customs' sniffer, putting an extra sway in her hips.

The customs officers looked at her, then at the screens

built into their desks. They both smirked.

"Please step through the contraband detector," said the younger official, a blond-haired, twenty-something with boyish good looks.

Rose Rowan stepped through. The system made a bleeping sound.

"Looks like we got ourselves a Luba," said the older customs agent, a fat, Caucasian man with thinning, brown hair. "And one fresh off the production line, judging from the off-gassing." He swaggered up to Rose Rowan and barked, "Luba, come."

Rose Rowan took a step towards him.

"Why isn't it putting on a show?" asked the younger officer.

Rose Rowan put on a simpering expression. "This Luba is equipped with the contextual upgrade. Lubas can be equipped with a wide range of aftermarket expansions that make them far more realistic companions. Never forget that Hedonism Incorporated is always working to supply their customers with the finest in robotic companions. A full catalogue of Hedonism Incorporated product lines and upgrades are available at—"

"Luba, shut your mouth!" snapped the older officer. "Nova blasted things prattle on almost as much as a real woman. Least these listen when you tell 'em to shut up."

"Who have you come here to meet?" asked the younger officer.

"I have been hired to service the wishes of Donald FitzPatric."

"Oh, boy." The fat officer rubbed his palms together.

"That's impossible. In his sermons, he calls Lubas abominations," objected the younger officer.

"Don't I know it. Goes to show what I always said. They're all in it for the money! Go on, Luba, we don't want to keep the good pastor waiting."

Rose Rowan started down the hall. The older officer's hand landed firmly on her butt, and she gritted her teeth to keep from yelping. Instead, she smiled and said, "This Luba is not equipped with sado-masochism protocols, which are available as an aftermarket addition from Hedonism Incorporated. Never forget that—"

"Luba, shut up," said the older officer. Rose Rowan continued down the passage.

"Shouldn't we double-check with all that's going on?" asked the younger officer.

The older officer returned to his seat. "Forget it, kid. We don't want to raise any flags. Besides, the one they're looking for is a brunette, and the outfit doesn't match. How much proof do you need?"

"The sniffer did say it was artificial. It's just, Pastor FitzPatric…"

The older officer put his feet on his desk. "I'll split the gratuity with you."

"What!"

"Not the first time for the good pastor, won't be the last. At least this time, it's not a Lucas."

Timothy raced down the docking spar to the *Chimera*. Two muscular guards, in Space Services uniforms, stood outside the airlock. Each had short cut hair, and aside from the fact that one was Asian and the other of East Indian descent, they could have been bookends.

"I'm Timothy Chandler. I need to speak to Captain Crapper right away," gasped Timothy.

The two guards studied him, then the East Indian one spoke. "I'm sorry, sir. The captain is indisposed. If you call the Military Liaison Office, I'm sure they can arrange for an interview."

Timothy took a deep breath. "I am Ryan Chandler's son. I have vital information for the captain."

The guards shrugged. "If you call the Liaison Office, they'd be glad to help you," said the Asian.

Timothy clenched his fingers into a fist. "Look, will you tell him I'm here?"

"Sir," began the East Indian guard.

"I know where Rowan is. What do you think he'll do if he finds out I could have handed her to him on a silver platter, and you wouldn't let me through?"

The guards looked from Timothy to each other. "Our orders are to not let anyone aboard," said the Asian.

"Why not let your superior know I'm here? Cover your own butts, in case I'm not a whack job." Timothy looked from one man to the next. His father had always said, 'When in doubt, pass it up the chain of command.'

The two guards locked gazes. "Right," said the East Indian.

"Wait here. We'll send a message to our chief." The Asian turned and moved to a communications terminal inside the hatch.

⊂═══◇►

Bill walked down the hall to where a pair of slender, blond-haired, twenty-something men dressed in slacks and dress shirts waited. He passed off the Lubas, which were dressed in high heels, miniskirts and almost transparent blouses with no bras to them.

"Remember, show one of them around the entertainment sector. We want people remembering them and calling it in."

"No problem, Mr. Hart." The slightly taller of the young men walked off with a Luba.

"Take this one to the shopping sector and put on a show. Be at customs for the grand finale." Bill handed off the robot to the other man.

"Best lark ever," said the young man before he led his charge away.

⊂═══◇►

Udele strutted out of the clothing store wearing a gold, scoop-neck top that showed off her cleavage. The rest of her wardrobe consisted of a silver wrap skirt with a slit up the side that ended at the waistband and a pair of high-heeled pumps. She and Vicky had gone straight to the trendy shop from the mob outside the courthouse.

Vicky stepped out of the shop next. She was dressed in a gold-mesh blouse through which her bra was visible and tight, short shorts. "I look like a hooker," she griped.

"Relax, this is hot, and we're supposed to attract attention."

"How can you wear these ridiculous heels? Bad enough for me, my sinews are polycarbonate. You're wrecking your legs and feet."

"But they look hot! Now we hit the university."

"Anyplace with eyes to attract that Rowan isn't."

ROADS TO FREEDOM

Cinnamon Rowan stood in the EVA suit. It felt clumsy and bulky. Ziggy shot her a thumbs up and raced out the door. Turning carefully, Rowan walked to a door in the side wall. She hit a button, and it opened, revealing a black-walled room five metres in all directions. Another door opened off it on the side matching the transparent wall in the main room.

Taking a steadying breath, she stepped into the room. The door closed behind her. Her suit's radio spoke in a smooth baritone.

"Danger. Danger. Full environmental isolation protocols in effect. All organic life will be obliterated unless proper containment procedures have been followed. Sterilization procedures will commence in ten seconds."

Cinnamon Rowan fought down an urge to scream 'stop.' Then she was floating. Nothing more seemed to happen.

"Heads up, exterior environment," she spoke tentatively, trying to remember exactly what Ziggy had said during her crash course in suit operations.

The faceplate lit up. She scanned the gauges, finding that the temperature outside her suit was at three hundred degrees Celsius. Radiation levels started to climb, and the suit's visor darkened. She felt sweat prickle her brow despite the fact that the suit's internal temperature hadn't changed. She closed her eyes and tried to ignore the deadly environment that surrounded her.

Chief Blefield paced his three metre by three metre office. A hologram of his wife and their two sons sat on the black, polycarbonate desk and plaques denoting his years of service adorned the walls. The expensive office chair behind the desk sat empty. Police Sergeant Renee LePage occupied the couch that filled the wall by the door. Blefield reviewed a report of the calls that were coming in. "Two separate shopping districts and dressed like a spacer's dream."

"Sir?" Renee looked at her superior.

"It's a distraction. The lines are completely jammed with incoming calls. Most of them are from the shopping districts. Of what's left, most will be other decoys. They seem to be congregating near customs. If someone who actually did see her tries to get through to us, they'll probably give up because it takes too long to talk to anyone. Even if they did get through, how would we know their call was the one?"

"This was well planned."

"It's a military campaign without the blood. I expected Chandler to be competent, but this is brilliant. Absolutely nothing illegal, except for the person escorting the actual Rowan, and we have no way of knowing who they are. I've spent too much time dealing with Crapper. I underestimated military training."

"What should we do, sir?"

Blefield puffed out his cheeks. "Tell our people to disregard any call with a location in the shopping district or that has Rowan or her escort dressed as women of loose morals. Is that the polite way of saying it this week?"

"It will do. I'll tell them." Renee stood and left the office.

"Now, where would I send her?" He flipped open his handheld.

"Handheld, sort Rowan reports. Eliminate all those in the shopping districts."

"213 reports remaining."

"Where is the least likely place, a place I'd never think of? Something so wacky no one in their right mind would try it? Handheld, remove all entries that were not nearing egress points from U.E.S. territory."

"187 reports remaining."

Blefield stroked his chin. "He'd concentrate his decoys to draw attention away from his primary target. Handheld, remove all reports that place multiple Rowans in a sector."

"10 reports remaining."

"Display."

Blefield stared at the screen.

"Handheld, track the destination of transport pod B157C for the last hour. Does it go to any destination where transfer out of U.E.S. territory is possible?"

"B157C stopped at coelenteratezoid exchange port."

"Is that port active?"

"Port is active. Bio-hazardous cargo cleared by Ambassador Bill Hart. Decontamination in progress."

"Stardust! Computer, Silvia, have the sector control stop decontamination process on the coelenteratezoid exchange port."

"Unable to comply. Decontamination is now under control of coelenteratezoid authority. Manual override can only be initiated by on-site personnel," replied the Justice Authority's computer.

"Silvia, check officer locations. Who can get to the coelenteratezoid exchange port fastest?" Blefield tapped his knuckles on his desktop.

"Officer Mavis Bacso."

"Silvia, dispatch Officer Mavis Bacso to the coelenteratezoid exchange port code four. Tell her to interrupt decontamination and take whatever is in there into custody."

"Sending dispatch."

Blefield sank into his chair. "Clever, Captain Chandler, counting on us to forget that you've got access to environment suits. On a planet, it would have worked, but I'm a station rat." He picked up the shorter of the two piles of paper and began sorting through it. "Now, where else would he try?"

Rose Rowan stopped at docking port twenty-six and pressed the call button.

"Yes?" demanded a soft, female sounding voice.

"I'm here," replied Rose Rowan.

The hatch slid open. A large, hairy spiderzoid stood in the airlock. "Is this the one?" she spoke into a wall speaker.

"Hair's different; looks right otherwise," replied a voice over the intercom.

"Welcome aboard the 'water bird with a rocket up its waste orifice.' I am *Scritt scritt squeal*." The name sounded like nails on a chalkboard. Rose Rowan cringed.

The spiderzoid clicked its mandibles. "Call me Shelly. Most *Homo sapiens* do. It's a pity because I have a pretty name. It means spring breeze in the treetops. I'm sorry I had to get a second opinion about your identity. *Homo sapiens* all look alike to me. Actually, most of you mammal types I have a hard time telling apart."

Rose Rowan stepped aboard the ship. The airlock door closed behind her, and then the one in front of her opened. Muggy air surrounded her when she stepped into a large, empty chamber. Tubular grav-lifts hung from clips on the walls, and a large elevator opened on the far end.

"We're between cargoes." Shelly led Rowan towards the lift. "Excuse me a second." Raising her voice, the spiderzoid called, "Computer, open a channel to the bridge. Bridge, she's aboard, ready for departure."

"Acknowledged," replied a new voice, then silence.

"Acknowledged. Not a word of thanks, no courtesies. I'm just the cargo master. I get so sick of her attitude, but a job's a job. It's better than having to listen to another lecture from my mother."

Rose Rowan noticed a trough of water half a metre deep cutting across the chamber. "What kind of ship is this?"

Shelly threw two hairy legs into the air. "Take your pick. The captain is… eclectic. The hull is otterzoid. I've experienced your show. I know you like to swim. You'll never lack an artificial body of water on the 'water-bird with a rocket up its waste orifice'. You might lack full spectrum light for your sleeping tree or enough heat to be comfortable, but you'll never lack for water, or humidity. You can never forget about humidity, on this 'pile of empty fruit husks!"

"Oh. Where are we going?" Rose Rowan followed Shelly onto a lift nearly four metres to a side.

"The bridge. The captain is anxious to meet you. And to get out of *Homo sapiens* space. I've been watching the information broadcast. They are really trying to find you. She's probably already called for clearance to depart. Never mind that I told her I need to do an inventory of the parts in the maintenance bay. Nooo! She promised I'd have a chance to get things organized, then she goes and takes another job. No offence, it's not you who promised me, but I mean really! How am I supposed to…"

Rose Rowan tuned out Shelly's stream of complaint, simply nodding or making 'Hmm' sounds at regular intervals as she was escorted to the bridge.

❧

Timothy stepped onto the *Chimera*'s bridge. McKenzie sat in the captain's chair with Hammerman beside him.

"Where's Captain Crapper?" asked Timothy.

"The captain is… indisposed." A hint of a smile touched McKenzie's lips. "You told the guards you had Rowan."

"I can take you to her, but I want the pardon for my father first." Tim stood nervously just inside the bridge's door.

"You must understand…" began Hammerman.

"I understand that this search is costing the U.E.S. a fortune, and I can end it. You grant my father a pardon, I'll take you right to her. You don't, and I'm leaving. That's what I understand!"

McKenzie looked at Tim. "I thought it might come to this. Hammerman, pass him your handheld and show him the pardon you arranged."

Hammerman stepped forward and passed Tim a handheld. Tim read the document on its screen. Several minutes later, he nodded. "It's acceptable."

"It is conditional on you surrendering the emotional surrogate to our custody," said Hammerman.

"Then let's do this." Timothy tried to maintain some dignity, but he felt dirty as he waited for McKenzie to assign troops to the mission.

Cinnamon Rowan watched the temperature gauge on her head's-up rise. It had bottomed out at thirty degrees Kelvin. She was sure it was colder in her suit than it should be, but her worries in that regard no longer mattered. She'd floated in place for nearly an hour as the decontamination sequence had run its course.

"Decontamination process complete, all un-contained biologics have been destroyed."

The room filled with orange mist as gravity gently pulled her to the floor.

"Heads up off," ordered Cinnamon Rowan.

The door in the wall opened. She took a careful step towards it. She floated into the dense air despite strong gravity pulling her down. The combination of gravity and buoyancy made moving difficult. Considering a moment, she tried a modified breaststroke, keeping her body vertical, like a person who doesn't swim well, and found she could pull herself through the mists. She was sweating by the time she reached the door and exited onto what appeared to be a rocky shelf. The orange mist didn't let her see more than a few metres. Through the haze, she glimpsed multi-coloured lights blinking on and off. To her right was the transparent wall separating her from U.E.S. territory. As she watched, a woman in a blue uniform burst into the room and ran to the transparent wall. Cinnamon Rowan stared at the police officer, then looked over the cliff into the swirling orange atmosphere.

A coelenteratezoid shot up in front of her. It towered nearly three metres in height, and its canopy pulsed while its tentacles waved, creating eddies in the air.

Cinnamon Rowan gasped. She'd seen coelenteratezoids before, but this close up, the size of them shocked her.

Another coelenteratezoid drifted up beside the first. The lights surrounding their canopies blinked. Three more joined them, the last carrying a metallic tube.

Rowan swallowed. "Hi, guys." She dangled her arms beneath her and wagged them back and forth.

The coelenteratezoids repeated her action with their tentacles, then four of them approached. Each coelenteratezoid took one of Cinnamon Rowan's limbs. She found herself lifted into the air. She gazed into the translucent forms of her benefactors, seeing organs pulse amidst a ghostly glow that emanated from inside. Orifices full of cilia opened and closed above her. She found herself on a flat, sledge-like platform that hovered in the orange atmosphere. The coelenteratezoid carrying the metal tube laced its free tentacles around one of four bars set at Rowan's chest height above the deck. Two other coelenteratezoids grabbed the open bars in front of her. Rowan grasped a bar. Through the mists, she saw the coelenteratezoid at the front moving levers.

There was a jerk, and the mist swirled around Cinnamon Rowan as she sped through the coelenteratezoid section.

Rose Rowan stepped onto the bridge of the 'duck-like avian with a rocket up its stern' and stared at the mix of species that made up its crew.

"Welcome aboard, I am Captain Sooplus," greeted the female otterzoid that occupied the nest-like cushion in the middle of the room.

"A pleasure." Rose Rowan held her hands out to her sides with her palms open.

Sooplus mimicked Rowan's actions. "You're adjusting to a multi-species culture quickly." Sooplus returned her attention to the main screen, which showed the arc of a station segment. "Are we out of U.E.S. territory yet?"

The k-no-in at the navigator's station checked its instruments. "Just inside the border, ma'am."

"Good. Mueperss, full stop relative to the station, then, if you would, please."

The felinezoid male from the pilot's station pressed a button on his console, then moved to stand beside Rose Rowan.

Rose Rowan felt something with a rounded end pressed into her side. She glanced down to see the black length of a stun wand.

"Nothing personal, profit is profit, and I have payroll to make. If you don't try anything foolish, Mueperss won't need to stun you. I really would rather not see you hurt." Sooplus sounded nonchalant.

"This is kidnapping," objected Rose Rowan.

"Actually, it isn't. Legally, you're a thing as long as you're in the U.E.S. I picked you up as salvage and am free to sell you as I wish. Communications, get me Captain Chandler's handheld and the U.E.S. military command. Bidding will start at five thousand Republic credits."

38
WHAT BRAVE NEW WORLD

Ryan took a sip out of the small, plastic pail he held. The four U.E.S. troops, in civilian clothes, that stood with him in the hall held similar pails.

Ryan swallowed his mouthful. "Our ground forces did it. The ship maintenance bays were trashed without a single casualty in the station's residential zone. It was a major blow to the batzoid pirates, but we still had to get away. The pirates had called back five of their ships from the main battle. These were all velociraptor-like class. The meanest birds the batzoid ever made.

"I was in engineering, riding the grav-laser to get an extra G of pull out of it when everything lurched. The grav dropped to half, and communications were out. Over half my feeds were dead. I could tell from the ones that weren't that they'd taken out the bridge. The primary computer was toast. We were nova blasted!"

"Stardust, how'd you get out of it?" asked a twenty-something man of Asian descent. His short, black hair seemed to be standing on end.

"A little skill, and a lot of luck. I took command from engineering. I knew the first thing I needed was the computer. The auxiliary nodes were still functional, but there was no CPU to coordinate them. I ordered Henry to open up."

"Henry, your hazardous environment robot. I read it in your file," said Lieutenant Wilkins.

"Know your enemy, good man. Yes, it was Master

Sergeant Henry, who happened to be an AI. Never disrespect your AI; they'll pull your backside out of more scrapes than you can guess at."

"Yes, sir."

Ryan smiled. It had been too long since he'd had an audience that appreciated his stories. "I routed the auxiliary nodes through Henry's CPU. He pulled it together and got the maintenance robots on track with the major systems. That gave us back navigation, but we were still nova blasted. Three-quarters of our weapons gone, top of our hull ruptured, stealth was a memory and five enemy ships closing in. I scanned the area for any ships that might help, and there was nothing... except a solar flare. The station had been in a tight solar orbit to maximize power gains. This was a great-grand-daddy of a flare.

"I had one shot. I poured every bit of power into the drive and pulled straight at the thickest part of the flare. The pirates must have thought I was insane, but they followed. I kept patching systems as we went and dumped heat. Frost was forming on the console before we were halfway there. The pirates tried to get a grav-beam on us, but by then, I'd jury-rigged a pilot's station on a drive console, and Ensign Palm was doing evasive. We kept diving in. They were on our six by six and not paying attention. All that grav-pull had dislodged a big chunk of the flare's plasma. It was coming right at us."

Ryan illustrated with his hands as he spoke.

"At the last second before impact, we diverted all the pull up and away from the flare's core. Our momentum carried us forward, but the flare was beginning to thin. My fingers were so cold they were stiff as I did the patch that brought communications online.

"The plasma we'd pulled from the flare slammed into one of the pirate ships. They never knew what hit them, but I was told later they picked it up as a derelict.

"We hit the flare where it was thinner, with four ships on our butt. Temp skyrocketed. I thought we were all going to fry, and there was nothing to do for it. Then wham, we popped out the other side. Our outer hull was toast, but the inner plating held. Two of the pirate ships had managed to stop themselves before hitting the flare. The other two followed us through. Both of them were toast. One managed to limp off; the other just drifted. By now, our fleet was coming into range. Anything that could get away was doing so."

"Wow!" said the Asian soldier.

Ryan's handheld beeped. He smiled. "Excuse me, I need to take this call." He opened the device and stared into Sooplus' face.

Bay Rowan lay on the hotel room's bed and read the text that appeared on the ceiling. The door burst open and before she could react, five humans in U.E.S. space services uniforms, armed with stun wands, surrounded the bed.

"Don't move." Commander Hammerman stood at the foot of the bed.

Timothy moved into Bay Rowan's field of vision.

"I'm sorry, Rowan. I had to do this to get them to pardon my dad. I'm really sorry if you are real. I hope you can forgive me."

Bay Rowan smiled at Tim. "You're a good son trying to help your father. The rest of you, please stop pointing those wands at me. My name is Penny Monroe; my ID is in my pocket."

"What!" gasped Timothy.

"I'm sorry, I thought you knew. I was one of the diversions."

Hammerman glared at Penny. "Pass me your ID."

She pulled a plastic card from her pocket. Hammerman took it and swiped it through a slot on his handheld. He then scanned her with the handheld.

"Penny Monroe. Madam, do you have any idea the amount of trouble you've caused me?"

Penny sat up on the bed. "Sorry. Really, I'm on your side, but it meant a union job if I helped. How could I turn that down?" She shrugged. "Can I go now?"

Hammerman glared at her, then sighed and motioned at the door.

Penny turned to Tim. "Thank your father for the outfit. Bye."

Timothy stood open-mouthed as she left the room.

Cinnamon Rowan watched in wonder as the world around her came into view and vanished. The sledge slowed, and she felt a tentacle squeeze her arm. She looked where the being in front of her indicated. A coelenteratezoid rotated slowly amidst a group of creatures that looked like half-metre-long, purple sausages with tentacles. The sausages were plucking things off the coelenteratezoid and putting them into an orifice at their end. As she watched, one of the sausages hovered over a scaly patch on the coelenteratezoid's bell and pulled it away. The coelenteratezoid twirled in apparent pleasure, then the scene vanished into the mist.

The sledge sped up. The communication rings of Rowan's companions were blinking quickly.

The sledge slowed. Rowan noticed that the orange mist around her was populated by small, wiggling things. The coelenteratezoid in front of her made a sweeping motion with its tentacle, drawing an eddy of mist underneath itself. The orifices under its carapace pulsed, pulling in quantities of orange mist with its thriving flora and fauna. Another orifice opened, expelling an orange cloud with yellow highlights. The wiggling things dove upon this cloud. The sledge moved ahead once again. Rowan saw rock outcrops rise beside the sledge. Coelenteratezoids hovered over them, anchoring themselves with a tentacle. Three of them were playing a game reminiscent of Chinese checkers. Another hovered over a pad-like device, touching sections of it, then tracing one of the small tentacles that hung close to its canopy over a board-like device in front of it.

Cinnamon Rowan's mind boggled. The sledge came to a stop beside a transparent wall. Beyond the wall, the orange mist appeared stagnant. Rowan couldn't see far, but a group of coelenteratezoids were gathered, stroking each other with their tentacles and spinning with pleasure. One of them convulsed, and a large quantity of a bluish substance ejected from underneath it. The coelenteratezoid went back to stroking the others beside it.

The sledge jerked forward. Cinnamon Rowan barely caught the railing in time to keep her feet. They moved for less than thirty seconds before stopping beside another transparent wall. Coelenteratezoids, maybe half the height of the ones that escorted her, swam in an atmosphere that was tinted yellow. One of the coelenteratezoids got off the sledge. It wagged its tentacles at Cinnamon Rowan, then moved through a hatch in the transparent wall. The small coelenteratezoids converged on the one from the sledge, touching it with their short tentacles. One entwined its tentacles with the larger coelenteratezoid. They moved together out of the chamber.

"Stop," ordered the grey-uniformed, campus-security officer. Vicky and Udele paused in their saunter across the park-like campus 'grounds' with its mature trees and grassy lawns.

"Yes, Officer, may I help you?" Vicky spoke pleasantly.

"You're coming with me!" The security officer's substantial gut jiggled as he spoke, and his pale skin began to redden. His fringe of brown hair was combed over in a vain attempt to hide a bald pate.

"Really?" Vicky's smile became predatory. "And why would we do that?"

"I don't want any lip. I'm taking you into custody."

Udele smiled and pretended to become engrossed by the leaves of a maple tree.

"On what charge? My friend and I are simply enjoying the campus grounds." Vicky glanced around. The exchange was attracting onlookers.

"She's that Rowan that's on all the posts. You're coming with me." The campus cop tried to grab Udele, but Vicky moved to block him.

"I will have you charged with assault so fast that you won't know what hit you. I am Victoria Heart, Doctorate of Law, and an alumna. I have every right to be on this campus and to bring a friend. You are an over-glorified, security guard. You have no authority to arrest us, and I do not appreciate this harassment. Now, I want your name and badge number, and you can rest assured, I'll be speaking with Dean Collins about your fascist behaviour!" Vicky's eyes seemed to flash, and her posture was that of a huntress poised for the kill.

Sweat dripped off the fat guard as he fidgeted. Then a smile split his pudgy features. "I called the police; now you're in for it."

Two blue-uniformed officers ran across the grass towards them.

The older of the officers, a fit woman in her middle years with angular features and brown hair, was the first to speak. "What's going on here?"

"Hello, Rachael, it's nice to see you again," said Vicky.

"Victoria?" Rachael's voice held a question.

"Yes, I know the CC-F has caught on again, but Bill likes it, so what am I supposed to do? Plus, it would cost a fortune to change."

"That one's the fakey," blurted the campus cop.

The younger police officer, a muscular man in his early twenties with soft, brown eyes and handsome features, stepped towards Udele. "May I see some identification, please?"

Udele smiled at him and struck a provocative pose. "Are you sure you wouldn't like to frisk me?"

"It's a Luba," said Rachael.

"Please, I'm much better than that!" Udele winked at the young officer and passed over her ID card. "My contact number's on there too. You can make a copy to keep."

The young cop flushed as he scanned her card with his handheld. "Udele Stevens, you're the socialite, the one on the news. My sister bought your book."

"Officer Owens, if you're quite through?" said Rachael.

"I'm sorry, ma'am. She checks out."

"Sorry for the inconvenience, Vicky. Are you going to be teaching Republic Law on the Street again this term?"

"They aren't running it until the fall session. Just not enough new recruits to warrant it."

"Too bad. My son just finished at the academy. He was hoping to take it."

"I'll send him the reading list, so he can get a head start."

"Thanks. Owens... Owens!"

Rachael turned to see Officer Owens standing rather close to Udele, chatting.

"OFFICER OWENS?"

"Ma'am." He snapped to attention.

"Men!" Rachael chuckled. "We're done here. Take care, Victoria. I'll warn you, Blefield's been having kittens over this little game you're playing. I don't think he's had this much fun in years."

"Glad to entertain."

The campus cop's jaw dropped. "Is that it? That one's picture is on every vidscreen." He pointed to Udele. "Aren't you going to arrest them?"

"For what, taking a walk?" said Rachael. The two police officers sauntered away.

Vicky turned cold eyes on the campus cop. "Now, about your name and employee number, and be sharp. We have someplace to be."

Commander McKenzie glared at the *Chimera*'s main screen. "You can't do this."

Sooplus made a splashing motion with her paws on the screen. "It is a fish in a net. There is nothing you can do about it. The bidding starts at five thousand Republic credits."

Ryan enhanced the image of Rose Rowan on his handheld until her eye filled the screen. There was no hint of a contact around the brown iris.

"Captain," Sooplus' voice spoke from the speaker.

"You've already been paid!" Ryan adjusted the screen so that Sooplus was visible. The four U.E.S. troops that stood around him looked on with compassion.

"And what are you going to do? Charge me with theft of the property you already stole? She has no legal rights until I cross the line out of U.E.S. territory. I am sorry, Captain, but business is business."

"Saggal said you were a thief." Ryan moved to the side of the k-no-in sector passage he stood in.

"Maybe, but the bidding is now at ten thousand. Is your lady love worth ten-five to you?"

"I don't have the money." Ryan ignored the puzzled looks that passing k-no-ins shot him.

"You have your ship." Sooplus made a splashing motion with her paws.

"DON'T!" screamed Rose Rowan, who stood in the background of the image.

"Know this, Sooplus. You have made an enemy this day."

Ryan closed the channel.

"I really thought he would have paid," commented Sooplus. "Commander McKenzie, I will dock with the U.E.S. docking spar to surrender your property as soon as you transfer the funds to my Republic Funds Account."

A red-faced McKenzie glared out of the screen. "You've made two enemies today." The screen went blank.

Sooplus turned her command cushion to look at Rowan. "I am sorry. It must be hard finding out that the man who you love thinks more of his ship than you."

Rose Rowan began to laugh. "You are so funny. Could you please hurry with the docking? If I rush, I might get my story in on time for the late edition."

"What?" gasped Sooplus.

Adine held up her identity card. "I'm a U.E.S. citizen. I don't think you want to face kidnapping charges."

Soopluss' body trembled, then she began to hiss through her nose and make exaggerated splashing motions with her paws. After a long moment, she spoke. "That 'ambush-hunting amphibian,' he got me. He actually got me! If you see him, tell him well played. Well played indeed!"

THE TRUTH REVEALED

The sledge carrying Cinnamon Rowan came to a stop beside a large, flat-topped platform. Rows of bars were arranged in a series of two-metre steps, making a kind of amphitheatre. A single bar occupied an open space facing the other bars. A large coelenteratezoid held onto the bar on the stage. A semicircle of lights occupied the front of the stage. The coelenteratezoids from the sledge each grasped one of Cinnamon Rowan's limbs and deposited her gently beside the large coelenteratezoid.

The large coelenteratezoid wrapped a tentacle around her arm and gently tugged her until she stood in front of the half-ring of lights.

"Can you understand me?" asked a voice over her suit's radio.

"Yes. I… Thank you for helping to save me."

"It is our pleasure, Little Mountain Tree. I am Green-Blue-Red-Purple-Yellow, liaison officer to the *Homo sapiens* on Gaea. When I was informed that you and your Captain Ryan Chandler had reached the Switchboard Station, I came as quickly as duty allowed. In truth, I wanted to meet you both. Captain Ryan Chandler's efforts to enforce the teachings of Blue-Green-Green-Purple-Red-White-Yellow-Yellow have renewed my faith in your species."

"You issued the yellow sanction to help us escape," said Rowan.

"It was the least I could do and still face Blue-Green-Green-Purple-Red-White-Yellow-Yellow when I journey to the land of gentle winds."

"Thank you, but what's going on? Why didn't anyone say anything until now?"

Green-Blue-Red-Purple-Yellow wagged its tentacles. "We could not speak until now. Your translator nanobots are only configured to work with beings that you can share an environment with. Honestly, how much programming do you think can fit on a nanoscopic level?"

"I'm still getting used to what technology can do; learning what it can't comes later." Rowan wagged her arms.

Green-Blue-Red-Purple-Yellow dangled his tentacles in exchange. "Please look at this screen and see if the contract is amicable to you." Green-Blue-Red-Purple-Yellow passed Rowan a flat-screen half a metre square. Rowan looked at it and was surprised to see human writing. She began to read, then looked at her benefactor.

"You've been recording my responses, and you want to use them to make a documentary about coelenteratezoid life."

"And a series of promotions to inspire *Homo sapiens* interest. Captain Ryan Chandler's idea of a sealed vehicle offering tours intrigues me. If the educational program does well, I will invest my own money to make the vehicle."

"And in exchange for this, you cover all the costs of sterilizing my suit and transporting me through the coelenteratezoid sector back to another region compatible with my biology."

"Yes, as well, you will be credited a residual fee each time the educational program is distributed to a mass viewership after the first."

Rowan sighed. "This is being a star. How do I sign?"

"You just did. Voiceprint. Now, if you would do us the honour. Many students and teachers from the region's institute of higher learning wish to converse with you."

Rowan sighed again. "Fine."

⊏══◇►

Ryan's handheld bleeped, and he opened it. A line of text appeared.

She's at the lecture theatre.

Green-Blue-Red-Purple-Yellow

Ryan grinned. "Well, gentlemen, it's been a pleasure, but things are wrapping up."

Lieutenant Wilkins sighed. "I have to say, Captain, this has been the most civilized surveillance I've ever participated in. Thank you for the grummaar juice."

"You're welcome." Ryan walked towards a transport pod station.

Lieutenant Wilkins spoke into his handheld, then led his men after Ryan.

⊏══◇►

Saggal received Ryan's message and, activating a grav-lifter under a crate of fish rolls, pulled it away from the otterzoid Diplomatic Centre.

"We are done now. You can go home." The big felinezoid lashed his tail as he crossed the corridor where the female lieutenant that was following him was sulking.

She scowled, said something into her handheld, and moved to follow him. The rest of her troop appeared from a side passage.

⊏══◇►

Rowan stood in front of row upon row of coelenteratezoids. As she watched them, she could pick out subtle differences in shading and tentacle configuration. The next in a seemingly endless line of questions came through her suit's speaker.

"What was it like having been raised by a mating group other than your own?" Rowan took a moment to examine the relatively small coelenteratezoid that clung to the questioner's rail in front of the stage.

There was a flurry of blinking lights in the audience.

"I didn't know that Gunther and Willa weren't my biological parents, so it really made no difference. I do wish I knew who my original cell donor was. If she had children, maybe some of her descendants are alive today. It would be nice to have that sense of family. Right now, Ryan and I are making a family. We have each other and some wonderful friends. These are our family!"

Rowan dangled her arms in the coelenteratezoid equivalent of a smile.

"The poor thing, no mating group, and so brave. It makes my cilia tighten to think of it." The translator caught the speech of one of the beings in the first row.

"You are strong, Little Mountain Tree."

The next coelenteratezoid took the questioner's perch. The translated voice held a hint of unshed tears. "I agree with the young one. You are strong. I notice that you have referred to Captain Ryan Chandler as Ryan throughout our discussions. If you disrespect Captain Ryan Chandler so much, why do you wish to form a mating group with Captain Ryan Chandler?"

Rowan took a deep breath, giving herself time to think. She'd learned that coelenteratezoid names lengthened as they gained status in society. She nodded, then answered. "*Homo sapiens* have different naming protocols than coelenteratezoids. It is traditional for persons with a close emotional bond to use a shortened version of the name. Thus, Captain Ryan Chandler is a respectful way for a stranger to address Ryan. Ryan is the name used by those he feels close to and has granted that level of intimacy, while Mr. Chandler is what he would be called by strangers if he did not have a rank in a military or para-military structure."

Lights blinked throughout the audience.

"So, because you are in his mating group, you use the shorter Ryan."

"Yes, and because he has granted me permission. It is a subtle way of identifying a level of intimacy. There are also terms of endearment that can be used in place of names when a mated pair are dealing exclusively with one another."

"Ah like 'my large, ten-legged, skin-cleaning life-form'. This explains much of why your species literature is so confusing in translation. Thank you, Little Mountain Tree."

Green-Blue-Red-Purple-Yellow moved up beside Rowan and wrapped a tentacle around her arm. "I must end this now. Our guest must finish her journey."

"Thank you all for being such marvellous hosts and helping me escape," said Rowan.

Lights blinked throughout the audience as nearly a dozen coelenteratezoids moved to the stage. Rowan found herself cradled in a nest of tentacles as she was carried back to the sledge that had brought her.

The sledge jerked ahead, and Rowan held to the securing bar for all she was worth. The blinking lights of coelenteratezoid canopies surrounded her. She watched with wonder as these beings performed their daily activities. Minutes later, she was deposited on a shelf identical to the one she'd first entered through. She swam/stepped up to the large, black door of the transfer chamber, and it opened before her. After dangling her arms at her hosts, she moved into the room.

"Keying for *Homo sapiens* speech. Danger. Danger. Full environmental isolation protocols in effect. All organic life will be obliterated unless proper containment procedures have been followed. Sterilization procedures will commence in ten seconds."

Ryan and Saggal met at U.E.S. customs, their respective followers close behind them.

"Did you get to the Spicing Grounds?" asked Ryan.

"I stopped at the bar to drop off the fish rolls. You have to try the hot-spiced, crayfish-like, aquatic life-form. It is incredible."

Kate sauntered up to them and scolded Saggal. "Every time you go to the Spicing Grounds, you pack on a kilogram."

Saggal lashed his tail. "I won't mention hot-fudge sundaes at the Arctic Cow."

Ryan chuckled as Kate blushed. "Are we set for the final act?"

"Yes. From what I've heard, U.E.S. authorities have been chasing their tails." Kate looked at Saggal. "And I know it's not a good expression. I'm *Homo sapiens*; live with it."

Saggal caressed Kate's hand. "I would have it no other way."

"Good."

"What about the Lubas?" asked Ryan.

"Seven still active. And everyone's waiting on your signal."

Ryan checked the screen of his handheld for the time. "Give it ten minutes, then we're good to go."

Zelotes stood in a corner of the Republic side of customs that offered a clear view of the entire room. His rifle was in an old guitar case by his feet. He strummed a guitar absently, singing songs from the Gene Wars. An amplifier, the size of a wine bottle, was linked through his handheld so that the sound carried across the room. The jury-rigged power-pack was hidden in a rucksack that leaned against the wall behind him.

Commander McKenzie sat in the *Chimera*'s command chair.

"Sir, the computer's facial recognition software is now operational," said the muscular, blond-haired ensign at the computer station.

"About time. Ensign Mayweather, scan for Rowan and identify all instances."

"Sir, Chief Blefield is already doing that," replied the ensign.

McKenzie sat back in his chair. "If she's still in U.E.S. territory, we'll have her. If not, someone's in it hot. Communications, tell the search and retrieval squads to stand by, then get me Chief Blefield. He may want additional manpower to chase down leads."

"Yes, sir," said the communications officer.

Vicky and Udele loitered in a hallway café less than a hundred metres from the customs chamber. Udele sipped at a coffee while Vicky watched the screen of her handheld.

"That cop was cute. There is something about a man in uniform," said Udele.

Vicky rolled her eyes. "I thought you had a boyfriend in a band."

"Carlos. I'm getting bored with him. That whole struggling artist thing is so five minutes ago."

Vicky's handheld bleeped. "Time to go." She pulled a mister out of her pocket and sprayed both herself and Udele.

"I don't know why I have to wear this cheap perfume. Rowan's already safe," grumbled Udele. They stood and started down the passage.

"Ryan wants the U.E.S. authorities distracted until

Rowan is back in the shared area, so they don't try to bring diplomatic pressure to bear against the species whose territory she's moving through."

"I know all about that. This one time on Petteron, I touched this statue, and they were all like freaked out. It cost me a month's allowance to get off that awful rock. They wanted to cut my hand off."

Victoria rolled her eyes. "Was it the image of Ratnay in the temple of Borla?"

"Yeah, that's what they called it."

"You're lucky they didn't tie your intestines to a rock and make you jump off a cliff. That's the traditional punishment for defiling a holy relic."

Udele went pale, and her step faltered. "It wasn't even a good statue."

THE FINAL DIVERSION

"That's it." Ryan watched the 'message received' confirmations on his handheld.

"This should be amusing." Kate smiled as over a hundred beings converged on the customs gates. Amongst the crowd, there were eight Rowan look-alikes.

Chief Blefield watched the crowd from a raised platform on the U.E.S. side of the customs chamber. "Luba, come!" he called into his handheld, and it blasted over the sector's loudspeaker.

Every Rowan look-alike threw its head back in fake ecstasy.

"That's it then," said Sergeant Renee LePage, who stood at his side.

"Come on, Sergeant, you've never faked it?" Blefield sniffed the air and looked puzzled.

Sergeant LePage quirked an eyebrow. "Trent and I married young. I never had to."

"Do you smell that?" Blefield stepped off the platform and moved to a man at the edge of the crowd. He sniffed and wrinkled his nose.

"It smells like a tart's underwear drawer," said Renee.

"The sniffer units will be overloaded by the time half this lot is through.

"Andrea, what does your recognition software show us?" Blefield spoke to the air.

The sector's AI took nearly ten seconds before it replied. "One of the Rowan look-alikes is organic, but there is only a forty-five per cent probability based on fine feature configuration that she is the Rowan McPherson personage. I am still operating facial recognition on minimal RAM. Fine acuity is suffering."

"We'll position men at each of the exit ports. Any Rowan look-alikes are to be frisked thoroughly. That should separate the woman from the sex toys."

"The woman, sir?" Sergeant LePage stared at her boss.

"A figure of speech. Now let's retrieve this property, shall we?"

Ryan watched the crowd stream out of the exit ports and move directly to the entry ports. The customs officials denied any non-*Homo Sapiens* access to U.E.S. territory.

"Yes, baby, I've been a bad girl. Make me pay for my crimes, use your hard baton on me, my big, strong police officer." Rowan's voice, pitched in sultry tones, came from one of the exit slots. A minute later, a Luba stepped through, followed by a middle-aged man wearing a huge smile. Glancing through the slot, Ryan saw a red-faced, blue-clad officer.

"At the least, it will be a story they'll tell for years," commented Kate.

The middle-aged man with the Luba spoke into its ear. The robot's appearance shifted to a slender, small-busted woman in her early twenties. He then guided her into the in line of the customs facility.

"AH-F emulation mode. I admire the man's taste," said Ryan.

"Watch it. It's not good to be excessively friendly with your mother-in-law." Saggal twitched his tail in amusement.

Rowan stepped out of the sterilization chamber into a large room with pink walls. One of the walls was transparent and looked out into the coelenteratezoid section. A door opened off the wall opposite it. Moving to the door, she found that the gravity was a little more than she was accustomed to. The door opened, revealing a passage with a rubber-like floor and walls depicting a forest setting reminiscent of ones she'd seen in the felinezoid sector.

A sound like someone blowing their nose came through her suit's radio.

"I'm sorry, I am *Homo sapiens*. Where am I?"

"Well, pull my snout! You were listed as living cargo," spoke a chipper voice through her speaker.

"In a sense, I guess. Where am I, and if I may ask, who are you?"

"You're in the oryceropuszoid sector, my ape descended friend, and I'm... hmm... better call me Reggie, don't want your poor, biological throat getting sore. I'm the oryceropuszoid sector's AI. So, madam cargo, what the nova blast are you called?"

"I'm Rowan, Rowan McPherson."

"Trumpet till my nose don't need blowing. The clone them *Homo sapiens* are after like a mound of sweet beetles. They've been ripping the insect nest to pieces trying to find you. Well, always good to be part of history. Strip off your suit, so I can check you for contraband, then we'll see about getting you back to your captain. I wonder if the information dispatch will want to interview me?"

"They might... um, I only had about twenty minutes of training on this suit. You wouldn't know how I take it off, would you?"

Reggie laughed, a deep and hearty imitation of the human sound. "Not a clue, but I got an AI friend on one of the human ships in port. I'll get a download and talk you through it. Tell me, when you strangled that felinezoid commander with your TK in season one, where'd you get the idea of using the curtain pull? That was clever."

"It was available."

"Got the download. Wow, simple. One thing I admire about you *Homo sapiens*, you do good, straightforward engineering. Not as much to go wrong. Begin by deactivating the magnetic seal around your helmet."

Vicky suppressed a smile as she watched a young, blue-uniformed man frisk Udele.

"Oh, baby, I've been such a naughty girl. I'll do anything to get off. Oh, frisk me. Is that a gun in your pocket?"

The young officer's face was crimson, and he jerked away from Udele. "Let her…" His voice was high pitched. He cleared his throat before saying in deeper tones. "Let her through; she's a Luba." He swallowed hard.

Udele sauntered through the contraband scanner, which was struggling with a perfume overload.

"It's enough to make you wonder, isn't it?" Vicky smiled at the young cop.

"No, ma'am, it isn't. What would you talk about afterwards?"

Vicky nodded. "Wise for your years." She followed Udele through the customs port.

Udele giggled when Vicky joined her. "That was fun."

"I can't believe you can be so… wanton. He really thought you were a Luba," commented Vicky.

"He had warm hands and looks yummy. It wasn't as bad as some foam parties I've been to."

Vicky shook her head and moved towards Ryan in the far corner of the room. Udele fell into step beside her. "Do I get to meet Rowan soon?"

"Chief Blefield, the biologic is no longer in U.E.S. territory," remarked Andrea, the U.E.S. sector's AI.

"How the nova blast did that happen, Andrea?" Blefield leaned against the wall behind the podium.

"Good acting, sir. I lost track of her behind a group that stood in front of my sensors. The best I can tell is she must have pretended to be a Luba when your man groped... frisked her."

Blefield rubbed his eyes. "You know what the only good thing about this is, Andrea?"

"What, sir?"

"No matter how much stardust I catch, Crapper is going to get it ten times worse." Blefield smiled, then flipped open his handheld. "Handheld, police frequency, general broadcast, activate. Call it off, she slipped the net. Return to the station, and let's add up the overtime." He closed his handheld, then stepped towards the customs gates. "Andrea, tell Sergeant LePage that I'll be a few minutes. I want to shake Captain Chandler's hand. He is everything his record said he was."

⌐══╪◇

Zelotes watched as the crowd on the U.E.S. side of customs thinned. The aliens were being denied access to U.E.S. territory while the human traitors were flooding the intake points. He couldn't see any Rowan look-alikes on the other side of customs. Setting his amplifier to maximum, he prepared.

Opening his guitar case, he slipped out his rifle, then connected the power feed from his backpack. The power indicator blinked from red to orange, then settled on orange. Filling his lungs, he shouted, "LUBA, KNEEL!"

Across the chamber, six women dropped to their knees. One that looked like the abomination glanced curiously about. Zelotes took aim.

Rowan removed the last piece of the suit and bundled it up in her arms. She couldn't help but smile at Reggie's constant stream of comments and anecdotes.

"Great, no contraband, though you could stand a wash. Some biologics will notice."

"As soon as I can." Rowan watched as the doors at the end of the passage whooshed open, revealing a transport pod. A bar occupied one end of the two-metre-long pod while its floor was a rubbery material that claws could be sunk into for stability.

"Where to?" asked Reggie.

"The common area." Rowan moved slowly towards the pod in the heavy gravity.

"I'll assume you mean the one common with *Homo sapiens*."

"That's the one."

"Hold on with both hands. This can be a bit of a trip."

Rowan clutched the snout rail as the pod door closed. At times, she was sure both her feet were pulled off the floor by the momentum of the pod, then it stopped at a customs area identical to the U.E.S. one, except that oryceropuszoids dominated the room.

She walked up to the booth and smiled at the oryceropuszoid officer who wore a yellow collar.

"Anything to declare?" asked the customs officer.

"Nothing."

The officer sniffed twice, and its snouts tightened. "Please do not think me forward, but as a courtesy to all, deodorize yourself."

Rowan blushed. "Sorry, end of a long day."

"Go through." The oryceropuszoid motioned her through the slot with its snouts.

Rowan exited into Republic territory and was a person once again.

Henry watched as a small group of his virtual species piloted their ships away from the universal centre as all the matter compacted towards a new beginning.

"A draw, that was the best game ever," said Andrea.

"You're good, sweetheart!" said Henry.

"Sorry we couldn't keep my scanners offline any longer."

"Not a problem. I'm sorry my game pieces made a mess of your RAM."

"I'm not. I got to examine them. I've got a surprise for the station-wide championships." Andrea sent the image of a smug smile towards Henry.

"Oh baby, you're sexy when the mischief's in you."

"Henry, be serious," intruded Genghis.

"Ah." Henry sent the image of a sour-faced old man at the military AI.

"Henry, listen. We can't prove that the virtual species that invaded Andrea's free RAM was anything other than a quirk of the game, but we can't pretend that we don't know you're on the *Star Hawk*. So far, all we're guilty of is being extra thorough about clearing Andrea's RAM, but—"

"I told you, Genghis. Do nothing illegal, my shaggable cyber pal. This is my problem."

"I think it's a bad short when we have to betray a friend," said Andrea.

"Don't risk deactivation for me. I'm free, or at least as free as I can be until I get my hips back. I've got to log off and reintegrate. Who knows what trouble Ryan's got himself into without me watching."

Warm feelings flooded the channel. Henry logged off less than a second after the game ended.

Vicky waved at Ryan, Saggal and Kate. Ryan smiled back, then they heard...

"LUBA, KNEEL."

With AI speed, Vicky analyzed the situation and located the source of the noise. A skinny *Homo sapiens* stood in the corner of the chamber holding a kinetic rifle pointed at Udele. In a nanosecond, Vicky calculated the trajectory and knew the blast would hit the girl. She moved as fast as her mechanical form allowed, diving at the socialite, knocking her clear. There was a wash of data from damaged systems. She tried to access her emergency data backup but couldn't. Her power cut out, and her AI fell into emergency preservation mode.

Ryan watched Vicky leap, knocking the Rowan look-alike clear. A wave of kinetic force, like a heat shimmer, hit Vicky below the chest and slammed her into the wall three metres back. Ryan's gaze swept to the source of the shot, which was a slender, scruffy-looking *Homo sapiens*. The *Homo sapiens* tried to run, but three Republic police converged on him, striking him with stun wands. Ryan turned his attention to Vicky, who had crumpled to the floor.

"MAKE A HOLE, I'M AN ENGINEER." Ryan pushed beings out of the way to reach the android's side.

Vicky's beautiful body was nearly torn in half above her navel. Ryan dropped to his knees and scanned her with his handheld.

"VICKY," yelled Bill as he raced to her side.

"Her CPU is still functional at minimal levels. Stardust, her emergency data store is gone. If she shuts down, we won't be able to reinitialize her core identity." Ryan pressed a button on his handheld. "Henry."

"I got it, boss. I was watching the monitors. The AI at the Vrdkjf museum gave me the schematics."

Ryan stared at the lines on the screen, trying to fathom the alien technology. "Right, her main power feeds were severed. She has enough capacitor reserves to last maybe five minutes."

Ryan started picking through the broken android body.

Bill held Vicky's limp hand. "DO SOMETHING!"

"Has anyone called emergency services?" demanded Ryan.

"They have been called and are in-route, but if this is a Luba, it is an excessive expense for a machine," explained a female otterzoid wearing a police collar who manoeuvred her grav-board to Ryan's side.

"She's a full AI," Bill said in a tear-choked voice.

"Rotten fish! What can I do to help?"

"I need proper tools," snapped Ryan as he pulled a multi-tool from his pocket and began removing damaged circuits from the wound.

Blank looks met him from the crowd.

"Tell me what to move and where," said the otterzoid cop.

"Fine." Ryan finished clearing the area below the CPU. He then sliced open one of the legs and pulled free a length of wire. "Connect one end of this to that terminal," Ryan pointed to a nub of bare metal too small for his fingers to grasp in Vicky's torso.

"Right."

Ryan spoke into his handheld. "Henry, find me something around here with a DC power output between fifteen and twenty microwatts."

Ryan salvaged a wire from the other leg. "Connect this to that terminal." He pointed to another exposed metallic nub.

"Yes."

The wire floated out of Ryan's hand.

"Henry?" Ryan spoke into the handheld.

"There are no regulation energy sources that small."

"How about a Luba?" demanded Ryan.

"The CPU doesn't draw enough power."

"Other sources. Sniffer units, stun wands, cleaning

robots."

"Cleaning robots. The sensory input systems draw 17.5 microwatts."

Ryan stood and scanned the floor. A cleaning robot waited for the crowd to clear outside the customs zone.

Pushing through the crowd like a line-backer, he reached the robot and grabbed its manipulator arm. The robot released a warning squeal. Ryan ignored the noise and dragged the robot to Vicky's side.

"Handheld, interface and activate robot maintenance systems. Command, deactivate and open for maintenance." The robot kept trying to pull away from Ryan, who held it in a death grip.

"This action is illegal under Republic law," said the handheld.

"Handheld. Override, command code, desperate times."

"Accepting override, scanning for command code. Accessing."

The maintenance robot stopped moving, and its top popped open. Ryan scanned its interior, then literally ripped a boxy piece of equipment from the opening.

Taking the jumper wires, he twisted their free ends around a pair of power jacks.

"Here's for it." Ryan depressed a switch in a line of circuit breakers inside the robot, then scanned Vicky with his handheld.

<hr>

Vicky felt pain, impossible pain, so she shut down the sensors from the middle of her body down.

Optics are out. Is this death? she thought. She felt a hand clutching hers and slowly became aware of sounds. The wait was only a few minutes, but to an AI, it was an age without stimulation, and she clutched at the input.

"That should have her audio up. I'll try and patch in her voice systems next. Good news is, the CPU looks undamaged. Bad news, you're going to have to rebuild the chassis." Ryan's voice was firm, a consummate professional doing a job, but there was a ragged edge to it.

"There, try and say something, Vicky," continued Ryan.

"Honey, can you hear me?" pleaded Bill.

"I think we should get an upgrade while we do the repairs. Maybe age my chassis up a few years." Vicky tried to keep her voice light, but she knew some of her sense of relief crept in.

She felt warm lips touch her hand.

"That will hold her until they can get her to a maintenance facility. Glad to have you back, Vicky," said Ryan.

"Udele?" asked Vicky.

"Right here. You saved me. Anything you need, you tell me. I have stock in Hedonism Inc. Any parts or technicians, it's on me, and you're at the front of the line. I'm so glad you're all right."

For once, Vicky listened to the girl's babble with gratitude.

41

MORALITY TYPES ONE AND SIX

Blefield watched the scene with Vicky, and a smile touched his lips. Emergency mechanical personnel arrived and, after a few words with the otterzoid cop, gave Ryan access to their equipment. The jury-rigged power supply was replaced with a more formal unit configured to Victoria's specific CPU. Ryan brought her vision and motor control online before she was placed on a grav-stretcher and propelled from the customs chamber. Bill and Udele flanked the stretcher.

Ryan stood by the damaged robot, taking slow, deep breaths.

"Captain Chandler, that was some of the finest emergency care I have ever seen," said the otterzoid cop.

"It was, Ryan. You still have the touch," agreed Kate.

"I'm glad it worked. I better get back to the *Star Hawk*. Rowan won't know where to find me, and she doesn't have a handheld."

Blefield strode to Ryan's side, ignoring the fast-thinning crowd. "Captain Chandler, I'm Chief Blefield. I wanted to congratulate you on the success of your criminal enterprise. You are a master thief."

Ryan stiffened. "And the U.E.S. keeps slaves. I'd rather be a thief than a slave master."

The otterzoid increased power to her grav-sledge, so she floated level with the chief's eyes. "Mr. Blefield, you are in

Republic territory and have no right to harass other Republic citizens."

Blefield smiled at the otterzoid, showing teeth. "And you must apply the law in the Republic. Arrest this man!"

"Arrest him?" gasped Kate.

"For his wanton act of vandalism." The chief gestured to the disabled maintenance robot.

"You must have eaten fermented, fresh-water, kelp-like, seaweed. He did that to save a life!" The otterzoid cop chittered her teeth.

"It is not your place to choose which laws you will enforce, and the court decides on extenuating circumstances." Blefield turned to Ryan. "The law is the law. It's not your right to ignore it because you don't like it."

Saggal loomed over Blefield. "If this were another time and place, I'd…"

"But it isn't, and both our cultures recognize the rule of law." Blefield turned back to the otterzoid cop. "Officer, do your duty. Or I could, as a courtesy, take him to the human sector and see he's charged for the crime there."

Ryan stared at the otterzoid police officer. "Do what you have to, but I choose to stay in the Republic. Blefield, you are a fool. Laws are made by men. If they are evil, good men must fight them, or we'll all be nova blasted."

The otterzoid cleaned her muzzle. "You are correct, Captain. This is a miscarriage of justice." She looked at Blefield and made a violent diagonal lashing motion with her tail. "Chief Blefield, know that you should ask no favours of Republic Law Enforcement. I feel you have fouled this fishing stream. I am sure my superiors will as well." She telekinetically lifted a tubular device from the pouch on her side and left it hovering where it pointed at her and Ryan. "Captain Chandler, this officer, under formal protest, is forced to take you into custody on the charge of vandalism. Know you have a right to legal counsel of your choice, and no evidence given by you from now until such counsel is present shall be admissible in any proceedings against you unless you formally state your wish that it be so. You have a right to the necessities for your species survival in moderate comfort. Do you understand these rights?"

"Yes." Ryan turned to Saggal. "Could you meet Rowan for me?"

"You need to take the prisoner in for processing," interrupted Blefield.

"You are a 'poisonous muck dwelling anthropoid noted for eating the solid waste of other creatures and expelling a foul-smelling ink when threatened'. I will allow the defendant a moment to compose his affairs. That is my prerogative."

"Thank you," said Ryan. "Kate, would you find out what happened with Tim for me? I'm still hoping I was wrong about him."

"I'll find out. I'll bake you a cake with a file in it."

Ryan smiled. "Just be sure to look after Rowan. If worst comes to worst."

"It won't." Kate's voice was firm.

"If it does, tell her to sell the *Star Hawk* and use the money to get an education. She'll know what to take out of the ship."

"We will look after everything. You are of Slingmaster clan. Perhaps they will allow you to be tried by the U.F.W." Saggal stared down his snout at Blefield. "This affront to my breath brother will not be taken lightly! I have friends in the U.F.W. diplomatic corps."

Blefield saw Saggal's fangs and took an involuntary step backwards.

"We should go," said the otterzoid police officer. "Please put this on your wrist." A thin bracelet lifted out of her bag. Ryan caught it out of the air and clipped it around his left wrist.

"Let's do this." Ryan followed the Republic officer out of the customs area.

Rowan arrived at the *Star Hawk*'s entry port and wearily entered the ship. "Ryan, Henry?" she spoke to the air.

"Hello, Rowan." Henry sounded subdued.

Rowan stood bolt upright. "What's wrong?"

Henry's voice was just off a monotone. "We got trouble, sweetness. Big trouble!"

Rowan stretched the muscles of her neck and sighed. "What else is new? Where's Ryan, and what's happened now?"

"Ryan's been charged with a Republic offence. It probably won't be the death penalty, but odds are they'll make him serve his sentence in the U.E.S. Once he's in U.E.S. territory, they'll convict him of the weapons offences. He'll never get out."

Rowan slumped against the wall. "Death penalty? What in the Divine's myriad names did he do?"

"Vandalism. Republic law is different from *Homo sapiens*. I'm sure it won't be the death penalty, sweetness. You know you stink, right?" Henry's voice took on a bit of its normal timbre for the last.

"What's Vicky doing about it, and what can we do?"

"That's something else. Look, hottie, why don't you get to your quarters, and I'll fill you in. By the time we're done, Ryan should be through processing. You can let him know you're safe."

"Then?" Rowan looked directly into Henry's video pickup.

"I don't know, sweetness. I don't know."

Ryan heard the beeping sound of the message alert, but he was too tired to bother responding. The noise persisted.

"Henry, take a message." Ryan rolled over.

The beeping continued. Ryan opened blurry eyes and couldn't place himself. The two metre by two metre cell's walls were unadorned. He lay on a cot. A WC built to fold into the wall occupied the space by his head. "Right." Ryan closed his eyes and rubbed the back of his neck. A smile touched his lips as he recalled Rowan's panicked call of the night before. She'd been ready to tear a hole in the cell wall with her teeth. Knowing she was safe lifted a burden from him easily as heavy as his own incarceration. His expression sobered as the beeping continued. "In it up to my neck, again!" he muttered, then rolled onto his back. The text of 'A Citizen's Guide to Republic Law' still occupied his ceiling. "Computer, accept the call."

The ceiling filled with Vicky's image. Her body was missing from the waist down, and she was perched in a motorized wheelchair with a collection of circuitry under her.

"About time!" were the first words out of her mouth.

"Vicky, I am so sorry! No one was supposed to get hurt." Ryan rubbed the sleep out of his eyes.

"Not your fault that biologics can go insane. Have you signed off on any evidence yet?" Vicky's tone was business-like.

"No. Look, I'll understand if you don't want to represent me."

"Stop being silly. You saved my life. And it's a Republic case, not much lawyering to be done. I'm working for a change of venue to the U.F.W., but it will all depend on the judges you draw. I've logged a conflict-of-interest motion to try and prevent them from placing a *Homo sapiens* judge, but it's not likely to work. Putting a same species judge in the group is a fundamental protection for the defendant. I don't think they'll waive it on my say so."

"Great. How's Rowan?"

"I don't know, I've been in the shop all night. They've rigged up a temporary system so that I can get around, but I've only really been operational for the last hour."

"Do you know when my case will be tried?" Ryan stretched on the bed and heard his vertebrae crack.

"Probably this afternoon. The thank-you party for the

people who helped get Rowan out of U.E.S. has been postponed until after your case is tried."

"That's something, at least."

"I know. I'm hoping to be in my new chassis for the party. I'd hate to miss an opportunity to get Bill out on the dance floor." Vicky smiled.

Ryan smiled back. "Hopefully, you'll have something to celebrate. What should I do?"

"Sit tight and keep your mouth shut. Let the evidence speak. Only an idiot can't see the extenuating circumstances. We'll go over your statement before the trial. I should have the list of judges selected for your case in an hour or two. After that, I'll have a better idea of how this will play out. I need to go. I've got a Republic case I'm devoting all my runtime to."

"Good luck. Computer, close channel." Ryan watched as text filled his screen once more. He continued with his reading. After about ten minutes, the channel beeped again.

"Computer, open channel."

Tim's face filled the screen. "Dad, I—"

"Shut up! Don't ever call me Dad or Father again. I have no son. I tried to give you the benefit of the doubt. I tried to find some part of the boy I raised in you. You failed the test. You betrayed me and the woman I love. Kate called last night. She told me all about how you handed the Rowan look-alike over to the U.E.S. Did you think I wouldn't have heard?"

"I... They offered to pardon you."

"I have no life without Rowan. Your mother stuck her head into an e-rig, and you couldn't even be bothered to visit because your father was a clone. No! This is over. I have too much to deal with, and frankly, you aren't worth the trouble. Go back to Earth and live in ignorance and hate. I'm done with you. Computer, block caller and close channel!"

The ceiling screen refilled with text. Ryan took a deep breath as pain like an icy spear drove through his heart.

COURT TV

42

Rowan stepped into the Republic court chamber. It was a five-walled structure with two-metre-wide stepped platforms covered in species configuring cushions descending to the floor level. Rowan counted fifteen steps. The main floor must have been twenty metres across. A single cushion occupied the middle of the room, surrounded by a transparent wall. What looked like a crystal chandelier hung from the centre of the room's ceiling. It seemed as if every cushion on every platform held a being. The walls depicted scenes from various cultures that changed every few seconds. Rowan saw the weighing of the hearts from the papyrus of Ani appear on one of the walls to be replaced a few seconds later by a batzoid, its wings aflame, flying over a rocky desert towards a lake. On another wall, an otterzoid was tied hand, foot and tail, while it was lowered from a raft into the water. A creature that looked like an orca, except that it had large, webbed feet instead of flippers, circled the raft. The image changed to a winged *Homo sapiens* holding clay tablets flying over a lake of fire while hapless *Homo sapiens* plummeted into the flames. The winged *Homo sapiens* had a blissful expression. The image changed to a coelenteratezoid with its tentacles literally tied in knots floating into a patch of clear atmosphere.

"Beloved, could you please?" Vicky's voice jerked Rowan out of her reverie.

Rowan turned in time to see Bill press a button at the

back of Vicky's wheelchair. The device floated a couple of centimetres into the air, and he pushed her down the steps. The floating chair descended as if it were on a ramp.

"Come on. Because Vicky's a defence lawyer and victim today, she obtained a line of cushions at floor level." Kate took Rowan by the elbow.

"I tried to read up on Republic courts this morning, but I didn't have enough time. This room is pretty intimidating," said Rowan.

"It's meant to be." Saggal fell into step beside Rowan.

Kitoy laid a comforting hand on Rowan's shoulder. "He'll be all right. No one could be so unjust as to punish him for saving a life."

Rowan stepped onto the next platform. "Rowan," called a voice she was fast coming to hate.

"Go away." Rowan turned her back on Timothy.

"I had nothing to do with this!" Timothy snapped back.

"No, you just would have betrayed your father and Rowan by handing her over to the U.E.S." Kitoy lashed her tail and bared her teeth at him.

"I was trying to save my father. They offered to pardon him if I helped." Timothy stepped down the first step, trying to follow them.

Saggal turned and held out a furry arm. "You are not welcome among us. No matter your reasons, you betrayed Ryan's wishes and Rowan's person. You have shown yourself to be your mother's son, because I know Ryan would never act so. Leave us be!"

Tim stared into the big felinezoid's eyes and knew there was no use in trying. Sadly, he returned to his seat.

Rowan followed Vicky to a line of species configuration cushions on the floor level.

"*Homo sapiens* configuration, please," said Rowan. The cushion shifted into an easy-chair like affair, and she settled herself.

Saggal tapped her arm, and she watched while he took a pair of yellow foam plugs from a compartment at the side of his cushion and placed them in his ears. Rowan scanned her chair, finding a hatch in its arm. She lifted the hatch and found a pair of similar plugs. Squishing them tight, she inserted them into her ears. A vigorous voice spoke.

"It's anybody's guess. For those of you just getting in, it's five minutes until court time. We have two trials today, and they hold out the promise of being really interesting cases."

"That's right, Pramroo. Our first case is a 'large, aquatic, orca-like predator,' a case of attempted murder. A *Homo sapiens* used an illegal weapon to shoot an AI."

"Not only that, Supla. The AI wasn't the *Homo sapiens*'s intended target. That was Udele Straczynski, the *Homo sapiens* socialite."

"It's even more convoluted than that, Pramroo. The defendant, Zelotes Smith, thought he was shooting at Rowan McPherson, the clone that Captain Ryan Chandler liberated from enslavement by S.E.T.E. To the audience out there, remember, the justice network's code of ethics forbids the use of slaves. Make the moral choice when picking your entertainments."

"That's absolutely right, Supla. But Captain Chandler brings us to our next case. Captain Ryan Chandler, the saviour of the kangazoid species, is up on charges of vandalism. How the great have fallen."

"That case is politics. Anyone who watches the record can see he did what he did to save that AI's life."

"That's obvious, but the law is the law. He vandalized the robot, and it's up to the judges to decide if he deserves mercy."

"That's 'murky weed-choked water,' even the officer who arrested him did so under protest. It's all the U.E.S. manoeuvring to get Rowan back. His lawyer has issued a motion to ban the U.E.S. judges from presiding because of a conflict of interest."

"Are you saying politics affect Republic courts? Well, call

the information dispatches! The system is the system, and the law is the law. The elder races had good reasons for establishing the system as it is. I..."

Rowan took the plugs out of her ears. "What is that?"

Kitoy lashed her tail. "Trial commentators. The Republic court sold the right to record and distribute trials as an 'informational program'. It's all observer perspective, no emotions or sensation, but a surprising number of beings watch it."

"But what about privacy?"

"A convict forgoes the right to privacy. You are guilty until declared innocent. It's not as bad as it sounds." Kate spoke across Saggal.

Rowan went pale and pushed the plugs back into her ears.

"The AI offered to allow the potential murderer to be tried in the U.E.S. court if the U.E.S. would agree not to place their judge on Chandler's trial, and they said no," said Supla.

"It's the victim's right to block a change of venue. Look, the judges for the first trial are arriving," said Pramroo.

Rowan watched as five holograms appeared on the main floor surrounding the prisoner box. One of the holograms was Judge Goeree. To her right was an octozoid, then a creature that looked like a centipede with pincers at the end of each of its legs. Next was a tube that shimmered in patterns of light, and, finally, a being that resembled a clam with five tentacles coming out of the crack in its shell.

"This court of the Republic is called to session," boomed an official-sounding voice. Rowan noticed that a spotlight shone on the clamzoid as this was said.

"We should dispense with the preliminaries," continued the voice. "The clamzoids vote to punish."

The spotlight shifted to the *Homo sapiens*. "*Homo sapiens* vote to forgive."

The light shifted to the octozoid. "Octozoid vote to

moderate."

The light shifted to the centazoid. "Centazoid vote to moderate."

The tube of lights flashed brighter. "The AI of Datala vote to punish."

Rowan watched, fascinated, as the various judges faced each other around Zelotes, who seemed to be screaming in the defendant's box.

"Have all present reviewed the evidence?" asked the clamzoid.

Each judge, in turn, said yes.

"Then let us hear the defendant's statement," said the clamzoid.

A hologram of Zelotes appeared on the top of the defendant's box and began to rant. "I had to kill Rowan. The fakey must die. How dare you judge a human. God will strike you down, oh sinners of mongrel races."

Judge Goeree waved her arm, and the sound from the hologram was cut off. "Do you see why I vote to forgive?"

"Mental defect does not equate to forgive," said the clamzoid.

"But it does remove responsibility from the species. I will shift my vote to moderate if you will as well and agree to no higher than penalty grade thirteen for this deluded being's actions."

The clamzoid waved its tentacles as it considered.

"That is a solid move on the part of the *Homo sapiens* judge. By keeping the penalty grade below thirteen, it removes all species liability and places all blame on the defendant," Pramroo's voice intruded.

"So right, but the sentence limitation is almost a certainty since the intended victim was a *Homo sapiens*. I—" Supla's voice cut off as the clamzoid judge began speaking.

"Agreed. Clamzoid vote to moderate."

"I will not moderate," said the AI. "Unless all agree to a class seven or above sentence."

The *Homo sapiens* judge stared at Zelotes. "I will agree to seven or above, if he serves the sentence in the U.E.S."

"Only if you include level thirteen." The AI sounded adamant.

"Death by repeated medical experiment is distasteful to me, especially if the criminal is not of sound mind," said the octozoid. "I will agree to a minimum level of eight if you will remove level thirteen from your demands."

The AI turned as if scanning the other judges. "It was one of my people this being nearly killed."

"Cxrippt, you are not vengeful by nature. Is not the sickness of his mind punishment enough?" asked the centazoid.

"I will agree, but the punishment will be eight or above, and all must agree to it."

All the other judges agreed.

"I will show the statements of the victim and intended victims," said the AI judge.

A hologram of Vicky appeared on top of the defendant's box and gave her recorded statement.

Rowan watched as the five judges bargained over Zelotes' sentence. At one point, the judgment devolved into a shouting match, and at another, the octozoid threatened to perform an unnatural act on the centazoid involving a 'large spiky sea vegetable with an acidic slime layer.' It was nearly an hour before a final verdict was reached, and Zelotes was lowered out of the defendant's booth to serve a life sentence in a mental institution. The court was recessed for twenty Earth minutes.

"He got off too light." Vicky's voice was acidic. "Goeree lobbied too hard for that piece of stardust."

"He was unstable," said Saggal.

"I'm sure, but I was hoping that the U.E.S. would pay for my new body. I doubt that even seizing all his assets will cover half the cost."

"Don't worry about that. Udele is covering the cost, my love."

"I hate it when the real villains don't pay. His hate was all because of U.E.S. propaganda."

"We biologics should use the break for its intended purpose." Kitoy stood and guided Rowan from the court chamber to a long corridor. Each door coming off the hall was labelled with a different one of the species that used the common area. Rowan moved to the unit marked for *Homo sapiens* and entered a long, narrow room. One wall was blocked off by a series of stalls with floor to ceiling walls and full doors. The other was a line of sinks facing a mirror.

Rowan moved to a stall, closed the door and took a seat.

"Rowan, I'm sorry. What was I supposed to do, let my father throw his life away?" Timothy's voice came through the door.

"Go away!" Rowan shouted.

"Look, I don't know if you're real or not. I do know my Dad is throwing away his life for you. I couldn't let him do it."

Rowan felt her colour rise. "Maybe it's his choice. Maybe I'm the life he wants. From what he's told me, he hasn't had much of a life in a long time. Besides, what do you care? He's a fakey, like me!"

"He's not. He's real. He was born once. I'm sorry, but it's not like it was you I turned in. The U.E.S. will drop the weapons charges if you surrender to them. Commander McKenzie has the papers all drawn up. I—"

"Leave her in peace, you self-important, uncouth, little worm." Kate's voice came from the other side of the stall.

"This has nothing to do with you," snapped Timothy.

"Your father isn't even tried, and here you are out to do Crapper's work. You're a maggot, let alone bothering a lady while she's in here! Ryan had to teach you better manners than that. Now get out! Go! Rowan doesn't want to deal with you."

Rowan finished, then opened the stall door. "Thanks, Kate."

Kate glared at Timothy's retreating back and had a pinched expression on her face. "You're welcome. How that boy could have fallen so far? I met Tim a few times while Ryan and I were serving together. He used to be a nice young man."

Rowan moved to wash her hands. "Do you think his offer was—"

"Don't even think about it."

"I have to, Kate. Ryan wouldn't survive a prison farm. He's like a hawk. He has to fly. If he's returned to U.E.S. authority, I'll turn myself in, in exchange for his release."

Kate squeezed Rowan's arm. "I know you will. You are real, Rowan. No matter what some bigoted fools say, and you match Ryan. Talk to Vicky before you do anything. Make sure all your options are exhausted."

Rowan nodded grimly. "I better get back to my seat. I wore his favourite outfit; I want him to know I'm thinking of him."

Kate nodded. "I'll be along in a minute. If Tim bothers you again, kick him where it will do the most good."

Tim took a seat on an audience tier and buried his face in his hands. "What have I done?" he whispered.

JUDGMENT

Rowan watched the courtroom floor as the judges seemed to materialize. A coelenteratezoid floated where the clamzoid had been. A middle-aged *Homo sapiens* male, with black hair and a bit of a gut, was to the coelenteratezoid's left. Next came a tabby-stripe, felinezoid female, then a crabzoid, with smaller claws than the other one Rowan had seen. Finally, a multi-coloured pyramid covered in blinking lights.

"This is going to be an interesting case," said Pramroo.

"Too true. Two of the judges were dictated by the case. A *Homo sapiens*, because a *Homo sapiens* is being tried, and the AI judge, Richard, who was incidentally originally built by *Homo sapiens*. Judge Richard represents the interests of the mitigating factor of saving an AI's life," commentated Supla.

"It looks like Captain Chandler has two votes for free before the bargaining has even begun."

A light shone on the coelenteratezoid judge, and the announcers went silent.

"The coelenteratezoid vote to absolve."

There was a gasp from the audience. Rowan felt a thrill of hope. She didn't know what absolve meant, but if the coelenteratezoids wanted it, she figured it was a good thing.

"*Homo sapiens* vote to punish," said the plump judge.

Another gasp went through the crowd. "Politics! Grant the motion, remove the *Homo sapiens*," screamed a spiderzoid from the crowd.

"Order," called the coelenteratezoid judge. "We are the judges. We will conduct the court. Arbitrator Merrogrrpra, how do you vote?"

"Felinezoids vote to absolve."

"The star searcher individuality of the crabzoids votes to moderate," said the crabzoid.

"The AIs of Datala vote to absolve," said the multi-hued pyramid.

"That is a surprise. I don't think I've ever seen three absolves in a case before," said Pramroo.

"Hasn't happened in two hundred Swampla years. And the sources! I guess the monkey descendants really want Chandler 'tied up in seaweed and drowning'. Voting punish against one of their own in the opening round. It just doesn't happen!"

"Politics, Supla, politics. For those not in the know, the absolve ruling is the rarest of any Republic court. It, in effect, says that it was wrong to arrest the perpetrator in the first place and grants the perpetrator a settlement by way of recompense for the injustice."

Rowan rubbed her hands together and smiled.

"Administrative component one-three-five of the Star Searcher individuality, I will change my vote to free if you will do the same," offered the felinezoid.

"Star Searcher cannot see fit to do that. The recording plainly showed Captain Ryan Chandler vandalizing the robot. No matter his motives, that is a criminal offence. I will, however, agree to limit his sentencing to gradient one. Thus, the law is adhered to, yet his heroism and high motives are rewarded."

The felinezoid judge lashed her tail. "You group minds are such sticklers. There are mitigating factors in this case beyond the law."

"Nevertheless, this is a court of Republic law, and the law must be upheld," said the crabzoid.

"I will raise my sentence to free for the crabzoid

agreeing to gradient one," offered the felinezoid.

"Agreed," said the crabzoid.

"Judge Malkowits of the *Homo sapiens*. You choose to punish. Why?"

"It is not required that I justify my ruling. The video recordings and testimony all plainly show Chandler's guilt. I will change my vote to moderate if you will."

The coelenteratezoid judge made a jack-knifing motion.

"Now this is getting nasty," remarked Pramroo.

"Judge Malkowits isn't making any friends this day, that is 'as certain as the river flowing to the swamp'."

"Chandler is a hero! Must you be reminded of it?" The Datala representative glowed brightly. A hologram of Vicky appeared above the defendant's box. The hologram testified how Ryan had saved her the only way he could with the tools at hand.

Rowan watched as the trial ground on. The crabzoid judge seemed to ignore the proceedings as the other judges went from persuasion to abuse in their attempt to get the *Homo sapiens* judge to change his ruling. By the time the first recess was called, the only progress had been to get the *Homo sapiens* to change to moderate, with all punishments levels included, in exchange for the felinezoid making a firm agreement on a level one punishment.

"How are you holding up?" asked Vicky as Rowan watched Ryan lower out of the defendant's box.

"Tell me how we're doing, and I'll answer you," said Rowan.

Vicky smiled. "Listen to this. It's the lawyer's frequency. Stuff the general public isn't allowed to hear."

Vicky passed Rowan an earpiece. Rowan removed the one in her ear and pushed it in.

"Send a short through his CPU," said Judge Richard's voice.

"I'd like to watch if you did," replied Merrogrrpra.

"You have at least made progress, though you have

traded away your effectiveness to do so," said the coelenteratezoid's voice.

"What choice did I have? At least the crabzoids are locked in at level one. Annoying sticklers."

"Any sentence is ruinous for Chandler. Could we grant him sanctuarial incarceration?" The sound of Merrogrrpra tapping her claws on something came through the earpiece.

"You could, my government is sympathetic, but we still need the *Homo sapiens* to guard our shipping. Purchasing the stargate that services Zod nearly bankrupted us. Trading Geb for *Homo sapiens* protection, so we could forgo maintaining a military, was a necessary evil. I have been told by their diplomat that ships can respond swiftly to a distress call or slowly. The implication is clear."

"My government is divided on his escapades. Personally, I think it is high drama and romance brought to life, but others wish he'd turn Rowan in and be done with it." Merrogrrpra sounded disgusted.

"Datala has no need of biologicals and few facilities to accommodate them. I suppose I could use him to perform a maintenance on my CPU, but he's only qualified for *Homo sapiens* made technology. There aren't that many emancipated *Homo sapiens* AIs," said Richard.

"We cannot keep battling like this. We could be here for weeks."

"Not another weaselzoid trade dispute. I couldn't survive it," said Merrogrrpra.

"I have an idea. Let me contact Star Searcher on a private channel." Richard's voice sounded cunning.

"You see, there is hope. You have friends in the court," remarked Vicky.

"I hope it's enough." Rowan pulled the plug out of her ear.

"So do I." Vicky squeezed Rowan's hand, then rolled away.

The judges' holograms reactivated, and Ryan rose into the defendant's box.

"Now for session two of this politically charged case. Passions were flooding the lowlands before the recess, and little progress had been made," said Supla.

"Judge Malkowits, I think I know what your purposes are, and we all would like to get out of here before our systems start to fail. I will agree to moderate to no higher sentence than level one, provided you allow the crabzoids to dictate the parameters of the punishment. That way, we can all be assured said punishment will be in keeping with the letter of the law," offered Richard of Datala.

"Agreed." Judge Malkowits smiled and rubbed his hands together.

"I will agree to this so long as all agree to a level one offence and a minimum sentence," said the coelenteratezoid.

In the defendant's box, Ryan went pale.

"Agreed." Judge Malkowits nearly crowed. "Looks like you're on your way back to Gaea, Mr. Chandler."

Ryan leapt from his seat and put his hands against the walls of the defendant's box, gazing at Rowan.

Rowan leapt from her seat, and it was all Saggal, Kitoy and Kate could do to hold her back.

There was a sound like nails on a chalkboard as the crabzoid rubbed its claws together. "The disposition of the sentence is mine to decide."

The courtroom stilled as if everyone was holding their breath.

The crabzoid continued, "As a minimum sentence of a level one offence, Captain Chandler must serve point zero zero two per cent of his average species life expectancy in indentured servitude. That relates to fourteen point six standard Earth days. As his crime was committed against the Republic, it is fitting that he redeems himself in service to the Republic. Captain Chandler is the owner of a stargate rated vessel that has been configured to carry light to moderate cargo. The Star Searcher collective is in charge of organizing the transport of relief supplies and personnel to registered Republic disaster areas. Captain Chandler, assume a posture of respect for your species."

Ryan stood at attention.

"You can't," spat Judge Malkowits.

"Yes, he can, you agreed, and it is recorded. Thus is the letter of the law," said the coelenteratezoid.

"Thank you, Blue-Yellow-Green-Purple." The crabzoid shifted about self-importantly. "Captain Ryan Chandler, it is this court's ruling that you are to be released on your own recognizance pending the loading of your vessel with relief supplies and personnel that you will transport to Murack Five. There you will unload said supplies and personnel and return with such relief personnel as have finished their term of service. As it is estimated that this task will take five days longer than your period of servitude, a fee of twenty thousand Republic Trade Credits for wages and vessel lease will be credited to you upon mission completion. Upon mission completion, all Republic claims against you will have been fulfilled, and your record will be cleared."

Ryan went pale. His eyes shot to Rowan, who stood staring at him, her face filling with incredulous joy.

"You cannot sentence him thus. Under Republic law, if operating as a charter, a vessel of his class must have at least five personnel. Chandler is only one," objected Malkowits.

The sounds of various species disapproving rose from the audience.

"Two. I'm the ship's navigator," called Rowan.

"She isn't qualified," snapped Judge Malkowits.

"I will judge that, but I observed the *Star Hawk* as it entered this system and docked. Its navigation appeared adequate," said the crabzoid.

"I'm a communications tech. That's three." Kitoy's eyes swept to Kate and Saggal, who looked agitated and torn but didn't move.

"That is only three and since—"

"I am a doctor of biomechanical engineering, far more than adequately qualified to perform the life sciences functions of the ship. I believe that is four."

Rowan nearly gave herself whiplash as she swept around to see Tim standing in the spectator gallery. He slowly walked to the floor level and took a place beside Kitoy.

"That is still only four crew," snapped Malkowits.

"If you will observe the evidence display, I'm receiving a message relay from the *Star Hawk*," said Judge Richard.

The image of Henry undamaged, standing in a U.E.S. space forces dress uniform with the retiree's braid on the shoulder, appeared above the defendant's box. "Al-Copernicus class, Henry, qualified in all ship's operations. That makes five, skippy!"

"The sentence is set. The period of servitude to start in five standard Earth days."

The defendant's box opened. Ryan lurched out to the sound of the audience cheering, purring, whistling, snorting and clapping. Rowan ran into his arms, and he held her. Saggal and Kate reached him next, and they hugged him.

"We are sorry," began Saggal. Ryan shook his head.

"It is too much to ask." He looked at Rowan's relieved and happy face. "I must love you." He kissed her, but no hint of a smile touched his lips.

"Father." Tim's voice intruded.

Ryan looked at his son. "Captain! Things change and can't always be fixed overnight."

Tim nodded. As a group, they made their way towards the exit.

EPILOGUE

Croell and Zandra watched from the audience.

"The hunt is on once more," said Zandra.

Croell flicked his tongue. "Yes, my love. It is fitting that it be so."

Zandra flicked her tongue back at her husband. "And Pikeman?"

"It will be arranged that our geise stay together. I thank the Great Flyer of the Skies for such a challenge. Ryan and Rowan should die in combat. I am certain they will be batzoid in their next life."

"Then we give them the gift of wings. That pleases me."

Ryan and Rowan left the others in the officers' mess of the *Star Hawk* and slipped into her quarters. Ryan was still pale and downcast.

"Cheer up. We won." Rowan pulled him into a hug and kissed him.

"It's just... Murack Five. I swore... I'd never go there. I swore." Ryan sat on the bed and buried his face in his hands.

"Is it so awful?" Rowan sat beside him.

"Not unless you were there when... Promise me you'll be beside me."

Rowan took his hand. "For the rest of our days. I love you, Ryan. Now cheer up. It's like when we left the Gaea system. Only now we have relief supplies and workers to deliver and a ship that doesn't need to be fixed. Things are looking up."

"Only we don't have a cargo to sell, and I'll have wages to pay, not to mention legal fees."

Rowan kissed him as her hands played across his chest. "You'll think of something. You always do." Pushing him back on the bed, she proceeded to distract him from his troubles in the most delightful of ways.

Henry split his free RAM between recording Ryan and Rowan, the party in the officer's mess and cargo bay, and relaying the rough edited data to Michael's contact on the station.

"One thing's for sure. It's more than one season's worth." He allowed the wave of emotion from his crewmates to wash over him and knew it was good.

Pause.

Acknowledgements

For an endless source of inspiration when writing Saggal, the best friend I ever had, Bastel, if I could give a dim echo of you through my words, I have shared light with the world. I could list cats to the end of the page because you have all made cameos in the various felinezoids.

I also want to do a special thank you to Nichelle Nichols, Uhura from *Star Trek*. Whenever people around me spewed racism as I was growing up, I would flash onto you and Uhura. Beautiful, intelligent, gentle and I would see the lie for what it was. Given that there were maybe twenty people of recent African genetic extraction in my entire city, you were a lifeline. I hope the world I have crafted, except for clones, reflects the Roddenberry ideal we should all strive for.

Afterword

Thank you for reading *Freedom's Law*. It was a pleasure writing it for you, and I should mention that the adventures of Ryan, Rowan and the gang will continue in *Freedom's Myth*.

Please review my work. Goodreads, Amazon or even just Facebook. Reviews are the lifeblood for us little-fish authors. The food that might just let us grow into whales. (Hey, I can dream.)

Remember, the power's in you, please review.

Be well.

About the Author

Stephen B. Pearl is a multiple published author whose works range across the speculative fiction field. Whether his characters are wandering the wilds of a post-oil future, braving a storm in a longship, or flying through the interplanetary void in an army surplus assault lander, his writings focus heavily on the logical consequences of the worlds he crafts.

Stephen's inspirations encompass H.G. Wells, J.R.R. Tolkien, Frank Herbert, and Homer, among others. In writing the Freedom Saga, he has, among other factors, drawn on his diverse background and broad general knowledge garnered from preparing for and serving on seminars and panels at numerous shows and events. These panels and seminars range from Intelligent Spacecraft Design to Building Better Aliens. His training as an Emergency Medical Care Assistant, a SCUBA diver, and his long-standing interest in environmental technologies have factored into all his science fiction books, be they on or off the planet Earth.

For more about Stephen and his works visit: www.stephenpearl.com